Only the Lonely

Only the Lonely

Ted Darling crime series

'blind dates end in bleeding hearts'

L M Krier

Contents

Chapter One   1

Chapter Two   10

Chapter Three   19

Chapter Four   28

Chapter Five   37

Chapter Six   47

Chapter Seven   57

Chapter Eight   66

Chapter Nine   76

Chapter Ten   85

Chapter Eleven   94

Chapter Twelve   103

Chapter Thirteen   113

Chapter Fourteen   122

Chapter Fifteen   132

Chapter Sixteen   141

Chapter Seventeen   151

Chapter Eighteen   159

Chapter Nineteen   168

Chapter Twenty   178

Chapter Twenty-one   188

Chapter Twenty-two   197

Chapter Twenty-three   207

Chapter Twenty-four   217

Chapter Twenty-five   227

Chapter Twenty-six   237

Chapter Twenty-seven   246

Chapter Twenty-eight   256

Chapter Twenty-nine   265

Chapter Thirty   275

Chapter Thirty-one   284

Chapter Thirty-two   295

About the Author

L M Krier is the pen name of former journalist (court reporter) and freelance copywriter, Lesley Tither, who also writes travel memoirs under the name Tottie Limejuice. Lesley also worked as a case tracker for the Crown Prosecution Service.

The Ted Darling series of crime novels comprises: *The First Time Ever, Baby's Got Blue Eyes, Two Little Boys, When I'm Old and Grey, Shut Up and Drive, Only the Lonely, Wild Thing, Walk on By, Preacher Man.*

All books in the series are available in Kindle and paperback format and are also available to read free with Kindle Unlimited.

Contact Details

If you would like to get in touch, please do so at:

tottielimejuice@gmail.com

facebook.com/LMKrier

facebook.com/groups/1450797141836111/

https://twitter.com/tottielimejuice

For a light-hearted look at Ted and the other characters, please consider joining the We Love Ted Darling group on Facebook.

Discover the DI Ted Darling series

If you've enjoyed meeting Ted Darling, you may like to discover the other books in the series:

The First Time Ever
Baby's Got Blue Eyes
Two Little Boys
When I'm Old and Grey
Shut Up and Drive
Only the Lonely
Wild Thing
Walk on By
Preacher Man

Acknowledgements

Thanks to all those who helped with this fourth book in the DI Ted Darling series, beta readers Jill Pennington, Emma Heath, Kate Pill, additional editing Alex Potter, Alison Sabedoria.

Special thanks to Chris Gillies for expert advice on the martial arts scenes.

To my brother

Peter

1948 - 2016

Chapter One

DI Ted Darling paused with his right hand on the door of the main office. It felt good to be back. He'd only been gone for two weeks but he hated any time away from his team. Even on rare holidays with his partner, Trevor, half of his mind was always wondering how things were going back at the nick without him.

Then he opened the door and went in. Only his sergeant, Mike Hallam, was at his desk, surrounded by several untidy piles of paperwork. It was still early, but Ted knew it would not be long before the rest of the team arrived. Ted was an easy-going boss who led by example. He was never late so his team were the same, out of respect for him.

Mike Hallam leapt up from the clutter, like a drowning man coming up for air, and his face broke into a wide smile.

'Boss! Am I glad to see you back.'

He extended a hand and shook Ted's warmly, then nodded in the direction of Ted's left hand, still bandaged after a recent serious knife injury which had needed extensive surgery.

'How's the hand doing?'

Ted lifted his arm and waggled each finger in turn. His thumb was a bit more reluctant to show its party piece, but he did manage to move it a little.

'Getting there,' he said. 'It's certainly a lot better than it was. So, how have things been?'

Mike groaned.

'Work-wise, fine. Nothing we couldn't handle, and we're

1

pretty much on top of most of the paperwork, although it may not look like it from my desk. It's just that we all missed you, boss. The Super's been trying to be supportive, but every time she trots up here to make sure we're managing without you, she makes everyone so nervous we turn into bumbling idiots.'

Ted laughed aloud. That was exactly the reaction their senior officer, Superintendent Debra Caldwell, universally known as the Ice Queen, provoked in him, too. He knew she would be in her office, if not now then shortly. He also knew that his first port of call needed to be to go and see her to let her know he was back and had been medically passed as fit for duty. He just couldn't resist seeing his team members first.

The door opened behind him and the rest of the team came trooping in together, all looking as pleased as Mike had done to see that their boss was back. DCs Rob O'Connell, Sal Ahmed and Virgil Tibbs all shook his hand. Even Trainee Detective Constable Steve Ellis plucked up the courage for a brief handshake. Their most rebellious member, DC Jezza Vine, had more reason than most to be pleased to see him back. She threw protocol to the wind to fling her arms around him in a brief hug and give him a swift peck on the cheek.

Ted had a quick glance towards the whiteboard to see what cases were ongoing. It looked as if things had been surprisingly quiet.

We had a body in the river, with multiple knife wounds, but we think we've got that more or less wrapped up already, boss. There was a sudden death at the weekend but I don't think it's one for us, unless anything unusual shows up with the post-mortem.'

'Right, I should go and let the Super know I'm back, then you can fill me in on anything I need to know after that.'

Ted knocked briefly on the Ice Queen's door and went in when she called out. Even his stiff and formal boss seemed pleased to see him and her smile appeared to be genuine.

2

'Ah, Inspector, did you smell the coffee? It's nearly ready. Please sit down and tell me how you're feeling now. I must say, you're looking very well, a lot better than when I saw you last.'

Ted sat, hastily making excuses for his casual attire. The Ice Queen insisted he wore a suit and tie to work always, which he hated. He'd done his best, but with the bandaging still on his injured hand, he hadn't been able to fit it down the sleeve of his suit jacket. Instead he was in an open-necked check shirt with a soft cotton poplin field jacket, the poppers at the cuff of the left sleeve open to allow room for the strapping.

'Ma'am, I'm sorry for the civvies. I can't get my suit jacket on over this,' he lifted his hand in evidence, 'and Trev is never awake early enough to tie a tie for me...'

Her smile was almost friendly as she waved away his apology and said, 'It's really good to see you. For a moment, I was worried you weren't coming back. So I'd have been just as happy to see you if you were in your pyjamas.'

'I don't wear any,' Ted risked, with a cheeky grin.

'Indeed,' she said, back to her businesslike self, setting out the coffee and sitting down opposite him. 'First of all, I must say your team have been exemplary. They have coped really well in your absence, especially with DC Brown still off on sick leave as well. I really have been most impressed. You've trained them very well.

'In fact you and your team have been the subject of various discussions at high level during your absence and I have some exciting proposals to put to you about the future.'

Ted wondered if he were dreaming. Just then, Freddie Mercury interrupted their thought processes by announcing that he had had a perfect dream. It was the ringtone on Ted's mobile phone, announcing an incoming call. One of Ted's rare moments of rebellion was to have the distinctive ringtone instead of a classic, neutral one.

'You'd better see if you need to take that,' the Ice Queen told him.

Ted pulled the phone out and looked at the screen. Despite Trev's offers of help, he'd never got round to having different tones to differentiate between callers.

'Professor Nelson,' he said, looking questioningly at the Ice Queen.

She nodded at him to take the call. If the senior forensic pathologist was phoning, it was likely that Ted's team had another suspicious death coming their way.

'Good morning, Professor,' Ted said formally.

He and Elizabeth 'Bizzie' Nelson had become good friends and were on first-name terms, but Ted always kept things professional in front of anyone else.

'Ah, Edwin, I assume you're not alone? I'm sorry to disturb you but I have something on my autopsy table which was supposed to be straightforward but which, on closer examination, looks as if it may be something for you, after all. How soon could you come down here so I can explain everything and show you why I think that? I'm just finishing up the post-mortem so it's a good time for you to see for yourself, if you're available.'

Ted took the phone away from his ear and said, 'Ma'am, Professor Nelson has a possible suspicious death and wants me to go down there as soon as possible. Would that be convenient? Could we continue our discussion later on?'

The Ice Queen sighed and looked slightly disappointed, but nodded her agreement. Ted told the Professor he was leaving shortly and would be with her as soon as traffic conditions allowed.

'Are you fit to drive?' the Ice Queen asked him, looking at his injured hand.

'As long as I don't change gear too often,' Ted joked in reply. 'I just have to remember not to pull the handbrake on too far or I struggle to let it off again. I'm sorry to have to dash away. I look forward to hearing the news you have for me as soon as I get back.'

Professor Nelson met Ted at the door of her post-mortem suite in the bowels of the hospital. She assured him he had no need for coveralls as she had finished her examination. She, too, greeted him warmly and shook his hand, asking how he was feeling and how he'd enjoyed his time off.

'It was good. I did a lot of walking, a lot of thinking. I needed time to get my head straight. I missed Trev like crazy, though, and I couldn't phone him often as the phone signal is dire down there. It's the longest we've ever been apart.'

'And he was like a little lost puppy without you, too. He asked me to dine with him a couple of times, just for the company, which was sweet of him, and a real treat for me.'

Ted handed her one of his Fisherman's Friend lozenges and took one himself before he followed her into the room. It helped to mask the smells that inevitably went with the job of rooting around in the most intimate parts of a body, in search of a cause of death.

The large, brightly lit room had three stainless steel tables, only one of which currently housed a body, that of a man. A white sheet was pulled up to his chin so Ted could only see his face, which was gaunt, with hollow cheeks. It looked grimy beneath the thick stubble, and the dark hair was long, lank and greasy.

'We haven't completely cleaned him up yet,' the Professor was telling him. 'There's no known next of kin, so we're still waiting on an identification. We'll make him look more presentable for that, if we get one.

'I was told that he's an unemployed man of forty-seven, Stan Marshall, a known alcoholic. That's confirmed by his state of malnutrition which, sadly, is often a feature. I didn't attend the scene as it was thought to be just a simple case of excessive drinking leading to his death. A straightforward, but none the less tragic case of alcohol poisoning.'

Ted wasn't sure where she was going with this. So far there seemed to be nothing in it for him or his team. But he had faith in Bizzie. If she thought something was wrong, then it almost certainly was.

'So what led you to think otherwise?' he prompted.

The Professor picked up what looked rather like an innocent Tupperware container, with a tight lid. She held it out towards him and Ted instinctively swayed back away from it. He had a horrible feeling it was going to be stomach contents and he was never good at dealing with the smell of those. Hesitantly, as she thrust it insistently closer, he prised up the lid, chewing frantically on his lozenge.

Surprised, he looked at Bizzie as the fumes reached his nostrils and asked, 'Whisky? But isn't that what you might expect to find?'

'Ah, Edwin, I always forget you're a non-drinker and clearly a Philistine when it comes to good Scotch,' she smiled. 'I'm a whisky drinker, enough to be able to tell, even after it had been sitting in his stomach for a time, that this is not a bargain of the day bottle from a supermarket shelf. I've had it tested to confirm my thoughts. This is a very good quality single malt, a bottle of which retails for more than twice what this unfortunate man was likely to be drawing in benefits per week.'

Ted shrugged.

'A lucky scratch card win, perhaps?'

'The last time I treated myself to a bottle of malt of this quality, I had to buy it from the duty free shop at an airport. Where would our Mr Marshall have got his hands on one? It's not for me to tell you your job, Edwin, but I would certainly be intrigued to know what the first responding officers at the scene found there. I wasn't involved, nor were your Crime Scene Investigators, as no crime was suspected. I would respectfully suggest that it would be worth a few moments of someone's time to go back to the unfortunate Mr Marshall's flat and have a look for the bottle.

'He drank almost all of it, very quickly, which is what

killed him. But if someone knew him, and for some reason wanted rid of him, they would surely know that giving a bottle of good whisky like that to an alcoholic was like putting a small child in a sweet shop.'

Ted was still looking less than convinced so she continued, 'In isolation, I may not have thought it at all strange. Like you, I'd probably have thought a lottery win, or that he'd somehow managed to steal it from somewhere. But his address rang a bell, so I looked back through our case notes.

'Mr Marshall lived in Sabden House flats. A couple of months ago, we carried out a post-mortem on another resident from there. This one was a known drug addict. He died from an overdose of heroin. Again, nothing unusual on the face of it. Except that this particular heroin was of a purity and strength like nothing we've ever seen here before. Exactly the same sort of thing. Guaranteed to kill someone who wasn't used to anything like it, in a very short space of time.'

Now she had Ted's full attention. He was looking at her intently as he said, 'I know Sabden House. It's where they moved Honest John when they took the old tower block down. It's a small place, not many flats there at all, so two deaths like this in such a short space of time is certainly unusual.'

He saw Bizzie's quizzical expression and explained that Honest John was the station's local confessor. Whenever any major crime was made public, he was always the first to phone up and confess to it, always insisting, 'Honest, it was me.' The truth was that he was a sad and lonely figure whose clinical obesity prevented him from ever leaving his flat and who craved whatever attention he could get.

'It's up to you how you want to go forward with this, Edwin, but I'm going to flag it up to the coroner as suspicious. Meanwhile, I'll send you all we have on this case, and the previous one, so you can look at the two in more detail. And please do keep me posted. I would be particularly interested to know exactly which whisky this was. I believe that murder by single malt is very rare.'

As soon as he got back to the nick, Ted went in search of the Ice Queen to find out just what exciting news she had for him. He couldn't begin to guess what it could be but he imagined that, whatever it was, it was going to involve a lot more paperwork for him. Everything these days seemed to involve more paperwork. That and the constant round of cutbacks all conspired to make his job even more difficult than ever.

She was on the phone when Ted put his head round the door so he waited outside until she called out to him to come in. Although their relationship was slowly settling down, it was still formal and awkward. Ted never felt totally relaxed in her company as he had done with his former boss, DCI, now Detective Superintendent, Jim Baker, who was also his close friend.

'Please come in and sit down. I really am pleased to have you back. I was worried that you perhaps had other plans. I take it you are back to stay?'

Ted nodded, so she continued, 'In that case, I want to tell you about the plans which involve you and your team. The top brass are most impressed with your performance. Between you, you have the best clear-up rate for serious crime within the force.

'The idea, therefore, is that we expand your team and, as well as covering this area, you become a mobile unit to cover the whole force area as needed. In the event of serious crime in any other division, you would be drafted in to help and to increase numbers.

'The new unit will be under the direct command of Superintendent Baker, so you would be answerable to him when out on secondment, and to me when based here in Stockport. You'll need a couple of new team members, too, but we can discuss those finer details when you've had time to digest the idea.

'Your team will certainly need a second sergeant and you will also need another inspector. That's because, as I'm sure you will have realised, as you will be going in as Senior Investigating Officer to other divisions, you will need to hold the rank of Detective Chief Inspector.'

Chapter Two

Trevor was in the kitchen of their home in Offerton, cooking something which was smelling delicious, when Ted got home from work. For once, Ted wasn't feeling exhausted. If anything, he was excited about the news he'd been given, but more than a little apprehensive about Trev's reaction to his promotion and new role.

He hoped his partner would be pleased that he'd made DCI, especially as it was unexpected. But he knew, too, that his new responsibilities risked taking him away more, and he hated to be apart from Trev. Their relationship was rock-solid, based on mutual trust. Ted's problem was that he worried constantly about Trev being much younger than him, not to mention extremely good-looking. Ted always felt he restricted the fun his partner could be having because of his being so much older, the nature of his job and the way he was. Trev was a natural party animal; Ted was a quiet people watcher.

He reminded himself yet again how lucky he was when he was welcomed home with a hug and a kiss from Trev, and six purring cats rubbing affectionately round his legs. He returned the kiss and, with a flourish, produced a bottle of good French wine, which he handed to Trev. Ted never drank alcohol but he loved to see his partner enjoy good wine in moderation.

'Oh wow, this is nice. Are we pushing the boat out for a special occasion? It's only a chicken liver risotto, I'm afraid, I didn't know we'd be celebrating anything.'

Ted gave a self-effacing smile and said, 'Believe it or not, you are now looking at a Detective Chief Inspector. Acting, for the moment, of course, but hopefully to be confirmed, if I don't make a total balls-up of my new role.'

Trev's hug this time was a bone-crusher which nearly lifted the much smaller Ted off his feet.

'That is fantastic news! Well done you. I can't wait to tell Shewee, she'll be as made up as I am,' he said.

Shewee was his younger sister, Siobhan's, nickname. She'd only recently come into both their lives and had quickly become a fan of both her big brother and of Ted.

'And don't forget to tell your mum, soon. She'll be so proud of you. Look at us, you a DCI, me a business partner. Just like proper grown-ups. Who'd have thought it?'

'It's more money, of course, which will help with the business loan, but there's a downside, inevitably. I'm going to be part of a new mobile unit covering the whole force area, headed by Jim. So that means I'm probably going to have to go away quite a bit, and you know I hate leaving you. I'll be going in as SIO, which is why I needed the promotion. I'll need a bit of clout, muscling in on other teams' patches. I don't imagine it will all be plain sailing.'

'You'll be brilliant,' Trev told him insistently, sounding proud. 'You know how good you are with people. You'll have them eating out of your hand in no time. And if they don't, you can just frighten them into submission with some nifty Krav Maga moves.

'Anyway, you won't be going all that far away. Where's the worst place they can send you? Owdham? Boory?' Trev asked with an exaggerated northern accent for Oldham and Bury.

He and Ted were from completely different social backgrounds. Trev had been educated at good, international schools and had a neutral, well-spoken accent. Ted was from Lancashire but had spent most of his life in Stockport and had a slight, though discernible, accent, with the characteristic flat vowels of the area.

'I just worry about leaving you. You're young, you're drop-dead gorgeous, you should be having more fun than you get, shackled to a boring, middle-aged copper.'

Trev turned away to stir his risotto and lower the heat under it. When he looked back, he asked, 'Is this you fishing for compliments? You know I love you, you know I accept the job because it's a part of you. If you have to go away, I'll miss you, but that's fine. I'll be here waiting, when you get back.'

Then his vivid blue eyes took on a mischievous sparkle as he asked, 'Or do I need to prove to you why I don't want or need anyone else?'

Ted's smile was slow and suggestive as he replied, 'I may need a lot of convincing.'

Trev laughed as he turned the heat off under the pan and pulled it aside.

'These chicken livers are going to be as hard as the very devil,' he grumbled, but he followed his partner out of the kitchen without complaint.

Inspector Kevin Turner, Ted's opposite number in Uniform, shot to his feet and snapped a parade-ground salute as Ted knocked briefly at his door and walked into his office the following morning, after his own team briefing.

'Morning, sir,' he barked, still standing to attention.

Ted laughed self-consciously and said, 'Shut up and sit down, you idiot,' taking a seat himself. 'Word certainly travels fast in this nick. I've only just told my team.'

As Kevin sat down, grinning, Ted noticed the involuntary wince and the hand that went up to massage his stomach.

'I can see the guts are still giving you a problem. You need to do something about them, and soon.'

'You have the smug, self-satisfied look of a man who got lucky last night,' Kevin said, totally ignoring the remark. 'I take it you and Trev enjoyed a celebration of your promotion?'

'Seriously, Kev, never mind your pip envy, now I've

figuratively got three to your two. What are you doing about your stomach troubles?'

Kevin sighed, reaching in his top drawer for a tube of over-the-counter antacids, a couple of which he sucked down greedily.

'As it goes, I've got an appointment at the end of next week for the dreaded gastroscopy. Trouble is, I know I'm going to bottle it. I'm really bricking myself, just at the thought.'

He looked hopefully at Ted as he asked, 'I don't suppose there's any chance you could come with me, Ted? I just need someone to hold my hand. Not literally, but someone to wait with me, stop me doing a runner.'

Ted hesitated.

'You know I would, if I could, Kev. It's just that with this new team to sort out ...'

'The Ice Queen's already asked me to fix up a pool car, for when you have to go away. You can't rock up on someone else's patch in that Dinky toy of yours. I could just really do with the company, and it needs to be someone I can trust to keep their mouth shut. I'd never live it down.'

'I know just the person, and he's available. You need Maurice Brown. He's still on sick leave.'

'Maurice?' Kevin Turner echoed, sounding horrified at the suggestion.

'Believe me, there's a lot more to Maurice than the overweight skiver most people think he is. He's perfect for anyone who's ill or upset. Seriously, I've seen him in action. I'll ask him for you. He'll do it, and he's the soul of discretion. He knows things about me that no one else in this nick does.

'Now, I didn't just pop in here to see you salute me. I actually need to talk to a couple of your officers, if that's all right with you. Whoever responded first to a sudden death at Sabden House flats at the weekend.'

Kevin was quickly on the phone, asking for the two PCs to come to his office as soon as possible. He had the paperwork with their report on his desk, which he pushed across to Ted. He'd only just finished his own morning briefing and not all of his officers had yet left the station.

'I didn't think there was anything in it for us. Certainly not for you,' he said. 'From the initial report it looks as if the man was a known alcoholic. A neighbour had noticed his curtains drawn for longer than normal and knocked on. When there was no response, they called us and two of my lads went round.'

'Professor Nelson found something a bit out of the ordinary at the post-mortem,' Ted told him, and quickly filled him in on all the details. He explained about the earlier case in the same small block of flats.

'I just wanted to ask your officers if they'd happened to notice an expensive-looking bottle of Scotch which was a bit out of place. Depending on what they tell me, I may go round and check the place out for myself, just to make sure.'

There was a knock at the door and on Kevin's instruction, two young PCs came into the small office. It quickly started to feel crowded. Ted knew all the officers in the station by name, which earned him the respect of everyone. PCs Stuart Harkness and Ian Cresswell greeted both senior officers and stood looking expectant. Kevin nodded to Ted to go ahead.

'The sudden death at Sabden House at the weekend,' Ted began. 'It may not be all it first seemed to be. I wondered if you could think back to your first impressions and tell me if there was anything, anything at all, which seemed unusual or out of place.'

The two looked at one another. PC Harkness was the elder of the two by a couple of years so by unspoken agreement, he replied for both of them.

'The place was a mess, sir. Looked like it hadn't been cleaned in ages. Didn't smell very nice, either. The neighbours told us the man was a pi ...'

He caught himself just in time, realising neither senior office would accept him calling the deceased a piss-artist. He

14

corrected himself neatly.

'A persistent drunk, sir. What we saw pretty much confirmed that, from the number of empty bottles about.'

'You didn't happen to notice one particular empty bottle which looked different? Like it might have been expensive?'

Both men shook their heads. In reply to Ted's further questions, they told him there was a set of keys for the flat being kept, together with the man's other personal effects, until any next of kin had been traced. Ted thanked them and let them go.

'Right, I'd better go and see the Ice Queen for this strategy meeting about the new team,' Ted said, then laughed at himself. 'Words I never imagined myself uttering. I'll phone Maurice for you, as soon as I get a minute. You'll be fine with him. He's a right clucky mother hen, and completely discreet.'

Before they got down to the nitty-gritty of discussing the new team and how it would work, Ted mentioned to the Ice Queen the death at the flats and the reasons Professor Nelson was not satisfied it was simply a case of another alcoholic drinking himself to death.

She listened attentively, as usual, then said, 'That is certainly strange, but I don't see how it can be a matter for your team. Unless there was any evidence that someone physically poured the drink down his throat, I can't at the moment see what actual crime was committed. The heroin case, of course, is different. At least there would be an offence of supplying a Class A drug, if ever you could find out who did so. But again, unless a third party administered the drug, that's the only offence there would be.

'Look into it, certainly, but I wouldn't tie up too many valuable resources on it for now. They're scarce enough as it is. And this other death, the body in the river, with the stab wounds? Is that case under control?'

'Yes, ma'am, the team are fairly sure it's gang-related and

they hope to bring in a suspect later today. A juvenile, with previous form for assault.'

'Now that you're a DCI, just one rung of the ladder below me, I don't think there's any need to call me ma'am when no one else is around,' she said, to Ted's surprise, serving up coffee for both of them. 'So, on to the main point on the agenda for this morning. The creation of this new team.

'As I said, you need a second sergeant, giving you one to travel with you, one to stay behind and help run things for your new inspector. I have some feelers out for someone to fill that position and you will, of course, have a say in who is appointed. I think it's a good moment to look at existing members of your team for someone to make up to acting sergeant. Who would be your choice?'

'Rob O'Connell,' Ted said, without hesitation. 'Maurice is the longest-serving but, although he has many qualities, leadership is not the strongest of them. Rob is a good officer. He knows his stuff, he's taken control of crime scenes in the past. He would be ideal.'

'Excellent. There's enough in the budget for a new DC to replace him. Next, young Steve. Has he done his two years as a trainee yet?'

'Not quite...' Ted replied, and stopped himself just before he added the customary 'ma'am'. They'd been on formal terms for so long it was going to be a hard habit to break.

'From what I saw of him while you were away, he seems both intelligent and competent. I would say that all he is lacking is a little confidence in himself. What if we were to take away the T for Trainee in his title and replace it with an A for Acting? Might that give him enough of a boost to help him to blossom forth?'

Ted smiled his pleasure. He agreed with her assessment of Steve and was delighted with the idea of rewarding his diligence and hard work.

'And making the best possible use of skills, I would like to see him develop his abilities in computer work. So much of what we are confronted with these days involves computer skills. I have secured a small budgetary allocation to build this team up. Part of it will go towards a civilian Computer Forensics Investigator, who can work with young Steve on that side of things.'

Ted was impressed. It was clear that this new team was being taken seriously, with money being spent on it when resources were so tightly constrained.

'I would suggest that you move into the office which is still standing empty since DCI Baker vacated it. Then somehow we can cram the new inspector and one of the sergeants into your old office. This should then free up enough space, with a little lateral thinking, in the main office for the new DC, and the CFI. Part of the team will, of course, not be in the office a lot of the time, when they're mobile, so it shouldn't feel too overcrowded. There may need to be some hot-desking, though.'

Ted was nodding his enthusiasm. It was all starting to sound promising and more than a little exciting.

'So now we come to DC Brown. I understand he has another two weeks to run on his sick leave. The question is, do you see him as a fit for this new, enhanced team? Is there a productive role for him, bearing in mind that what we are aiming for here is a standard of excellence?'

Ted leaned back in his chair to gather his thoughts before speaking. Yes, Maurice was a skiver who would always try to slope off for a pint if he could. He was neither the brightest nor the most efficient copper on the force. But Ted had seen the other side of him often enough to know that it was invaluable. The Maurice who could comfort and support anyone, man or woman, when they were hurt or upset.

It was in no small measure due to his kindness and compassion that Jezza Vine had been able to find her place in the team. Maurice had been the one to pick up the pieces when first Steve and later Jezza had been seriously assaulted. Ted also knew that although he was slow, he was methodical and could plod patiently through witness statements or lists, carefully cross-checking, meticulously collating, often finding things others had missed. The idea of the team without him appalled Ted.

'I hope you're never in a dark enough place to find out, but if ever you are, and you're lucky enough to have Maurice to hand, you'll know exactly why I want to keep him on my team. Whatever the cost.'

She nodded her understanding.

'Very well. I trust your judgement, and it's your team. If you want to keep him, I'm sure I can crunch a few numbers to make it so.'

She was interrupted at that point by the phone on her desk. She answered it, then said, 'Yes, he's here.'

As she passed the handset to Ted she said, 'It's DS Hallam.'

'Sorry to interrupt your power-talk, boss, but we just got a shout. A body's been found at a hotel, definitely a suspicious death. Multiple stab wounds ...'

'The same as your body in the river from the weekend?' Ted interrupted him.

'No, boss, something much more. The first officers attending, who called it in, apologised and said the crime scene is contaminated because everyone so far who saw the body lost their breakfast. It sounds as if you might need more than one bag of your sweeties for this one, boss.'

Chapter Three

They went in Mike's car, Ted glad of the opportunity not to drive, to give his injured hand more recovery time. Both men were apprehensive about what lay in wait for them, from the scant information they had so far. Mike, in particular, was nervous.

'I should warn you, boss, I don't have the strongest of stomachs at the best of times,' he said apologetically. 'I'll try my utmost not to add to any crime scene contamination, but if it's very gruesome I may not have much choice.'

'Let's not go in with any preconceptions. It may not be as bad as we fear. Suck on one of my menthol sweets when we get there. I know you're not keen on them but I find they do help.'

The hotel was part of a low-cost chain and always seemed to be popular. There were certainly plenty of vehicles on its parking area. Mike left his car there and the two men headed inside to the reception desk, warrant cards in their hands. The young woman at the desk was looking shaken.

'DI Darling and DS Hallam,' Ted told her as they held up their ID. 'We're here in connection with the sudden death.'

'Oh yes, it's absolutely dreadful. We've never seen anything like it,' the woman replied, her voice trembling. 'It's on the first floor, room 127, if you want to go straight up.'

Ted nodded his thanks and the two of them instinctively walked over to the stairs. There was a lift, but neither of them was anxious to get there any faster than they had to.

'It's DCI now, boss,' Mike reminded him, more to make conversation than anything else. His nervousness was mounting palpably, the nearer they got to their destination.

'I keep forgetting, and I've not got my new card yet,' Ted told him, also glad of the distraction, as they walked slowly up the staircase.

The corridor was clear apart from two PCs standing outside an open door. Ted noticed that it was once again PCs Harkness and Cresswell and felt sorry for them, having two sudden deaths to deal with in a short space of time. Seeing them approach, both stood up straighter and mumbled a brief, 'Sir, Sarge.'

Cresswell looked shocking, his face white, tinged with green. He also appeared mortified as he said to Ted, 'Sorry, sir, I'm afraid I was one who managed to throw up on the crime scene. I've just never seen anything as bad as that before and I didn't get out fast enough. I'm really sorry.'

'Don't worry about it,' Ted reassured him. 'We've probably all done it at least once in our careers. I know I have. Anyone who tells you otherwise is probably not being very honest.'

Through the doorway, Ted could see that Professor Nelson was there, working on a body next to the bed. All Ted could see of it from where he stood was a pair of bare legs. They looked like a man's legs. Forensic Investigators were also inside, working carefully and methodically.

'Is it all right to come in, Professor?' Ted asked, not wanting to trample any further over a crime scene without permission.

She looked up and saw Ted with his sergeant, so kept things formal. 'Can you both please cover up before you do, gentlemen? There's been enough contamination already, and hotel rooms are always a nightmare, with traces of so many people. Be careful where you step, too. At least three people have already puked in here, adding to our difficulties, including the poor young constable outside. I should warn you, it is a particularly nasty one, so I hope you have plenty of your lozenges.'

The two men put on the protective wear which one of the investigators handed to them, put lozenges in their mouths, inhaled the menthol vapours gratefully, then stepped into the room, carefully avoiding splatterings of vomit on the carpet in several places. There was blood everywhere, starting from just inside the door and leading to the bed, alongside which the body lay. Both men steeled themselves to approach, taking more deep breaths to steady themselves.

'Can I just say that if you are going to throw up, and there's no shame if you do in a case like this, the bathroom is just there and we've already finished in there, so try to hang on. If you can't, at least puke into an evidence bag,' Bizzie Nelson instructed them heartily.

The first thing they saw was that the victim was wearing only a bathrobe, which had fallen open, revealing a mass of stab and slash wounds to the torso. Then their gazes travelled upwards to the face. Or what was left of it. The whole head seemed to have been pounded into mush, the features beyond recognition, the skull battered and deformed. Ted had a horrible feeling that the jelly-like substance which he could see was leaked brain matter. He sucked hard on his lozenge and willed his stomach contents to stay where they were.

Mike Hallam was not quite so fortunate. He spun round and lunged frantically for the bathroom, from where they heard him hurl up whatever was inside him, continuing to dry heave for some time afterwards.

'What the hell was done to him to produce injuries like that?' Ted asked, somehow unable to tear his eyes away from the horror.

'His head has quite simply been kicked and jumped on until it exploded like a watermelon,' the Professor told him, in her usual direct way. 'This is one of the most frenzied attacks I can ever remember seeing. There are multiple stab wounds, for a start. A very savage attack, which would have killed the victim. But it then looks as if the killer has completely lost control and just jumped up and down repeatedly on him in a real eruption of anger.'

Mike Hallam reappeared at that point, wiping his mouth with a handkerchief and looking ashamed of himself.

'Sorry, boss, sorry Professor,' he excused himself. 'That has to be the worst one I've ever seen.'

Ted switched immediately into senior officer mode, taking control, glad of the opportunity to do something other than to stare in horror at the battered remains of the victim.

'Right, Mike, call in some of the team, whoever is free. Rob, definitely, and whoever else you think. Ask for some more officers from Uniform, too. There might be quite a lot of guests in a hotel this size and you'll need help to get contact details for all of them plus the staff. You go down to reception to meet them. Find out all you can about who our victim is from the booking records. I want this entire floor cleared of guests. Is there a dining room here?'

Mike nodded, and Ted continued, 'Good, get them all assembled in there and ask the management to give them coffee. Then you and the team need to take statements from everyone, including the staff on duty. Especially whoever was first on the scene. A chambermaid, perhaps? And take young Ian with you, he's not looking too clever. Make sure you and he get a hot drink.

'I'll see what I can find out from here, then come down and join you. Leave Stuart on the door for now, to stop anyone coming to have a nosy round. Get the whole area taped off and post uniformed officers to keep it clear. And make sure all the staff know not to talk about this to anyone, especially the press, if they get wind of it. Try to convince the guests of that too, if you can.'

Mike gave him a grateful look, relieved not to have to stay in the room any longer than he needed to. He went back out into the corridor, already taking out his mobile phone to call reinforcements.

Ted turned back to the Professor.

'Right, what can you tell me so far? Do you have an approximate time of death, please?'

'I would say between midnight and two in the morning, but I'll be able to be more accurate after the post-mortem. It's clear from the state of the bedding that someone had recently had sex, and there are short dark hairs from our victim, as well as several long blonde hairs, on the pillows.'

A look of intensified horror spread over Ted's face as he realised the implications of what she was telling him.

'You're surely not telling me that the killer could be a woman? Would a woman be capable of inflicting injuries like those?'

'Physically? Yes, I see no reason why not. The good news there is that there are footprints on what remains of the head and face which might give you some valuable information, when we've had time to examine them more thoroughly. Emotionally, could a woman do it? Sadly, such violence is not quite as rare as one might prefer to think with the so-called fairer sex.

'I can also tell you that the victim had been in the shower just before he was killed. There are still traces of shower gel and shampoo on him, so he hadn't had time to rinse himself. But he may have washed himself enough to remove any useful DNA traces of his sexual partner.'

Ted was looking slowly around the room, letting his eyes take in the slightest indication of what had happened.

'So, the initial knife attack took place by the door, but was it someone trying to get out, or someone the victim had let in?' he mused aloud, then, to the Professor, 'What about the weapon? Anything you can tell me about that?'

'Again, I'll know more after the post-mortem, but my initial thoughts are that it could be a standard kitchen knife. You're the detective, of course, but I suggest you have a look at the door handle and see what that tells you.'

Ted followed her advice, turned and walked to the door, pushing it to so that he could examine the handle on the inside. He studied it carefully, then self-consciously took out his reading glasses to bring it more into focus. He was still not comfortable being seen wearing them, so he put them back in his pocket before he turned again to face the Professor.

'I take it that the residue is shampoo, or shower gel? So, our man was in the shower, something or someone took him over to the door, which he either opened or tried to prevent someone else from doing so, at which point he was stabbed.'

The Professor nodded agreement.

'The force of the first stab wound knocked him backwards. His attacker continued to stab him as he staggered back. Then when he either fell or, I suspect, probably tripped against the foot of the bed, they leapt on him and gave him a final, mortal, stab wound to the throat which severed the jugular vein. Then the kicking began. It was certainly prolonged, to have inflicted so much damage.'

'Any ID anywhere?'

'His wallet is on the desk or dressing table or whatever you would call it, over there under the window. We haven't touched any personal effects, until you or someone from your team got here. From what I've seen of what remains of him, I'd put him somewhere between mid-forties and mid-fifties, but his documents should give you more detail.'

Ted picked his way carefully to the other side of the room, avoiding the blood and vomit as best he could. He was gloved up, so he carefully picked up the wallet and slid out the driving licence inside.

'Duncan Waters,' he read aloud. 'Lives in Southampton. Aged forty-six, so you were spot on. I wonder what he was doing up here?'

'Perhaps he was whatever the politically correct word is

now for a travelling salesman?' Bizzie Nelson speculated.

'I'll take the wallet with me, get our young Steve to run his details through PNC and anywhere else that might give us a lead. I'll just bag it up, then I'll get out of your way and let you carry on. Can you let me know when you'll be doing the post-mortem and I'll come myself. I don't think it's fair to inflict it on Mike. He's already suffered enough.'

Ted was relieved to get out of the room with his stomach contents intact. He paused to have a few words with the PC still on the door and promised to find someone to bring him up a cup of tea.

As he made his way towards the stairs, he got on his phone to young Steve with the details he had so far of the victim, asking him to run whatever checks he could. He also told him he might have another small job for him when he got back to the office. Next, he called the Ice Queen to give her the initial details he had so far on the case.

'Although this is on our patch and the new team is not fully up and running yet, this is exactly the sort of case which will come under its remit. Please give DSU Baker a call and fill him in on the details, at least, as a courtesy.'

Jim Baker listened in silence while Ted gave him all the information he had so far on their current case.

'Christ, Ted, that sounds like a bad one,' he growled. 'I don't envy you, being there for that. Let's hope it's just a one-off. Bad enough if it is, but if it's just some violent crime of passion and you wrap it up with your usual speed and efficiency, that'll be something. Keep me posted, and let me know when you've got your new team members. I'd like to come over to say hello, and perhaps you and I can have a quick drink together to celebrate your promotion. Congratulations on that, Ted, it was well overdue.'

Ted and the team spent their time taking statements from everyone they could find, and checking details. No one in the neighbouring rooms was admitting to having heard anything.

But the manager was keen to tell them that one of the features of the hotel was its soundproofing, so guests could get a good night's sleep, without hearing everything which happened in the next room. Ted had already asked for CCTV footage covering the times the Professor had given him, with an hour's margin of error either side.

The management kept the team well topped up with coffee, and a plate of sandwiches appeared at one point. Neither Ted nor Mike could so much as look at them, after what they'd seen.

Once they'd broken the back of the early enquiries, Ted and Mike went back to the office, leaving Rob in charge. It was a good opportunity for the team's newly appointed Acting Detective Sergeant to step up to the mark.

Steve had already found out a lot of information by the time Ted got back to his office. He'd put together the beginnings of an impressive folder. But Ted had something else he wanted to do before he really got stuck into the current case. He decided it was worth an hour out of the office to check up on the flat in Sabden House, where the alcoholic man had been found dead. He wanted to take Steve with him to see how he acquitted himself in the field, as he tended to be such a computer geek, who always preferred to be in the office.

Ted had picked up the keys for the flat where Stan Marshall had died. On the short drive to the address, he explained to Steve that Professor Nelson had raised a few doubts about the cause of death.

'I just want to check it out for myself, see what I think, and I thought it would be an opportunity for you to use your powers of observation, which I know are good. I want you to tell me your first impressions, let me know if you see anything which doesn't look right to you. Then we can compare notes.'

Steve went pink, as usual, but was clearly pleased to be out on a job with the boss. As Ted opened the door, they both stepped into the small, untidy flat, first putting on gloves and shoe covers, in case it did turn out to be a crime scene. Ted turned on the light so they could see better. The PCs had been right about one thing. It did smell bad in there.

Steve stood perfectly still just inside the door, letting his eyes travel slowly around the chaos and squalor. Ted was doing the same, wondering if the young man would pick up on what he had seen for himself, probably because he had an idea in his mind of what he was looking for.

Finally, the young man spoke.

'Sir, I don't know a lot about whisky, but I've never seen a fancy wooden box like that one over there on any bottle I've ever seen on a supermarket shelf. So just looking round this flat, which I think is a council tenancy, my first thought is how would someone living like this afford to buy something like that? And if they didn't, who gave it to them and why?'

Ted smiled slowly.

'Steve, you have just proved why it was fair to drop the Trainee from your title. You've got just the right sort of enquiring mind for this type of work. Well done, that's good work. Right, now we need to bag up that box and the bottle, if we can find it, then get it checked for prints and anything else it might tell us.

'Now, there's just another quick call I want to make before we go back to the nick.'

Chapter Four

Ted led the way back down the stairs from the first floor, where Marshall's flat was situated, then along a corridor, looking at the numbers on doors, before stopping in front of the one at the end. He made no comment to Steve as to their reasons for the second visit. Instead, he knocked firmly on the door and stood back to wait.

After what seemed like a considerable time, Steve said, 'Nobody at home, sir?'

Ted shook his head.

'He's there, it just takes him a bit of time to get to the door.'

Eventually, they heard the sound of slow, shuffling footsteps and heavy breathing. Then someone was undoing a series of locks and the door swung open just enough to allow a man's full moon face to peer warily at them.

'DI Darling, John. Remember me? And this is DC Ellis. Can we come in, please? I want to ask you a few questions.'

Steve was surprised by the look of absolute delight which split the man's face into a beaming smile as he opened the door wider and moved awkwardly back into an open doorway to allow them to enter. It was not the usual reaction to an unannounced visit from the police.

'Come in, Inspector Darling, please come through to the sitting room.'

The man was quite tall but his extreme obesity made him look gigantic in the dark, narrow hallway which ran the length of the poky flat. It was some time since Ted had last seen him, not since his move to this accommodation from the old tower block where he used to live. He was shocked at how much his size had increased since their last encounter. He now moved painfully slowly and with obvious difficulty, his breath wheezing with every step, and when he reached the door to the living room, Ted noticed he had to position himself at a careful angle to be able to fit through the opening.

He led them into a surprisingly neat and tidy room. A table held all the medication and equipment necessary to manage serious diabetes. There was also an open book, which Steve noticed was in Russian.

'Would you like to sit there on the sofa? It's a bit low for me so I tend to sit here,' the man explained, slowly and carefully lowering his immense bulk on to a specially-made sturdy wooden chair at the table.

'John, we're here about a murder. Can I ask your whereabouts from between about ten o'clock last night and around four this morning?'

The big man sighed.

'I knew you'd get me, Inspector. And you have. Yes, I did it, honest, it was me.'

'Can you just confirm your shoe size for me, John?' Ted asked him. 'And have you got the pair you were wearing last night, please?'

The man looked taken aback. He was wearing shapeless felt slippers, their sides cut open to allow access for his badly swollen feet.

'Er, yes, I take a size ten and a half. They're out in the hallway. Just one pair, my everyday ones.'

Ted nodded to Steve who went out of the room and returned shortly with a smart pair of brogues, impeccably clean and highly polished. Both men could see immediately that there was no way they would have fitted on to John's feet in their current state.

Ted took the shoes and made a solemn show of turning them over and carefully examining the soles. Then he handed them back to Steve to return to the hallway.

In a softer, less formal tone, Ted said, 'Are you all right, John? How are you doing? Is the new flat suiting you? I see you've got the curtains closed. Is there a reason for that?'

Steve stayed tactfully in the hallway while the boss was talking to Honest John. He knew the man was their local confessor. It was his way of getting the attention he craved, confessing to every crime he heard about on the patch. He wasn't quite sure of the reason behind the boss's pre-emptive strike in visiting, before the latest sudden death had been made public, but he knew it would be a sound one.

'It's not so good here, Mr Darling,' John said quietly, a wistful note in his voice. 'They thought they were helping me, putting me on the ground floor. But the local kids come and peer at me through the window and shout things at me. Horrible things. So I keep the curtains closed.'

Ted took out one of his cards and handed it to him.

'Here's my card, in case you haven't got one. Let me know if ever I can do anything to help you, John. And I'm glad to say that, based on my examination of your shoes, we can eliminate you from our current enquiries. Don't worry, we'll see ourselves out. You take care, now.'

They'd come in Ted's own car, a small Renault Scenic. He hadn't yet taken possession of the service vehicle he'd been allocated for his new role. On the drive back to the station, he asked Steve for his thoughts on his first encounter with Honest John.

'Sir, was there a reason you didn't tell him you're now a DCI?' he asked to begin with.

When Ted laughed and admitted, 'I keep forgetting,' Steve gave his initial impressions.

'Well, sir, I was surprised at how clean and tidy everywhere was. And how well kept his shoes are, when he's clearly not able to wear them now. I saw that he has one of those grabber things for picking them up to clean but he clearly never puts them on. I rather thought, with his problems, he'd live in the same sort of state as the other man.'

'You're not the first to think that. Honest John's a great example of why we should never pre-judge anyone, especially in this job. He can hardly get about, but he's always cleaning and tidying up, as best he can. Did you see the book? He speaks fluent Russian, used to have his own import/export business. Quite a high flyer.

'Then his only son died of leukaemia, very young. John went completely off the rails. His wife was of Russian origin and she went back there. John started to comfort eat, and you can see the result. Remember, there's usually a story like that behind every human tragedy. But despite all he's been through, he keeps himself and his home as clean as he can, within his physical limitations. The reason he keeps calling us to confess is that he craves attention, and company. I like to keep in touch with him, make sure he's as all right as he can be.

'How's Maurice doing now, by the way? When does he hope to be back?'

Steve lodged with DC Maurice Brown, who was on sick leave after a serious knife incident which had nearly cost him his life.

'Making good progress, sir, he should be back the week after next, with any luck.'

'Right, Steve, when we get back, I want you to prioritise our body from the hotel. Find out everything there is to know about him, particularly what he was doing here. You'll be getting some help any day now, in the shape of a new computer expert. But I also want you to do a bit of digging into Sabden House in respect of the two deaths from there. John's on a secure tenancy. Find out if the others were as well. Have a check around, see if there are any plans afoot to do anything with that building which might give somebody some kind of motive for wanting to free up flats occupied by secure tenants.'

Ted got the team together when they arrived back at the end of the day, for a catch-up on the day's progress. Mike had started a whiteboard with what information they had so far on the victim from the hotel, Duncan Waters. A further search of his wallet had revealed that he was a sales rep for a company selling photovoltaic panel installation packages.

There would be no photos of this victim up on the board. Once they received all the shots from the scene of crime, they would be put in folders for all the team to see but not kept on public display. There was no telling who might come into the main office from time to time, like the cleaners, and Ted didn't want to inflict those images on anyone unless it was essential.

'Now we have the ID, we need to get on to Southampton to contact the next of kin and let them know. Rob, can you see to that, please? Whoever it is will need to come up at some point to identify the body in some way. I'm waiting to hear from the Professor about when the PM will be. I've said I'll take that one, unless anyone wants to fight me for it?'

There was a ripple of amusement from the team. They appreciated the boss's attempt at humour in a case which was hard for all of them. They appreciated even more him attending the PM himself without delegating, as some senior officers had been known to do in similar circumstances.

'Still nothing at all from any witnesses who heard anything?'

'Boss, the room next to the victim was empty that night. The victim's room was at the end of the corridor, if you remember, so only one adjoining room. The couple in the room opposite had been to a family gathering where they drank quite a lot of wine and were sleeping like logs. They admitted they wouldn't have heard anything,' Rob told him.

'What about access? Can anyone just walk into the hotel at

any time?'

Rob shook his head.

'After ten o'clock at night you need the code to the keypad at the door to operate the lock. That's issued when you check in. There were some guests who had already checked out before the body was discovered. We're trying to track them down to talk to them.'

'And who discovered the body? Was it someone coming in to clean the room?'

'Yes, boss. Interestingly, the swipe-card for his door had been returned to the reception desk so they thought he'd checked out. It was a pre-paid booking by credit card. That's why the cleaner used her pass-card to get in. She thought he'd already left. When she found him, she threw up then went to get the manager, who did the same thing. That's when they called 999.'

'So the killer, presumably, picked up the card from somewhere in the room and left it at reception when he went? That seems like a rather cold and calculating act, after such a frenzied attack. Anything from the CCTV to indicate who the killer might have been?'

'Jinxed there, boss,' Rob told him. 'The system's been playing up for some time. It kept cutting out last night, and there are chunks missing from the crucial timing. That seems to be genuine. We had a quick glance at some other dates and it's clear it's been an ongoing problem that's not yet been fixed. We're not going to get anything from that.'

'Right, well, we need to find out everything we can about the victim and his whereabouts in the hours leading up to his death. I'll leave you to get on with that before you all knock off, then we'll come at it fresh tomorrow. I'm going to talk to the Super to see about our new team members. We might be glad of some extra help with this case. Good start, though, well done, everyone.'

The Ice Queen was at her desk when Ted went down to find her. She offered him a seat and a coffee. He sat down but shook his head and said, 'No thanks, no coffee this late in the day or I'll be pinging off the walls all night.'

He gave her his initial report on the case, sparing her the worst of the details, though stressing that it was a frenzied attack, the worst he and many of the others had ever witnessed.

'I certainly don't envy you this one. I hope it's something you will be able to wrap up quickly. I'll make sure we have a press release ready. I wouldn't want any details or wild speculation of this to be bandied about in the papers too soon and cause widespread panic.

'Now, on the subject of your team members. I've managed to source a DI, a DC and a CFI who look good on paper and are available immediately. Obviously, you'll want to look at their files and probably interview them for yourself.'

She pushed three files across the desk to Ted, who briefly scanned the first page of each then said, 'I'm no good in interviews myself so I don't tend to judge people on their performance in them. If you've read through their files and think they would be a fit for the team, let's start them and see how we get on. After all, on paper, I would have been mad to accept DC Vine, but she's turning out to be an excellent officer, a real asset to the team.'

'Which is largely down to you and the way you manage people,' she smiled.

'My only reservation is why they're available, if they're good. As long as there's a valid reason for that, I'd be happy to go for them.'

'The computer expert has recently moved to the area. I think the combination of her and young Steve Ellis could be our secret weapon in a lot of things. I imagine, for example, your victim today has a laptop, which will need rummaging through? And a phone? It means we can now do a lot more of that here, without having to outsource and put up with the consequent wait.

'Both DI Rodriguez and DC Jennings are casualties of staffing level reductions in various divisions. Roles are being reshuffled and those two were outstanding amongst the list of officers looking for other positions. Would you like me to arrange for them to start tomorrow, if possible? It might be a good idea to have all three start at the same time, then you can do a single induction and it won't take you away from valuable operational time.'

Ted's head was reeling as he drove home at the end of the day. He could scarcely believe that in such a short time he had found himself promoted and about to head up an expanded team on what was looking like a challenging case. Even if this killing proved to be a one-off, it was still, in terms of the means of death, one of the worst he had encountered to date.

He was definitely not looking forward to the post-mortem, and he'd had a call from Professor Nelson, just as he was leaving, to say that she had scheduled it for early the following morning. It meant he'd had to hand over the induction of his new team members to Mike Hallam.

There would have to be some rapid rearranging of offices and furniture, and the Ice Queen had promised early delivery of a new computer for their CFI. After consideration, Ted had decided to keep his old office, judging it too small to accommodate two people. His new DI could move into Jim Baker's vacated room, with Mike Hallam to keep him company.

Trev was in the kitchen when Ted arrived home and the kettle was on. Having turned down coffee, Ted was keen for a mug of green tea. The two exchanged a hug and Trev asked, 'How was your day? I've not started cooking yet, I wasn't sure how long you'd be. Well, I've thrown some jacket potatoes in the oven and it's lamb chops, which won't take long. Is that all right for you?'

Ted bent down to stroke cats vying for his attention as he replied, 'That sounds good, as long as my chop is not even remotely pink. I've seen enough blood today to last me for a while. And I've got a particularly gruesome PM to look forward to tomorrow morning. Oh, and I'm getting new team members tomorrow. How do you pronounce this name correctly?'

He picked up a handy pen and scribbled on the back of an envelope, pushing it towards Trev who read it and said, 'Depends. Some people Anglicize it and say George, but in Spanish or Portuguese it would be Jorge,' with perfect mastery of the rasping H sounds for J and G.

Ted had a tentative go himself.

'I don't want to start off by not knowing how to pronounce his name,' he smiled.

'What are they like?' Trev asked, checking the potatoes and putting the grill on ready for the chops.

Ted shrugged. 'You know me, I prefer to keep an open mind about people, so I've barely glanced at their files. Whatever they're like, they'll all need to be able to hit the ground running with a case like this one as their baptism of fire.'

Chapter Five

'How the heck are the next of kin going to be able to identify him?' Ted asked Professor Nelson, as he got his first close-up look at the battered remains of the face which had belonged to Duncan Waters.

'Luckily one of his eyes is still intact,' she told him breezily, looking closely and appraisingly. 'What we usually do in cases like this is rely on judicious padding and bandaging, and leave only the most presentable parts on show. The relatives stay in the viewing gallery, of course, so they don't see a great deal anyway. We usually manage to give them something they can recognise. We'd probably leave a hand exposed if there was a distinctive ring or other feature, for example. Although our man here wasn't wearing what looked like his wedding ring. That was in the drawer of the small unit next to the bed.'

'You know I don't like to jump to hasty conclusions, Bizzie, but if that was the case, I'm guessing there's a good chance that the long blonde hairs in his bed didn't belong to Mrs Waters. Trev and I don't do rings but I know most people who do tend to leave them on, and certainly when going to bed with the partner they represent.'

'Are you going to be all right with this one, Edwin?' she asked briskly. 'Only none of it is very pretty.'

Ted was already sucking on the first of his Fisherman's Friend lozenges, which had got him through some difficult and gruesome situations. It was as much the comfort factor of remembering happy times with his father, the two of them fishing up at the canal or at Roman Lakes and never catching anything. Just enjoying each other's company, while his father munched on his lozenges to ward off the cold and damp.

'You're not going to stick things under my nose and ask me to sniff them again, are you?' he asked suspiciously. 'As long as you don't, I'll probably be fine. Hopefully. But not guaranteed.'

The Professor chuckled, then became her usual professional self as she set about skilfully getting the body of Duncan Waters to give up its innermost secrets.

'Is there any news on your whisky drinker of the expensive taste?'

'You were right about the whisky. Something expensive with the Highland Park label. We went back and found the bottle, and the fancy box it came in. I'm getting them checked for prints, but even if we find and identify any, there's still a long way to go to make any kind of case for us, and this killing needs to take priority.'

The Professor nodded her understanding as she worked.

'I think the most we can hope for with the drinker is a misadventure verdict at the inquest, unless you get very lucky with fingerprints. But even so, it's surely not a crime to give someone whisky, even if you know or suspect that it may kill them?'

'It would be a very complicated case to bring, as the Super has already reminded me. I don't want to abandon it, though. It's so cynical, if those deaths really were caused deliberately. But for now, I need to concentrate on Mr Waters. This is bad enough if it's a one-off, but if this killer has more than one victim in mind, it doesn't bear thinking about.'

'From what I can see so far, I can tell you that more than one of these knife wounds would have proved fatal on its own. The last one, to the neck, would certainly have killed him. The combination of all of them together would have caused him to bleed out in much less than ten minutes. Some of the wounds severed arteries, which caused catastrophic blood loss. I think you now know, at first hand - no pun intended - what the effects of arterial bleeding are.

'There is some small comfort in the fact that Mr Waters was dying when the kicking to his head began and he probably lost consciousness before much of it was done to him.'

'Can you tell me any more about the footwear yet?'

'All I can safely tell you for now is that they were a size forty-four European, which equates to nine and a half in old money, so not all that big. Still probably more likely to suggest a man than a woman. Also that they were something like a work boot, with heavy tread soles, and I wouldn't rule out steel toecaps, because of the extent of the damage. We will be able to give you the exact make later on.

'It's good to see you back, Edwin, and seemingly in such good form. How is the arm doing? When will you be able to lose the bandaging?'

Ted grinned guiltily and said, 'Don't say anything to my boss but it could come off now, really, or at least I could manage with a much smaller dressing. It just gives me a valid excuse not to wear my suit to work. I always feel much more functional in casual wear.'

Bizzie laughed delightedly. Ted always marvelled at her ability to go from serious and professional Professor of Forensic Pathology to the warm-hearted and caring individual he knew her to be.

'Your secret is safe with me,' she promised. 'I'll email you all my findings later on but for now I think I've given you all I can. Death was the result of several stab wounds, plus the serious trauma to the head. You'll get exact details of the knife later, with my conclusions in full detail. So now I better let you go and get on with trying to find this killer, just in case they are planning more of the same.'

Ted was glad to get back into his own clothes and to leave the smell of the mortuary behind him as he drove back to the station. He was keen to meet his new team members, assuming the Ice Queen had managed to arrange for them to start at such short notice. Despite the difficult morning so far, he felt surprisingly optimistic, keen to get on with the task in hand.

Ted was just back to work after extended sick leave for the knife injury and subsequent surgery. He'd needed a complete break to give him time to think about his career. Policing seemed to get harder by the day, with more and more restraints on officers. Ted had never been a rule-bender; he'd never needed to be, and he despised a bent cop as much as anyone else did. But constantly being hit with enquiries into every move he and the team made had sapped his morale after the last case.

Although he hated being apart from Trev, he'd gone to Wales for two weeks, to stay with his former DS, Jack Gregson. Ted loved to walk. Jack could walk a bit and was encouraged to do so by his doctor. But sometimes his Parkinson's disease would cause him to freeze up, so he couldn't go far.

The two men had settled into a comfortable daily routine. Both would walk, slowly and companionably, down to a nearby hotel which had a bar and restaurant open to non-residents, in time for morning coffee. Ted would leave Jack safely installed while he went off to walk the tracks of nearby Brechfa Forest, coming back at lunchtime so they could eat together and talk about old times.

Once they'd eaten, Jack would walk home slowly by himself while Ted went off to explore further afield, desperate to discover some of the wide open spaces of Llanllwni Mountain, which were the nearest things locally to his preferred desolate and windswept uplands of the Peak District at home. Then when he got back, the kettle would be on and they would talk some more until Jack's daughter came home and got the supper on, often helped by Ted.

The break had done him more good than he'd thought it would. Now he was back, secretly thrilled by his unexpected promotion and the new responsibilities that went with it. He was determined to make his expanded team a force to be reckoned with. And their first task was going to be to catch the killer who had had the effrontery to commit such a violent act on his patch.

Before he went upstairs to meet the new team members, Ted took a moment to catch up with Kevin Turner. He'd spoken to Maurice Brown and was able to report that he was happy to go with the inspector to the hospital and do whatever hand-holding duties were necessary.

'And seriously, Kev, you really can trust him. He knows how to keep a secret. It'll cost you a few pints, but he's just what you need to make sure you're all right. I hope it all goes well for you.'

The new DC was the first person Ted saw when he went into the main office. She'd taken over Mike Hallam's old desk, now he was moving in with the new DI. She stood up when she saw him come over to her desk to introduce himself, shaking his hand.

'Morning, boss, I'm DC Jennings. Megan. I'm just getting up to speed with the current case. Not a nice one. I hear you're just back from the PM?'

Ted liked what he saw. She looked to be around mid-thirties and her grey eyes had a direct, searching look which made him suspect she was formidable at interviewing witnesses and suspects.

They exchanged a few words then, as Ted crossed the office to where Steve was now sharing work space with the new computer expert, he could see that his newly made up Acting DC had got it bad. The young man shot to his feet, peeling his adoring gaze away from his new work colleague with evident difficulty.

'Sir, this is our new CFI, Océane. This is our boss, DCI Darling,' he made the clumsy introduction.

The young woman unfolded languidly to her feet with the feline grace of one of Ted's cats and held out a hand for a somewhat cursory handshake. She was tall and incredibly slim, with dark auburn hair in wildly rebellious curls, pulled back into a thick ponytail, and her eyes were almost as intensely blue as Trevor's. She smiled as she trotted out an explanation she must have had to make many times. Ted knew to his cost the problems of having a somewhat unusual name.

'Sorry, my mother is an ageing French hippy.'

Ted was surprised to see that there was already an impressive new computer sitting on her work station. When the Ice Queen promised to do something, she certainly didn't hang around, and she always delivered.

'I'm sure Steve's told you that we should be getting our latest victim's laptop and phone any time now. It will be your main priority to pull off any and every piece of information you can for us from both of them.'

'If it can be done, I'll do it for you. If I can't do it for you, then it can't be done,' she told him.

It should have sounded arrogant. Coming from her, it was simply a statement of fact.

Two down, one more to meet. Ted wondered if his luck could hold for his third new team member. He liked what he had seen of the first two. Now he headed to Jim Baker's old office in search of his new DI, who was going to be his right-hand man whenever he was away from the nick with the mobile unit. It was essential that they got on and were singing from the same hymn-sheet. If the new inspector came in with his own ideas of how Ted's team should be run, it could be disastrous.

Ted walked in without knocking. This office too had been rearranged, space made for two people to work at the large desk. The man behind the desk stood up to shake Ted's outstretched hand. He was early forties, not too tall, which Ted was pleased to see. He already had to look up at all his team members, except Jezza Vine, being short himself. DI Rodriguez had a slightly olive complexion and surprisingly light brown eyes. His beard was impeccably trimmed, leaving his cheeks clear.

'So, Jorge, is it?' Ted asked, sitting down in the seat opposite him, the place he'd occupied most days for his talks with the old Big Boss. It felt strange to realise that he was now, effectively, the Big Boss himself.

Rodriguez smiled his appreciation of Ted's efforts at pronunciation but said, 'Jo is fine, boss. If you're not used to it, you can give yourself a sore throat trying to pronounce it like that. I have a Spanish father and an Irish mother but I was born and raised in Bolton, so it quickly became Jo, at school. Jo for the whole team, if that's okay with you? I know the team already call you boss so I'm happy to be Jo.'

Ted nodded.

'Whatever you like, it's a relaxed team. As long as everyone does their job and shows a bit of respect, I don't mind first names. I'm Ted, when it's just the two of us. Boss is fine in front of the team.

'Now, I always like to get this part out of the way early on as it can, just sometimes, cause a few problems. I take it you know I'm gay, and I hope that doesn't bother you?'

'It should do, boss, me being a good Catholic boy. But it won't worry me at all, as long as we're clear on the fact that I'm not and never will be.'

Ted laughed out loud. He had a feeling that he and Jo were going to get on fine, if the early signs were any indication.

'What about you? Married? Family?'

Jo turned round a framed photo, which he'd put on his desk, so that Ted could see it. A family group. Lots of happily smiling faces.

'Good Catholic boy who does what the Pope tells him,' he smiled. 'So I have six kids, three of each.'

'Blimey! I thought having six cats was hard going.'

The ice firmly broken, the two men got down to the serious business of discussing the case so far. The more they talked, the more confident Ted became that Jo would be a good choice to be left at the helm when he had to go away. Unless he had a serious vice which he was good at concealing, he seemed as if he was going to be an excellent fit for the role.

'What are your initial thoughts on a suspect?' Jo asked him.

'I'm really hoping that we're not looking at a woman as the killer,' Ted told him frankly. 'I know I should know better, in this job, but the idea that a woman might be capable of such savagery as that turns my stomach. Luckily the boot size rather suggests a man.

'We'll know more when we get all the forensic results in, but if the blonde hairs in the bed were not his wife, then perhaps he was playing away and we're looking for a jealous husband? It's early days yet, so we don't really have enough information to start speculating. Once the family have ID'd him, or what's left of him, and we have his phone and computer, we should be able to start putting together a clearer picture of how he spent his last hours. That should make it all a bit clearer.

'Get Mike Hallam to give you all the details on this, and on the other ongoing cases we have on our hands.

'Right, today being Wednesday, it's my day for sloping away early, with the full knowledge and approval of the Super. My partner and I run a self-defence club for schoolchildren, and it's usually my night for some judo practice myself, though I'm not up to much at the moment,' Ted added, getting to his feet, and holding up his bandaged hand.

He didn't add that the other reason he left early was for a counselling session, before his martial arts. Few people knew about that, and he wanted to keep it that way. He was doing much better lately, but he still kept up the sessions, when time allowed.

'I'll see you in the morning. In the meantime, Mr Sulu, you have the conn.'

Jo went up even further in his estimation when he replied, 'Aye, Captain.'

A lot of Ted's vintage film and TV quotes went over many people's heads.

Jo grinned as his new boss left the office. He'd heard he was easy to work with and he was encouraged by what he'd seen so far.

Ted and Trev always liked to walk to the gym which housed the dojo they attended. It took them about half an hour and was a good means of warming up gently. It wasn't always possible, with Ted's job, but he had timed his counselling sessions to allow for the walk, when he was free.

As they walked, he told Trev about the new team members and how optimistic he felt that the team might go from strength to strength. Trev was pleased to see his partner so upbeat once more. He'd been to some dark places with recent investigations. It was nice to see glimpses of the old Ted.

When Ted had finished talking, Trev told him, 'Willow and Rupert have invited me to a party this weekend. It's on Saturday night, with some friends of theirs. The thing is…'

Ted chuckled.

'Let me guess. The thing is, the presence of a copper might just severely cramp the style of the beautiful people at such a party?'

Willow and Rupert were friends of them both, who worked as models. Their social circle was a bit above where Ted felt comfortable, but he knew that Trev would love such an event.

'Would you mind if I went? I won't do any stupid stuff, you know that. Perhaps a glass or two more wine than usual and maybe just a bit of blow. But I promise you it won't be any more than that. Rupe's the designated driver, and he's very sensible so you don't need to worry on that score. The friends live in…'

Ted cut him short.

'No, don't tell me, it's best if I don't know. I know you'd love to go so that's fine. Just please promise me you really won't do anything stupid? No snorting, no pills, nothing like that.'

Trev hugged him and said sincerely, 'I don't. I won't. Promise. Swear down.'

Ted laughed.

'All right, no need to go overboard. I believe you. Go. Have fun. I'll be fine.'

'Why not ask Annie round for supper? I could cook something to leave for you, if you're busy. She'd love to hear all about how clever her son is to make DCI. I'll have a much better time if I know you've got some company while I'm out partying.'

Chapter Six

Ted's first job of the morning, after the team briefing, was to go to the hospital to meet Duncan Waters' family when they arrived to identify the body. Without wishing to add to their grief and distress, he was keen to ask them some questions while they were in the area. He preferred to do it himself, rather than rely on officers he didn't know, from the force local to the family, and Southampton was a long way to go to do so.

He decided to take the new DC, Megan Jennings, with him. It would give him chance to get to know her a little better and see how she operated. He also thought she might be useful in helping the victim's widow through a distressing time. Ted always worried he would say the wrong thing in such circumstances, although all who knew him said how good he was with people.

He'd been told that the deceased man's widow had come up the evening before, with two teenage sons. They were staying at a hotel, though not the one in which Waters had been murdered.

After the formal identification, Bizzie would lend him her small office to talk to the family, rather than him having to ask them to go with him to the police station. He didn't envy the widow the task in hand. He was glad that she at least had her sons with her for mutual support, although it was clearly going to be as difficult for them as it was for her. He knew Bizzie's team would have done everything in their power to make the body presentable for the identification, but he imagined it would not have been easy, given what they had to work with.

Ted had arranged to meet the family in the hospital's main reception area and escort them himself down to the mortuary where they would make their identification. He felt that it was the least he could do, as Senior Investigating Officer on the case.

As soon as he saw the widow, it confirmed the suspicions he already harboured that the blonde hairs in the dead man's bed where not those of his wife. Mrs Waters' hair was short and dark, probably no longer naturally so. He introduced himself and DC Jennings to her and to the two tall, older teenage boys with her, who identified themselves as her sons, Jason and Ben.

On their way downstairs he explained, picking his words carefully, that because of extensive injuries, her late husband's head and face would be heavily bandaged when she saw him. He saw the family safely installed in the viewing gallery. Then when Mrs Waters nodded in response to his question if she was ready, Ted signalled for the curtains to be opened to give a view into the post-mortem suite. Duncan Waters' body was lying on the steel table nearest to the window.

Ted was heartily relieved to see what a good job had been done of the body. The judiciously placed heavy padding and bandaging gave no hint of the devastation which lay underneath. The intact area around one eye and part of the cheek below were about all which was readily visible, together with a hand, wearing the wedding ring which had been replaced to help with identification, on top of the sheet which covered the corpse.

Mrs Waters staggered at the sight and her sons protectively took hold of an arm each to support her. Tears sprang to her eyes and she nodded several times, struggling to speak. In the end, the older boy had to speak for her.

'That's him. That's my father, Duncan Waters.'

'Thank you. I'm sorry we had to put you through this, but it was essential to get a formal identification, to help with our enquiries. Would you mind just coming with me for a few moments, while I ask you some questions?'

Ted ushered the stunned family out of the gallery and along the corridor to Bizzie's office. There was not much room, and not enough chairs for everyone. Ted made sure that the woman was sitting down and as comfortable as possible, offering her a glass of water, before he began. He was pleased when, without a word, DC Jennings slipped quietly into a seat next to the woman. As if reassured by her presence, Mrs Waters placed her hand into the officer's and squeezed it hard for comfort. It was clearly what she needed.

'First of all, Mrs Waters, please accept my sincere condolences for the loss of your husband, and let me assure you that we are doing everything in our power to find out who did this to him,' Ted began. 'We've recovered his car and that is being subjected to forensic testing so we can't, unfortunately, release it to you yet. We will inform you when you can collect it.'

'I can't drive,' the woman said anxiously. 'And Jason's only recently passed his test, he doesn't even have his own car yet. It would be a long drive for him ...'

'It's all right, mum,' the older son interrupted soothingly, putting a hand on her shoulder while she clung even harder on to DC Jennings' hand. 'That's not important now, we can sort it out. Uncle Laurie will come and get the car, I'm sure.'

'Mrs Waters, what I need to know for now is, can you tell me anything about your husband's trip up here? When did he come? How long was he planning on staying? Do you know anything about who he was meeting?' Ted asked, as gently as he could.

He always hated to intrude, but any information she could give them could be vital.

She looked desperately from one to another. DC Jennings let her keep clinging frantically on to her hand. With her own spare hand, she fished out a packet of paper tissues which she held out to her. Ted was liking what he saw of how his new team member behaved towards a bereaved woman. She was smiling encouragingly at her now.

'Er, he drove up on Sunday night,' Mrs Waters began hesitantly, taking a tissue, which she first dabbed against her eyes and nose, then squeezed into a damp and shapeless mess. 'He had clients to see in the area. He phoned me when he arrived, like he always did. He planned to stay three nights in Stockport, he said. Then he was going on to Birmingham, spending two nights there. He told me he would be home on Friday afternoon.'

Her voice broke as she realised that her husband would not be coming home on Friday. He would never be coming home again.

Her words confirmed the information they already had from the hotel records, about the length of the booking. What Ted needed now was something more, anything she could tell them to point them in the right direction.

'Thank you, that's very helpful. Now, I'm sorry to have to ask this, but did your husband have any enemies? Had he had trouble with anyone recently? Did he tell you of any difficulties with anyone?'

She looked puzzled now, turning her gaze from one to the other of them, as if seeking some sort of reassurance.

'You really think someone killed him, then? Deliberately, I mean?' she asked imploringly, wanting him to say it was all a mistake, it had simply been some dreadful accident. 'I can't think of anyone who would want to harm Duncan.'

Ted's warm hazel eyes sought hers and held contact as he said quietly, 'Mrs Waters, I'm sorry but there is no possible doubt that your husband was killed deliberately. I'm very sorry. Thank you for all your help, and let me assure you once more that we will do everything we possibly can to bring his killer to justice.'

He stood up and everyone else did the same. As the woman

turned to leave, the older son, Jason, said quietly to Ted, 'Can I have a quick word with you, please? In private?'

'Yes, of course. DC Jennings,' Ted said, taking out his wallet and extracting a note. 'Please would you be kind enough to take Mrs Waters and Ben up to the canteen and get them a drink of something, and one for yourself. Jason and I will come up and find you shortly.'

As the others left the room, Ted indicated to the boy to take a seat and sat down himself, facing him.

'Now, what can I do for you?'

'My father was a piece of shit,' the boy spat, his face contorting with surprising vehemence. 'My mum thinks Ben and I didn't know, but we're not children. We knew exactly what he was like. He was always chasing after other women, wherever he went, especially when he was on the road, like he was a lot of the time.

'Mum just pretended everything was all right. She's very nervy, totally dependent on him. Like you heard, she never even learnt to drive. She must have known, though. Dad even picked up an STD one time, so she must have known. Even she isn't that naïve.

'He used to leave his phone and his laptop lying around. Mum's useless with anything like that, but me and Ben saw stuff. That's how we knew all about what he was like. If someone's killed him, it could be because of all these other women.'

'Thank you for being so frank with me, Jason,' Ted told him. 'It could be very useful to the enquiry. We will, of course, be looking closely at his laptop and phone, but what you've said gives me a useful line of enquiry to start pursuing.'

'He was on lots of dating sites online. He was always going on there, boasting about how hot he was. He also had one of those phone apps. You know, for casual sex, no strings attached.'

Ted certainly didn't know, although he'd heard of such

things. He'd been in a monogamous relationship for more than eleven years. He definitely wasn't shopping for anyone else, not even window-shopping.

'Thank you for this, Jason, it really has been very helpful.'

The boy jutted out his chin defiantly. Ted guessed he didn't yet need to shave daily. Despite having passed his driving test, he still looked too young to be taking on the responsibilities of supporting his widowed mother.

'I'm not sorry he's dead,' he said, and it made him sound suddenly childish. 'I'm just sorry for my mother and what she's going through. But Ben and I will look after her. And then perhaps she might finally find someone who treats her like she deserves to be treated.'

On the drive back to the station, Ted filled Megan Jennings in on what the older son had told him. As was his way, he was also keen to give feedback on how she'd handled the situation.

'I like the way you dealt with Mrs Waters. I'm not very good at knowing the right thing to say and, on her own admission, Jezza is not exactly the tea and sympathy sort. She does have other excellent qualities, though.'

'No worries, boss. I'm a single mum. I have a boy of eight, Felix, who's mad about Minecraft. I can be quite motherly, when necessary. Here's your change, before I forget.'

She fished coins out of her pocket and at Ted's request, dropped them into the side pocket of his field jacket.

'I wondered what was going on with the family dynamics. I could tell that Ben was seething about something. The vibes coming off him were like Felix when he's on restricted Minecraft access. Or when it's not sausages for tea.'

Ted smiled to himself at the mental images that came into his head at her words. It sounded cosy and domestic, a far cry from what they were dealing with on this case.

'So do you think our man's death was related to his playing the field, boss?' she asked.

'I never like to speculate too soon, but it's certainly a strong possibility. We'll feed it back to the team and see what else anyone can throw into the mix.'

Not all the team members were in the office when they got back, but Ted assembled those who were. He prised Steve off his computer and away from Océane. She told Ted in passing that she now had Duncan Waters' phone and laptop and was working on those. Her eyes never left the screen, nor did her quick fingers quit the keyboard while she spoke.

He was left with Jo, Rob, Jezza, Megan, Steve and himself. He succinctly reported all the information they had discovered from interviewing the family, with particular emphasis on what Jason had told him.

'That confirms what I'm discovering so far,' Océane piped up from her work station, still not taking her eyes off the screen. 'I'll have more for you shortly, but there are certainly plenty of dating sites and more than one casual bunk-up app.'

'Thanks, Océane. Which brings us to the possibility that Mr Waters may have been killed as a result of his lifestyle. I don't like to think of a possible female killer, with anything as horrific as that but…'

'Not just women, boss,' Océane chimed in. 'At least one of the apps is decidedly AC/DC. Looks like he may have taken what he could get, where he could get it.'

Ted shook his head in disbelief. Whenever he thought he had plumbed the depths of human depravity, something else would come up to prove him wrong.

Jezza surprised them all by starting to sing, a crooning sort of song.

'Do you remember, when we met, that's the day, I knew you were my pet …'

'Jezza? Something you want to share with us?' Ted asked.

'Sea of Love, boss. Brilliant film. Al Pacino and Ellen Barkin. Blokes on the dating scene are getting their brains blown out so Pacino goes undercover. It turns out to be the jealous ex-husband of one of the women, picking off men who've dated her.'

'A jealous husband is a possibility,' Ted conceded. 'Océane, is there anything on there yet about where Waters was fixing up meetings? Anything which could have been intercepted by the husband, or partner, of whoever he was arranging to meet?'

'Plenty of steamy stuff here all right, and details of meet-ups. When I find the ones for his time up here, I'll print that off first and circulate it.'

Ted caught sight of Steve's wistful look and wasn't sure which he was missing the most, being at his computer, or being in close proximity to Océane. He was certainly gazing with cow eyes at both.

'What about the older son, boss? Jason?' Megan asked. 'Do you like him for a suspect? After all, on his own admission, he hated his father and was used to checking his phone and laptop to find out what he was up to.'

'One hell of a bluff, him offering me all that information, though,' Ted replied. 'He could easily have said nothing, then later denied all knowledge of what his dad had been up to. But we should certainly look into it. Let's get someone round to where they're staying and at least check out his shoe size, for a start. Megan, can you go, while they already know you? Can you also ask for an up to date photo of the victim. I'm guessing the ones on these sites might not be all that accurate.

'We also need to find out how feasible it would be for Jason to have got up here from Southampton by public transport, as his mother said he doesn't have a car. Unless, of course, he had help from someone. Perhaps we need to find out more about this Uncle Laurie he mentioned. Brother, or brother-in-law of the deceased? If he knew what our man was up to, did he do something about it?'

'About four hours by train, direct, just over nine on a coach, one change.'

Océane again. She seemed to have the ability to tune out what they were talking about and get on with her work, whilst at the same time hearing any bits that needed quick information from the computer she was working on. Ted was impressed. Steve was almost drooling.

'Anything on Waters' car yet?' Ted asked.

'Nothing yet, boss,' Rob told him. 'We're still waiting on forensics. In particular, we're waiting to hear if the owner of the blonde hair was ever in the car. In other words, did he go out and pick someone up in his car to take back to the hotel.'

'And anything from other guests at the hotel?'

Rob shook his head.

'No one admits to seeing or hearing anything. The others are out chasing up a few we've not spoken to so far, and pinning down the rest of the staff who've not yet been interviewed.'

'Right, let's get on with what we have got. We need that recent photo of him, so we can start showing it around, try to find out where he went, where he ate out, if he did. Anything like that.'

'Sir, I've printed a photo off from one of his dating site profiles as a starter,' Steve told him. 'But you're right, it may not be genuine.'

'I've just checked it. Definitely edited and enhanced, so you'll need a genuine one,' Océane confirmed.

'Good work,' Ted nodded his satisfaction. 'Now, before I forget, let's get together in The Grapes at close of play tomorrow. All of you. Jo, Megan, Océane, you too. It's a bit of a tradition. We go there from time to time, for a get-together, a bit of a morale boost. First round is always on me. Steve, make sure Maurice knows to come and join us. And the Big Boss is coming over. He wants to meet the new team members and see the rest of you again.'

There was a pause, then Jezza voiced what the rest of them were thinking.

'Er, boss, you are the Big Boss now.'

Ted smiled in embarrassment.

'I suppose I am. I'll just never get used to me being the Big anything.'

Chapter Seven

Océane clearly knew her stuff. Before much longer, she came to find Ted in his office, tapping on the door before going in and sitting down in response to his invitation.

'Right, there's still a long way to go, but I do have the names and email addresses of the women he'd arranged to meet up with while he was in Stockport,' she began, putting a few printed sheets on his desk. 'The email addresses don't help us much at the moment. I'll explain why.'

'That's excellent, thank you. How are you settling in? I hope the team are all making you welcome?'

'So far, so good. Your Steve is very bright. He can do most, but not all, of what I can do,' she told him.

'I imagine he can, but we also need to prise him away from his computer a bit and get him out there, to scenes of crime,' Ted replied. 'He's got the makings of a good officer. He just needs more experience in the field. That's where you come in. Free him up a bit by doing the computer work.'

'I'll have a lot more for you later in the day, but this is just for starters, to give you something to go on. Your Mr Waters was a dirty dog. He'd set up meetings with three different women on Monday evening, half an hour apart, in two different pubs. And that was just day one. The detection bit is not my remit but my intuition suggests he invites three then goes off with the one he fancies the most and who is up for it.'

Ted nodded. It seemed likely enough.

'So have you any way of tracing who these women are for

us? I take it we'll need court orders for things like their email provider or whatever, to disclose details to us?'

'Yes, for their ISPs. Internet Service Providers,' she clarified, to make sure he understood. 'The trouble is it's not quite as simple as that. To ask an ISP for records, we first need evidence of illegal activity. And as far as I know, the kind of messages we're talking about here are not illegal. However, I thought that with the timings and venues, you could at least be making a start on tracing where your victim went. Although I imagine the ones for the next day will be irrelevant, as he never met them. Just give me a bit longer though, I have a cunning plan.'

Ted liked the way she grinned at him when she said it. It was infectious. He couldn't help but return it. He asked her to expand on her plan.

'Well, some people are incredibly naïve and not at all Internet savvy.'

Ted held up a hand.

'That would be me, for one,' he said sheepishly.

'I'm guessing you don't know much about social media, then?'

When Ted shook his head, she continued.

'Facebook, in particular, wants people to use their real names on there. Many people, for one reason or another, like to use a nickname, something other than their own name. But Facebook periodically have clamp-downs and insist on proof that the name someone uses is their own.

'Just on the off-chance, I started searches on the names these three women gave in their emails. Well, two of them. One just goes by 'Snookybunnyface'. I got lucky with one of them. Anne Forfar. Facebook obligingly found me the profile of an Anne Forfar, who comes originally from Scotland. It wasn't too much of a quantum leap from there to find an Anne Angus who lives right here in Stockport.'

Seeing Ted's querying look, she continued, 'Forfar is a

town in Angus. It was an educated guess, worth trying a search on, and it paid off. They always say the best cover story is as close as possible to the truth. I have the address for you, from the electoral register. It's one coincidence too many for it not to be worth your time to at least go and talk to her, don't you think?'

'Very definitely, I think,' Ted said, looking admiringly at his new team member. 'Can you make my day complete by telling me she has long blonde hair in her profile picture?'

'I'm afraid not, boss,' she laughed. 'Her avatar is a rather cute-looking Shih Tzu puppy, with a sparkly bow in its hair.'

'Ah well. Still, this is a great start, Océane, thanks for that.'

'Oh, Steve could have done most of that for you. So now I'd better go and do some really clever stuff that he doesn't know how to do, to justify my place on the team. Oh, and another thing. Your Mr Waters wasn't using that name for his online antics. He was calling himself Duncan Allen. He had a separate email in that name.'

She rose and went out of the office, Ted not far behind. He looked around the main office to see who was available.

'Jezza, can you come with me, please? We have a possible name for someone who may have met up with Duncan Waters on Monday evening. Are you at a point where you can break off?'

She looked at the substantial heap of paperwork on her desk. Ted could see that she was wading through witness statements taken so far from guests and staff at the hotel.

'Desk-bound with this lot, or a trip out into the real world and the fresh air?' she mused aloud. 'I'm in, boss. Your car or mine?'

He opted for Jezza's Golf, pleased that she had, after all, decided to keep the vehicle in which she had been abducted and assaulted. He knew she was tough, but he was still impressed with how well she seemed to be recovering from the ordeal. He'd persuaded her to start seeing the same therapist he went to for counselling, knowing how much she could help.

They were heading for an address in Woodsmoor. The house in question turned out to be a well-presented semi in a quiet residential road. As they parked and went into the driveway, Ted could see a small dog barking at them from the windowsill of the front room.

'Is that one of those Shih Tzu things? And do they bite?' he asked Jezza.

Jezza laughed at him.

'It's one of those Tibetan types, boss. I don't really know the difference with those breeds. And what's it going to do? Savage your ankle?'

Ted rang the doorbell as they both took out their warrant cards and held them ready. The bell was a fancy one which played Westminster chimes, slowly and ostentatiously, immediately setting off a further frenzy of yapping from the small dog which, from the sound of it, had now rushed to the door and was lying in wait for intruders.

They heard a woman's voice, inside the house, remonstrating with it.

'Doodle! Doodle, you naughty boy, stop that noise at once. Go in your basket. Basket, Doodle.'

Doodle clearly had other ideas because, when the woman opened the door, she had the wriggling and still vocal small dog tucked firmly under one arm.

'Anne Angus?' Ted asked. 'I'm Detective Chief Inspector Darling, this is Detective Constable Vine. I wondered if we might just have a few moments of your time, in connection with a routine enquiry, please?'

She looked in bemusement from one to the other. Police officers turning up unannounced on her doorstep was obviously a new experience. The little dog redoubled its struggles, obviously keen to get at the newcomers, but whether in friendship or fury, Ted was unable to tell.

'Yes, I'm sorry, of course, do please come in. Please go into the front room. I'll just go and pop Doodle in his basket. He's very friendly but he does like to climb all over people. And he can sometimes get rather frisky with men's legs. Please go in.'

Jezza was clearly having difficulty in not laughing, seeing the look on the boss's face. The two of them went into an obsessively neat and tidy room. There was not so much as a crease in any of the cushions. They both stood waiting for an invitation to sit down.

The woman bustled back into the room, minus the small dog, one hand unconsciously tidying her hair. Ted noticed it was blonde, though probably not naturally so, in a wavy style which finished just below her jawline. She was small, slim and not unattractive, probably in her early forties.

'Do please sit down. May I offer you something to drink? Some tea, perhaps? And how can I help you?'

They both sat down on the sofa, perching on the edge, rendered uncomfortable by how immaculate everything seemed. The woman sat in an armchair near the old chimney breast, now open and containing an artfully arranged tall copper vase of fresh flowers.

'Nothing to drink, thank you, it's just a quick call. Is it Mrs Angus?' Ted asked and, when she nodded briefly, he continued, 'I understand that you have recently been in contact with a man calling himself Duncan Allen.'

One hand flew to her face and she looked shocked, her cheeks colouring.

'How did you know...?'

Ted skirted the question and continued.

'I believe that you may have met with Mr Allen, in Stockport, on Monday evening. Is that so, Mrs Angus?'

'That was the plan,' she said, through pursed lips. 'I've been divorced for some years. I've been optimistically looking for Mr Right, using various dating sites online which seemed respectable enough.'

'Tell me about Duncan Allen,' Ted said encouragingly.

Her expression turned bitter.

'Well, I'll never know if he was Mr Right or not. He simply never turned up, and never sent word. We arranged to meet at that pub near the market place, the one which does good food, at six-thirty on Monday. He apologised for it being rather early but said he had a client to meet later that evening. He suggested we meet for a drink and, if we found we got on, have something to eat together. I wouldn't normally go in a pub by myself but it seems to be quite respectable there.

'I went and sat there like a fool for more than half an hour, waiting for him to show, but he just stood me up. He'd given me a mobile number to call if I couldn't make it for any reason but it went straight to voicemail when I tried it. I sent a few texts and then a few emails but there was nothing from him in reply.

'I was really disappointed. He had seemed so nice in our email exchanges. I was looking forward to meeting him. He always asked after Doodle and was very interested in him.'

'What did he tell you about himself?'

She sighed.

'He sounded ideal. He said he was a widower, no children. He claimed to love small dogs, but not to be able to have one because his job took him away a lot. He said he advised people on investing in sustainable development projects, which I found fascinating, as that's what I'd like to do with the small amount of money I have.'

'Did anyone come into the pub who could possibly have been Duncan Allen?' Ted asked. 'How were you going to recognise one another?'

She gave a small laugh and looked embarrassed.

'Oh, that was a bit silly, really. I have a little pendant necklace with a Shiz Tzu on it. I was wearing that. As for him coming in, I kept looking, every time the door opened, hoping it would be him. There was a man alone at the bar when I got there. He looked nice, but not like Duncan's photo. After I'd waited a good few minutes, I went to get myself a drink and I made sure he could see the pendant. But he didn't say anything, so it wasn't him. In fact, I think he was waiting for someone and may have been stood up himself.

'While I was there anyway, I thought I'd have another drink and perhaps a bar snack, so I stayed some time. It was well after seven when the man at the bar got up to leave. He'd been looking at his watch a lot, and keeping an eye on the door. In fact it must have been getting on for half past seven by then. There was only one other single man in the bar, but he seemed in a hurry, not as if he was waiting for anyone. He finished his drink quickly and went out not long after the first man. After that all the men there, or who came in, had company.

'Do you know anything about him? Do you have any idea why he stood me up? Has he been in an accident, or something?'

Her voice sounded hopeful, wanting there to be a plausible explanation for why her date had neither shown up nor made contact.

'We were looking into him in connection with something else,' Ted said evasively. 'He was clearly unavoidably detained for his meeting with you.'

'Unavoidably detained as in picked up another blonde who was hotter stuff and didn't have a randy lap-dog called Doodle, you reckon, boss?' Jezza asked jokingly as they got back in her car for the short drive back to the station.

Ted smiled.

'It was the best I could come up with. What about this investment in sustainable development, then? Is that what they call selling solar panels these days? His designs on her were more likely to be his commission on selling her some panels, it seems. I keep seeing in the paper how people can sometimes be left with a big shortfall between what the panels cost them and what they generate in income, with these schemes.'

'Yeah, you'd think it might just occur to people that good old sunny Stockport doesn't quite rival somewhere like the Riviera for sunshine hours per year. But then again, our Anne was clearly a bit gullible, believing all that stuff Duncan spun her, which clearly carefully matched what she wanted to hear. Do you think Duncan was the man at the bar, boss? That he was checking her out, didn't fancy what he saw, so moved on to his next meeting?'

'It's a possibility. It's also possible that his next date didn't turn up, if they were due at, say seven. Océane said the first two meet-ups were arranged for the same pub, half an hour apart. So then he moved on to his seven-thirty appointment in a different pub. He was certainly a cool customer, arranging two meets so close together in the same place.

'It's also just about possible that the man who left straight after him was our killer and he was following him. What we need now is the details of who those other two dates were with, if Océane can find that for us.'

The afternoon was nearly over when they got back to the station, so Ted called the team together to update them on progress so far.

'I don't reckon Anne Angus as a suspect at all at this stage,' he told them. 'She's petite, smaller than me, and her feet are small. I'd need a lot of convincing to imagine her kicking a man's head in while wearing big, steel-capped boots. What we desperately need now, Océane, is a lead to the two other people Waters had arranged to meet.'

'It's what I've been working on, boss, amongst finding out what else was on his phone and laptop. I was lucky with the Angus woman. I've not yet been lucky with the other two. Waters had been in contact with all three for a week or so before his visit up here, clearly keen to set something up.

'What I need to do next is to run a reverse image search, using their avatars from the various sites. Anne Angus's was a dog, at least the other two are humans, although one is just a rather suggestive mouth with very full lips. That way I can find out where else they pop up and I may get more of a lead out of that. If not, I've got a few more ideas.'

'Boss, I've got up-to-date photos of Duncan Waters on my phone now, from the family. I'll get them printed out. Needless to say, it looks nothing like his photo on the sites. And Jason Waters is in the clear. Wrong size feet, and he was in a job interview on Monday. One of those all-day ones, where they get all the candidates together at the same time to observe their interaction, then interview them one by one, so he has plenty of witnesses,' Megan Jennings said.

'Just on the off-chance, I checked on the younger boy, too. Ben. He was certainly seething with enough hate to do it, if nothing else. This was all just in conversation, you understand, I was simply chatting to them. He's a cross-country runner, on a local team, and they had a special training session on Monday afternoon which he had permission from his school to attend. That will effectively alibi the uncle as well as he drove him there because his dad was away and his mother doesn't drive. I'll phone Southampton and get someone to discreetly check out those alibis for us.'

'Excellent, Megan, thank you. Right, time to call it a day for today. Tomorrow, we'll sort out who goes round with the photos to where he'd set up his meets, and further afield, to see if we can pin his movements down more precisely. I want to know more about the man at the bar, if that was our victim, and about the other man, who followed him out. Someone may well remember something.

'And don't forget, The Grapes for a quick one, or two, after work tomorrow. I don't have to remind you to be sensible about who's driving. Good work so far, everyone. See you all tomorrow.'

Chapter Eight

DC Megan Jennings was the last to arrive for the Friday morning briefing, erupting through the door in a breathless flurry of apologies, although she was only two minutes past the appointed time.

'So sorry, boss,' she panted. 'Felix is convinced we have a visiting fox in the garden, and I couldn't prise him away to school until he'd been all round putting out bowls of food and clean water for it. I'll make sure it doesn't happen again.'

Ted hid a smile. He liked his officers to be on time, especially working a difficult murder case, but he was amused by the warm pictures of domesticity he was getting from Megan. He also appreciated her sincerity in apologising.

'It's fine. Just try not to let it affect your work. We've got a wily fox of our own to catch,' he said dryly. 'Before I forget, we need to sort out DNA from the family, to eliminate traces of them from the victim's hotel room.'

'Already sorted, boss,' Megan replied, taking off her coat and sitting down at her desk. 'I mentioned to them that it would be necessary, and when I spoke to Southampton I asked them to sort it out, soon as. I thought it might be slightly more tactful, doing it that way, as they're not really prime suspects. I hope that was all right, boss? I should have checked first.'

She always seemed so eager and anxious to please. But then Ted knew who her previous senior officer had been and could understand why. Not someone who gave praise or credit, even when it was well earned, and who ran the team on a blame culture. Not Ted's style at all.

'That's fine, Megan, I think that's probably exactly how I would've handled it myself. They're not in the frame at the moment, so you did the right thing,' he reassured her and saw her obvious sigh of relief.

He wondered what it must be like to work on a team where you were always expecting to get a bollocking for everything you did or didn't do.

'Right, this morning's task is to pin down as much as we can of our Mr Waters' last movements. Mike, you assign who goes where, but this is what I want covering. I want further statements from all the staff at the hotel about if and when anyone saw him, either going out or coming back in on the night he was killed. If you've already asked, ask again. Jog memories. We need to know.

'Océane, can you tell us the times and locations of his dates and any detail at all you've got so far on who he was meeting, please?'

'Right you are, boss,' she said, looking up from her computer. 'First off, Anne Forfar, or Anne Angus as we now know she is actually called. They were supposed to meet in the pub at six-thirty. Then at seven, in the same bar, he was supposed to be meeting a woman who calls herself Linda Lovelace, but I think we can be fairly certain that's not her real name. She's the one who's all mouth in her avatar.'

There were some blank looks from the younger members of the team so Jezza, their walking edition of Trivial Pursuit, supplied helpfully, 'Linda Lovelace. Former porn star. Starred in Deep Throat in, I think, from memory, 1972.'

The longer-serving members of the team all knew that Jezza's general knowledge came from her need to answer the incessant questions of her autistic younger brother, Tom.

Mike Hallam gaped at her and asked incredulously, 'Surely your Tommy hasn't been asking you about Deep Throat?'

Jezza chuckled.

'Don't forget Tommy doesn't recognise the same social boundaries as most people. If he sees or hears something, he asks me about it, whatever it is.'

There was general laughter before Ted brought them back to order.

'All right, focus, please. Who was number three, Océane?'

'Number three is the famous Snookybunnyface, and that really is all I have on her for now, if it is a woman. They've exchanged a lot of steamy emails, though I have to say that Linda's are the most graphic when she replies to any of them. Snookybunnyface usually signs herself off as just Snooks. They were due to meet in the next pub along the road, at seven-thirty.

'I have nothing much to go on yet, just a partial face photo and yes, it is a blonde, with long hair, but it may not be her. I'm trying a reverse image search to see where else it crops up, in the hopes of finding her on social media or somewhere, under her real name. The problem is that a lot of these sites offer protection for personal details so you can't always do that, but I'll keep trying.

'And I take it we are going to look at any street CCTV from around the pubs in question? Is that one for me? Steve is certainly more than capable of doing it.'

'I'm in this weekend, sir, I could do that, free up Océane for other stuff?' Steve supplied helpfully.

'Good, Steve, do it. Start today, if time allows. We need it all checking,' Ted told him, watching him blush furiously at the acknowledgement from Océane.

'Just another thing, boss,' Océane continued. 'The victim had no phone contact at all with the Linda Lovelace person, only email. I haven't yet read through all their smutty messages, but their contact and the arrangement to meet were all by email only. And Linda's were all from throwaway mail addresses. Literally. A different address every time, though the same name. A nightmare to trace. Luckily the victim was in phone contact with Snooks, so we have her number, at least.'

'I could get in touch with her, boss,' Jezza suggested eagerly. 'Give her a call, or send her a text, claiming we'd met somewhere. Try to fix up a meeting?'

Ted shook his head firmly.

'Too risky yet, on too many counts. Not least of which because it could be seen as entrapment, as you well know, which needs clearance. There's no sense in us slipping up this early on so we can't even take the case to court once we find our murderer. And we don't know for sure that this Snooky is a woman. She could be a man, and our murderer. We'll have to think of another way forward for now. I'd need to get permission from on high for anything like that.'

'Boss, someone needs to go through all the exchanges between the victim and the people he met. I can print them out, but that's a job anyone can do, whereas if you want me to dig out his innermost computer secrets, that isn't,' Océane put in.

Once again, it could have sounded arrogant, but Ted knew she was right.

'That's one for the weekend, if we're quiet. I'll be coming in myself at some point, so I can do some of it. Right, so, for now, we need to take Mr Waters' photo, the correct one, from pub to pub, see if we can't pin down his movements. We also need to trawl through all the witness statements looking for anything to help us, and picking out questions that still need to be asked.

'If you sort out people for those, Mike, I think, on reflection, maybe Jo and I should pay a visit to the hotel. Perhaps a bit of rank might rattle them into remembering. I can't believe no one saw or heard anything. They may just need a bit of prodding to realise what they can remember.

'Jo, I just need to go and chase the Super up about court orders for email providers, if that's even a possibility, and see if we can't get a trace of Snooky from her phone number, too. Then I'll be right with you.'

'Ah, Ted. Coffee?'

It was taking some time for Ted to get used to the newly informal meetings between him and the Ice Queen. He nodded and sat down as she continued, 'How are your new team members shaping up?'

'Good choices, ma...' he so nearly called her ma'am. It was still deeply engrained. He couldn't yet quite bring himself to call her Debs all the time. 'Océane is very impressive. She's already found out a lot of useful information for us,' he said, giving her the details so far.

'What are your early theories? I'm hoping there are no indications so far that this is something other than an isolated killing?'

'I'm a big believer in Occam's razor. I try to keep assumptions to the bare minimum. But the most obvious ones to draw are that either someone knew what Mr Waters was like and was exacting extreme punishment on him, perhaps on behalf of the family. Or that the husband or partner of one of the people he had arranged to meet had intercepted his messages and killed him in jealous rage.

'That's why we really need authority to follow up on the owners of the email addresses. Even Océane is struggling at the moment to find out who Snookybunnyface is, not to mention Linda Lovelace. We need Snooky's identity from her mobile phone number.'

'I will push for it, as hard as I can, but you know these things take time,' she reminded him.

Jo Rodriguez was talking on the phone when Ted went back up to his inspector's office. Mike was in the main office, assigning tasks. To Ted's surprise, Jo was speaking in Spanish and the rapid-fire conversation sounded heated. Ted didn't understand a word of it. Jo made an apologetic face at him and clearly wound the conversation up as fast as he could, then rang off.

'Sorry, boss,' he said apologetically. 'The wife is Spanish, too. She was just reminding me what shopping to pick up on the way home tonight.'

Ted laughed.

'That was a shopping list conversation? I'd hate to hear you having a full-blown argument, in that case. Right, let's you and me go and see if we can jog some memories at the hotel. Are you happy to drive?'

It was a good opportunity to get to know the team member he'd be leaving in charge whenever he had to move to another division to head up an enquiry there. Ted was a keen observer of people and felt it was often possible to tell a great deal about someone's character by how they drove. Jo's style was definitely hot-blooded and flamboyant. He kept within the speed limit, just, but he was clearly a risk taker and some of his language got a bit colourful. Ted noticed he had a gold canine tooth, which gave him something of a rakish air. Mildly, he asked him to tone down the language and was met with profuse apologies.

'I just like to keep it respectful, within the team. Wouldn't want standards to slip when I'm away and you're in charge,' Ted said, then was interrupted by his mobile phone.

He groaned as he looked at the caller display.

'Alastair! I was just thinking I should phone you,' he began, holding up crossed fingers towards Jo to cover the white lie. 'I know we haven't been able to give you much at the moment, but I will send something your way, just as soon as I can.'

Ted ended the call as quickly as he decently could, then grinned guiltily at Jo.

'All right, you caught me out. I'm not keen on the press, and that was our local reporter. Everyone calls him Pocket Billiards. I'll leave it to your imagination as to why.'

Jo was still laughing when they arrived at the hotel and he parked his car. Once inside, Ted was able to see his new DI in full-on charm offensive and he had to admit, it was impressive. With his ready smile and a flash of the gold tooth, people seemed to warm to him and were happy to talk.

They didn't get much further forward, although the young woman on reception did tell Jo that Duncan Waters was openly flirting with her when she gave him his key-card on arrival. Ted didn't recall having seen that in any of the witness statements to date.

'He was a bit of a charmer, like you,' she laughed, in the face of a cheeky wink and another flash of the gold tooth from Jo.

'Well, he certainly won't be charming anyone else, eh, boss?' Jo commented, as they drove back to the station. 'Let's hope Océane can find out who these other two women are before too long, then we can at least interview them. I must say, she's certainly very hot...' he left a suggestive pause before adding, 'with a computer.'

'And strictly off limits,' Ted warned him dryly. 'Another thing I'm not at all keen on is office romances between team members. It has a nasty habit of getting in the way of police work.'

'Me, boss?' Jo was all wide-eyed innocence. 'A good married Catholic boy with six kids? When do you think I'd have the time? Or the energy?'

There was some degree of progress by the end of the day, when the team members came back in to report, before gathering in The Grapes.

'Boss, we got a positive ID on our man in the first pub. The bar staff remembered him hanging around and checking his watch. One of the young women said he was trying to chat her up. They also remember Anne Angus. Working in a pub, I suppose they get good at identifying someone who's been stood up on a blind date. She stood out a bit as she ordered a St Clement's and it's rather old-fashioned these days,' Mike Hallam told them.

In response to some blank looks, he told them, 'Orange juice and bitter lemon.

'They confirm she didn't follow our man out when he left. She'd ordered food and stayed to eat that. One of the bar staff thinks they saw another man leave just after him but the description doesn't help us much at all. Medium height, medium build, darkish hair. Wearing a dark fleece with some sort of a logo on it. It's not much to go on. She only remembered him because he'd sat nursing half a pint for quite some time, watching everyone who came in.'

'We picked up the trail of our man at the next pub, boss,' Rob took up the story. 'One of the bar staff recognised his photo and said he came in about half seven. It wasn't very busy at that time, so he remembered. He said the man bought a drink then went to a table where there was a woman with blonde hair who had clearly been waiting for someone.

'Our man went over to her, said something, then sat down with her. The same barman said there was a lot of very hot and steamy body language going on. They just had a quick bar snack and seemed in a hurry to leave. He said they left some time before nine o'clock. He didn't specifically notice anyone else leaving at the same time or hanging around watching, but he said they were starting to get busy by then.'

'Excellent, that's a good start. Any description of the woman? Did they know her?'

'The barman didn't know her, although he's seen her around before. And yes, a description.'

Rob hesitated, knowing what a stickler the boss was for respect.

'Don't shoot the messenger, boss, not my words, and I'll paraphrase them a bit. He said she was short, blonde, curvy, gobby and he compared a certain part of her anatomy to a large round fruit.

Even Ted had trouble keeping a straight face at that.

'Right, well, that's a start. Océane, anything new from

your side?'

'Negative on Linda Lovelace. The name is all I've got to go on so far for her and it's not advancing me very far at the moment. Snookybunnyface did attach a coy photo to one of her emails but it's artful stuff, you can only see an eye and part of a cheek and I'm betting they aren't hers anyway. It's similar, but not quite the same, as the one she uses on the dating site. The best I've come up with so far, in trying to find her anywhere online, is a 'Snooks' who's joined a group for former students of a school here but hasn't posted anything yet.'

'So can one of us join the same group and try to strike up conversation with her, try to draw her out and find who she is?' Jezza asked.

Océane answered, as it was her domain.

'Theoretically, yes. But I'm CFI on this so it's me who has to prepare the report to say what information we obtained and how it was sourced. There could be ethical issues with an idea like that, and I imagine, boss, it would have to be cleared from higher up?'

Ted nodded then stood up from where he was, as usual, perched on the edge of a desk.

'Right, let's wrap it up for today and adjourn to The Grapes. I hope everyone's able to come? Steve, is Maurice coming?'

'Probably already there, sir, you know him. He's not drinking at the moment, though, because of his medication.'

Maurice Brown was indeed already there, so was Jim Baker, the former Big Boss and now the officer in charge of Ted's newly expanded team. Ted hadn't seen Maurice for nearly a month and was astonished at the change in him since his operation. He'd been trying to lose weight for some time and had clearly finally succeeded. He looked much better for it.

Ted made the introductions and there were handshakes all round. Jezza surprised him by greeting Maurice with a warm hug and a kiss on the cheek. He knew the two had become good friends, but they seemed to be closer than ever.

It was a good chance for Ted and Jim to catch up on the day's progress. Ted didn't usually like bringing work into the pub, but he needed to keep Jim up to speed. When he'd done so, the two men stood in companionable silence, watching the team relaxing. It was a way to see how the new members interacted.

'You're going to need to keep your eye on that one,' Jim grunted, nodding to where Jo was deep in conversation with Océane, all sparkling gold tooth and twinkling eyes.

'Jo?' Ted asked. 'Happily married man with six kids, he tells me.'

'I wasn't meaning him,' Jim said dryly. 'She looks like trouble. She certainly isn't putting up any resistance to his charms. And Maurice and Jezza look very cosy.'

Ted looked across the bar to where Maurice was perched on a high stool, Jezza right next to him, the two of them laughing and chatting like the good friends he took them to be. Then he saw what had probably been staring him in the face for some time and he had not yet recognised. Steve was standing near to the two of them and the look on his face was unmistakable, even from the other side of the room. Blatant jealousy.

Ted groaned inwardly. That kind of triangle was the last thing he needed on the team, with a difficult case to manage.

'You're a good copper, with a good eye for detail, Ted,' Jim told him. 'Just make sure, because your own relationship is so steady, you don't miss out on the signs of other dynamics brewing up. Not what you need right now,' perfectly echoing Ted's own unspoken thoughts.

Chapter Nine

'I'm sorry I need to go into work today, especially with you going out tonight,' Ted told Trev when he took him up a cup of tea on Saturday morning. Trev was never an early riser. Even on work days, he was usually on the last minute. Ted had already been up, seen to the cats, unloaded the dishwasher and put everything away.

'Yes, but not straight away?' Trev asked pointedly, pulling back the duvet on Ted's side of the bed. 'Stay a bit longer. Or come home at a decent time, then we can have a bit of time together, like an old married couple. Before I go out, and your mum comes to supper.'

Ted smiled, but peeled off his sweat pants and slid back into bed. 'I will try to get back at a decent time, then I can clean the house. My mother will faint at the sight of all the cat hairs, and it is my turn.'

'I know you. You say you'll be back in good time but you'll get held up at work and it will be the usual mad scramble to get everything done. You're only ever on time for work stuff, never for your own life. I'll sort it, and cook supper for you both before I go out. But in payment for that...'

He put his tea on the shelf next to the bed and moved closer to Ted, draping an arm possessively over his chest.

'Your tea will go cold,' Ted warned him.

'Let it,' was all that Trev replied.

Ted got to work slightly later than he had intended. Steve and

Jezza were both on duty, working away in the main office. Jezza looked up from a sheaf of print-outs as he walked in.

'Boss, I'm going through the emails between our victim and the three women from up here, especially Snooky. I haven't started on the texts yet, that's next on my agenda. Snooky hasn't told him much about herself, apart from some lurid physical description and some of the very creative ways she likes it. But she must be local to here. She's got the knowledge. She knew straight away, when he suggested meeting up, which were the best pubs to meet in. Detailed knowledge, too, not just a Google search type. And he will certainly have been targeting people in Stockport for when he was up here. He'll have probably been looking for someone in and around the town centre, purely for convenience, but that's just a guess.'

'Does that help us much, though, without an actual name and address?' Ted asked.

'Think about what the barman said, boss. He thought he'd seen her before, and his description was quite a detailed one. Maybe she drinks in local pubs, if she's in the habit of meeting up with strangers from the Internet. What if I went round a few pubs and bars, where younger women hang out? Just go in, have a drink, start chatting, and ask about Snooks? Someone is bound to know her. I can't do the same for Linda Lovelace, though. I might get more than I bargained for.'

Ted was already shaking his head before she had finished speaking.

'It's risky, Jezza. We don't yet know if she could be the killer, or acting as bait for the killer, to draw his victim in.'

Jezza was clearly having difficulty curbing her impatience. She was always headstrong.

'But boss, when I've got a babysitter for Tommy, I do sometimes go out on the lash, you know. So what's to stop me asking around anyway, while I'm out there? Surely it's worth a shot?'

'I'm what's to stop you, Jezza,' Ted said firmly. 'You've told me, I've said no. I've evaluated the risk and I don't like it, without further intelligence. Going ahead and doing it now would be directly disobeying the order of your senior officer. Is that clear?'

Ted didn't really want to be having this conversation in front of Steve, even though he knew he was probably blissfully unaware of what was going on around him, as he usually was when he was focused on his computer.

Jezza was not a quitter. Once she had the bit between her teeth, she took some stopping, as Ted knew to his cost.

'Okay, so what if I go with someone?'

Ted sighed. He was going to have to discuss it with her in detail; he owed her that.

'Come into my office,' he told her, leading the way and heading straight for the kettle.

The onus was always on him to ensure the safety of his officers, as well as his own. Snooky may have been incidental to the murder, but he didn't yet know enough to be sure. He was busily mentally writing the report for if he agreed and anything happened to Jezza. He quite simply couldn't justify the risk, even to himself.

'We'll be going round all the pubs and clubs asking about her, and about Linda, as a matter of routine,' he began, waving his box of green tea at her in invitation.

She nodded, but cut in, 'Boss, going round the pubs in office hours talking to the staff will be as much use as a chocolate teapot. It needs someone going at night, when the good-time girls are out on the pull. That's the only way to find Snooky, without court orders on the email addresses.

'You know I can get the gear on, put all my piercings back in, colour my hair, and no one would begin to imagine I'm a cop. It's the best and the quickest way to find out who Snooky is, and she may well be the last person to have seen Waters alive, before the killer.'

Ted put a mug of tea in front of each of them and sat down.

In a sense, she was right. But her safety was his responsibility. It would be his career on the line, not hers, if anything went wrong, and at this stage they didn't know for sure if their killer was male or female, nor if they were only targeting men.

'All right,' he said. 'Bring me all the email exchanges between Snooky and Waters, and the others. Let me read through and evaluate before I decide. The texts too.'

Jezza chuckled.

'I've only glanced at those so far but they're definitely sexts not texts. They'll make your hair curl, boss. They're more than a bit steamy.'

He ignored her comment and continued, 'If, and only if, I then decide it's the right course of action to take, you go with someone.'

'Who, though, boss? No offence, but if I take any of the blokes on the team, I'll look like I'm out with my other half, or my pimp.'

'Not acceptable, Jezza,' Ted told her sternly. 'If you don't like male officers calling you a bird, please don't call them blokes. Equality cuts both ways.'

She had the decency to look contrite as she mumbled a brief apology.

'I was thinking of a female officer, now we have Megan on the team. But it will all depend on what I decide after reading through the exchanges between the victim and this Snooky. And if not Megan, who might have childcare issues, we could perhaps consider Susan Heap. She's been of great help in the past.'

It was Susan Heap who may well have saved Ted's life after the knife attack. She was one of the first responding officers from Uniform branch, who had done everything in her power to stem a serious arterial bleed until an ambulance arrived.

'Er, boss, I'm trying not to sound judgemental here but, seriously? Megan? She looks a bit, erm, a bit mumsy, to be out on the toot with me, when I'm dressed up in the part.'

'You are being judgemental, DC Vine, and I won't have it,' Ted warned her. 'And it isn't like you. Is everything all right? Is there anything you want to talk about?'

She shook her head.

'No, sorry, boss, just me being a cow, I think. I'll go and bring you copies of all those print-outs. There's plenty more for me to look at, with the Linda Lovelace ones to start on. I also thought it was worth going through the ones with Anne-Doodle, just on the off-chance there's anything there, although I think that's a very long shot.'

His exchange with Jezza had left Ted feeling a little anxious about her. She had been so much of a lone wolf when she had first joined the team, he wondered if it was nothing more than two new females coming onto what she now thought of as her territory, and disturbing the dynamics. He hoped he didn't get called away to another division until the team had settled down with its new members.

She was certainly right about the exchanges between their victim and Snooky. After the first few, they quickly got down to sexting at its most graphic, leaving nothing to the imagination.

Ted knew it was almost impossible to form an accurate opinion of who was behind messages online. He'd been on courses about child grooming, so he knew that the seemingly youthful voice in an innocent chat room could be that of a middle-aged man. But some instinct told him, the more he read, that these exchanges were probably nothing more than what they appeared to be. Two consenting adults setting up a bit of fun.

Once he'd read through the Snooky sexts and cleared some of his own paperwork, Ted started to think about bagels for his lunch. He wanted to spend a quiet half hour with both Steve and Jezza, in an informal setting, to see if he could figure out what was gnawing at the pair of them. He offered to treat them to lunch, took their orders and sent Jezza and Steve into his office to brew up while he was out.

Ted made sure he sat on the same side of his desk as the other two. He wanted this to be relaxed, not a boss talking to officers under his command. They all knew he was approachable. He just liked to emphasise the fact when he could.

He kept the conversation as light as he could, asking how they were getting on with their new team members, all the time using his keen powers of observation to look for any tell-tale signs. Steve was, as ever, awkward and on edge but that was normal for him. His replies were mostly monosyllabic, but he opened up more and went pink singing Océane's praises. Ted hoped she wasn't going to break his heart. He clearly had it bad.

He watched Jezza's reaction, looking for signs of any jealousy there. All he saw was an indulgent fondness, like that of an older sister for a younger brother who had a serious crush on someone. He wondered even more about the look he'd seen on Steve's face in The Grapes on Friday. He'd have to leave it for now, though. They had bigger fish to fry.

It wasn't long into the afternoon before Jezza knocked on his door and came in, armed with more print-outs.

'Boss, I've started now on all the text messages from the victim's phone. Océane didn't flag it up, but there's a text here in his Drafts folder, to Anne-Doodle, to say he'd been delayed and would be in touch as soon as he could. With an apology.'

Was there a hint of reproach in her tone about Océane, Ted wondered? Or was he starting to get paranoid? He nodded to her to sit down.

'But he didn't send it? When was it written?'

'Written at 7.45 but not sent for some reason. Maybe he was in a mobile black spot? Meant to send it later but never did, for some reason? Had his hands full with Snooky? Didn't fancy Anne-Doodle enough for a bunk-up but still figured he could flog her some solar panels?'

'Ah, Jezza, so cynical for one so young,' Ted smiled. 'Except I've never had phone problems near there. It's a pretty good signal area. Even if you were right, it doesn't advance us very much, I fear.'

'The thing is, boss, I know she's not a relative, but do you think someone should tell Anne-Doodle he's dead? Maybe knowing that he was going to contact her might make her feel better about herself? Rather than her having just being stood up?'

'Mrs Angus,' Ted corrected automatically, but continued, 'That's a kind thought, Jezza and yes, I think you might be right. I'll call round there on my way home, to let her know. I might also try to warn her, tactfully, that's it's just possible that our Mr Waters was more interested in selling her a solar installation than anything else.'

'Do you want me to come with you, boss?' Jezza asked him, a mischievous twinkle in her eyes. 'To protect you from the savage Doodle? He might give your ankle a severe gumming, or even hump your leg.'

'Don't push it, DC Vine,' Ted growled, trying to sound fierce. 'There's plenty of paperwork I can send your way to keep you occupied.'

Chuckling, she stood up and made for the door. Ted was pleased to see the glimpse of what he considered to be the real Jezza, the one with a good heart, who cared about people. As she was leaving, he said, 'I'll do it, and thanks for suggesting it.'

Doodle was on his customary spot, barking frenetically at the intruder from the bay windowsill. In response to the Westminster chimes, Mrs Angus came to the door, once more with the struggling little dog clamped in her arms.

'Oh, hello again, Inspector, please go into the front room

while I put Doodle in the kitchen. I wasn't expecting anyone so I'm afraid it's in a bit of a mess.'

Ted noticed that her definition of a mess was one fallen petal from the flower arrangement in the open hearth. He felt guilty, thinking of the hairy carpets at his own home, which Trev was going to have to see to for him as he was already running later than he'd planned.

The woman came back in, minus the dog, and immediately went guiltily to pick up the petal, which she tucked into a pocket, before sitting down, indicating to Ted to do the same. She sat with her knees demurely together, her hands placed one on top of the other in her lap.

'What can I do for you, Inspector?' she asked.

Ted didn't bother to correct her.

'I just thought I ought to come and tell you that the person you know as Duncan Allen is dead.'

One hand flew up to her face as she said, 'Oh my goodness! It was him, wasn't it? In the hotel? I read in the paper that a body had been found. It said it was at a hotel. He told me he was going to be staying in a hotel but not which one. And I read that the police are treating the death as suspicious. I just didn't make the connection. Is that it? I'm a suspect?'

Ted hastened to reassure her.

'At the moment, Mrs Angus, we have no reason to disbelieve what you have already told us, and it has been confirmed by staff at the pub. I just thought you might, perhaps, like to know that Mr Allen had made an effort to contact you, to tell you that he had been delayed.'

'I didn't get any message from him,' she said, looking confused.

'For some reason, the message was never sent. But it was in the Drafts folder on his mobile phone, so he had thought to at least tell you he was delayed.'

'And was he really Mr Right? Were the things he told me about himself true? He was single, unattached?'

Ted hesitated. There was little he could tell her without breaching confidentiality or giving out information that was not yet in the public domain.

'Mrs Angus,' he began gently. 'From my limited experience of such things, people are seldom what they pretend to be in online encounters. My advice to you would be to exercise extreme caution with anyone you arrange to meet.'

Seeing her face fall, he went on, 'But I'm sure you will find someone. You're an attractive woman, you'll no doubt find a Mr Right before too long, if you're careful.'

When she coloured slightly and raised her hand to pat her hair, Ted realised he may possibly have gone too far in trying to comfort her.

'You're really very kind, Inspector, and I imagine you had no real need to come here to tell me this, to make me feel better. Tell me, do you like small dogs?'

'Ah,' Ted said awkwardly, his stock phrase when he wasn't quite sure what to say. 'I'm not very good with dogs, even small ones, I'm afraid. I'm a cat person. My partner and I have six.'

This time, she went bright pink with embarrassment.

'Oh dear, I'm so sorry, how very stupid of me...'

'No, not at all, I'm sorry if I gave you the wrong impression,' Ted said, rising to his feet and preparing to leave. 'I just thought you might prefer to know that he hadn't simply stood you up. I really hope you will find someone suitable soon, but please, do be careful. Especially of anyone who mentions being in investments. They may not be all they seem.'

She also rose to her feet to show him out. Her tone was bitter as she said, 'A double-glazing salesman?'

'Something like that,' Ted smiled, as he shook her hand in farewell.

Chapter Ten

Ted left his car on the driveway, ready to go and collect his mother after he'd had a shower and changed. He was running late and he hated to be late. It was just that, as usual, he'd got tied up at work. The extra detour to see Mrs Angus had been enough to make the difference.

He hurried through to the kitchen, full of apology. Trev was putting the finishing touches to the table, adding a small vase of flowers as a centrepiece. He'd obviously realised Ted would be later than he promised and had already showered and dressed, ready to go out.

'I've set the kitchen table, I thought that would be cosier for the two of you,' Trev said in greeting.

'Oh my God, you look and smell good,' Ted told him admiringly, moving closer for a hug. 'Are you sure you want to go out tonight?'

Trev laughed and pushed him gently but firmly away.

'Down, boy. I'm going out, and you're going to eat with your mother. And you needn't look so worried, I'm not going out on the pull.'

It was not worry over Trev's faithfulness that made Ted anxious. It was his own insecurities. Whatever he was wearing, Trev was quite simply stunning. Now, with his jet black hair still damp from his shower and curling more wildly than ever, he was sensational. Even casually dressed in good jeans, an open shirt and tailored jacket, it was easy to see how he'd been offered modelling work on a trip to Berlin with Rupert.

As if reading his thoughts, Trev gave a throaty chuckle and said, 'Surely this morning was enough to convince you I've no need to look elsewhere? Now, I knew you'd be on the last minute, which is why I grabbed a shower and got ready. I'll go and pick up Annie, you get yourself ready.

'Fish pie and sticky toffee pudding in the fridge ready for you, away from thieving cats. Just heat them up, make sure they're hot right through. And there's clotted cream for the pud. Now give me the car keys and go and get ready. I'll fetch your mother then leave you to it, as soon as Rupert and Willow swing by to pick me up.'

Ted enjoyed his evening more than he thought he might. His mother was ridiculously proud to hear, from Trev, of his promotion. Ted would never have dreamt of mentioning it. He told her little of his police work. There was not much he could tell her. Most of it was too shocking. He did want to touch on the current case, in broad detail, though. He didn't for a moment imagine his mother might be suddenly tempted to start dating. After all, she had stayed single ever since she had left Ted and his father more than thirty years ago. But he was anxious to warn her about the kind of scams people got sucked into, which could end up costing them thousands of pounds.

After a pleasant evening, Ted drove her home, then settled down to clear some of the routine paperwork he'd brought home with him. He imagined Trev would be late back and he didn't want to be found waiting up for him like an anxious parent, so once he'd made some progress, he went upstairs with a book. Not a great reader, he did sometimes indulge in some Ian Rankin crime fiction, always wondering, whenever he did, how John Rebus kept his driving licence, never mind his job.

He must have dozed off, the open book still on his chest, his reading glasses slowly slipping off his nose, when he heard noises downstairs. He slid out of bed, pulled on sweats, and went quietly downstairs.

Trev was busily making toast, grinning widely, humming happily and totally tunelessly to himself. He started when he sensed Ted pad quietly into the kitchen behind him.

'Oh, sorry, did I wake you? I'm making toast. I want toast, with honey. D'you want toast?'

He only just managed to catch the slices as they popped out of the toaster, then set about spreading honey liberally, though not entirely accurately, over them.

Ted smiled indulgently. He was pleased his partner had clearly had such a good time.

'No toast, thanks, I've no room after that supper you made us. Did you have a good time?'

'Wonderful!' Trev beamed owlishly. 'Brilliant! Have some toast.'

Ted shook his head.

'No toast. And you're all right?' he asked pointedly.

'Wonderful!' Trev repeated. 'I may just be a little bit squiffy, and maybe a teeny bit stoned, but I am all right.'

'You haven't brought anything back with you?' Ted hated having to ask, but he needed to be sure. Like most coppers, he could selectively ignore knowing that someone occasionally shared a spliff at a party, but possession of drugs was something different altogether.

Trev lifted his arms up and held them out at shoulder height, honey dripping everywhere from his bitten piece of toast.

'Nary a thing, officer. But you might have to strip-search me to be sure.'

Ted was smiling, despite himself.

'I'm sorry, but you know I have to ask. I'm a policeman.'

'I know, I've seen your truncheon,' Trev told him and collapsed into helpless giggles.

Patiently, Ted set about cleaning up the honey, much of which had run up the sleeve of Trev's good jacket. Then he ran him a tall glass of cold water and held it out to him.

'Drink that, before you come to bed. It'll dilute the wine a bit and reduce the hangover.'

Then, aware he really did sound like Trev's father, he added softly, 'I'm glad you had fun. You deserve to.'

Ted had warned Trev that he intended to go into the office again the next day. He hadn't yet finished going through everything Océane had recovered from the laptop and phone and he wanted to do that before Monday morning's briefing with the full team. He had a gut feeling there was something there which might point them in the right direction.

He got up later than usual for a work day, finished off clearing up downstairs, then took tea up to Trev. It was, as ever, strong enough to trot a mouse across, with just a suggestion of milk.

Trev was still sleeping like a baby, spread-eagled across most of the bed. Ted put the mug down on the shelf next to him, perched lightly on the edge of the bed and gently shook his shoulder. One brilliant blue eye opened reluctantly, looked at him, then a lazy, suggestive smile spread over Trev's face as he rolled slowly onto his back.

'You're not going out just yet, are you? Stay a bit longer.'

Ted shook his head regretfully.

'I'd love to, I really would. But I need to get on top of this case. So far, we've only got one victim. I really don't want to risk our man striking again before we've made any progress. I'll be back as soon as I can, promise. I'll text you. Drink your tea.'

'You can send me a sext, if you like.'

Ted was still smiling at the thought as he drove out of the cul-de-sac where they lived and headed for the station. Steve and Jezza were in again, and Ted knew that Maurice would be looking after Jezza's brother, Tom. Maurice was brilliant with children. Even the often difficult Tommy loved going to spend time with him, and managed to cope with Maurice's often lively twin daughters. Steve and Jezza would take days off in lieu in the week, so there was always someone on call, every day. It was how the team always worked, with a serious case ongoing.

The three of them exchanged greetings, then Ted asked if they had anything new for him.

'Sir, can you take a look at this, on the CCTV?' Steve asked him, looking for the relevant bit to show to the boss.

Ted pulled Océane's chair across and sat next to Steve, looking at the screen. He could see straight away that it was from the camera nearest to the pub where Waters' first two meet-ups had been arranged. The images were, as usual, grainy, but he knew that, with enhancement techniques, it would be possible to get greater detail on anyone they wanted to study.

He noticed that Steve had selected a time shortly before six on Monday evening, more than half an hour before Mrs Angus had said she was due to meet Waters. Few people went into the pub that early in the evening. One of them was a man who was reading a newspaper as he walked.

Steve let the tape run a few moments then looked at the boss expectantly.

'Tell me what you see, Steve, and I'll tell you if I see the same thing.'

'Well, sir, as the man comes into camera shot, he's just taking his paper out from under his arm and starting to look at the back page as he walks towards the pub. That wouldn't look unusual, of itself. But I think the height he's holding the paper looks wrong.'

'Wrong in what way?' Ted asked, impressed that Steve was voicing exactly what he was thinking himself.

'Well, sir,' he said again, 'usually if you're walking along reading a paper, you sort of have it folded over, so you don't block your own view completely.'

He reached for a red top on his desk and held it up to show what he meant.

'His isn't folded, and he's holding it quite high up.'

'He could be short-sighted,' Ted suggested, playing devil's advocate.

'He could be,' Steve conceded. 'He could also be very aware that there are CCTV cameras there. The way he's holding the paper not only masks most of his face, it also hides the front of the fleece jacket he's wearing. And if you remember, we've got witness statements of a man in the pub, wearing a fleece with a logo, who left shortly after the victim.'

Ted nodded.

'I agree with you, Steve, that's a strong possibility. Well spotted. We need to find out more about logo-man. We'll need to go back to the pub and press the bar staff for any detail at all about what that logo is. It may be nothing, just a brand label, but there's an outside chance it's work clothing, with a company name on it. Anything else?'

Steve was flushed with pride at the praise.

'Yes, sir,' he said, fast-forwarding through the tape. 'Not much more than five minutes later, we have our Mr Waters, going into the pub, here. Then just before six-thirty, Mrs Angus going in, just as she and the witnesses said.'

'And leaving?'

'Exactly as Mrs Angus said, sir. Waters left just before seven-thirty, followed shortly afterwards by logo-man,' he was speeding through it again as he spoke. 'Acting just the same way with his newspaper. Then we've got Mrs Angus leaving quite a bit later on, as she said.'

'Good work, Steve. Jezza, anything from your side so far?'

'I've run out of mind bleach, reading this stuff, boss,' she told him. 'I think there is something, but I'm not sure, so I really would like your take on it as well. I've started on the Linda Lovelace stuff now, so would you mind reading through it yourself and telling me if anything strikes you about it?'

'That's what I was planning to do this morning. In the meantime - and with my limited experience, I don't even know if this is possible - I'm hoping between the two of you, you can compile something for me. I want some sort of a profile of the type of person Waters was contacting, then the same for Snooky, Anne Angus and Linda. Then trickling down from there, if you follow me. A way to look for links, target words and phrases, that sort of thing. Is this making any sense?'

'Perfectly, boss,' Steve beamed happily.

It was the sort of thing which was right up his street.

'For example, let's assume that Mr Waters really was interested in lap-dogs, which seems improbable. Was he searching on people with a similar sort of interest? Is that the sort of thing you mean, sir?'

'Steve, you're a genius,' Ted told him. 'You even know what I mean when I don't know myself. Right, I'm going to shut myself away to read the steamy stuff so you can't see me blush with embarrassment.'

Ted read carefully through everything, twice over. He saw what Jezza was getting at. He hadn't realised how much the morning had got away from him until Jezza tapped on his door and stuck her head round.

'Me and Steve want to treat you to lunch today, boss, as you bought ours yesterday. Smoked salmon and cream cheese bagel?' she asked.

Ted laughed.

'Am I as predictable as that? Yes, please, and it's kind of you both. I'll get the kettle on.'

Ted was a rarity amongst officers of his rank for his willingness to spend down-time with his team members. Some senior officers argued that it reduced respect to be too matey. Ted thought the opposite. His team members thought the world of him but they knew that he could, and would, still kick backsides if anyone was out of line. He didn't believe in disciplinaries. He preferred to deal with matters himself, in his own way.

When they'd finished eating and were enjoying a drink

together, Jezza asked, 'So did anything strike you, boss? About the Linda stuff?'

'It did. It reminded me of scenes of crime I've been to which have been staged. Where a killer who thinks he's a bit clever has set things up to be what he thinks it should look like, or what he's seen on television. The Linda stuff just doesn't quite ring true to me. I hasten to add that it's definitely not my area of experience, but I'm just not buying it. It comes across all wrong.'

'Exactly what I thought, boss!' Jezza sounded pleased that they were both on the same wavelength. 'It's like when you read a book. Like all that crime fiction trash I had to read recently. When it's written by a woman trying to sound like a man, or vice versa, and getting it horribly wrong, so it just sounds cheesy.'

'It just wasn't authentic to me, somehow,' Ted said, aware that he was getting himself into an uncomfortable situation which was likely to have Steve going bright red and he himself squirming a bit. 'It really isn't something I'm familiar with, for obvious reasons. But I read it several times and compared it to what Snooky wrote. It wasn't the same.'

'It was like someone writing what they thought sounded right, not what actually was,' Jezza agreed. 'Know what I think, boss? I think our Linda is definitely a man. I think she may be logo-man on the CCTV and if that's the case, I think he's the killer. He waited in the bar for Waters to come along, followed him to his next meeting. Waited and watched, followed him back to the hotel, with Snooky, if that's who it was. Waited again for them to finish, then went in and killed him.'

'It's possible,' Ted said guardedly. 'But we don't want to get ahead of ourselves. It's all conjecture and supposition at this point. We need an ID of logo-man for a start. Steve, is it possible to find out who else Linda Lovelace is talking to on these sites? Just in case we can get any idea of who else they may possibly be targeting?

'Depends on privacy settings a lot of the time, sir, but I'll see what I can find out. If I can't do it, Océane will be able to.'

Ted stood up and cleared away the remnants of lunch. He gathered up routine paperwork to put in his briefcase as he said, 'Right, I'm going to leave the two of you to get on and I'm going home to try and spend a bit of time with Trev. See you both tomorrow.'

Trev was ironing in front of the television when he got home, not needing to look at subtitles to follow the foreign film. He spoke several languages fluently, having lived and been educated in a few different countries. Ted greeted him with a hug and a kiss.

'You're back at a decent time. Was I totally outrageous last night?' Trev asked.

'Amusing, rather than outrageous,' Ted smiled. 'Do you fancy going out for a bit of a blow somewhere, while I've got the time and there's some daylight left? Are you all right to drive the bike, or do you want me to?'

Trev laughed.

'I wasn't that bad, officer. I'll be well under the limit by now. Just promise me you won't breathe a word to Shewee. It would ruin my credibility as the big brother trying to keep her on the straight and narrow if she ever found out I came home tiddly and slightly stoned.'

'Give me five minutes to change and let's head up to the High Peak. Might as well make the most of it, before I find myself with another murder on my hands.'

Chapter Eleven

Reluctantly, Ted had to abandon pretence and revert to wearing the suit he hated for work. He really could no longer use the excuse of bandaging on his arm. It was visibly so much better. The scarring was still impressive, although he was assured it would improve, and he already had most of the use back. He was told that if he kept up the exercises, he would regain at least ninety per cent of normal function.

The team had two solid days of steady, plodding, routine police work which individually didn't seem to amount to much, but by the Wednesday morning briefing, there were some signs of progress.

'Boss, we've still not got a definite ID on Snooky,' Rob began, 'but we found one or two bar staff who reckoned to have seen her. One knows her as Snooks but one woman said she thought her real name might be Suki.'

'Suki's an unusual name, so that might give us a lead,' Megan Jennings suggested. 'If we can pin her age down as much as we can from the descriptions, do you want me to try ringing round local schools, to see if any of them had a pupil called Suki at the right time? Especially the school Océane already highlighted? It might be a complete dead-end, but you never know. I might just get lucky.'

'Anything's worth a try while we're still waiting on tracing her through her email and mobile phone,' Ted agreed.

He liked Megan's enthusiasm. Before he could say anything further, he was interrupted by his mobile phone. Jim

Baker calling.

'Morning, Super.'

'Morning, Darling.'

The two men never tired of the old joke.

'Looks like your man may have done it again, Ted. I need you and some of your team to get over to South Manchester, as soon as possible. Your old pal Cyril Foster's patch.

'Foster and his DS are already on the scene, with Scemes of Crime. You and some of yours swing by the nick first, introduce yourself, take some of his team, then head for the hotel. I'll arrange visitors' passes to be ready for you at the front desk of the station. It seems like exactly the same MO, from the early reports I've had. Amazingly, someone has clearly read circulating emails, for once, and made the connection, so I got an early shout.

'I'm tied up in meetings at the moment, but I'll try to get over there to join you later if I can. I know there's history between you and Foster, and I know what he's like.'

Ted groaned. He had certainly butted heads with the man a few times, not least because of Foster's sexist and homophobic attitude. It was not a coincidence that his team had almost always been exclusively white and male.

In Ted's opinion, he was the worst type of old-school copper, who thought anything went, as long as it brought results. He knew the type well. His predecessor at Stockport had been the same.

Foster had been subject to more than one investigation by Complaints because of his attitude, but no one ever felt brave enough to testify against him, so he somehow kept getting away with it.

'You don't need me to tell you not to take any crap from Foster or any of his team. Your main priority is the killer, of course, especially if it is the same person. But if you were able to deliver any of their heads on a platter to Complaints at the same time, it would certainly bring you a few extra

Brownie points.'

Ted laughed.

'No pressure, then? Right, boss, I'll see you there at some point in the day.'

The team members were looking expectantly at him as he ended the call, wondering if it might be a shout for the new team. It had clearly been the old Big Boss calling.

'Right, everyone, the A Team is go. Another body; sounds like the same MO. Another hotel, this time South Manchester, so we're mobile. Foresnsics are on site, with the local DI and DS. We just have to swing by their nick first before joining them, compare notes quickly, bring everyone up to speed.'

He looked around the office, deciding who to take. Steve and Jezza were both on a day off today. 'Jo, you're in charge. If it's all right with you, Mike, I'll take Rob on this one, with Virgil, leave you with Sal and Megan to carry on here.'

Mike smiled his gratitude.

'Fine by me, boss. If it's anything like the last one, I'm quite happy to pass on it. Save me from disgracing myself again.'

'Right, Rob, you and Virgil get the keys to the service car. We might need the blues and twos if there's heavy traffic. I'll be right with you, when I've just let the Super know.'

Ted let Rob drive. They made excellent time, with the occasional use of the car's siren to give them a clear run where they needed it. On the way over, Ted gave Rob and Virgil a word of warning.

'DI Foster runs his team in a particular way and I should warn you, Virgil, that black officers, and women, have tended to have a very short life expectancy with him. Just get on and do your jobs, as I know you can, but please report to me on any grief anybody in the team gives you.'

Pausing only to sign in, Ted and the others took the stairs two at a time up to the CID office on the first floor. There were four officers waiting there for them. Pointedly, no one even made a show of standing or even straightening up as the SIO on the case came in. The looks being thrown at Ted were decidedly hostile.

Ted moved to the front of the room, flanked by Rob and Virgil.

'Morning, everyone. I'm DCI Darling, these are DS O'Connell and DC Tibbs. I'm SIO on this case because it may well be linked to one we're already working on. I want to get to the scene as soon as possible, but I also wanted a few minutes to introduce myself first. You'll all be wondering why you've been saddled with a short, gay bloke from Stockport.'

Ted's usual light-hearted ice-breaker barely raised a smile from the four stony faces which looked at him. He knew Foster's team would be hard nuts to crack and he hoped he wouldn't have to waste his time dealing with attitude issues when he should have been going after the killer.

'Well, it's orders from on high so you're stuck with me. Until I get to know you, please tell me your name and rank when you have anything to say. And for the record, I don't like to be called guv, so either sir or boss will do.'

'We already have a boss,' one of the four men said truculently.

He sat with his arms folded across his chest, knees wide apart, feet pulled back under his chair, his expression aggressive. Ted knew all four officers present were DCs. He didn't like to judge, but knowing who their boss was, he was not optimistic about working with any of them.

'I'm sorry, I didn't catch your name?' Ted said quietly, his tone questioning, knowing full well the man hadn't given it.

'Terry Coombs,' he said, his tone sneering. 'DC. And DI Foster is our boss.'

'Well, DC Coombs, sir will do very well for me. Now, I imagine DI Foster has already told you who he wants on this?'

'All of us for now, with as many Woodentops as we can rustle up,' Coombs told him, deliberately not calling him sir.

'Uniformed officers, please, in my presence,' Ted told him

calmly enough.

It was clear that the man was going to be trouble.

'Right, let's go. DC Coombs, you're with me, your car. The rest of you, with DS O'Connell.'

As soon as they were on their way, Ted half turned in the front passenger seat so he could look at Coombs while he spoke to him.

'Right, DC Coombs, let's get a few things straight, while it's just the two of us. I'm here to catch a killer.'

The man opened his mouth to speak but Ted cut in.

'Be quiet, and listen carefully. You're busy playing who can piss highest up the wall. Well, let me tell you something. It's me. I can piss higher than any of you, that's why I'm SIO on this case.'

Coombs' knuckles were going white where he was gripping the steering wheel and his voice was angry as he spat, 'You can't talk to me like that, you little prick. You're not my guv'nor.'

'I just did. And I've not finished yet. I don't like people who are judgemental, especially not police officers. It doesn't make them good at their job and I only want the best people working a case like this, under me. I'm just putting you on notice that I'll be watching you, and so far, you've got some way to go to stay on this case.'

Coombs lapsed into angry silence for the rest of the drive.

The hotel where the body had been found was near the town centre and didn't have its own car park. Instead, the DC parked in a nearby municipal multi-storey then led the way, still saying nothing, to walk the short distance to the hotel.

He took what was presumably a short-cut, through a ginnel behind some shops.

There was a uniformed presence in front of the hotel. Ted showed his ID to a young constable who greeted him with a polite, 'Sir,' and gave them the room number. They went into the hotel, Coombs still maintaining a sullen silence.

Rob O'Connell and the others were waiting at the reception desk. There was no sign of the local team's detective sergeant, so Ted addressed his own.

'Rob, witness statements from all of the staff and any guests still around,' Ted told him. 'And anything and everything they have on the victim. You know the form. Ask about CCTV, too. Maybe we'll get lucky this time.'

When Ted and DC Coombs went upstairs, there was another officer from Uniform branch outside a bedroom door which stood open. Inside, Scenes of Crime Inestigaters in coveralls were still working, and Ted could see from a pair of naked legs near the foot of the bed that the body had not yet been taken away. He took out his Fisherman's Friend lozenges and slipped one in his mouth, which brought another sneer of derision to Coombs's face.

DI Foster appeared from the doorway of what was presumably the shower room. He was wearing latex gloves and had on shoe covers, a pencil in his hand, with which he was busy poking and prodding at objects of interest. He looked up when he saw Ted and DC Coombs pause outside the door, waiting for permission to enter.

'Morning, Ted. Put covers on and you can come in but watch where you walk. SOCO have pretty much finished this floor area and the pathologist has been and gone, but there are bits of blood and brain splattered everywhere.'

Ted nodded to him in return.

'DI Foster,' he said, hoping his formal tone might remind the man that Ted now outranked him and was SIO on the case. 'What can you tell me so far?'

Foster was not much taller than Ted, with weasel-like features and thinning hair in a comb-over. A somewhat scruffy short raincoat emphasised the old-style cop image. Ted knew he was not far off retirement and that his sole aim in life was to keep plodding on until he could draw his pension. Ted neither liked him particularly as a person nor rated him as a detective, but he was professional enough to keep his feelings to himself.

'Richard Hutchinson, according to his reservation details. Not local, he's from out of town. Harrogate. Pathologist reckons he was killed shortly before midnight last night. Found by the cleaner when she came in to do the room. He was due to leave today. His business cards, on the desk over there, call him a Health and Safety consultant.'

'Cause of death?' Ted asked, not yet having gone close enough to look for himself.

'Multiple stab wounds, followed by someone kicking the shit out of his head and face. His own mother wouldn't recognise him.'

'Laptop and mobile phone?'

'Also on the desk thing, over by the window.'

'I'll take them back with me. We have a CFI on the team who's working on the ones from the first case. Get them bagged up for me and I'll sign for them. So, if the cleaner let herself in, presumably she thought he'd checked out? DC Coombs, can you ask at reception if his key, or card, or whatever they have here, had been handed in.'

Coombs hesitated and looked towards Foster.

'Boss?' he asked, pointedly asking for his permission.

It was borderline insolence, but Ted didn't have time to deal with such petty behaviour now. He fully intended to mark Coombs' card for him when he got the opportunity, though.

'The DCI's the gov'nor on this one, Terry, best do as he tells you.'

Then, as Coombs disappeared off downstairs, Foster said to Ted, 'Take no notice of Terry; he means no harm.'

Ted looked him squarely in the eye as he replied, 'But I do take notice, Cyril,' dropping the rank now Coombs had left them. 'And I don't like what I see so far.

'Right, let me have a look at our victim, then you can tell me how you're reading the scene.'

This time the dead man was wearing only the less than

generous-sized towel provided by the hotel, tied round his waist. There were several frenzied stab wounds to the torso, with some defensive injuries to his right arm. Once again, there was a stab wound to the throat, which had clearly resulted in catastrophic blood loss. And as before, the killer seemed to have lost all control once his victim fell to the ground. The damage to the face was possibly even worse on this occasion. Ted had no idea how this body was going to be made presentable enough for identification.

Ted found it hard to gauge the exact height of the prone body, but the man didn't look tall and his build was medium. It was almost impossible to judge his hair colour because of the amount of blood. Ted steeled himself to look closer. Part of the scalp had been peeled away, presumably as a result of his head being stamped on.

'Wedding ring?' Ted asked.

'Not wearing one,' Foster replied.

Curbing his impatience, Ted asked, 'Have you looked for one? In the room, or in his clothing? There's a reason why it might be significant.'

Foster shrugged indifferently.

'Not everyone wears one.'

Ted asked one of the Investigators still working on the scene if he could look in the bedside drawer, and in the man's clothing. Sure enough, when the drawer drew a blank, the man found a wedding ring in the jacket hanging on the clothes rail.

'This could be relevant, based on what we know so far in the other case,' Ted said, then walked across to the entry door, pushed it to and had a look at the handle on the inside. He went back again to the body and looked at the hands and at what remained of the hair. Then he looked across at Foster and said, 'Tell me what you see.'

Foster looked slightly disinterested.

'Picked up the wrong person for a bit of how's your father? Or refused to pay a tart for services rendered so she lost it and took her own payment?'

'You think a woman did this?' Ted asked in a neutral tone. 'What about his wallet? Are his credit cards still there?'

'I haven't looked yet,' Foster admitted. 'I just got his name from reception.'

Ted had always suspected the man was next to useless. He wondered how he had ever made detective inspector. Again, he turned to the Investigator, who found the wallet and reported that there was cash in it and several credit cards.

'Whoever killed him was almost certainly not in the room with him. The victim let them in. As with the last case, this victim appears to have been disturbed when taking a shower, gone to the door to let someone in, and been stabbed almost immediately.

'Right, let's get down there and start interviewing people, see if we can get any more information before we head back to your nick. Superintendent Baker is coming over as soon as he's free, for a progress report.'

Foster looked at him as if he had made an obscene suggestion.

'Interviewing witnesses? I usually leave that to my lads and to the Woodentops.'

Ted looked at him hard, trying to keep the distaste from his voice.

'Inspector Foster, I like to keep it respectful always. Uniformed officers, please. And an extra couple of pairs of experienced hands can only be a good thing in helping us to wrap things up here for now, surely?'

As Ted turned to go out of the door, he distinctly heard two things. The first was at least one of the Crime Scene Investigators stifling a snort of laughter. The second was Foster spitting between gritted teeth, 'Jumped up little prick.'

Chapter Twelve

When Ted got back down to reception, he finally saw the man he took to be Foster's DS, who had so far been conspicuous by his absence. He had a Mars bar, partly unwrapped, stuck between his teeth, and a cup of coffee in each hand, from the vending machine he was standing in front of. He thrust one of the coffees at Foster and took the chocolate out of his mouth so he could speak, although he completely ignored Ted.

'Thought you might fancy a brew before we head back, boss.'

Foster accepted the coffee and took a noisy slurp before he said, 'This is DCI Darling. My sergeant, Jock Mackenzie. Have you met?'

Mackenzie gave a brief lift of the chin and a muttered, 'All right?' in greeting.

Ted hadn't met him, but his reputation preceded him and it was no better than Foster's.

'We're not ready to go back yet, any of us,' Ted told them. 'I want to get statements from everyone before we leave. Some of these hotel guests will be from well out of the area. I don't want to be having to chase them up all round the country once they've left.'

'You can safely leave that to the lads and the W …' DS Mackenzie only got as far as the first consonant before Ted rounded on him, tired already of the total lack of respect from this team.

'We'll get through this much more quickly and efficiently if everyone pitches in. I'll phone one of my team to start running PNC checks now because we'll want to find his car, for one thing. And DI Foster, you might want to warn your team that I will not tolerate disrespect in any form. Uniformed officers are to be referred to as exactly that, likewise Community Support Officers. I do not want to hear any more references from anyone to Woodentops, nor to Plastic Policemen. Clear?'

He turned to go and heard the DS mutter something of which he didn't catch much except for the word 'twat'. He spun lightly on his feet to turn back and looked directly at Mackenzie.

'I'm very approachable, DS Mackenzie. If you disagree with any aspect of my handling of this case, please feel free to say so to my face, rather than behind my back.'

Not unusually, Mackenzie was taller than Ted. But something in the way the smaller man held himself and looked at him made him stay quiet. Ted turned back and went in search of where his team and the officers from Foster's were hopefully interviewing staff and potential witnesses. Foster drained his coffee, tossed the cup into a nearby bin and caught him up.

'Lighten up, Ted. We'll get someone for this.'

Ted stopped and faced him.

'Let's be clear on something from the outset, DI Foster. I don't want someone. I want the person who did it.'

He knew that, as well as too many unsolved serious crimes on his books, Foster had also had some wrongful arrests. He had a bad habit of picking a suspect then trying to make a case stick. Ted reckoned he must have friends in high places to have hung on to his job. He wondered if funny handshakes were involved.

Ted found his team in the dining room, patiently interviewing people. Scanning the room, he could see there was no sign of DC Coombs, nor of another of Foster's team, whose name he did not yet know. He could only see two of the local officers, looking bored and going through the motions of taking details. He waited until he could catch Rob's eye. When his own newly promoted DS came over, Ted drew him to one side to ask about progress.

'They're a bunch of useless skivers, boss, to put it bluntly. Virgil and me have been going through the staff and whatever guests are still here. Coombs and another one sloped off on a fag break at least ten minutes ago and I've not seen them since.

'So far, there's not much of any real use, although there is some CCTV footage we should be able to look through. The woman I've just been speaking to, who was in the next room to our victim, said she heard someone in the corridor last night around midnight. She thinks she heard someone saying they were from maintenance and that there was a problem with the plumbing, but I haven't followed that up yet. We've not yet talked to the manager. He's been running round in square circles trying to deal with panicky guests, so I thought I'd leave him till later.'

'I'll go and find him and ask him about it.'

He went back to the local DI and said, 'You and DS Mackenzie liaise with DS O'Connell on what still needs doing. Once we've covered all bases here, then we'll think about regrouping back at the station. And one of you can start by finding DC Coombs and the other one and putting them to work.'

Ted was not going to be winning any friends. It didn't bother him in the least.

He found an extremely harassed-looking manager on the front desk trying to placate guests who were wanting to check out early. They were clearly alarmed by the police presence and news of what had happened. In reply to Ted's question, the man gave his name as Simms.

'I'm sorry to bother you, Mr Simms. I know this is a difficult time for you, but we do need to get as much information as possible early on, while it's still fresh in people's memories. One of your guests has told my officers there was some sort of a problem with the plumbing late last night. You had to send maintenance up to the first floor to fix it? Can you tell me anything about that, please?'

The man looked at him in surprise.

'First I've heard of it. We don't have anyone on at that time of night to do anything like that.'

'I see,' Ted said neutrally. 'It's possible, of course, that the lady was mistaken. If you do happen to hear of anything which might explain it, can you please let me know? Here's my card, if I've already left when you find out.'

He went back into the dining room and found Rob talking to a man. He excused himself, drew his DS aside again and asked about the woman who'd told him about a maintenance man.

'She's over there having some coffee, boss,' Rob pointed to an older woman, clutching a cup and saucer.

The hotel had put coffee and biscuits out for guests who were being interviewed.

'I'm just talking to her husband now, although he didn't hear anything. Mr and Mrs Stanley.'

Ted went across to where the woman was just finding herself a seat. He took out his warrant card as he approached her.

'Mrs Stanley? I'm DCI Darling. Would you mind if I joined you for a moment? I could do with a coffee myself.'

He got himself a cup and pulled up a chair to sit down next to her.

'My sergeant tells me you heard someone outside your room last night. I wondered if you'd mind telling me about it, as well?'

'Well, I think it must have been about midnight. I was having difficulty getting to sleep. My husband snores so much. I got up to go and find one of my sleeping pills, from my bag in the bathroom. I could hear the sound of running water through the wall from the next room. The walls are a bit thin, you can always hear when the person next door is taking a shower.

'Then I thought I heard a knock on the door of the next room, and the water was turned off in the shower. Someone outside on the landing said something, but I didn't catch it all. The door to the room is a bit better at muffling sound. It was something about the plumbing needing maintenance. I didn't hear much else, just a bit of a bump at some point as if someone was moving something. I suppose they may have needed to do that to get at where the plumbing problem was. Then I put my earplugs in and got back into bed so I didn't hear anything more, I'm afraid.'

It was well past what would normally have been lunchtime before Ted was satisfied they had all the information they could get for now. He proposed they regroup back at the station for a debrief, with a stop to pick up some food on the way back there. One of Foster's men took sandwich orders and money. Ted had received a text from Jim Baker saying he hoped to be there within the hour.

Coombs was clearly still sulking when he and Ted started the walk back to the car park. Rob O'Connell and the others had gone on ahead, with the sandwich order, as had DI Foster and his DS. Out of courtesy, as the SIO, Ted had wanted to have a final word with the manager before leaving.

Just as Ted and Coombs were turning into the ginnel, they could see ahead of them a group of three teenage hoodies, who appeared to have a young man pinned up against a wall. Ted saw straight away the flash of broken bottle in one of their hands. To his surprise, Coombs made to do an about turn and walk away.

'Call back-up, now,' Ted told him, already moving forward, shouting, 'All right, break it up. Police! Back off and leave him alone.'

The three youths turned deliberately to look at the short

man in a trenchcoat, who was approaching them. Ted could see that two of them were black, but the hood the third was wearing obscured too much of his face to reveal anything much about him.

'Yeah? Or what you gonna do about it, little man?' one of them asked tauntingly.

Ted was still moving slowly towards them. He'd not yet heard the DC make a phone call, so he barked at him, 'Call it in, Coombs. Now.'

Then he pulled out his warrant card and held it up towards the youths.

'I'm a police officer. Step away and put the bottle down.'

With a provocative gesture, the one who had spoken swung the broken bottle towards the terrified young man up against the wall. In a reflex action, he brought his right arm up to protect his face and the jagged edge of the glass bit through his sleeve, causing blood to start dripping through the ripped fabric, as he started to sob in pain and terror.

Finally, Ted heard Coombs make the call, asking for back-up. The youths heard it, too, and lost some of their certainty. Ted was standing his ground, not too keen to risk further injury so soon after the last time, but fully prepared to wade in and protect the injured youth if it became necessary. He knew instinctively he couldn't count on any help at all from Coombs.

The ringleader was carefully weighing up his adversary. He was streetwise enough to tell that he was not the pushover he had looked at first sight. Something about the way Ted was calmly standing there, poised for action, rang warning bells in his head. That and the wail of a siren, distant for now but clearly getting closer, and fast.

In a last defiant gesture, he hurled the broken bottle towards Ted's head before the three of them turned and disappeared at speed up the ginnel. Ted effortlessly avoided it with no more than a precisely timed sway of the body, then he moved closer to the victim, now cowering back against the wall and sliding down into a sitting position.

'It's all right, I really am a police officer. I just need to get some pressure on that wound for you to stop the bleeding,' Ted told him calmly, crouching down to his level.

'Don't touch me!' the young man almost screamed in panic.

'Coombs, phone an ambulance,' Ted said sharply then, gently, to the young man, 'It's all right, I'm not going to hurt you. I just need to get that bleeding under control.'

The young man shook his head frantically.

'No, it's not that. I'm HIV positive.'

Coombs was making the second call. Ted now saw him take a swift step back, as if he thought the infected blood was suddenly going to target him, like a heat-seeking missile.

'It's fine, don't worry. I have gloves,' Ted said quietly, pulling some out of his pocket, where he always carried at least two pairs, and slipping them on. 'I'm Ted, by the way. What's your name?'

'Jamie,' he replied, his voice quavering.

'Well, Jamie, just press this hanky against the bleed for me. It is clean. My partner always makes sure I have a clean hanky for just such an occasion.'

He made eye contact with the youth, who didn't look more than about eighteen. He could tell that he had understood the message.

'It turns out my partner wasn't quite as open and honest as I thought,' Jamie told him, as Ted took his tie off and wound it round the handkerchief to get some even pressure on the bleed. Luckily, it didn't look too bad, but Ted didn't want to take any risks.

'Ambulance and Woodentops are on the way now, so we can get going,' Coombs said from behind him, clearly more interested in his dinner than in the welfare of the victim.

Ted ignored him, hoping Coombs would not be foolish enough just to abandon him and go back to the station without him. He might break the habit of a lifetime and put him on a disciplinary if he did. He already had plenty of cause.

'I'm sorry to hear that, Jamie. I'm going to stay with you until the ambulance gets here, although I'm hoping that siren is it on its way. Is there anyone I can call for you, while we wait?'

Jamie shook his head.

'I'm on my own at the moment. Anyway, all the numbers were on my phone, which they stole.'

It wasn't too long before they saw the ambulance pull up near to the end of the ginnel, then two men in green headed down the passageway towards them. Ted made the introductions, quick to stress Jamie's HIV status, then waited until the young man was safely taken away and loaded into the ambulance. He removed his gloves carefully, relieved to see they were still intact, and gave them to the paramedics for safe disposal.

'What about your tie?' Jamie asked him, anxiously.

Ted gave him a conspiratorial grin as he said, 'I hate wearing a tie. You've given me a good excuse not to do so for the rest of the day. Good luck, Jamie. With everything.'

As the ambulance pulled away, Ted rounded on Coombs.

'The next time I tell you to make a phone call, you make it immediately. Don't make me repeat myself. And don't ever refer to uniformed officers in that disrespectful way again in my presence. Am I making myself clear, DC Coombs?'

Coombs gave him a sullen grunt in reply, which could have meant anything, before turning and walking off down the ginnel. Ted got his phone out as he followed him and made a call to Jim Baker.

'Where are you, Ted? We're all here ready to start the briefing.'

The Big Boss didn't sound too pleased.

'We just got delayed by an active wounding. Victim's now safely on his way to hospital. I'll be there shortly, if I don't stop to commit murder on the way.'

'Problem?'

'Pain in the arse, more like.'

As they got near to the level where Coombs' car was parked, the DC said scathingly, 'You not being bothered about catching AIDS from him. Is that because you've already got it?'

Ted stopped in his tracks and looked at him, hard. Anyone who knew him would have seen instantly that his usually warm hazel eyes had changed to a dangerous shade of green, reminiscent of the broken shards of the bottle.

'You are on very dangerous ground there, DC Coombs. I suggest that you think extremely carefully before you say anything else.'

'Yeah, or what?' Coombs asked sneeringly, his tone not unlike that of the hoody earlier. 'Like I said, you're not my guv'nor and I'm not taking orders from a jumped up little bum-bandit like you.'

At that, Coombs seemed to have wound himself up into such a state that he completely lost it and threw a wild punch at Ted's head. With four martial arts black belts to his name, Ted knew so many ways to deal with such an attacking move. He preferred instead simply to slide out of range and watch, with a certain satisfaction, as Coombs' fist connected, hard, with a concrete pillar. The man yelped as the blow took the skin off his knuckles and a loud crack suggested that he had probably broken at least one bone.

'I'll drive, then, shall I?' Ted asked calmly, as Coombs nursed his hand in pain.

Detective Superintendent Jim Baker, head of the new team, was waiting impatiently for Ted and Coombs to arrive. Coombs was red in the face, looking furious, and cradling his hand across his chest.

Ted smiled innocently and said, 'Sorry, boss, we got held up doing some proper police work, hands on stuff. But we've handed over to Uniform now, so we're all yours.'

At a nod from the Big Boss, Ted filled all those present in

on everything they knew to date of the death on their own patch, plus the similarities with the one they had just come from.

'I don't want to start jumping to any conclusions yet, not before we've studied CCTV footage or anything else. But we have logo-man at our scene, and there's a witness here saying they heard a reference to maintenance. I can't help thinking there may be a link there.

'We'll take the laptop and phone back with us and get the contents analysed.'

He'd given them to Rob to put in their car.

'I want to know full details of the post-mortem, as soon as it happens, and I want to speak to next of kin myself, so keep me posted. But for now, I think we'll head back to Stockport and come back here tomorrow.'

One of the DCs waved a paper bag at Ted and said, 'Did you want your sandwich?'

Ted shook his head, despite having paid for it. He had a strong suspicion that at least one of Foster's team would have spat in it, if not worse.

Chapter Thirteen

Ted wanted to catch a few words in private with Jim Baker before he left. He sent Rob and Virgil on ahead to the car, asking them to pick up a sandwich and some coffee for him from the nearest shop. When he replied to Rob's question about why he hadn't fancied the sandwich he'd paid for earlier, the two of them went on their way laughing.

Jim Baker had been loaned the use of an office the size of a broom cupboard. There was barely enough room for the two of them to sit down. Ted filled his boss in on everything so far. When he came to the part about the incident with the broken bottle, Jim interrupted him.

'Bloody hell, Ted, are you all right?' he asked anxiously. 'Are you sure it was safe to do that?'

Ted shrugged, unconcerned.

'I'll be fine. I had gloves on, and they were still intact when I took them off. But I will go to the drop-in centre as soon as I get back to Stockport, just to be on the safe side. They'll tell me how long I have to wait before I can be tested, and I can get the results there almost instantly when I can be.'

'And what about Coombs? If you want him booted off the team, just say the word. More than happy to trust your judgement. I don't think much of Foster, and I'm not in the minority. It stands to reason none of his team will be up to much or they wouldn't stay with him and put up with his shit.'

'Leave him, for now. I'll keep him close, where I can keep an eye on him, for the time being. He may just be a coward, but the way he was ready to leave well alone smacked more of bent cop to me. I know he's homophobic, he's shown me enough evidence of that already. But I wondered if he has an arrangement with some of the local gangs, to turn a blind eye to certain crimes. He certainly didn't seem concerned about a GBH and theft by three thugs on one young man.'

'Wouldn't surprise me,' Jim responded. 'This team needs a massive boot up the arse. We've been down this route before, you and I. Foster's just treading water, ready to retire. It would be a political hot potato to drop him now, so close to his pension, without very good reason. But if you give me even half a reason I can work with, I'd be happy to do it.

'Oh, and tell me about Coombs' smashed up hand. Was that anything I should know about?'

Ted smiled.

'Having made several unkind comments about my anatomy and asking my HIV status, he lost it and unwisely threw a punch. I just dodged it. Nothing more than that.'

'He threw a punch at a senior officer?' Jim demanded angrily. 'More than enough reason to kick his arse off the team, and out of the force.'

'Let it go for now, Jim. Just the school bully, flexing his muscles. If it gets any worse, or he starts on any of my team members, I'll make it official. For now, you know me. I'm more than capable of taking care of myself.'

Jim grunted reluctant assent, then continued, 'Where do you want to base the enquiry? I'm assuming you're happy the two deaths are connected? So with one here and one in Stockport, do you want to move everything to one central location?'

'From what I've seen so far, I would be surprised if we're dealing with two different killers. I hope not, at any rate. It sounds daft but, I don't really want this lot mixed in with my team any more than I can help. So just for now, until I see how it pans out, I'd prefer to hop between the two stations, if you agree.'

'Your enquiry, Ted, you run it how you see fit. I'm just here to add what clout I can and to take the rap if it all goes tits up. Which I know it won't. You've never let me down yet, although you've given me a few scares on the way. Good luck with the clinic. Let me know what they say.'

Ted pulled his mobile out on the way to the car, to call Trev.

'I'm really sorry but I've no idea what time I'll be back,' he told him. 'I don't think I'll get there in time for the kids' club. Would you mind taking my kit down for me, just in case I can get there for judo afterwards? I'm really in the mood for some lively randori, after the day I'm having.'

Trev chuckled suggestively.

'I'm liking the sound of that.'

Ted had only been away from his own team for a few hours, but it felt like days. He was pleased, but not surprised, to find everything running smoothly and peacefully in the clearly capable hands of Jo Rodriguez, helped by Mike Hallam. Everyone was quietly working away at their desks, the atmosphere completely different to that which he had experienced in the other station.

Ted told them everything they had to date from their day's findings and confirmed that it had all the hallmarks of being the same killer. He asked for any updates.

'Boss, first off, I got all the details available from PNC and sent them through to South Manchester. I tried a follow-up phone call, as a courtesy,' Sal told him. 'What a barrel of laughs they are, on that team. Would I be over-reacting if I said I got the feeling that my name being Ahmed may have been the reason I didn't get a thank you?'

Virgil laughed, a rich, dark rumble.

'Oh, I was welcomed with open arms and kisses on both cheeks by all those good white boys,' he said ironically.

'If any of you want to make an official complaint at any

time, please come and see me. I won't have anyone subject to any kind of prejudicial behaviour. I was on the receiving end of plenty of it myself today. I decided to let it go for now. I'm more interested in catching our murderer. But seriously, if any of you are bothered by it…'

When nobody said anything, Megan Jennings put in, 'Boss, Océane and I have been working together to find Snooky. We've not quite done so, but we have made a bit of progress. I rang round the schools and, amazingly, I did find two Sukis of about the right age. Jo and I have been out to try to track them down, but there wasn't anyone in at one address and we were told that the other one has married and moved to Australia, so I think it's a fair bet that she's not the one we want.'

Océane took up the story.

'Megan gave me the other name, Suki Jackson. That was her name at school, so there's a possibility she's changed it since, if she got married. So far, I've found nothing in that name on things like the electoral role. So I've been looking on social media and I've found a Suki Su-su. I've narrowed down her IP address to this side of Manchester but I can't yet get the exact physical address, although where Jo and Megan went and found no one at home is in exactly the right area.

'Now, we get into ethics issues again if I, or anyone on the team, starts trying to Friend her or Follow her on social media, in an entrapment sense, in the meantime. A lot of her posts are private, but her check-ins are not always private.'

Seeing Ted's look of blank incomprehension, she quickly explained that people could use a phone app to show where they were at any given time, especially when they had arrived at somewhere significant.

'As a result, we now at least know the name of the pub she likes to go to most Friday evenings, by the look of it. So if we don't find her any other way, there is that possible way forward. The old casual encounter in the pub with off-duty police officers trick.'

116

'Good work, all of you,' Ted smiled round at his team.

What a difference in initiative and enthusiasm to what he'd been confronted with earlier.

'We've brought back more work for you, Océane, in the shape of the mobile and laptop of our second victim, Richard Hutchinson. I'm hoping you can work your magic on that once more and see what we're working with here. I'd be very surprised if the two cases were not linked.

'And thanks again, all of you, for your work today. I know it's not been an easy day for some of you. I'd take you all for a drink after work if I didn't have somewhere to be.'

'Comes from the top down, boss,' Rob told him frankly. 'Can't imagine anyone wanting to try to make an impression on DI Foster or his DS, from what I saw today. You're a good boss.'

'Stop it, you'll make me blush,' Ted grinned, but he was pleased. He tried to lead by example and it was always good to get feedback that it was working. 'Right, I need to brief the Super on where we're up to, then I'm off. See you all tomorrow.'

He'd already phoned ahead to cancel his weekly therapy session with Carol, as he'd known early on he was not going to be in time for it. Luckily she understood the demands of his job and other than asking how he was feeling, had said nothing about the late cancellation. He was just about to head downstairs when his mobile rang and the screen told him it was Professor Nelson calling. He took the call as he went out into the corridor, pausing at the top of the stairs.

'Afternoon, Bizzie, do you have something for me?'

He hadn't been informed of a sudden death on his patch. It was possible that it was another one that had started out looking innocent enough then had given the pathologist cause for concern at the post-mortem.

'Good afternoon, Edwin. We have another drugs overdose from Sabden House. Once again, the cause of death was heroin more pure than anything which we routinely see. I'm flagging it up as a possible suspicious death. You might well want to send someone round to have a look at where it happened.'

'Give me all the details and I'll hand it over to my new DI, Jo Rodriguez. I already have several places to be at once. I'm just back from another death very similar to our hotel guest. Once I get the PM report for that, I'll send you a copy for comparison.'

'That's a worrying development for you. I'll look forward to seeing the report, in a professional sort of way.'

Ted went in search of Jo, who was back in his own office. Quickly, Ted laid out details of the previous two deaths at the flats.

'There may be nothing to it, only coincidence, but it's strange that in the three cases we now know of, the quality of the gear, both the heroin and the alcohol, was so high. That would suggest it was outside the usual price range of the victims, so it certainly merits looking at. Can I leave that one with you to check on? Go and have a look at the scene, see if anything jumps out at you.'

Ted put his head round Kevin Turner's door on his way to see the Ice Queen. He wanted to make sure he was not thinking of ducking out of his hospital appointment on Friday, and to reassure him that Maurice Brown was still more than willing to go with him.

'I heard you had to go abroad today. Cyril Foster's patch? That must have been worse than the body. I don't hear anything good about that lot. My mate up there is tired of trying to get him to show a bit of respect for his uniformed officers and to stop treating them like his personal lackeys. For all your faults, at least you're polite.'

'Often under great provocation. And what faults? I don't have any,' Ted laughed. 'I'm sending Jo round to Sabden House to look at this latest sudden death there. Professor Nelson has marked it as possibly suspicious.'

'My lads said it just looked like a drug overdose. The deceased still had the needle in a vein.'

'It wasn't a criticism. Just that the Professor phoned me a few minutes ago with the PM results and the quality of the heroin is suspiciously pure, like the last one. We'll need to take a bit of a closer look. Can you ask your officers attending to have a word with Jo? It will do tomorrow, though, this is on the back-burner a bit. Our murderer is taking priority, especially with another killing almost certainly down to him.

'Make sure you go and get sorted on Friday. Maurice is programmed to come looking for you, if not. And trust him. He's a good man.'

Next stop was the Ice Queen's office. He gratefully accepted her offer of coffee. He didn't seem to have eaten or drunk much during the day. He was answerable to Jim Baker for the murder away from their patch but as a courtesy, he filled the Ice Queen in on the similarities. He also told her about his need for an HIV test. It was just to cover himself. He was not remotely concerned about any possibility of it showing up positive.

'I think I have to wait up to three months for anything to show up, but I'll go to the drop-in centre now for advice. I should be clear. I had gloves on and I didn't come into contact with any of his blood.'

He asked for any update on personal detail disclosures from Internet Service Providers or mobile phone companies for the murder case. The Ice Queen told him she was still waiting on any development, and reminded him dryly that, unlike on the television, such things often took time.

Ted brought up the fact that they now had a possibility of tracing Snooky through the pub she favoured on a Friday evening. He mentioned the idea of Jezza and Megan going in there to see what they could find out.

'She's not a suspect, as such,' he stressed. 'I don't see them as being at any degree of risk. Just two colleagues on a night out.'

The Ice Queen considered thoughtfully.

'And you've thought carefully about the possibility of a link between Snooky and your logo-man? I'd be happier if there was someone else there, just to keep an eye on them, in case.'

'I have the perfect solution,' Ted told her. 'DC Vine was most anxious not to have anyone cramping her style. I've seen her in action before now, looking nothing at all like a police officer, so I can understand her reservations. But I have what might just be the perfect way to keep an eye on them both, without blowing their cover.'

On his way out, he put his head round Kevin Turner's door once more and said, 'You, me and Maurice are going to meet up for a drink on Friday night. Celebrate you getting sorted out and Maurice gearing up to come back to work on Monday. I just need to keep a little covert eye on young Jezza while she does her stuff of not looking remotely like a copper, to try to track down a witness we need. So I need cover of my own and you two can be it.'

When he mentioned the name of the pub they would be going to, Kevin stared at him in horror.

'In there, on a Friday night? Are you mad? We'll get eaten alive. It's always full of sex-crazed, man-hunting women … On second thoughts, count me in. What time?'

Ted didn't have long to wait at the drop-in clinic. He never liked to play the police card, if he could avoid it, by expecting special treatment. But when he explained the circumstances, he was seen quickly.

As he'd thought, he was told he would have to wait for some time to know if he had been infected, but the nurse dealing with him was quick to reassure him that, from what he had told her, his risk was probably slight.

She carefully examined the impressive scar down his hand and inner forearm, left by the recent knife attack. She pronounced that it posed no real hazard as there was no broken skin left visible. She advised him to have a simple finger-prick test immediately, to check his current status, although he assured her he was low risk. He and Trev were in a mutually monogamous relationship, but he consented to it anyway. It came back clear, as he knew it would.

He left, promising to return in no more than three months, for a follow-up test, with the proviso that he might need another after a further twelve weeks, before he could be sure he was completely clear.

Once he'd finished at the clinic, Ted saw that if he got a move on, he'd just about have time to get to the club before the adult judo session started. It was a discourtesy to be late, one he tried to avoid. But he was seriously in need of some fast, physical action after a stressful day. He hadn't been able to do much recently, because of his hand. It would feel good to work out to the point of being breathless and sweating.

Trev had walked down, as usual, so went back in the car with him. Ted told him about his day, about the necessity of the HIV test and the need to be careful until he knew he was definitely clear.

'Oh, we'll be careful all right,' Trev told him. 'Just as long as you're not proposing abstention as a means of caution.'

Chapter Fourteen

Ted called an early morning briefing with his own team the following morning. He wanted to keep things moving along on the murder on their own patch before he went back up to Foster's, to see what progress could be made there.

The team was up to full strength again, with both Steve and Jezza back in. Océane came in early, although she was not obliged to. Ted was impressed by her apparent enthusiasm for the job. She promised to call him as soon as she had any information from the phone or computer of the latest victim.

'It's not like on telly or in books though, boss,' she warned him. 'I can't just magically download everything off his phone in an instant and solve the case for you. Not even the FBI can do that. But if I can get into both the phone and the laptop, I'll be able to see his emails, that sort of stuff, which might give us a start.'

'Benny from Luther would do it,' Ted said with a smile, as Océane sighed and clicked her tongue in mock exasperation.

Then he continued, 'Rob, you and Virgil come with me again, and we could do with an extra pair of hands. Who's up for it? Jezza, do you think you could cope with our misogynist friends north of the Mersey?'

Jezza flashed a wicked grin.

'Shouldn't you be asking if they can cope with me, boss?'

The whole team laughed. None of them doubted for a moment that Jezza was quite capable of dealing with the likes of Foster's team. She'd proved it on more than one occasion since she'd joined them.

'And what are you doing Friday night, Jezza?'

'Boss, you sweet-talker, you, are you asking me out on a date?' Jezza teased him.

Ted smiled indulgently. He didn't mind the easy banter of his team because he knew he had their respect.

'Megan, too, if you're available? The two of you, in the pub, for a girls' night out, asking around for Suki or Snooky or whatever she calls herself. But on the orders of the Super, and I entirely agree with her, you'll be chaperoned, just in case. Inspector Turner, Maurice and myself will be sitting in a corner, trying not to cramp your style, but keeping an eye out.

'Right, Jo, you're in charge here. Keep me posted, as usual. We're off to enjoy the welcoming smiles and open arms of our colleagues. We'll hopefully be back for a catch-up at the end of the day.'

On the way over in the car, Ted told his team members that the widow of the dead man, Richard Hutchinson, would be coming at some point, to make an official identification. It was certainly not going to be possible from what remained of his facial features; they would be relying heavily on his dental records. But the dead man had a tattoo, which was going to help, especially as it was a name. Ted just hoped it was the wife's name, which would move things along nicely for the enquiry.

He was also anxious to have a word with his team members, especially Jezza, about Foster's lot.

'So far I've not seen anything to commend any of them, from the top down. I've already experienced their homophobia. Virgil, I imagine you've come in for some racist remarks and Jezza, be prepared to encounter the sort of sexism which has no place in any police force in this day and age. It makes our job harder, but I can hardly have them all kicked out at once in the middle of a murder enquiry. But, as I said before, if any of you want to make an official complaint at any time, come and see me and I will take it further. Jezza, just no resorting to kickboxing, all right?'

There was not much sign of activity when Ted and the others arrived and picked up their visitor passes. Foster and his team were simply sitting around waiting for his arrival. Coombs was even reading a newspaper. They were without doubt the sloppiest team Ted had ever encountered. He was going to have to give them a massive shake-up to get any results out of them.

They barely stirred as Ted and the others walked in and moved to stand by the whiteboard. Ted could see at a glance that nothing had been added since he had left the previous day.

'Morning, everyone,' Ted began, and introduced Jezza.

He could see the resident team were eyeing her up like a roomful of hungry predators. She merely glared back at them, her look defiant.

When there was no reply from any of them, Ted said again, more forcefully, 'Good morning.'

Only Foster and the youngest-looking of the DCs responded, reluctantly, but it was a start.

'Right, where are we up to? What do we know, from the witness statements so far, of Mr Hutchinson's last movements? And what's happening about the next of kin and formal identification?'

Foster replied, 'The wife is flying in from Milan this morning. She lives there, part of the time. I'm sending the W...' he actually thought better of it and corrected himself, 'officers from Uniform to pick her up from the airport and take her straight to the morgue, to identify what she can of him and his personal effects. The PM isn't until later today; it's the earliest they could do it.'

'Where would you usually talk to next of kin?' Ted asked him.

'Depends. At the morgue, or back here.'

124

'Right. I want you and DC Coombs at the mortuary for the ID, and DI Foster, you're back there for the PM. DC Coombs, you're in charge of logging his personal effects. Then please arrange for Mrs Hutchinson to be brought back here, and DC Vine and I will talk to her. Do we know yet if she was in Milan at the time of death?'

Blank looks all round. Ted wondered if this shower actually knew anything about basic police work. No wonder their track record was so poor.

'I'll ask her that when I speak to her. Now, what about last known movements? What's come up so far from witnesses?'

More blank looks. Eventually the youngest DC spoke up.

'The girl on reception said the victim asked directions to the Red Lion when he went out.'

'And has anyone checked out yet if he actually got there?' Ted asked, although he was fairly sure of the response.

In fact, there wasn't one. He looked round the room, his anger rising. It was almost as if the other team didn't care whether or not the killer was caught.

Eventually, Coombs spoke up, his tone, as usual, scornful. He had at least put down his newspaper, but that was the only indication he gave of any interest in the case.

'Good luck with that. It was singles night at the Lion. The place would have been packed out. Doubt if any of the staff would be able to tell you who was there, certainly not a stranger from out of town.'

This time, Ted's silence spoke volumes, for anyone with the intelligence to see how his expression, his whole demeanour changed. His voice was glacial when he finally cut the silence.

'Nobody thought to mention this earlier? Even after I told you all yesterday that our victim in Stockport was into online dating and we believe there's a strong possibility he may have met his killer going on a blind date in a pub?'

He looked around, inviting comment. No one said anything, but the DC who had taken the witness statement had the grace to look uncomfortable. Ted looked directly at him and asked his name.

'DC Winters, sir, Graham.'

'I'd like a word with you, after we've finished here,' Ted told him, and saw the younger man squirm in his seat. 'For now, DS O'Connell, I'd like you to stay here and go through all the witness statements to date, to see what else has been missed. DC Winters can work with you, and DC Vine, for now, until she and I need to talk to the next of kin.

'DS Mackenzie, can you take someone and go and see what you can find out from this Red Lion place? We've not much to go on yet, until we get a photo and a decent description of what our man was like before someone rearranged his face. But try your best.'

Mackenzie nodded.

'Charlie, you come with me. Chris, you stay here and see if Acting DS O'Connell needs any more help.'

It was a pointed and unnecessary cheap shot, the remark heavy with sarcasm. Once again, Ted was forced to let it go in the interest of making a start on some routine police work.

'And what news of the victim's car? Has that been recovered yet?' Ted asked, more in hope than anticipation. It seemed this bunch were intent on doing as little as possible.

'We only got the details of it late yesterday afternoon,' Coombs said dismissively. 'I'll get it sorted now.'

'I know that DC Ahmed sent the information through early yesterday afternoon, and followed it up with a courtesy phone call,' Ted told him levelly. 'It should have been sorted before anyone left last night. Working a murder case is not nine to five. I hope everyone understands that?'

At that moment, Ted's mobile rang. Océane.

'I need to take this. It might be an update on intel from Mr Hutchinson's mobile and laptop.'

He stepped outside the office while he took the call. Océane briefly told him that although she hadn't yet looked at a great deal, she had found that their latest victim had recently been looking up singles nights and speed dating venues within reach of the hotel where he had been staying.

'He's another one who thinks 1234 is a good, secure code for his mobile phone, and doesn't bother with a password for his laptop. I'll let you know as soon as I have anything else.'

A stony silence greeted him when he went back into the main office. Apart from his own team members, it was as if he was climbing a high mountain, pulling the rest of them behind him on a cart with a flat tyre. He'd always known it would never be easy, coming onto Foster's patch and taking over as SIO. So far, it was harder than he had feared.

'Right, that was additional confirmation that our man was looking for singles nights and speed dating while he was here. DS Mackenzie, if you don't get anywhere at the Red Lion, I'm sure you know the other places to go into, around town, for that sort of thing.

'You know what needs doing. Please get on with it, and we'll have a debriefing this afternoon. DI Foster, if I can use your office to talk to DC Winters? And DC Coombs, get that car picked up and get Forensics on to it, just in case there's anything interesting that shows up.'

DC Winters followed Ted into the small office, looking slightly apprehensive. Ted took a seat but didn't invite him to do the same, so he stood, awkwardly, looking increasingly unsure of himself.

'Any particular reason why you sat on an important piece of information, DC Winters?' Ted asked him levelly.

'I didn't sit on it, I told my guv'nor, DI Foster,' he said defensively.

Ted looked at him, hard, for several moments. The younger man didn't look particularly stupid, but he must have realised how important the information was. Perhaps he had genuinely thought Foster was going to do something constructive with it.

'It was important. It could have given us an early lead. But I'm prepared to accept that you thought you were following correct procedure and that DI Foster would have passed it on to me. In future, though, just to be sure, could you please keep me in the loop at all times, so we can make some progress? Here's my card. You can phone me direct. We're not at school here. You're not telling tales. Just updating the SIO on the case. Are we clear on that?'

Winters looked at him, clearly surprised. If he'd expected to get his arse kicked, he'd misjudged Ted. He took the card and put it in his pocket, then, with a mumbled, 'Sir,' he turned and left the office in response to Ted's nod of dismissal.

It was early afternoon before their latest victim's widow arrived at the station. Ted and Jezza went downstairs to talk to her, in an interview room which had been made available for the purpose. Ted introduced them both and extended his condolences before beginning.

'Please, Inspector, or did you say Chief Inspector?' the woman asked, her English impeccable, but with a trace of an accent. 'Please don't waste your breath. Was Dickie's death something to do with his endless womanising? One jealous husband too many? Because I knew all about that, which is why I refuse to be a hypocrite and play the grieving widow.'

It was sadly not the first time Ted had encountered such a reaction. The woman sitting opposite him was attractive, her skin toned and tanned, even in winter, glossy black hair, artfully tousled, reaching her shoulders. Even Ted, who took no interest in fashion or designer labels, could see that her clothes were high quality.

Ted was monogamous by nature. He had never once cheated on Trev, nor had he ever been tempted to. He didn't like to judge, but at first glance, it was hard to understand why

Hutchinson had been repeatedly cheating on such an attractive woman.

'Mrs Hutchinson,' he began, trying to frame his questions carefully.

'Please call me Nadia,' she invited. 'And I imagine one question you are going to need to ask me is my whereabouts on the night my husband – I suppose I will now need to get used to saying my late husband – was killed. Well, I was in Milano, with my daughter. She's studying fashion there. We have a small studio apartment there, as well as the house in Harrogate, for her use. It's where I'm from, originally. I was staying with her. So I have an alibi.'

'You say you were aware that your husband was seeing other women ...' he began again.

'Dickie suffered from small penis syndrome,' she told him frankly. 'He wasn't very well endowed, so he had an irresistible urge to prove its ability as often as possible. I didn't bother divorcing him. It would have been too unsettling for Molly, while she was studying.'

Jezza skilfully turned a stifled snort of laughter into a cough behind her hand at the woman's words.

'Is your daughter your only child?' Ted asked, more to give himself recovery time than from any pressing need to know, except to check for possible suspects.

'I have two sons. One is a tree surgeon, the other runs a gastropub in Yorkshire. I imagine you'll want to know their whereabouts, too, as they were also well aware of what their father was like. I'll happily give you their contact details. I doubt very much if either of them killed him, although I wouldn't have blamed them if they had.'

'This morning must still have been distressing for you, Nadia. Were you able to identify your husband?'

'They didn't allow me to see his face. They said his injuries were too horrific. But I was able to identify all his personal effects. He also had a tattoo on the inside of his left forearm.

My name. He probably had it done so he would remember what it was. He was ridiculously proud of getting that tattoo. He had an extremely low pain threshold, he was nothing but a wuss.'

Her accent made the word sound almost comical.

'He moaned and whimpered about it for days afterwards. It must have given him some awkward moments with his other women. He probably told them he was divorced. Or a widower.'

'Were you aware of anyone in particular he was seeing?'

'I'm sorry to sound totally heartless, Chief Inspector, but I honestly didn't care. I was long past that stage. I would like to think he didn't suffer too much. He was, after all, the father of my children. But I would be being untruthful if I said I felt any more for him than that. I only found out after we were married that he'd been seeing someone else at the time and had asked her to run away with him before our wedding.

'I didn't need him, for anything. I have my own money. I certainly didn't need him for the indifferent sex. But the children have a certain fondness for him, which I don't discourage, so I lived with how things were.'

After they'd taken details of her two sons and daughter, to check alibis, and escorted her out of the station, Ted turned to Jezza and asked, 'What did you make of that, then?'

'Sorry for nearly losing it, boss. It just cracked me up, the way she said it. We certainly seem to be dealing with some low-life cheats in this case. If he had been off to a singles night or whatever at the pub, is it possible he might have run into our Linda Lovelace there, if that really is our killer?'

'If any of these clowns here get their act together and ask the right questions, we might find something out. And Océane will no doubt have a lot more for us by the time we go back. In the meantime, I want you to check into alibis for the whole family, including finding independent alibis for both mother and daughter.

'There's something else I think we should at least consider. If our victims were both serial womanisers, we need to look at any link, no matter how tenuous, between the families of both. There's just an outside chance that we're looking at a person hired to kill them, by someone in their own family.'

Chapter Fifteen

There were smug faces all round when Ted arrived on Foster's patch the following morning. He had Rob and Virgil with him again but had left Jezza behind. If they were held up for any reason, he wanted her to be ready to go hunting for Suki with Megan. Kevin Turner and Maurice were briefed and would be there to keep an eye on them, if Ted was not back.

Ted looked round the room, wondering what was going on. He did notice that DC Winters was not looking quite as pleased with himself as the other team members were.

'Has there been a development?'

DI Foster was positively smirking.

'You could say that,' he said, milking the moment for all it was worth. 'We have a suspect in custody.'

If his desire had been to shock Ted and his team members, he had succeeded. All three were left practically open-mouthed at the unexpected news.

'Would you care to tell us a bit more?' Ted invited. 'I don't, for instance, see a suspect name on the board.'

'We thought we'd wait for you to arrive to share the news,' Foster said gleefully. 'DS Mackenzie, DC Coombs and I picked him up last night, shortly after midnight. He claims to be a plumber, which fits with our enquiry. He's a Polack.'

Ted hated the derogatory term, as he did any lack of respect.

'I think you mean he's Polish, DI Foster,' he corrected, his tone warning. 'What's his connection to our victim?'

'He had one of his business cards in his pocket when we picked him up. And he had marks on his face, as if he'd been involved in some sort of a ruck. There were traces of blood on the passenger door handle of Hutchinson's Subaru. We'll be checking it against our suspect's DNA but I'm betting they will match.'

Ted was immediately suspicious. It all sounded so convenient. Too much so. He needed to know more, but he didn't like the sound of what he had heard so far.

'So how did you come across him?'

'Terry, Jock and me went out for a few bevvies together last night after work,' Foster continued, indicating DC Coombs and DS Mackenzie.

It made Ted even more suspicious, to know that there was possibly a close social link between the three men.

'When we were walking home, we noticed a van in a pub car park, and a man acting suspiciously. The van had a sign on it. Pawel the Plumber. We stopped to have a word with him. He got twitchy and tried to run off, so we arrested him and brought him in for questioning. We haven't started yet, though. Thought you might like the privilege.'

'Have his prints been checked against any on the business card?' Ted asked suspiciously.

'Getting that sorted now, along with DNA against the blood on the car,' Coombs said proudly.

The three of them looked well pleased with themselves.

'Did you at least ask him for his movements on the night in question?'

'He's living rough out of his van, parking it up anywhere he doesn't get moved on. No fixed address, doing jobbing plumbing. He just has a mobile number for contact,' Foster told him. 'He claims to spend his evenings in his van, doesn't go out much. No alibi for the time of either murder.'

'Right,' Ted said decisively, recovering from his initial surprise, but still sceptical. 'DS O'Connell and I will go and start interviewing him. The rest of you, we need to establish his movements and any connection between him and either victim. Also find out from the hotel here, and the one in Stockport, if they've ever used a plumber called … what's his full name?'

'Bosko. Pawel Bosko.'

'What do you make of it, Rob?' Ted asked, as the two of them made their way down to the interview room where Bosko was going to be waiting for them.

'It has fall guy written all over it for me, boss,' Rob told him, knowing he could always speak frankly in front of Ted. 'You've got no fixed address, you've just killed someone, possibly your second victim, you have a van. Why would you still be hanging around the same area? Especially in a van with plumber written on it, when you've used being a plumber as your way to get into a room, and you don't know if anyone heard you or not?'

'Let's not jump the gun until we've spoken to him, but you've pretty much summed up everything that's gone through my head about the arrest.'

The man who was waiting for them looked afraid. He made to rise as the two men came into the room, clearly uncertain. A constable in uniform was waiting just inside the door. The suspect was in coveralls. His own clothes had clearly been taken for testing. His face looked bruised and bloody.

'Please sit down, Mr Bosko,' Ted told him, introducing himself and Rob for the tape, which he immediately set running. He wanted this one by the book from the start. He was already uncomfortable about it. 'Has anyone offered you medical attention for the injuries to your face?'

The man raised a hand self-consciously to the inflamed area.

'Is fine. Is nothing.'

Ted turned to the constable, who was just preparing to leave.

'Has Mr Bosko been offered any refreshment, do you know, Constable? He's already been here some time. Has he had the necessary care?'

If the constable was surprised by Ted's concern and his polite tone, he covered it well.

'I'm afraid I don't know for sure, sir, but not that I'm aware of.'

'Perhaps you could at least bring him a drink, please? Mr Bosko, would you like something to drink? Some coffee, perhaps? Or water?'

The suspect was looking equally surprised. He spoke hesitantly.

'Coffee. Yes, please. Coffee, black, no sugar.'

Ted thanked the officer and sent him on his way to find the drink. Then he settled himself down for the job, looking levelly at the man opposite him.

Ted's secret weapon, and a large part of his success rate, was his interview technique. Because he was small and seemed insignificant, people were seldom wary of him. His tone was always calm, quiet and polite. People would often tell him far more than they intended to, their guard lowered when they saw no immediate threat in his manner. Although seemingly innocuous, he was tenacious. He took his time, hardly ever lost his temper, but with his relentless patience, he inevitably got far more from a suspect than anyone who went in shouting the odds.

'Just for the tape, Mr Bosko, can you please confirm your name and address?'

'Pawel Bosko. I don't have address yet. My friend said come to Manchester. Lot of people want good plumber. I am good plumber. It is true, I find work, but not yet enough money to have house or flat.'

Gently, methodically, Ted took him through a succession of bland questions, ones to which he would have no reason to lie. He allowed him pauses to drink the coffee which had been brought for him. Ted was watching carefully to see his body language when he was likely to be telling the truth. That way he could identify subtle changes – a twitch of a muscle here, a rapid eye movement there – which would give him a sign for when the man was lying.

'Do you know why you're here, Mr Bosko?' he asked.

'Those other police, they asked me did I kill man. I didn't kill anyone. I am not *morderca*. Not murderer.'

His face was suddenly closed down, wary, but Ted didn't detect any difference in the way he stated it. Although he was no gambler, Ted would have put money on the fact that he was still telling the truth. But he would need a lot more than his intuition to decide whether the man was innocent or guilty.

'Tell me about last night,' he said, his tone inviting confidence. 'What happened when the police officers arrested you?'

'I did some repairs at pub yesterday. They had big problem with toilets. No water. Big problem, for pub. I put my card in many places, in many pubs. They call me, I go there. Repair toilets. Good job. The boss very happy, said I could park in his car park for night and sleep in my van. I told him I have no home yet. He gave me good food, too. Very happy with job I did.

'I getting ready to sleep, and I hear people outside my van. I look out. Three men looking all round my van, checking things, kicking tyres. I did not know they were police, so I was anxious. I get out to speak to them.'

To break his train of thought and watch for any other signs of a change of delivery, Ted interrupted him to ask, 'Do you know a Richard Hutchinson, Mr Bosko?'

The man shook his head emphatically.

'I never heard this name. Those other police, they ask me same thing. I told them, no, I don't know this name.'

Ted was still not seeing any change in the man's features or body language. Either he was telling the truth or he could well abandon plumbing as a profession and take up acting instead.

'So can you tell me how one of his business cards came to be in your pocket, Mr Bosko?'

'No, sir, I can't tell you,' his voice was starting to sound shrill, going up in pitch, with an edge of panic. 'I don't know. I don't know this name, I don't know who this man is. I don't know why card was in my pocket. I never seen it before.'

Ted turned and looked at Rob, sitting quietly by his side. They exchanged a glance and Ted could tell that Rob was of the same opinion as he was himself. If the man was lying, he was doing it extremely convincingly.

'All right, Mr Bosko, try to keep calm. Now, can you tell me about the injuries to your face? What happened there? Had you been in a fight with someone?'

Bosko drained the rest of his coffee to steady himself before he replied.

'No fight, no. I'm not fighter. I'm just plumber. Good plumber, trying to start up business. When I got out of my van, policemen start asking me lot of questions. I was very afraid. They were aggressive. I thought I did something wrong. I thought perhaps it was not allowed to live in van, even when pub owner said I could park there.

'I told them I would go. Move van, find somewhere else to park, if I was doing something wrong. I turned to get back in van but they pull me back, then push me against side of van, hard. I was afraid. I thought I was in serious trouble. I tried to get away. One of them hit me, in my face.'

'Which one hit you, Mr Bosko?'

'Tall policeman, more hair than two others.'

DC Coombs. Ted would have bet on him being the violent one.

'What happened next? Tell me everything you can remember,' he said, his tone still calm and quiet.

'He tell me not to resist arrest and he hit me again. There was blood from my nose. He had on rubber gloves. He wipe my face with his gloves. Then another one, older one, not much hair, put his hand in my pocket, takes out a card and gives it to me to hold. He ask me if I know this man, name on card, but I told him no, I don't know him. Tall one hit me again. Then he says I am being arrested for murder.'

The man's expression never changed. His direct gaze didn't waver from Ted's face, not even to look at Rob, still sitting silent beside him.

'I do not know this man. I killed no one.'

Ted believed him. He really thought he was telling the truth. He saw nothing to make him think otherwise. He could see now exactly how Bosko's blood was going to be identified on the victim's car, and how his fingerprints would be found on the business card. Foster had collected up the cards in the hotel bedroom. If he hadn't logged them all in, it would have given him a handy spare one to plant in the pocket of the first patsy they found. The three of them must have thought all their birthdays had come round at once when the first stooge they happened on was genuinely a plumber.

'What size shoes do you take, Mr Bosko?' Ted asked, wondering if the sudden change of direction of the questions would show up a chink in his armour, if the man was lying.

The question clearly surprised him, but it didn't throw him. There was no flicker of recognition for why the information might be relevant.

'Size forty-five,' he replied.

It was a full size larger than the boot-marks on the first victim, and the size had been confirmed again by the post-mortem the previous afternoon on Richard Hutchinson. Bosko's own shoes and clothes would be tested, but Ted was fairly sure that his shoes would not be a match. The whole thing reeked of a stitch-up, but one it could be tricky to prove.

'Have you ever been to Stockport, Mr Bosko?'

He looked genuinely puzzled.

'Stockport? No, sir, I have not been. I just stay round here, so people get to know me. I know no one in Stockport.'

'How long have you been in the area?'

'Only a few months. I don't yet know area well. I don't have time for visiting much, with trying to start up business. Sir, I swear to you, I did not kill this man. I have never killed anyone. Never even hurt anyone. I am just peaceful plumber.'

'Well, if he's lying, boss, he should win an Oscar for it. He has me convinced. And it's easy to see how he's been set up. But to what purpose?'

'You know I don't pre-judge, but what I think we are looking at here is lazy, bent coppers who just want results, at any price. I'm going to need to call a conference with the Super now, see if he thinks we have enough to approach the CPS about charging Bosko. I'm taking it as a given that the bloods and fingerprints are going to come back as a match, and I think we both know how.'

Ted, as SIO, was in charge of the case on the ground. But Jim Baker was heading up the new unit, so final responsibility lay with him. Ted put a call through to him and arranged a time as soon as possible when the two of them could sit down together to discuss progress, before talking to the rest of the team. Once again they squeezed themselves into Foster's office, sending him out to the main office to do some paperwork.

'I don't like it at all, Jim. It's got stitch-up written all over it. It's clever enough, in its way, but I can't see CPS being happy with it. We've got a tentative and probably suspect link between Bosko and Hutchinson from the car door and the business card, if they're confirmed, as I've no doubt they will be. Now we have his DNA, we'll check it against both scenes of crime but I'm pretty sure we won't find a match there. Not unless those three goons have been tampering with evidence in a big way.

'Both Rob and I, independently, found Bosko credible. There was no sign at all that he was lying, not at any stage of the interview. You can see for yourself on the playback, if you need to. But I can't believe both Rob and I would have missed something, if there was anything there to see. I don't like him for a suspect, not at all.'

'I don't like any of it any more than you do, Ted,' Jim Baker growled. 'We all know your famous intuition is usually right, but we need more than that. If he is our man and we let him go, we're up the creek without a paddle. The unit could go down, and you and I might be issuing fixed penalties for the rest of our lives.

'I like it even less going into a weekend, with the added hassle that gives us applying for extensions if we need them. When's our twenty-four hours up?'

'Two o'clock tomorrow morning.'

'If I authorise another twelve hours, does that give us long enough to achieve anything?'

'I'll come back in first thing in the morning, probably with Rob, and have another go at him, but I doubt his story is going to change one iota and I personally think he's telling the truth. As for officers possibly tampering with evidence, that's one for you or Complaints, I imagine? But I think it's something that needs looking into, on the quiet, and urgently.'

Jim Baker nodded his agreement.

'I'm pretty sure you're right, Ted. I wish you weren't, but I have a feeling you are.'

'Oh, and Jim? I'll go and talk to the custody sergeant now, but can you issue an official edict with a bit of clout? I don't want anyone interviewing Mr Bosko except me and Rob. I have a feeling that if Foster, Mackenzie and Coombs go anywhere near him, he would finish up confessing to every unsolved crime in history, and probably claiming to be Jack the Ripper.'

Chapter Sixteen

Before Ted left to head back to Stockport, having updated Foster's team on what he and Jim Baker had decided, he wanted a quick word with DC Winters. So far, he was the only one of Foster's team who had shown any sort of a spark. Ted was particularly interested to know why he hadn't looked as pleased at the rest of the team with their suspect.

'I have a little mission for you, DC Winters, if you're interested,' Ted told him. 'But just for the moment, I'd like to keep it quiet, if I can count on your discretion. I understand your loyalties lie with DI Foster, but I'd just ask you to trust me on this one. Can I rely on you?'

'I want to see the right suspect charged, sir,' the younger man told him.

His answer, and the unexpected formality, told Ted all he needed to know about why Winters had not looked pleased about the suspect. If he didn't know, he certainly had a hunch that all was not as it should be. It was encouraging. Ted didn't like to think the whole team was rotten.

'I need you to go on a shopping trip for me. I'll authorise payment, of course, but I need it doing to be ready for me here first thing in the morning, when I come back to interview Mr Bosko. And I wondered if you would like to sit in on that interview, to see the fruits of your shopping? I'm hoping it may well be enlightening.'

Once in the car heading back south, with Rob driving, Ted phoned Jo to check how things were going back on his own patch.

'Not quite all quiet on the western front, boss,' Jo told him cheerfully. 'We've had a fatality. Looks like a domestic which got out of hand. We've got the boyfriend in custody but he's completely off his face, not fit to be interviewed. We've banged him up for now and I'm coming in first thing in the morning, with Mike, to question him, when he's hopefully come down off whatever it was. Everything's in hand, though, and I'd be surprised if he was going to try to deny it, although he may deny intention to kill.'

Jo was turning out to be a real asset. It was certainly taking some pressure off Ted to have someone senior at the helm while he was away in another division. As long as Jo's seemingly roving eye and twinkling gold tooth didn't lead to relationship problems within the team, he was glad to have him on board.

Ted left his car on the driveway when he got home. It was later than he'd hoped. It didn't leave him much time before he would have to go out again, to be at the pub to see if Jezza and Megan could find Suki.

He found Trev in the sitting room, stretched out full length in what looked like a press-up position, but with his weight resting on his forearms. He was holding the position without moving, throwing the muscles in his shoulders and arms into sharp relief.

'What are you doing?' Ted asked him curiously.

'Planking,' Trev replied. 'It's all the rage. And it's harder than it looks.'

'How long do you have to stay like that?'

'Until my muscles get too wobbly, which they are just starting to do.'

Trev lowered himself to one knee then sprang lightly to his feet. He was wearing sweat pants with a vest top, showing his clearly defined muscles and a body with not an ounce of spare fat.

'I have to work hard to keep my body in perfect shape. I live with an insatiable sex fiend,' he grinned as he greeted his partner with a hug.

No matter how hard Ted's day, Trev usually succeeded in making him smile, as he did now.

'Your body is already perfect. That's why I'm insatiable. But I'm going to have to love you and leave you yet again. I've got to go and chaperone Jezza in a dodgy pub full of rampant women. I've just got time for a shower and change, grab a bite to eat, then I have to go. Oh, and I'm sorry, but I'll need to work tomorrow, too. But I'll make it up to you as soon as I can.'

Trev was nuzzling his neck suggestively.

'I need a shower too, after my work-out. We could share, to save water. Then I could make you a bacon butty to eat on your way. And I'm going to call that favour in sometime soon. Shewee's trying out for the school eventing team and she wants me to go down to Somerset to watch her compete on Blue. I'd like you to come with me. But for now...'

Ted was only just on time to meet the others at the pub. Kevin Turner and Maurice Brown were already installed in a corner, their drinks in front of them, in a good position to give them a view of the whole room, which was already busy. With his peripheral vision, Ted saw that Jezza and Megan were also there, sitting near to a bunch of other women, talking loudly. He made no move to acknowledge them.

'How did it go, Kev?' he asked, sitting down, while Maurice went to the bar to get him a drink as the other two caught up.

'Ulcers. Can all be sorted with a few pills. And you were right about Maurice; he was bloody marvellous. To think I'd been worrying and bricking myself about it for weeks. Not very pleasant, but it's done and there's nothing to worry about.'

Maurice Brown was looking even better than the previous week, and Ted noticed that he was on soft drinks. He appeared

143

to be in his element, with a seemingly plentiful supply of single females. But the three of them were there for a specific purpose, keeping an eye on Jezza and Megan, and looking out for anyone who may have been the real killer. Ted was still convinced that Pawel the Plumber was not their man.

Jezza had been agreeably surprised to see how well Megan had entered into her role for the evening. She realised she'd been judgemental of her new colleague. To see the way the two of them were turned out, few people would have taken them for police officers. They were there specifically to try to find Suki, so they mixed with other women. But to keep up appearances, when either of them went to the bar, they would flirt outrageously with any men in their path.

Jezza had asked a few women already if they knew Suki but had so far drawn a blank. At the moment, women far outnumbered the men in the bar and Ted's trio were attracting a fair bit of attention, to Maurice's evident delight.

When the door opened to yet another group of young women, who headed straight for the bar, Jezza got up to join them and order more drinks.

'Hi, is Suki coming tonight, do you know?' she asked the one nearest to her.

The young woman pointed towards the other end of the bar as she replied, 'Suki? She's over there.'

Jezza laughed it off.

'God, sorry, bird, so she is. Teach me to be too vain to put my specs on when I go out on the pull.'

She collected the drinks she'd ordered, then made her way casually to the person who'd been indicated to her. She looked to be in her late twenties, blonde and attractive, busy attacking the tequila slammers with her friends.

As Jezza drew level with her, she let out a squeal of apparent delight as she said, 'Suki! Hi! Not seen you in ages. Where've you been hiding?'

Suki looked at her blankly, clearly struggling to put a name to the face which was greeting her. Dressed as she was, and with all her many piercings back in place, Jezza looked nothing like anyone's idea of a copper, even one off-duty who was trained in drama and an expert at blending in.

'Jezza,' Jezza supplied helpfully. 'We met in here, a few weeks ago now. I kept meaning to give you a bell. You were probably as pissed as me and forgot all about me.'

It was such a simple tactic, yet it worked more often than not. Suggest to someone that they had met you before and they would often believe that they had, without remembering when or where. Jezza had it off to a fine art. The two were soon chatting away as if they were long-lost friends just reunited, then Jezza skilfully steered her over to join Megan at their table.

'Don't look now,' Jezza said, with an elaborate show of casually ignoring people, 'but those three blokes over there keep looking at us. I reckon we've pulled. Three of them, three of us. Perfect.'

'Which one do you fancy, Jezza? The small one looks cute and cuddly,' Megan replied, throwing herself into the part and nearly giving Jezza the giggles in the process.

'I've got a thing for older men,' Suki told them. 'If I have to pick one at a time, although I'm open to other suggestions, I'll take the one in the middle. He looks a bit of a silver fox.'

Jezza lost it at that point, nearly snorting her drink back down her nose. Suki was eyeing up Kevin Turner, Megan had suggested Ted, which left her with Maurice Brown who, she knew, fancied the pants off her anyway, even if they were good friends and work colleagues.

They'd prearranged a signal with Ted, in case they succeeded in finding Suki, so he could come over. She wasn't a suspect at this stage, simply a witness, but they needed to talk to her and she might be wary if she'd made the connection between the man she'd gone to the hotel with and the press and television news articles about a body being found there. Jezza made direct eye contact with Ted across the crowded room and raised her glass towards him in invitation.

'Get your coats, gentlemen, we've pulled,' Ted told the others ironically, then added, 'Remember, Maurice, what we're here for is just to find and interview a witness. So don't get your hopes up.'

'Or anything else,' Kevin added, giving Maurice a suggestive nudge with his elbow.

The three sauntered over, trying to look nonchalant, then pulled up stools to join the three women. First names were exchanged to begin with, the conversation kept casual. The three men were sitting in such a way that none of the women opposite them could leave their seats easily. Then Ted switched into professional mode.

'Suki, I'm sorry if we've led you on, but we're police officers. We've been looking for you in connection with a death which you probably read about in the local papers. I believe you may have been with the man who died, a Duncan Waters, shortly before he was killed. You may have known him as Duncan Allen.'

Suki had gone white as soon as he began to speak. She whispered, 'Oh, shit.'

'You're not a suspect, Suki, we just need a witness statement from you, and we had trouble tracking you down. Hence turning up here tonight looking for you.'

'I've been avoiding my place for the time being. A small matter of outstanding rent and a not very accommodating landlord. I've been dossing with friends.'

'I'm sorry we're mob-handed; don't let that alarm you. Jezza and Megan were just here to find you. The rest of us were having a social drink, that's all. Would you be willing to come out to my car, with Megan, and tell us what happened the night you were with Duncan Waters?' Ted slid his warrant card across the table so she could see it. 'It's a bit unorthodox but we do need to question you. We might need you to come into the station at a later date to make a formal statement.'

She was looking from one to another in bewilderment.

'You're all coppers, all of you? And I suppose we've never really met before?' she asked Jezza.

Jezza grinned at her.

'We may have done, but we were maybe both too pissed to remember.'

'And you three aren't out on the pull?' she asked, still looking hopefully at Kevin Turner, who was smiling back at her appreciatively.

'I'm afraid not,' Ted smiled. 'I'm sorry for the subterfuge but we really do need to speak to you. Would you be willing to come outside? My car's not far and Megan can come with us.'

'I'm not into that kind of threesome,' she told him with a laugh. 'And I don't need a chaperone.'

'I think I might,' Ted told her candidly, but with a smile.

The three of them went out and got into Ted's car. He sat in the driver's seat, with Suki next to him and Megan in the back seat. He put the heater on as the night was chilly, and the interior light, so he could study Suki's face as she began talking.

She spoke frankly and without hesitation. She told them that she liked casual sexual encounters with older men, with no strings attached. She often used online dating sites and chat groups to meet up with them, as well as going to singles nights and speed dating.

She'd met Duncan Waters in a pub as arranged. There was an instant physical attraction between them, so after a meal together, they'd gone back to his hotel room and enjoyed what she described as some fairly lively sex. She told them she had left shortly before midnight when Waters had been alive and well. She'd not had any further contact with him and had never intended to.

'You didn't notice anyone else in the pub paying any particular attention to the two of you? Nobody behaving suspiciously? No signs of anyone following you?'

'I wasn't paying much attention to anyone else. We were both well up for it. We just wanted to get to his room and rip the clothes off one another.'

'Are you not worried by the risks of such encounters?' Ted asked her, as much out of curiosity as anything.

She shrugged, unconcerned.

'Some of my friends have done the whole get married, settle down, have kids thing. One of them is nothing but a human punch-bag but won't leave him. Another has a bloke who's always dipping his wick where he shouldn't and she's picked up STDs a couple of times from him. How is what I do any more risky than that?'

'And Duncan Waters was alive when you last saw him?'

'Most bits of him were, but one part was pretty much dead to the world,' she said, then caught herself up short. 'God, sorry, that sounds heartless. But he was fine. We'd had a good time but it was never going to be any more than just that.'

'Can anyone verify the time you left the hotel?'

'I called a taxi on my mobile from his room and they picked me up in front of the hotel. I can give you the details of the taxi firm, and they'll have it on their records. The driver was cute. I tried chatting him up on the way home, so he may well remember. Turned out I was wasting my time anyway. He told me he was gay and his boyfriend was a cage fighter, but he may just have been saying that.'

'And you can't think of anyone you know who might want to harm Mr Waters, because he'd met up with you? Partner, former partner, jealous boyfriend? Anyone who may have followed you to the hotel?'

'I'm really not into long-term relationships at all. Plenty of time for that later on, if I decide I want to do it. I can't think of anyone who would be bothered by me going off with someone else. I really can't.'

'We're going to need a formal statement from you, at the

station. We can arrange that for early next week,' Ted told her. 'But we need to be able to contact you, if you could give us an address, and confirm your current mobile phone number. And if you do remember anyone else in the pub at the same time, anyone who may have been looking at you, here's my card. Do please let me know.'

'I'm not being conceited or anything, but lots of men eye me up when I go out on the pull. If they didn't, I'd know I'd lost it. It's how I meet blokes a lot of the time. The Internet stuff is just for a bit of fun. I know that type are always married men, playing around away from home, and it adds a bit of a thrill.'

'Please be careful. It's a very dangerous game you're playing,' Ted told her earnestly, not wanting her to be another murder statistic, especially not on his own patch.

'Haven't I read somewhere that you're fifty per cent more likely to be killed by family or someone you know well than by a stranger?' she countered.

'Statistically, yes,' Ted conceded. 'But you're still taking a huge risk meeting up with people you don't know. Did Mr Waters mention anything to you about his domestic circumstances? About anyone who may have been watching him, or perhaps following him?'

She gave him a pitying look.

'That's not the kind of conversation we were having. I'm not interested in the whole 'my wife doesn't understand me' bit. It's just about casual sex, a one-off, no strings. Just a bit of fun. And it was fun, as it happens. He was quite imaginative.'

Ted knew, through his job, that people lived like that. He couldn't imagine anything worse. He thanked her for her time, took her contact details, and let her go back to her manhunt. He did wonder if she would succeed in getting her claws into Kevin Turner, although as far as he knew, Kev was happily married and didn't play away.

'Thanks for all your help, Megan,' he said, when Suki got out of the car and walked back towards the pub. 'And please thank Jezza too. Can you let Inspector Turner and Maurice know I'm going to cut and run now? Seeing the seamy side of life like that has made me realise more than ever how much I just want to go home and spend the rest of the evening with Trev.'

Chapter Seventeen

'You're back earlier than I thought.'

Trev turned the sound down on the film he was watching when Ted came in and sat down next to him, pushing cats around to make some space for himself on the sofa.

'We found the witness we were looking for, and I got fed up watching a bar full of people out on the pull and only interested in one-night stands. Why do people do that?'

Trev shook his head.

'No idea. I certainly don't need to go out shopping around when I have my own insatiable sex fiend on tap.'

Ted laughed.

'Tired and world-weary sex fiend this evening. And I have to be up and out early tomorrow. I'll try to be back at a decent time, though, and I'll pick up a takeaway, if you like, save you cooking? I just have to go in. Foster's lot have a man in custody and I'm convinced he's innocent. I can't leave him languishing there the whole weekend, if he is.'

Trev leaned over and kissed him.

'I love how much you care about people.'

'And I love everything about you. Except, perhaps, your habit of leaving your clothes lying around on the floor.'

Trev's look was one of mock offence.

'What? So next time you're dragging me upstairs against my will, you want me to stop, sort the laundry and hang everything up first?'

'I've never known you to protest,' Ted smiled.

It was just the sort of domestic normality he needed, after the day he'd had. Especially with the stink of possibly corrupt coppers in his nostrils.

Ted's first port of call when he got to Foster's nick the following morning was to go and see the custody sergeant. He wanted to make sure Pawel Bosko was being well looked after, and to tell her that he was going to be interviewing him shortly, with DC Winters.

'Has Mr Bosko had his breakfast, Sergeant?' Ted asked the officer behind the desk.

'He has, sir,' she informed him tersely. 'There are some of us within this station who follow the rules and take care of anyone enjoying our hospitality.'

'Yes, of course, I apologise, Sergeant,' Ted said hastily in the face of her reproachful look. 'I made an assumption and I shouldn't have done. It's something I deplore.'

The contrast when she smiled at his apology was astonishing. Ted found himself smiling back at her.

'I should just tell you, sir, that I had great pleasure in refusing DI Foster and DC Coombs an interview with Mr Bosko when they came sniffing round after you'd left. I've been wanting to do that for some time.'

Ted was pleased to hear it. He knew how difficult it could be when the likes of those two got above themselves and started bending the rules. The custody sergeant outranked Coombs, but there were certain CID officers who regarded all those in uniform, regardless of rank, as beneath them, as Coombs had already demonstrated.

When he went upstairs to the main office, Ted found DC Winters waiting for him, but no sign of anyone else. There was a brand new pair of leather work boots, with steel toe-caps, sitting on the desk next to him. Ted couldn't help himself. He reached out and lifted them off the desk, putting them on the floor, then grinned shamefacedly at Winters.

'It's an old superstition. You shouldn't put new shoes on a table. It brings bad luck. And I have a feeling that these particular boots are going to be very lucky indeed for our Mr Bosko.'

'You're thinking the size is wrong, sir? But is that enough to clear him?'

'Have you ever tried walking in a pair of boots a full size too small for you? Especially ones with steel toe-caps. There's just no way of forcing your feet into something that rigid, if they don't fit. Even if he succeeded, it would be likely to be painful. People may not have noticed a maintenance man going in to repair the plumbing. One who was limping painfully would stick in witnesses' memories.

'I'd like us to go down and start interviewing him now, but I don't want to spring the boots on him too soon. We'll leave them just outside the door. Then, if I pause the interview at some point and ask you to organise some drinks, please bring them back in with you, and we'll watch carefully for his reaction.'

'Am I asking questions, or just observing, sir?'

'If you could just watch for now, please, we'll see how we go.'

He could tell from the DC's reaction that he wasn't used to a senior officer using please when addressing him. Ted was interested to know why DC Winters has chosen this station and why he stayed. He was clearly not overly impressed with the recent actions of his DI.

Seeing how easy-going Ted was being, Winters risked asking, 'So when I bring the boots in, do I put them on the floor or on the table?'

Ted laughed.

'You got me there. Put them on the table, where he can see them. I'll just have to hope the old superstition isn't true. Right, let's go. I want you to watch our Mr Bosko very carefully, especially when you bring the boots in, and tell me afterwards what you think of his credibility.'

As usual, Ted set the tapes running before he so much as exchanged pleasantries with the suspect. If he was going to recommend letting the man go, he wanted back-up for his decision. There were already, to his mind, too many grounds for a skilled defence lawyer to suggest reasonable doubt. He was having difficulty with the idea that the man had been careless enough to get his blood on the victim's car door, and to keep hold of his business card, yet had seemingly left no trace of himself at the crime scenes.

Ted began by going patiently over everything he'd asked the man before. Bosko stayed consistent, his answers never varying from what he had already said the day before. Nor did his body language show any variation between seemingly innocent, unrelated questions and anything to do with the crime under investigation.

'Tell me about the business card, Mr Bosko. Can you tell me how the victim's card came to be in your pocket?'

'No, sir, I can't,' the man said frankly. 'I just don't know. I never saw it before policeman took it out of my pocket. It was not in my pocket last time I looked there. I never saw it before.'

'When the police officers searched you, did they ask you anything about what they might find in your pockets? And did they put gloves on before searching you?'

It would be standard police procedure to ask a suspect if there was anything in their pockets which could cause harm to an officer about to put his hand in there, and to glove up to protect themselves.

'They all had gloves. I notice when I got out of my van, they all have blue gloves on. I thought it meant they must think I have done some crime, and they were looking for evidence. But no, they did not ask me. The one who searched my pockets just said, I think, something like 'what have you got in here?' or some words like that.'

The more Ted heard, the less he liked it. He only had until

two o'clock to hold the man, without applying for a further extension. So far, he had nothing to justify such an application. He carried on doggedly, covering everything he could think of. He was still waiting on DNA results from the Stockport crime scene, checked against Bosko's, which were being rushed through as fast as possible for him.

'I think we'll just take a short break there for some refreshment. Mr Bosko, coffee for you? Tea for me, please, DC Winters, milk and two sugars, if you could arrange that?'

Ted paused the tapes, after saying what was happening. He noticed that Bosko immediately started to look nervous, as if fearing what might be about to happen to him, with the tapes switched off.

Winters came back in almost immediately, carrying the boots, which he placed on the table directly in front of the man. Bosko showed no reaction beyond a mild curiosity. Ted restarted the tape.

'Mr Bosko, you can see in front of you a pair of work boots. Do you own a pair like that?'

'No, sir, I do not,' the man said, making a move to pick one of them up. When no one stopped him, he lifted it up and turned it over. 'Not my size. They are size too small.'

'Nevertheless, I'd like you to try them on, please.'

The man looked at him, his expression puzzled.

'I don't understand. They not my size.'

'Please try them,' Ted repeated patiently.

The man put the boots on the floor, carefully opened each boot as wide as he could and attempted to slide his feet into them. He had quite a high instep, so he was having little success. His feet would go so far but no further. He looked up apologetically.

'Please keep trying, Mr Bosko,' Ted told him. 'Perhaps try standing up, to see if that makes a difference.'

He seemed to be trying genuinely enough, but he was not having any more success, even when he stood up and tried to force his feet down, wincing with the effort.

'Is like Kopciuszek,' he said.

'I'm sorry?' Ted queried.

'Is story. About prince who tries to find pretty girl who danced with him and lost shoe. She has bad sisters, who want to try the shoe, but it does not fit. I am like sisters. These shoes do not fit me. I'm sorry.'

'Cinderella,' Ted smiled. 'We have the same story. And yes, I agree. Those boots do not fit you. Thank you for trying.'

There was a knock on the door and a uniformed officer appeared with a tray of drinks for them. Ted thanked him, then told Bosko that they would leave him for a moment while he had his coffee in peace. He and DC Winters picked up their drinks and left the room.

'I need to make a phone call to the Super,' Ted said as they moved down the corridor. 'You stay outside the room. I won't be long. What are your impressions so far?'

'If he's a liar, he's a bloody good one, sir,' Winters said emphatically. 'And surely any defence lawyer would drive a truck through the case with the boots being the wrong size? Are you going to let him go?'

'That's my gut instinct, but I want to check it with the Big Boss first. I've no doubt he'll be in close contact with CPS, and I can't see them being happy for us to charge him on the basis of what we have so far, even with him having no alibi. We have no witnesses and nothing to place him at either scene, if my instincts are right. I'd like to get those DNA results back from my patch, to make absolutely sure, but it will all depend on the timing.'

He moved away out of earshot, taking a gulp of his tea as he went, pulling up Jim Baker's number and pressing dial. The Big Boss answered quickly.

'What's the latest, Darling?' Jim asked him, still finding time for their customary joke.

Ted told him everything that had happened in the

interview, finishing up with, 'It just doesn't stand up, pun intended. He couldn't even get those boots on, let alone walk in them, or kick anyone's head in with them. If I tried that theory out, any decent defence lawyer would do the same and that would probably be all the reasonable doubt a jury would need to get an acquittal if we tried to take it to trial.

'I'm hanging on, hoping to get the DNA results through, but I doubt there'll be anything there. What are CPS saying?'

'Pretty much the same as you, before I even go back and tell them about the boots. They don't think we have much of a case at all, with no witnesses, nothing to place him at either crime scene. Unless you suddenly get a confession out of him in the near future ...'

'The only way he's going to confess is if I go in there and practise some Krav Maga on him.'

'Don't even say it in jest, Ted,' Jim growled. 'No doubt that's pretty much what was going to happen to him, if you hadn't had the presence of mind to restrict access to him. Right, get back to him, see what else you can get out of him, but I'm not prepared to ask for further time without either a confession, correctly obtained, of course, or DNA evidence.'

Ted paused for a few words with DC Winters, outside the interview room, while they both finished their drinks.

'Loyalty is a good quality, DC Winters. But it's always a good thing to know when it might be misplaced,' Ted told him conversationally. 'If you have any ideas at all about how that card got into Mr Bosko's pocket, or how his blood came to be on our victim's car, it might be a good idea to tell me, in confidence. I need hardly point out to you that should it emerge, at a later date, that you knew anything and said nothing, you could be facing conspiracy charges, if anything serious, like tampering with evidence, has gone on here.'

'I don't know anything, boss,' he replied, surprising Ted with how he addressed him. 'Not for definite.'

'But you have your suspicions?' Ted asked astutely. 'Let's

carry on with Mr Bosko, for now. After that, I strongly suggest you and I have a long talk, perhaps over a sandwich.'

They went back inside and Ted continued his questioning. Bosko was unshakeable. His version of events never varied. Ted was just about to call it a day when there was a knock on the door and the same constable who had brought the drinks put his head around the gap.

'Sorry to interrupt you, sir, but your DI needs you to call him, urgently.'

Ted explained for the tape and excused himself to Bosko. Seeing the anxious look reappear on the man's face, he said, 'You have nothing to worry about, Mr Bosko. Neither myself nor DC Winters are going to do you any harm. If you prefer, I'll ask this officer to leave the room as well?'

Bosko's eyes had been riveted on Ted the whole time they had been speaking so he had barely glanced at the DC. He looked at him warily now but was clearly slightly reassured by what he saw.

'Is fine. I trust you.'

Ted went out into the corridor to phone Jo, who answered on the first ring.

'I thought you would want me to interrupt your interview, boss, as I have good news for your suspect there. In fact, it's a double whammy of good news for him, but less so for us.'

Ted invited him to go on.

'Firstly, the DNA came back as no match, which, I think, was what you were expecting. There's nothing at all to place your suspect at our crime scene. And secondly, our real killer is still out there, and back on our patch. Mike and I are just on our way out towards Cheadle. The call's just come in. Another hotel, another body, sounds like the same MO. So unless your man is a better escape artist than Houdini, went walkabout in the night then let himself back into his cell at the nick, I would say that just about clears him beyond all doubt.'

Chapter Eighteen

Ted could see that he had an incoming call waiting and wasn't surprised that it was from Jim Baker. He would also have been informed of a suspected third killing by the same perpetrator, as a matter of routine. Ted ended his call to Jo and answered Jim's.

'You heard, then? I was just about to phone you anyway, to say I was happy enough that our man here is innocent, even before Jo told me about the latest victim.'

He told Jim all that had gone on in the interview and how he had already made his mind up before the latest death.

'Is there any way we can suspend Foster and his two cronies for the time being, Jim? I don't want them anywhere near this case. At best, they're incompetent. At worst …'

'We could be looking at conspiracy to pervert the course of justice,' Jim Baker finished for him. 'Leave it to me, Ted. I'll get those three clowns in this afternoon for an intimate discussion with me and my good friend Gerry Fletcher. I know he's free; we were due to play golf together later on. He'll be even more formidable than usual, being kept from thrashing me yet again on the course.'

Ted gave an involuntary shudder at the mention of the name. He'd met the head of Complaints and Discipline for the force a few times, socially, through Jim. There'd never been anything against Ted to warrant investigation by C&D, although he'd recently had a close call. Fletcher was tall and muscular, ramrod-straight, silver hair cropped into a close crew-cut, steel grey eyes which bored like a gimlet. A former Welsh Guardsman, it was easy to imagine him being the terror of new recruits on the parade ground. Ted was always relieved he only had to converse with him over drinks or dinner rather than across the table in an interview room.

'I'll head off back to Stockport shortly, after I've given Mr Bosko the good news. I just want time for a quiet chat with DC Winters first. I don't think he's involved. I'm not sure he knows for a fact what went on, but I just want to make him understand how unwise it would be for him to speak to any of the other three before you do. I'll keep you posted.'

When Ted went back into the interview room, Bosko and Winters looked to be relaxed enough and appeared to be chatting about football. The plumber looked up at him hopefully as Ted sat back down and set the tape running once more.

'Mr Bosko, I'm pleased to be able to tell you that in light of information which I have just received, you are now free to go, and there will be no charges against you. Thank you for your cooperation.'

He would have loved to follow it up with an apology but he knew he was not allowed to. It would be ideal ammunition for any possible future claim for wrongful arrest. From the delighted beam which broke out on Bosko's face, and the way he grabbed Ted's hand in both of his and shook it enthusiastically, he could see that he was just so relieved at the news, he would be pleased simply to get back outside and go on with his life.

'Here's my card. If ever I can help you in any way, please feel free to call me,' he said, pushing one of his cards across the table. 'And if you ever do come to Stockport, let me know, so I can contact you if I need a good plumber. Thank you again for your cooperation. Someone will be along shortly to return all your possessions to you, and you will then be free to go.'

As he and Winters left the room, Ted asked him if there

was a canteen in the nick. He needed to get going shortly, but he could murder a cup of tea before he went. He was certainly not going to risk eating anything, based on the previous two scenes of crime. He hoped Mike Hallam would be all right this time.

'There's just a rest room, where we can brew up. If you want anything to eat, there's a sandwich place just on the corner. I could nip out for something?'

'I just need a cuppa. There's been another killing, on my patch again this time, which was another solid reason for letting Mr Bosko go. But I also wanted a quick word with you before I leave.'

Winters put the kettle on and showed Ted where everything was to brew up, sorting out coffee for himself.

'Are you on duty today, or did you just come in with the boots? Who else is on? I must admit, I expected to see more signs of life, with an ongoing investigation and no confession yet from the suspect.'

'It's always a bit, well, fluid, here of a weekend. The DI will probably pitch up at some point, and maybe the DS.'

'Can I ask you a personal question?' Ted asked him.

Again, the DC looked surprised that he would even ask before posing his question. He nodded warily.

'Why here? Why this nick, this team? They don't exactly have the best reputation in the force, and I can already see why.'

'It's handy. I live with my mum, sir. She's … she has health problems. I have to keep an eye on her, so I didn't want to move away. It's not what I would have chosen, and I don't agree with everything the DI and the team get up to. I just have to keep my head down and stick it out, for the convenience.'

Ted nodded his understanding.

'Fair enough. Right, I don't want this to go any further but the DI and DS, as well as DC Coombs, are going to be rather tied up for the rest of the day. Something related to this case.

'Now we know that Mr Bosko is definitely not our man, we need to pull out all the stops to find who is. I want you to get out there again and try to find anyone who saw Mr Hutchinson in any of the pubs, or maybe restaurants, starting with the Red Lion. I want witnesses who might be able to tell us who he was with and, more importantly, anyone else who was around. Particularly anyone who may have been watching them. You know as well as I do that the sooner we can get witness statements, the more likely they are to be accurate.

'Ring me later today, let me know how you got on, what you found out. We've wasted time looking in the wrong direction. Now I need you to get us back on track, take the case forward in the right one. It looks as if it's just you for now, so show me what you can do.

'I also need you to agree not to contact the DI or any of the rest of the team for now. If any of them phone you, just don't take the call. Can I trust you on that?'

Winters looked him directly in the eye.

'Count on me, sir.'

Ted drove directly to the hotel address Jo had given him, near to Cheadle. He showed his warrant card to the uniformed constable at the entrance door as he went in. Once inside, a pale-faced young woman on reception, looking visibly shaken by events, directed him up to the second floor. Mike Hallam was standing outside an open bedroom door, looking a bit green around the gills. He was chatting to another young uniformed constable.

'What have we got, Mike?' Ted asked, as he greeted them both.

'Jo kindly left me at the door, boss, when I told him what happened to me last time. He's in there with the Professor, and from what he's told me so far, it's exactly the same as the last one on our patch.'

Ted put his head around the door. He was surprised to see

Bizzie working away inside, near to where a pair of naked, hairy legs protruded past the end of the bed. She looked up as he tapped an already gloved hand against the door for permission to enter the crime scene.

'Ah, Chief Inspector, do come and join us. Just watch the markers have put out out where the investigators have not yet finished.'

'I didn't expect to see you here, Professor,' Ted replied, also keeping it formal in company.

'I drew the short straw as I didn't have a good excuse to hand when the call came in. And as I did the first one, it was thought appropriate that I should take this one as well. It's clearly going to be another murder so it needs a Home Office pathologist on it.'

Jo appeared from the shower room, looking remarkably chipper, seemingly unaffected by the blood spray and brain tissue Ted could see even before he went into the room.

'Almost certainly the same attacker, boss,' Jo told him. 'Pretty much the same MO as before, from the reports. Multiple stab wounds and serious injuries to the head and face, which the Professor confirms were caused by a man's work boot, almost certainly with steel toecaps. I was just checking in the shower room. It looks once again as if he was interrupted in the act of taking a shower and his attacker stabbed him almost the moment he opened the door.'

'Time of death, Professor?'

'I'll need to confirm it, but shortly after midnight again would be my best guess so far.'

Ted was looking carefully round the small room, not yet moving around. There was not a lot of space, with the crime scene investigators already working in a relatively confined area. He took a step further inside, just enough to see more of the body.

The dead man lay face down, between the bed and the wall. He had a towel around his waist. Another, which had

163

presumably been draped round his shoulders when he got out of the shower, had slipped to the ground next to him. He appeared to be of average height and slightly overweight. Even with his face squashed into the carpet and turned partly to the side, Ted could see the extent to which it had been ravaged. Once again, there was not going to be a lot for the next of kin to identify.

'Identity?' he asked Jo.

There was no need for him to go in and rummage round, getting in everyone's way, if his DI had already done a thorough job, and he had no reason to believe he wouldn't have.

'George Gildyke, from Suffolk. His cards say he's a financial advisor, but looking at the budget hotel and the labels in his clothes, I'm wondering if that's a fancy name for a life insurance salesman, boss. He was forty-eight. He's a nice organised sort, next of kin listed in his diary as Mrs Vera Gildyke, at the same address.'

'Wedding ring?'

'In his jacket pocket,' Jo told him with a grin. 'I suspect we're looking at another naughty boy playing away. His car keys were on the table there. It's a Ford, so I was just going to send Mike out into the car park to point them at any Ford he spots, see what else we can find out.'

Ted nodded his approval and passed the keys to Mike outside the door.

'See if you can find the car, after we've finished here, check if there's anything obvious to interest us inside it. Then get forensics on to checking it.'

He turned back into the room.

'No signs of the weapon in the room again, I imagine? Do we know what it was, Professor?'

'It's not been found in the room, and I don't like to guess, but the wounds look similar to the last one. I would say a decent type of kitchen knife. Easy enough to come by. I'll be able to give you the size of the boots which did the damage when I get him back, but again, it looks like the same as the previous one.'

Ted was busy looking at the inside door handle. As before, he could see signs of shampoo or shower gel there. It seemed to be the now familiar pattern of the man having been taking a shower just before he went to answer the door.

'Any signs of company in the bed?' he asked the nearest investigator.

'We've got long hairs, which were certainly not the victim's, and there are what look like semen stains on the sheets.'

'Laptop and mobile?'

'Bagged and ready to go to Océane,' Jo told him.

Ted was impressed, and feeling slightly redundant. He couldn't think of anything his new DI hadn't covered already.

'Witnesses?'

'Sal and Virgil are downstairs now, with a couple of Uniforms, talking to staff and any guests, to see what they can find out from them. Also asking about CCTV.'

'When can you do the post-mortem for us, Professor?'

'Not until Monday morning, I'm afraid,' she replied brusquely. 'There is somewhere I have to be tomorrow and it can't be altered. But I can start it at seven on Monday, for whichever of you gentlemen would care to join me?'

'I've got it, boss, if you like,' Jo told him. 'You've got enough on your hands with the rest of the case, I'm sure.'

Ted jerked his head to Jo to get him to join him, picking up Mike on the way. They walked together to the end of a corridor, which appeared a quiet enough place for Ted to bring them up to date with all that had been going on with the case in South Manchester.

Jo whistled and said, 'I've not heard anything good about Cyril Foster and his team, that's for sure, but this is sounding worse by the minute. Surely even he isn't stupid enough to think they'd get away with trying to fake evidence like that?'

'I think it's highly likely that if the Big Boss and I hadn't put a stop to them interviewing the suspect again, they'd have got a confession out of him somehow, so nobody would have looked too hard at the evidence and lack of witness ID.

'It means we're back to square one, with no suspect, and that team is down three members, so we're going to have to do some juggling. DC Winters is promising. With the right support, he might be all right, but I don't know about the others who are left. I don't know what their involvement was, or if they can actually do their jobs at all, never mind properly.'

Ted didn't like to spoil the team's weekend unless he had to, but now with three killings almost certainly down to the same person, he needed to get everyone together to take stock.

'I'm sorry to bugger up everyone's weekend plans, but I think I'm going to call a full team meeting for first thing tomorrow morning, with what remains of Foster's team. And since we now have two deaths on our patch, we'll host the meeting. Everyone there, all of ours and Foster's remaining three. Mike, can you ring round, please. Eight sharp, no excuses. Blame it on me. At least it means some of them can have the rest of the day to themselves, once we've assigned tasks. The Super has the purse strings on this and I think he'll stand the overtime, just to see some progress. I'll let him know.'

'Do you want Océane in on it too, boss?' Jo asked him. 'She did say she would be willing to come in outside her normal hours, if ever it was necessary.'

There was something about the way he said it that made Ted concerned once more that there might possibly be something, if not yet going on, then brewing up between the two of them. Not what he needed.

Ted nodded and continued, 'Jo, I think either you or I need to be overseeing Foster's team most of the time. And they need a DS to keep them in line. Mike, do you want it, or do you think Rob is up to the task?'

'Happy to do it boss, but I'd say why not let Rob have a

crack? It may be a baptism of fire for him, but it might also be just what he needs to get his teeth into,' Mike suggested, heading off towards the stairs to start looking for the victim's car.

Ted turned back to his DI.

'Jo, where are we at with the deaths at Sabden House? I don't want to lose sight of that with everything else that's going on. Three unusual deaths now in a comparatively small block of flats needs looking into.'

'We're on it whenever we have a spare minute, and anything else still on the books. Virgil's been asking around. He seems to have good street contacts. So far no one knows anything about heroin of that quality on the patch, although a few of them have asked him where they can score some.'

'I think it may be time to introduce you to our tame news-hound, Pocket Billiards. If anyone knows of shady dealings and secret planning applications involving that building, he will,' Ted told him. 'He may not have the nicest table manners you've ever seen, but he's like a dog after a bone for a good story, and he usually ferrets out all the detail. Handled correctly, he can save us a lot of legwork.

'Right, let's get started on checking witnesses here and retracing the victim's last known movements. Get Mike to call the nick local to the victim and ask them to let the wife know. And please remind me, before we all knock off this evening, that I'm meant to be picking up a takeaway. If I go home empty-handed, Mr Gildyke's death is not likely to be the only one you'll have to investigate. Especially when I tell Trev I've called an early morning meeting for tomorrow.'

Chapter Nineteen

Ted knew he shouldn't have been surprised that Foster's remaining team members turned up late for the morning briefing, but he was still disappointed. All of his own officers were in ahead of time. Even DC Maurice Brown had come in, although he was not officially back from sick leave until the following day. He was looking amazing, after his close encounter with death, and was welcomed back warmly by the whole team.

They were using the station's conference room on the ground floor, where there was slightly more room than in the cramped main CID office, with Ted's own extra officers as well as those from Foster's patch. Assuming they ever arrived, Ted thought to himself angrily, trying to keep a lid on his temper.

When they did finally roll in, only DC Winters had the grace to look contrite and mutter an apology. The other two, clearly Foster's men and anxious to prove it, sauntered in arrogantly and looked around for seats without saying a word, not even in greeting.

'Eight sharp was the instruction,' Ted told them. 'We have a lot of ground to cover and the later we start, the later we finish.'

'Just a bit further than we thought,' one of them, DC Charlie Eccles, said without a shred of remorse.

It was a pathetic excuse, and everyone present knew it. Yet more boundary pushing Ted could have done without. He decided to let it go once again, for now, at least. They had far more important things to discuss. But he did intend to have strong words with them before he let them go for the day. He was a fairly laid-back boss, who still managed to run a tight ship. He didn't like the blatant disrespect of their attitude.

'So, victim number three, George Gildyke. What do we know about him so far? Jo?'

The DI gave them all the details they had discovered at the hotel, and all that they had learned from talking to possible witnesses. Once again, it didn't amount to a great deal.

'The guy in the next room thinks he heard someone in the corridor saying something about maintenance, probably around midnight, but he was, erm, rather busy himself with a lady friend so said he didn't take much notice,' he added.

'We need to find Gildyke's lady friend. We should be looking at anything which links the victims to our man. Suki was adamant she has no jealous partner or former other half, but it could be someone she's dismissed as not being significant,' Ted was musing aloud. 'What is motivating our killer? Are the women the victims have slept with known to him in some way? Jealousy of some sort?'

'Have we got links with Linda Lovelace to all three yet?' Jezza asked.

There was a snort of laughter from both DCs Eccles and Chris Hope at the name, which was clearly not unknown to either of them, though possibly not in connection with the case.

'Linda Lovelace, darlin'? Is that what you think the case is all about?' DC Eccles sneered.

Jezza was just about to respond when Maurice beat her to it.

'I wouldn't make her angry, bonny lad. You wouldn't like her when she's angry.'

He said it mildly enough but the warning was clear behind his tone. He'd recently lost most of the spare flab he'd been carrying around but he was still solid and bulky. Although he knew Jezza could usually more than take care of herself, with her sharp tongue and kickboxing skills, he still felt strongly protective of her.

'That's enough,' Ted said sharply. 'Too much time has already been wasted on this case. We need to concentrate on the matter in hand. DC Eccles, am I to assume that you've not yet read the full file on the first case? If you had, you would know the significance of the reference to Linda Lovelace. Make sure you read up on it thoroughly, before you leave here today. And that goes for anyone else who's not up to speed.'

DC Eccles was clearly stubborn and didn't know when it was best to quit while he was ahead.

'What if the three cases aren't linked? We had a perfectly good suspect in custody, with DNA evidence likely to back it up, and the boss was hopeful of an early confession.'

Ted's own team saw the change in his body language, and spotted the danger signs of his eye colour turning a menacing shade of dark green. Eccles clearly had no idea of just how thin was the ice which he'd ventured on to.

'Everyone listen carefully, please,' Ted's voice was deliberately quiet so they all had to pay close attention to what he was saying. 'I'm not going to repeat myself. Pawel Bosko has been cleared of any suspected involvement in this case. That goes for all three of the murders. The available evidence was not safe and is the subject of a separate enquiry.

'We are proceeding on the basis that one man is responsible for all three deaths to date. Which means that what we are looking for is something which ties the suspect – the man we are referring to as Linda Lovelace, for now - either to the women involved, or to the three victims. Possibly both. We are also going on the assumption that the link is likely to revolve around online dating, casual sexual encounters, pub singles nights.

'So now would everyone please concentrate and think of

possible angles we've overlooked to date.'

He looked round the table expectantly. Océane spoke first.

'Clearly I've not yet had the time to look at the laptop and phone of the third victim, boss. But a possible link has occurred to me already.'

'Go on,' Ted encouraged her.

'I think a keyword here might be investment. Our first victim, Duncan Waters, sold solar panel systems. In between the smut I've had to wade through, he liked to portray himself as a knight in shining armour. One who could ride to the rescue of poor little women with more money than sense and show them how to invest in a planet-saving green energy system, which would see them in clover for the rest of their days.'

'But wasn't the second one, Richard Hutchinson, a Health and Safety consultant?' Rob O'Connell queried. 'Where's the investment aspect in that?'

'He liked to brag about having big clients in the financial sector. Banks, investment companies, that sort of thing. Part of his chat-up line was to hint at having his finger on the pulse of the financial world.'

'And our victim number three called himself a financial advisor,' Jo reminded them. 'But just from a first glance, I think he was more of an insurance salesman, and his so-called investment advice would probably consist of selling someone a life insurance policy.'

'So what if we're looking at someone who's set themselves a mission of avenging women who've been swindled out of their money by someone promising them gilt-edged investments?' Steve suggested. 'What if the motive isn't actually sexual at all but financial?'

DC Winters had been watching in evident fascination the way the team kicked around ideas. It was nothing like the team meetings he'd been used to with DI Foster. Everyone seemed to be free to say something, without fear of ridicule, so he plucked up the courage to make a suggestion.

'So you mean what if the women are almost incidental in this?'

Then, seeing the mocking glances of his two colleagues, who were looking at him as if he'd turned traitor or was trying for the creep's prize, he hesitated and dried up.

Ted was nothing if not encouraging.

'In what sense, DC Winters? Don't be afraid to put a theory forward, that's what these meetings are for. We're short on theories at the moment, so let's hear yours.'

'Well, sir, suppose it's the man who was scammed out of money? Suppose he's the one who lost his savings in an investment that went wrong? Someone he met online, through some seemingly innocent chat group, or social media, perhaps? He doesn't know exactly who the man is, so now he's targeting anyone mentioning investments in the hopes of killing the right person?'

Winters shifted uncomfortably in his seat when, at first, the only reaction was a snort of derision from his team-mates DCs Eccles and Hope.

Ted turned his gaze in their direction and said meaningfully, 'I'm sorry, I didn't hear any kind of suggestion from either of you.'

He turned back to Winters and continued, 'I think that's something we shouldn't overlook. We've focussed so far on the Lonely Hearts angle, with the dating scene. But that's a valid point.'

'Boss, we have had a couple of times in the past when women have come in complaining of having been scammed out of money online, if you remember,' Maurice Brown chipped in. 'And it's usually been someone too embarrassed to want it to go to court, because they've swallowed a line and felt stupid about it afterwards.'

Ted nodded.

'I remember one or two, certainly. Good call, Maurice. First thing tomorrow, can you dig out old files of anything like that, see what happened in each case. Good, that gives us another angle entirely to look into. Well done, DC Winters. And you too, Océane and Steve.

'Right, we need to find the women who were with these men before they died, see if there's any connection between them. Jezza and Megan, when are you interviewing Suki again?'

'She's coming in tomorrow after work, boss,' Jezza told him. 'I'm trying not to judge but I'm struggling to see her as an investment type. Although you never know. If she invested a packet and lost it, that could be why she's struggling to pay her rent now.

'Coincidentally, I do actually have some money I need to invest, to provide for Tommy. Maybe I could start looking around online…'

Ted was already shaking his head before she'd finished the sentence.

'Absolutely not, DC Vine, too fraught with danger on too many levels. It could compromise the enquiry. Find a proper financial advisor to make sure Tommy's taken care of.'

The team knew that Jezza had come into money when her parents died in a car crash, and that most of it was already in trust to provide for her brother's special needs.

'I know someone who could help you, Jezza,' Virgil told her. 'Nat Cowley used to work in a big investment company.'

'And didn't he nearly bankrupt them with reckless trading?' she laughed.

'Precisely the reason he knows what to avoid. I'll put you in touch with him.'

Ted smiled good-naturedly.

'All right, everyone, let's focus on the case,' he said mildly. 'I want witnesses found and statements taken as soon as possible, while details are still fresh in people's minds. Tomorrow, DS O'Connell and DC Tibbs, you go over to South Manchester and work with DCs Winters, Eccles and Hope. See if you can find whoever it was Hutchinson took back to his room. And keep trying to find anyone who saw our possible killer.

'Jo, you've got the latest PM, and I want to talk to the relatives of the third victim as soon as they come up from Suffolk to ID the body, see what that brings us. Mike, you get over to Cheadle with some of our team and start looking for the woman there, and anyone who may have seen anything.

'We'll skip a morning briefing tomorrow. You all know what you need to be getting on with. Instead we'll get together here at the end of the day. Six o'clock sharp, everyone. Now you know the way, DC Eccles, that shouldn't present you with any great problem, should it?'

Eccles merely grunted in response.

'And before the three of you go back,' Ted said, looking from one to the other of what remained of Foster's team, 'I'd like a word with you all, in my office, upstairs. Follow me.'

A grin passed from one to another of the original team members, who all knew to their cost about the boss's 'words' with team members. Even Megan and Jo had heard about that. Trying not to look too eager, Ted's team hurried up the stairs in the wake of the others, keen to see or hear Foster's cronies get their first taste of Ted in famous kick-trick mode.

Ted held the door of his office open while the three men trooped in and, finding nowhere to sit down, stood uncomfortably, turning to look back towards Ted to tell them where he wanted them. They turned just in time to see the famous kick-trick in action, a high flying karate kick which slammed the office door shut with such power it shook the partition walls of the small office. Even the noise it made didn't drown out the stifled snorts of laughter from the officers outside, in the main office.

Winters had gone positively white, while even the other two, who clearly considered themselves hard cases, were looking uneasy.

'Right, listen up. This is a serious crime enquiry. There's no place for incompetent or corrupt coppers on this team. I highly doubt if DI Foster and the others will be coming back to the team so for now, we're stuck with one another.

'I expect punctuality, efficiency and respect from everyone on my team. If you're not prepared to give those, put in for a transfer. I'll happily sign it. If you decide to stay, show me you deserve a place on the team.

'You will all be questioned, at some length, by Complaints and Discipline, so I suggest you get your notes in order. And that doesn't mean getting together and cooking up a bullshit story. You won't get anything past Superintendent Fletcher and it's important you understand that right from the start.

'Now you two,' he glared at Eccles and Hope, 'get out of my sight and wait in the car for Winters. And don't ever be late to one of my briefings again, without a very good excuse. Winters, you stay where you are.'

As the two men left the room and faced the walk of shame through the main office, Ted could hear more barely muffled laughter. He nodded to the chair tucked out of the way under his desk, facing him, and told Winters to sit down.

'Graham,' he began, his tone now softer, his manner more relaxed. 'If you're not very careful, those clowns are going to drag you down with them. Now, I may be wrong, but I don't think you're like the others. You showed me today that you have something more about you. This is your chance to prove it.

'It's up to you, of course, but I would strongly recommend you don't discuss anything with those two, and certainly not with the rest of the team members, who are under suspension. Write your own notes of what you know, what was said, even what you suspect. When you see Superintendent Fletcher, tell him the truth. Don't, whatever you do, try to hide anything or bend the facts. If you follow that advice, and you're not implicated, you'll be fine. But be in no doubt, if you are involved in any way, it will be uncovered.

'Right, you'd better go and join the Chuckle Brothers, and I'll see you again tomorrow. Good work today, that was a useful suggestion.'

There was still plenty of the day left and the weather wasn't too terrible, so Ted went shopping for a picnic on the way home. Trev was doing something with his bike in the garage, covered in oil but looking happily absorbed, when Ted got back. He left his Renault on the drive.

'Let's go for a picnic,' he suggested, leaning over to kiss Trev on the cheek, while he worked. 'Are you at a stage where you can leave it?'

'Give me half an hour to grab a shower and get changed, but the bike won't be ready to go out on. I'll need to finish off when I get back. If we're taking the car anyway, why not phone your mother and see if she's free?'

Ted made a face. 'I rather wanted a bit of us time. I know I've been neglecting you too much of late.'

'Call her,' Trev insisted. 'She may not be free, but if she is, she'd love it. Let's go to the seaside.'

'Are you mad? Have you seen the weather? It may not be raining at the moment, but it's not exactly beach weather.'

'Come on, stop being a boring old fart. Let's take her to Southport. Walk on Ainsdale beach and see if we can get a glimpse of the sea. Candy floss. Donkeys. The whole works,' Trev grinned at him. 'Do you good. A complete break from policeman stuff.'

'The donkeys will still be on their winter holidays, if they've got any sense,' Ted laughed. 'All right, all right, I'll ring her. Go and get ready.'

'And by the way, next weekend, you and I are going down to Somerset to watch Shewee compete. No excuses. I don't care how many bodies there are. You've got Jo now to stand in for you, and if you say you can't get the time off, I shall phone the

Ice Queen and Jim myself and make sure you can. And I mean it, Ted, if you let me down on this one, I shall divorce you.'

'We're not married,' Ted reminded him. 'I keep asking but you keep refusing.'

'Well, I'll marry you first, just so I can divorce you. Now go and phone your mother.'

Chapter Twenty

Trev was right about Southport. Ted's mother was free and delighted to be asked. The day brought back long-forgotten happy memories for Ted, of times before his mother had left him as a child.

Annie and Trev got on brilliantly and genuinely enjoyed one another's company. Trev had never known warmth or affection from his own parents, even before he told them he was gay. He'd not had much contact with them while growing up and what he had had was stiff and formal. Annie was warm and loving, happily returning his hugs, fussing over Ted to make sure he had a good time.

Trev was like a big kid at the seaside, insisting on drawing 'Trev loves Ted' with his heel in the damp sand. Ted had forgotten how much his mother loved to collect coloured pebbles and pretty shells. He carried them for her in a bag left over from their picnic in the dunes, sitting close together to shelter from the keen wind.

Ted would have loved more family time like this. The sort people with ordinary jobs enjoyed. The type of thing so often out of reach of coppers, and so frequently the cause of failed relationships within the force. He didn't hold out much hope of escaping for an entire weekend the following week but he would certainly try. At least Jo was proving to be reliable, though Ted was still worried by the evidently flirting looks that passed between him and Océane, and how they always seemed to manage some fleeting physical contact when they were discussing work. If the weekend away looked like even a remote possibility, he would try to have a word, just to allay his fears and reiterate the boundaries.

He felt considerably more relaxed going into his own nick on Monday morning, with the smell of sea spray still lingering in his nostrils from the day before. Rob and Virgil had gone over to South Manchester, and Ted was keen to do some essential catching up on routine work. He needed to touch base with the Ice Queen, for one thing. Although the current murder case was not her remit, as a courtesy he would keep her in the loop, and he would need to talk to her as well as to Jim about taking time off, if he could.

'The main problem is that I'll be about five hours away, if I go, so I can hardly rush back,' Ted told her.

'But you're confident DI Rodriguez is up to the job of holding the fort in your absence? Even if we should have another body in your serious serial case?'

'He's excellent, no worries there. A good find. I just don't like taking time off in the middle of a big case like this. But Trev is threatening to leave me if I don't,' he said with a laugh, 'and I'm not sure how much he's joking.'

'We can't take that risk,' she smiled in reply. 'I'd be happy enough to agree, if Superintendent Baker does.'

He needed to call Jim next, to find out how things had gone with Foster, Mackenzie and Coombs and their meeting with C&D.

'Mackenzie is singing like a canary in a coal mine,' Jim told him cheerfully. 'It wasn't him, guv, it was all that nasty DC Coombs and he couldn't do anything to stop him. He's clearly too stupid to realise that even if he escapes the conspiracy charges, admitting such a thing is not showing his leadership skills as a DS in a very good light.'

'And Foster?'

'Well, he really is stupid. So close to his pension, all he had to do was keep his head down and his nose clean. He's denying everything, even what day of the week it is, but he's implicated up to his neck. If your Mr Bosko would agree to testify, we could put them away for a nice long time and show the public that we do try to clean up our act.'

'What about Coombs?'

'I interviewed him myself. Now that is one nasty piece of work. And not your number one fan, Ted, either.'

'I'll try not to lose any sleep over it,' Ted responded ironically. 'Let me guess – something of the homophobic about him?'

Jim's rich chuckle came over the phone.

'Oh, yes, but as much as anything, I think he resents you being good at your job. He seems to me to be a lazy bastard, whose mission in life is to get results by doing as little work as possible. Then you pitch up and have the audacity to suggest he should do some proper police work. I'm prepared to believe it was all his idea, and that, as much as anything, it was to make your life difficult.'

He told Ted that the three were not yet in custody, while further investigation was going on into the false forensic evidence, but that all were suspended and under orders not to contact each other or anyone else from the team.

'I've got Rob and Virgil over there today riding shotgun on the Three Musketeers who're left,' Ted told him. 'Winters looks promising. Quite bright, good ideas, but probably just kept down by the others. I'm not sure about the other two yet. I'll reserve judgement on them until I hear what they've managed to achieve today. We've got a catch-up at six this evening.'

'I'll come over for that,' Jim told him. 'I want to make it abundantly clear how seriously Complaints are taking this matter. I know your team are solid, but it never hurts to remind everyone what lies in wait for them if ever they think of taking the easy option.'

Ted decided to raise the subject of his weekend away while

he had Jim's full attention. He knew he might well be busy later on when he came over for the meeting.

'I hate to ask, Jim, and I know it's not easy, with a big case ongoing, but Trev is threatening to divorce me if I don't go with him.'

'I thought you weren't married.'

'We aren't. I keep asking him, but he knows how uncomfortable it would make you, if I asked you to be my best man, and I wouldn't want anyone else.'

There was an embarrassed silence from Jim Baker, who was also one of Ted's oldest and best friends. It was true, and he knew it. Jim tried his best to be accepting of their relationship, and he liked and respected Trev. But the idea of the two of them getting married was always going to be one he would struggle with.

'Jim, it's fine, I was teasing you,' Ted assured him, to break the awkwardness. 'Trev and I are solid, you know that. We don't need the marriage label. Just he is threatening me with dire consequences if I don't go with him. It's some horsey thing for his sister. I don't know much about it, but apparently it's important to them both.'

'Then you should try to be there. Family is important and us coppers often forget about that. It's fine by me, if you're sure the team can hold the fort? And of course, you'll be contactable by phone at all times, if they need any advice?'

They finished off by discussing who was leading which part of the meeting later that day. Ted was glad Jim would be there. His presence would definitely impress upon everyone how seriously the force took any signs of trying to falsify evidence.

Ted's main task of the day was going to be talking to the next of kin of their latest victim. As the post-mortem was only taking place that morning, they would be going to the hospital later in the day to make the formal identification. They had been asked, and had agreed, to come to the station first to talk to Ted. There was little doubt about the identity of the body; the identification was just a formality. In a sense it would be easier to talk to the widow first, before she had to undergo the ordeal.

When Ted went out into the main office later, to find out if Jo was back from the PM, he found his DI perched on Océane's desk, his black-haired head leaning close to her auburn one as they talked. Ted noticed that Jo's thigh was close to Océane's mouse-hand as she worked on her computer, almost touching. He saw, too, the looks the two were getting from Steve. The green-eyed monster was much in evidence once again.

'How was the PM, Jo?' he asked, and noted the way the DI shot off the desk like a scalded cat. Time to have a word, before things got out of hand. 'Can you come into my office and fill me in, please?'

Ted went to put his kettle on, inviting Jo to take a seat as he went, and offering him a brew.

'Coffee, boss, please. And shall I shut the door, or is this going to be my kick-trick initiation?'

He was grinning broadly, clearly amused by the situation, when Ted turned back to him.

'Have you done something to warrant it?' Ted countered.

Jo laughed.

'No, but I can see how it might look as if I have. Boss, if I tell you something, can it stay between us, or it could totally blow any street cred I might have?'

'As long as it's not something that's going to affect the smooth running of the team, your secret will be safe with me,' Ted said cautiously, turning back to make the drinks and put mugs in front of them both.

'The thing is, I'm a hot-blooded Latin male. I love women. I mean, I really love women. The trouble is, my wife, Sofia, is even more hot-blooded Latin than I am. If I did anything, anything at all, she would cut off my sausage and serve it to me instead of chorizo in a paella. I know it, and she knows I know it. It doesn't stop me flirting though. I can't help myself, especially with someone like Océane around. But honestly, boss, that is as far as it will ever go. I swear. On the lives of the six children Sofia has presented me with.'

Ted smiled his relief. He believed him, and appreciated his honesty. It made him happier at the prospect of going away at the weekend. But he added a word of caution.

'I'm not entirely sure Océane sees it as just a bit of harmless fun though, so do watch what you're doing.

'Now tell me all about the PM, before the relatives get here. If Megan's around, I'll have her with me. Jezza's not the tea and sympathy sort.'

'Ah, Jezza, now there's another one,' Jo said with a wink.

Ted immediately became serious.

'Absolutely off limits, Jo. With good reason. Not so much as a flirt, please. Trust me on that.'

Jo heard the note of warning in the boss's voice and nodded in acknowledgement. He then ran through the PM details. Bizzie would send Ted her written report later in the day but for now, he needed the main points before he spoke to the relatives.

The details were similar to the other two. Bizzie Nelson had no doubt that both the knife and the boots were the same in all three killings, having been sent the report on the South Manchester victim. Once again, there were multiple stab wounds, several of which would have proved fatal, followed by the now-familiar boot injuries to the head and face. Although forensic analysis of the hotel sheets confirmed that there had been recent sexual activity, the victim had been showering just before his attacker struck so they were unlikely to find any evidence on the body to identify the sexual partner.

'We need to focus on finding the women in these cases,' Ted stressed, when Jo had finished speaking. 'They're definitely not suspects, at this stage, but they may well have seen something, perhaps without realising. Someone watching them in the pubs where they made contact. See what you can chase up.'

A call to Ted's desk phone let him know that the widow of the latest victim was downstairs in an interview room. He collected Megan and the two of them made their way down to find the woman. In fact there were two women in the room, looking alike, one perhaps five years older than the other.

'Mrs Gildyke?'

'Yes, I'm Vera Gildyke,' the younger of the two told him. 'This is my sister, Rosemary. She's my only family, we have no children. I hope it's all right to have her with me?'

'Absolutely, no problem at all,' Ted assured her. 'Please may I begin by offering you my condolences. I'm afraid there is little doubt that the deceased person is your husband. Asking you to identify him is a formality. I just wondered what you could tell us about him, and about his reason for being in Cheadle?'

The story was a familiar one. A husband who was away travelling a lot of the time, often staying away from home, in one budget hotel after another. No, she wasn't aware if he was seeing anyone else, although the look which passed between the two sisters at that point told Ted all he needed to know. Yes, they were happy, and their marriage was a good one. No, she knew of no one who might have any reason to harm George. There were no enemies that she was aware of. It didn't advance them a lot.

'Stories like these make me glad I'm single,' Megan remarked, as she and Ted went back upstairs together.

'Stories like these make me glad I'm in a stable relationship,' Ted replied.

Ted was hoping there may be fresh leads to feed back when they all got together at the end of the day. They were in the conference room once more, Ted and Jim Baker sitting at one end of the table, flanked by Jo and Kevin Turner. He was there to evaluate what help would be needed from his uniformed officers, and particularly from the Community Support Officers, who kept an ear close to the ground on their patch.

Jim Baker said his piece, then Ted asked for any feedback from anyone who had anything promising from interviewing potential witnesses.

Looking smugly pleased with himself, DC Hope drawled, 'I've got a possible. A couple in a pub who said they saw a man sitting in a corner reading a paper and watching what was going on in the room. They both remember he was wearing a dark fleece and had work boots on. I got a bit of a description from the two of them, but nothing much.'

Ted had always thought the expression 'face-palm' was just that; a turn of phrase. He felt a sudden, overwhelming desire to do it. Putting his elbows on the desk in front of him, he lowered his face into his hands, trying to rub away the sudden extreme fatigue which threatened to engulf him. He breathed deeply, to be sure of keeping his self-control.

'DC Hope,' he said, when he removed his hands. 'Please tell me that you didn't interview both potential witnesses at the same time? Are you familiar with the concept of co-witnessing and the problems that can present, with the two feeding off one another's account of what happened?'

Hope looked mutinous as he muttered, 'I thought it would save time...'

'No, DC Hope, it won't save time. It will simply, in all probability, result in the two people saying the same thing. Now tell me about the clothing. Did that just come up in conversation or did you suggest it to them in any way? In a busy pub, how did they come to notice the man's clothes and, in particular, his footwear?'

'Well, I may just have asked if he was dressed for a night out or still in his working clothes.'

'Reassure me, at least, that you remembered to ask them not

to discuss the incident further between them, before we take formal statements from them?'

Hope had no reply and deflected the question by making a show of looking through his notes.

Ted looked up and addressed all of them.

'All right, everyone. Please remember the basics. Separate witnesses before interviewing. Don't ask leading questions. And remember to caution them about discussing the incident.

'DS O'Connell, can you please arrange for this couple to be interviewed again at the station, as soon as possible? One at a time.

'Anything else? Anyone? If not, please, everyone, write up all your notes, in detail, and let me have them as soon as possible. There is something here we're all missing for now. I want to spend a day or two going through everything we've got to find what it is.'

With that, Ted wound the meeting up, after assigning tasks for the next day. He noticed that DC Hope was particularly anxious to scuttle out of the conference room as soon as possible.

Ted went back up to his office to collect his things. He was just getting ready to leave when Rob came and knocked on the still-open door of his office. He was looking anxious.

'Boss, I'm really sorry, I screwed up. I should have checked Foster's lot knew what they were doing, before I let them loose on witnesses.'

'Not your fault at all, Rob,' Ted assured him. 'Both Hope, or perhaps Hopeless may be more appropriate, and Eccles have got more years under their belts than you have. It was a fair assumption. Just remember you're the DS on this; you're there to see they do their jobs properly. This is a big ask for you, new into the role. Don't be afraid to ask for help if you need it.

'Meanwhile, get them together first thing tomorrow for a briefing. Tell them how you want the interviews run and make damn sure they do as you instruct them. Any problems, let me know. I'm hoping and praying to get away at the weekend, on pain of death from Trev if I don't, so I need to know I'm leaving the ship steering a steady course towards a result.'

Ted was not a drinker, but after the day he'd just had, he stopped on the way home to buy a bottle of ginger beer for himself and a decent bottle of wine for Trev. He would get as much enjoyment from watching Trev drink it, and it might gain him a few good marks, just in case he couldn't pull off the weekend away.

Chapter Twenty-one

Ted had set aside some desk time for himself, leaving the team to get on with their tasks. He'd let them know he didn't want to be interrupted for anything non-urgent until further notice. He hadn't made much headway before his mobile alerted him to an incoming call from Jim Baker.

'There have been developments, Ted, of an unexpected kind,' he told him, after they'd exchanged their usual light-hearted greetings. 'DI Foster is dead.'

'Really? Was it …?'

'Natural causes, fortunately for everyone. Apparently he had a heart problem he was trying to keep quiet about. He didn't want to be put out to grass before he got his pension. He was supposed to stop smoking and cut right down on the drinking. With all this going on, he'd started hitting both again, hard, and I don't suppose the stress of the enquiry helped. His heart simply gave up, it seems.

'Now this is where it gets really interesting. He lived alone, long since divorced, kids grown up and gone. He was found by DS Mackenzie, the person who was under strict instructions not to go anywhere near him, or to have any kind of contact with him. To his credit, instead of just legging it and leaving him there to rot, he did call it in, so at least Foster was taken away and will get a decent funeral.

'Mackenzie was on his own. We don't know, and never will, but if I had to speculate, I would say the two of them were out to do a deal where they would throw Coombs to the wolves

188

to save their own skins.'

'Nice company,' Ted commented. 'Sounds as if you could well be right. And it does seem, from what you told me, and from my own experience of Coombs, as if he was the ringleader and the other two just went along with him. So what now?'

'Gerry Fletcher and I will need to discuss it in detail, of course. But we may be able to use it to our advantage. If Mackenzie agrees to testify against Coombs, we could offer him a deal where we don't prosecute him. But whatever happens, his days in the force are finished, and he knows that.

'If he testifies, and if your Polish plumber agrees to do the same, we've got Coombs bang to rights and he could go down for up to a year for false allegation of a crime resulting in the arrest of an innocent person. It turns out he made a lot of enemies over the years with his attitude. Forensics, in particular, didn't like his high-handed manner. They had some interesting things to say on the provenance of the blood trace on the victim's car, and at what point Coombs drew it to their attention.'

'He deserves everything he gets. His type don't help the rest of us who try to be decent coppers. I'm not sure about Mr Bosko; he seemed nervous of the police. He might not want to draw attention to himself by testifying, although I hope he will. But if Mackenzie turns, there's surely enough without him?'

'Oh yes,' Jim agreed, 'I just want every nail I can possibly get for the lid of that bastard's coffin.'

Ted returned to his paperwork, only to be disturbed again by the briefest of knocks on his office door and the appearance of Bill, the desk sergeant. He didn't often venture up onto Ted's territory, so Ted knew it must be something important and, pushing his files aside, he put the kettle on and prepared to listen.

'I just wondered if you'd heard anything from Honest John lately, Ted?' Bill asked, sitting down. 'Only we haven't, and there have been a few deaths on the patch since I can last remember him calling. I wondered if I needed to send someone round? After all, one of the deaths has been in his block of flats, and he's not even laid claim to that.'

'You're right, Bill, now I come to think of it. My last contact was when I took Steve round there to introduce him. Last time we lost contact, his phone was out of order. He's not doing as well in the new place, either. He's getting bullied by local kids. I wonder if his social worker is keeping a close enough eye on him?'

'You know what it's like these days, Ted,' Bill took a slurp of the tea as he spoke. Ted had made it how he knew he liked it, dark and sweet, like treacle. 'Everyone's overworked and under-resourced. John is just the sort who could easily slip through the net. Do you want me to send a CSO round there to check?'

'I'll tell you what, I'll send young Steve, now he knows where John lives. I could do with getting him out of the office more. Especially now he and Océane are getting like Siamese twins over the computers.'

Bill laughed.

'Can't say I blame him. She is a very pretty girl. Out of his league a bit, though? He's so quiet I can't imagine how he's ever going to find himself a girl.'

'How are you, anyway, Bill?' Ted asked him.

He knew Bill was a lonely man, who lived for his work since the early death of his wife.

'Oh, I'm fine. I pass the time. Darts with some of the lads, too much television, and as many work shifts as I can get. They tell you it gets easier with time. It's not true, though. You just get better at pretending that it does.'

They shared a companionable silence while they finished their drinks, then Bill stood up to leave.

'Can you please ask Steve to pop in here, as you go out, Bill?'

Just as the young man came timidly into the office, looking anxious, Ted took a call on his desk phone, from the Ice Queen.

'I'm sorry to be the bearer of bad news,' she began, and Ted groaned inwardly. He had a horrible feeling that meant his plans for the weekend were scuppered.

'It's only just been landed on me. I have a divisional budgetary planning meeting first thing tomorrow morning. That means I'm going to need some figures from you today. Can we get together in my office in, say, an hour's time? I'm basically looking for a breakdown of hours, and whether your latest operation is all coming out of our budget or what can be offloaded onto Superintendent Baker's.'

She must have sensed Ted's silent cursing as she added, 'And let me just remind you, we only have DI Rodriguez because of budgetary cuts in another division. So if you want to keep him, I suggest you make a financial case for it.'

Ted was less than thrilled so his reply was a terse and formal, 'Ma'am,' then he turned his attention to Steve.

'Don't look worried, Steve, it's just something I need you to do for me. Sit down first, though, and tell me how you're getting on. Anything fresh to report?'

'Well, sir, I had a thought,' Steve began nervously. 'I mean, after killings like these, our man is surely going to be covered in blood, or worse?'

Ted nodded encouragingly. Steve had some good ideas. He was just sometimes a bit hesitant about voicing them. Ted rightly guessed that he would be even more reticent with the expanded team, and especially the incomers from South Manchester.

'So if he's used the cover of being a maintenance man to gain access to the bedrooms, he may well use overalls, which he can then peel off afterwards, just in case anyone sees him. Our only sightings to date, from witnesses and CCTV, have him in a fleece. So I looked again at the CCTV from the first killing. It's not easy to see, but Océane enhanced it. He definitely has a strap over the shoulder furthest from the camera. Some sort of a holdall, perhaps.'

'Excellent, good work, make sure everyone working on the case knows that. It might just be something else to give us a steer towards who he is,' Ted told him. 'In the meantime, I'd like you to nip round to Honest John's place and just make sure he's all right. He's been a bit quiet of late and it's not like him. Don't spend too long there, just check his phone is working and that he can contact the outside world, then let me know. I'll be in a meeting with the Super, but send me a quick text, please.'

Ted was glad that he always tried to keep on top of his paperwork, no matter how busy he was. It was a scramble, but he could pull together the figures he would need relatively quickly. Now he had Jo on board, he didn't want to risk losing him. Especially not if it meant that he and Trev could get the occasional weekend away together, like a normal couple.

The Ice Queen had her coffee machine on and, to sweeten the pill, she had sent someone out to get pastries for them. Ted had his phone on mute but midway through their meeting, he felt it vibrating and risked a glance at the screen.

'I need to take this. Sorry,' he told her. 'I'll be as quick as I can,' then, as he picked up the call, 'Yes, Steve? What's the situation?'

'Not good, sir,' Steve's voice quavered with uncertainty. 'I think John might be dead. I waited ages for him to answer the door; I remembered how slowly he moves. But there's no sign of life inside and there's a really terrible smell, sir. I thought it was drains at first, but it's not. It's not like anything I've encountered before. That's why I think he might be dead inside there.'

'All right, Steve. Now listen carefully. I'm going to send two uniformed officers, and they'll gain access to the flat. I can't leave here just at the moment, and everyone is tied up. So I need you to be my eyes and ears on the scene. Remember what we did the last time. I want you to look round carefully and see if there's anything which you think isn't right. If there is, get Uniform to call it in as suspicious and we'll send in the cavalry.

'Keep your head. Don't panic. And don't worry. I'd rather you called it in as suspicious and it wasn't than let it go as natural causes and it turns out to be something else. Keep me posted at all times.

'Sorry,' he said to the Ice Queen, 'I just need to sort this. Steve's on his own at the scene of a possible suspicious death. Honest John.'

'Of course. Let me speak to Inspector Turner for you and get his officers there. I assume they all know the address. You see if you can track down either DI Rodriguez or DS Hallam to get round there. Is DC Ellis going to be up to handling this on his own until they arrive?'

'I think so. He's sensible; he was with me when we looked at the last suspicious death scene at the same place. It won't be very nice if John is dead and smelling to high heaven, but I think he'll cope, for now. It's a good chance for him to show us what he's capable of.'

Ted tracked down Jo, who was nearer to Sabden House than Mike was, but would still need half an hour to finish what he was doing and get over there. Ted promised to join him as soon as he could, and went back to the figures. It was less than half an hour before he received another call from Steve.

'John is dead, sir. We've got inside now. Looks like it's been a few days. I've had a quick look round. I haven't touched anything, just looked, and something's not right at all. There's a big hamper of fancy food here in the living room, and it looks as if he'd been tucking into it. But his diabetic stuff, the medication and testing kits, isn't here, and I can't see it anywhere around, just at first glance. Shall we call it in as suspicious, sir?'

'I've never known John not to have his insulin to hand. He

was too organised. Good work, Steve. Yes, call it in. Jo's on his way over, he'll be there as soon as he can, and once I've finished in this meeting, I'll come too. But are you okay for now? Can you manage?'

'Yes, sir. It's not very nice, but I'll be okay. But sir, one thing that's worrying me, is how the heck are they going to get him out of here?'

It was the first thing that had gone through Ted's mind, too. It was going to need specialist equipment to remove the body of someone of John's size from the flat. He reassured Steve once more and turned back to the figures, although he was finding it hard to concentrate. He'd always liked John, appreciated the man's intelligence. He knew food was an addiction for him, but he was wondering where he would have got the money for a fancy hamper.

Although he tried to keep his attention on the paperwork, his concentration was broken. After about twenty minutes, the Ice Queen called a halt.

'Go, Ted,' she told him. 'Your mind's not on the figures. Leave me your notes and I'll finish off. I know you're worrying about DC Ellis, so go. Go and sort the crime scene. I'll make a convincing argument tomorrow so you get to keep your team up to its full new strength.'

She could be surprisingly sensitive at times. Ted threw her an appreciative smile and didn't need telling twice.

When he arrived at the flats, there was a fire appliance outside as well as an ambulance. It was clearly going to be a specialised operation. Steve and Jo were outside the front of the building, with two officers in uniform. Ted was surprised to see his DI was smoking, a small cigar. Jo came over to him as soon as he saw him, to fill him in on where they were up to.

'I didn't know you were a smoker.'

'Me, boss? As if,' Jo replied with a guilty grin, cupping his smoke in his hand to conceal it. 'I told Sofia I gave up when young George, our eldest, was born. I tell her what she wants to hear and what she needs to know. I find it's a good recipe for a happy marriage.'

Ted chuckled.

'If you keep telling me stuff like that, I'll start wondering whether I can trust you or whether you're just telling me what you think I want to hear. Right, tell me what we know so far.'

Jo had also had a look inside the flat and agreed with Steve. Something didn't look right.

'We can't get in there just now They're busy working out how they're going to bring him out. At the moment, they're thinking of taking the front window out and trying that way, so they've sent for a maintenance crew.'

'Poor John. What a way for him to end his days. He was an intelligent man, just brought down by grief. And it wasn't like him at all not to have his insulin to hand. He was always scrupulously tidy and methodical, almost obsessively so. I suppose it's too much to hope that the maintenance crew they send will include our prime suspect for the other deaths, in his day job?

'Steve, tell Jo what you've found out about our other case from the CCTV. I think you might be on to something there.'

They had to wait for quite some time until John's vast body was safely recovered and the flat made secure once more. The man would be transported to the morgue in a specially adapted ambulance, as the body was too big for any of the usual discreet undertakers' vans.

Scene of Crime Investigators had been called to the scene, as it was now being treated as a suspicious death. Jo and Steve had already looked round, so Ted put on gloves and shoe covers and went inside to see what he could spot. He'd visited John a few times over the years, though only once at this new flat. He was still used to his ways. There was no immediate sign anywhere of his blood testing kit or his insulin, which Ted knew was always carefully laid out close to hand. John moved slowly, because of his bulk, and never took the risk of being unable to reach his life-saving medication, should he ever need it urgently.

Ted found the hamper Steve had mentioned in the living room, on the table next to where John used to sit. He doubted John would have been able to carry it into the flat by himself. Someone had clearly delivered it and brought it in for him. Possibly the same person had moved the insulin out of reach.

Honest John had made quite a dent on the hamper, and looked to have put away the best part of a bottle of sweet dessert wine, as well as the food. Ted knew he wasn't supposed to drink at all, because of his medical condition. He'd also polished off a full box of expensive hand-made Belgian chocolates, amongst other tempting goodies. It must have had a catastrophic effect on his blood sugar levels, and without his insulin to hand, the result was a foregone conclusion. Ted just hoped he'd enjoyed every mouthful before he'd slipped into a coma.

'You did good work here, Steve, well done,' Ted told him when he went back out. 'I agree with all your observations. I can't see where John would have had the money for a hamper like that. Even if he had, he wasn't stupid. He knew he was taking a risk with the pizzas and crisps he usually ate, but I can't see him starting on chocolates and alcohol unless the temptation was put in his way.

'I'll take the inquest on this, Jo. I feel I owe it to John. And you and I need to go and have a chat with my friend Pocket Billiards next, about what is going on at this block of flats, and why someone clearly wants rid of the secure tenants.'

Chapter Twenty-two

Ted wanted to let the Ice Queen know the details of the latest death before she left for the evening. He knew she could well be unavailable all the next day, with her meeting, and he needed to run some ideas past her before she disappeared.

'We're now on the fourth suspicious death in that same small block of flats. It can't be coincidental. I think it's something we need to look into as a possible murder case.'

'I'm struggling, at the moment, to see how a murder case can be made out of someone buying a bottle of whisky for a known alcoholic, or supplying high-quality heroin to a drug addict. How could we begin to prove intention to kill?'

'With great difficulty, I agree,' Ted conceded. 'But with Honest John, it looks fairly certain that someone deliberately removed his diabetes medication. We couldn't find it anywhere in the flat, and that opens up possibilities for us.'

'Could he not simply have run out and been unable to get any more?'

Ted shook his head.

'It was on repeat prescription, which went direct to the pharmacy, and they delivered regularly. They were good to him, always kept an eye on him. He used to tell me he enjoyed their visits. And I checked with them. They'd been to top him up just last week. So it certainly indicates that someone may have removed it from the property.

'What I want to do now is go and find our local newshound and ask him what he knows about the building. See if he has any ideas of who might have a motive to want secure tenants out. Then that might lead us to who is behind it. So when I see him, he's going to want something juicy in exchange on our Lonely Hearts killer. Is it time to make good use of him once more, to circulate even a vague description of our so-called Linda Lovelace through him? Maybe issue a warning about the dangers of blind dating, especially with a killer on the loose? Without, of course, causing panic.'

'I certainly shouldn't have any trouble getting the hours we need if you are really saying you have two separate cases, with a total of, what is it now, seven victims in all? Are you going to be able to head up both enquiries, without compromising either of them?'

'I'd be happy, at this stage, to leave Jo and Mike Hallam to the Sabden House case. I'm impressed with what I've seen of Jo so far, and we already know that Mike is a safe pair of hands. I want to take Jo with me to meet our reporter friend, see what we can dig out. What I would like from you first is a statement, or press release, or something I can feed him about the Lonely Hearts case, to keep him sweet. Or as sweet as someone that obnoxious ever is.'

'Shouldn't that come from Superintendent Baker, as he's in overall charge of that case?'

'It should, ideally, but he's busy dealing with corrupt coppers and I don't want to interrupt him on that. Besides, he's with Superintendent Fletcher at the moment, and he's scary.'

The Ice Queen hid a smile, finding it difficult to imagine Ted being really afraid of anyone, although she, too, knew the head of C&D, and his formidable reputation.

'And I know all this means it's the worst possible time for me to want to take a weekend off, but it's only really Saturday, I'll come back in on Sunday as soon as I get back...'

'Nonsense, you should be entitled to the odd day off. We're all inclined to forget we have home lives, when working a difficult case. But we shouldn't. They're what keep us grounded. I'm actually hoping to try for a bit of family sailing this weekend myself.

'Leave the statement to me. I'll make sure you get it before tomorrow morning. We'll give him just enough detail to keep him cooperative. And well done with the improved relations you've forged with him so far.'

Trev kept asking Ted every day if he was still going to be able to get the weekend off. He was pleased to be able to pass on the Ice Queen's words when he got home that evening.

'But that does mean I'm not going to be able to make it to the dojo tomorrow. I need to get everything up to speed before you drag me away on this dirty weekend. I'll need to work late tomorrow and Thursday, if you want us to leave at a decent time on Friday.'

He'd been pleased to get home to extra hugs when he told Trev about Honest John.

'I know you were fond of him. I just wished I'd made the time to go with you to meet him one time. It sounds as if we would have got along. Just as well I made sticky toffee pud again for tonight. It sounds as if you're in need of some comfort food.'

Ted had often told his partner he should meet John. Russian was one of the languages Trev spoke, though not as fluently as some others. Ted had suggested he meet John so he would have someone to practise with. He knew John would have been glad of the intelligent company, even if only occasionally.

'The kids will all miss you tomorrow. I will, too. But I'll explain about work, and it's fine by me, as long as it means you'll be able to come with me at the weekend.'

'I'll miss the physical workout, if you keep making me sticky toffee pud. I'll need a way to burn off the calories.'

'Oh, I think we can always find other means of doing that.'

Ted called another early morning full team meeting for Wednesday. He was pleased to see that the three officers from South Manchester were on time. All three looked subdued, no doubt shaken by the news of DI Foster's death, and the implications of what was going on behind the scenes with their team. He was also impressed that once again, Océane had shown up for the meeting, when she was not obliged to.

The conference room was being used for the budget meeting, so they all crowded into the main office and it was standing room only for some. Ted mentioned first the Sabden House case, telling the team that they would now be investigating it as a possible murder enquiry, then asked for an update on their Lonely Hearts case.

'A bit of progress, boss,' Rob O'Connell told him. He'd been put in charge of coordinating witness statements for all three killings. 'We have a staff member at the hotel where Mr Gildyke was killed, who may just possibly have seen our prime suspect. The reception is manned through the night there, unusually for a budget hotel. She'd sloped outside for a quiet fag and passed someone who could have been the killer in the doorway as she was going back in and they were coming out.'

'There are advantages to a sneaky smoking break, then,' Jo put in, grinning meaningfully at Ted.

Ted smiled back, then asked, 'Description?'

'Not much of one, boss. Witness is five-six and said the man was about three or four inches taller than her, medium build. She didn't much notice what he was wearing but she said he had some sort of shoulder bag as it bumped against her when they both went through the doorway. It was sometime around midnight, is all she can say for timing, and they don't have CCTV on the front door, so nothing from that.'

'What about the women involved in the second and third cases? Are we any closer to finding them? Ted asked, looking round.

'Unfortunately, from the laptops and phones, I've not been

able to pin down any definitely planned meet-ups for either of the second two victims,' Océane told them. 'Both of those two, although active on the various dating sites, seemed to prefer to leave it to chance. Both of them had been searching online for pubs doing singles nights and the like for the days when they would be in the area.'

'So we're basically down to legwork on that side of things. I don't suppose we got lucky with DNA for either woman from the room or the sheets and found they have convictions and are on the database?'

'No such luck, boss,' Sal told him.

He was in charge of collating all the forensic evidence from the three crime scenes.

'So why is everyone so convinced this Linda Lovelace person isn't just another woman? And why that she must be the man in the pub?' DC Eccles asked.

At least he was showing something of an interest, although again he showed he was not up to speed on the case.

'Jezza and I have had the privilege of reading through all the email exchanges between Linda Lovelace and the first victim. It's not exactly scientific, but we both agree the wording is wrong for a woman. It's much more like a man trying to write like a woman,' Ted told him. 'That, and the timings, make it likely that Linda and the man in the pub are in fact the same person.'

'That and the blindingly bloody obvious factor of not giving the first victim a mobile phone number,' Océane said scornfully then, seeing the DC's face still looking puzzled, she explained, with barely concealed impatience, 'Well, if any of the men phoned so-called Linda and were answered with a gravelly baritone, it would be a bit of a giveaway, wouldn't it?'

'So with no phone number and only throwaway email addresses, how are we going to track down Linda? And more importantly, how are we going to get to the next potential victim before he does?' Ted asked the team.

'Boss, I've been digging through the files for people who've been in to report financial scams. Most of them never go on to press charges because they're too ashamed. One or two have, but those have gone to court and been resolved. Different person in each,' Maurice told them. 'That means publicity, in both cases. So if someone was after revenge for one of those, why the random killings? They would know the actual identities of the people involved.'

'Sir,' DC Winters began hesitantly. 'What about inquests? Have there been any cases recently where someone may have taken their own life because of some financial scam or another?'

'Very good point,' Ted told him. 'Maurice, can you add that to your list of things to check, please. Also I'll ask our reporter friend when Jo and I go to see him, hopefully today. Meanwhile, how are we going to get the jump on our killer before he strikes again? Because if he's hoping to target someone specific, he will probably keep going until he finds them. But if he's just randomly killing anyone who may be doing the same thing as whoever he has the grudge against, then we really do have a problem.'

'We could all get out there and hit the singles scene,' DC Eccles suggested. 'Then if we see someone who looks like the suspect, follow him back to the hotel and...'

Ted carefully unbuttoned the cuff of his left shirt sleeve, pushed it and his jacket sleeve back and held his arm up, palm towards the South Manchester three.

'I'm weapons trained, ex-SFO and I have black belts in four martial arts. This is what happened when I was trying to disarm a trained soldier with a knife,' he told them. The scar on his hand and forearm was healing well but was still pronounced. 'And I'll spare Maurice his blushes by not asking him to show you his scar from the same attacker.'

'Ugh, yes, who wants to see Maurice's belly right after breakfast?' Jezza grinned, prompting a chuckle from the team.

'Settle down, everyone. We're dealing with seven potential murders here. Let's keep it respectful,' Ted reminded them, then continued, 'It's a reasonable enough suggestion, DC Eccles. The problem is, we would have no way of getting back-up in place and we don't know this man's capabilities. All we know is that he is armed and his attacks are frenzied.

'The other thing we need to consider is that our man would appear to follow his target back to the hotel but then wait for the woman he's with to leave before he strikes. It could be that he doesn't want to scare them, or to implicate them. That to me tends to suggest that he's doing this on behalf of a woman, but that's just speculation. So he's hanging around somewhere, and he might well spot anyone watching him.

'For an operation such as you suggest to succeed, I would want back-up both inside and outside the bedroom and I can't, at the moment see any way of doing that. We would have to go down the route of running a sting, a honey-trap, and that's not always easy to run, or to get approval for. But it's a valid suggestion, thank you.'

Eccles looked stunned, both at Ted's revelation and at the unexpected praise. Ted always found he got better results with a bit of encouragement.

'Boss, we could at least try that way, without it being a sting,' Jezza began. She was comfortable enough with the boss to cut across him when he started to protest. 'Just hear me out before you say no. If we find out where the dating nights are in the area, we could start going to some of them, in twos, for safety. Then if any of us does see someone who could be Linda, we could call back up before we follow them. We only need to stop them on suspicion and do a search. If it's someone walking round with an offensive weapon in their possession, we could haul them in for that, then get fingerprints and DNA and we might get our murderer.'

'I'll think about it. It will need clearance from both Superintendent Caldwell, and Superintendent Baker, especially in light of what happened to me and Maurice. But I will definitely consider it. Steve, can you start drawing up a list of all the likely venues across the Greater Manchester area, then we'll look at dividing up who covers what. And that is only if I get clearance, which will certainly not be before next week at the earliest. Is that clear everyone? DC Vine? And it certainly won't be an excuse for a pub crawl on expenses.'

There were murmurs of assent, but Ted was not entirely convinced by Jezza's. She could be strong-willed and impetuous at times. He made a mental note to get Jo and particularly Maurice to keep a close eye on her, especially when he was away for the weekend.

As the meeting broke up, DC Hope sidled up to Jezza with a suggestive leer and said, 'Perhaps you and I could team up for a pub night sometime, darlin'.'

Jezza smiled sweetly at him and her tone was pleasant, although her milky-blue eyes flashed like Arctic ice as she replied, 'I'd rather eat my own eyeballs.'

'So what are you, Jezza the Lezzer?' Hope asked.

Maurice was not far away, near enough to overhear the exchange. He moved closer and said mildly, 'Like I said before, I wouldn't make her angry, if I were you.'

Hope's face broke into a sneer.

'So you two are at it, then? Well, you're welcome, mate. She's not my type anyway,' and he turned on his heel and made for the door.

Jezza was about to storm after him, with a face like thunder, but Maurice put out a gentle arm to stop her.

'Just let it go, Jezza. Like my old grandfather used to say, you can't expect more than a grunt from a pig.'

Ted called Pocket Billiards as soon as he got back to his own office. He wanted to set up a meeting at lunchtime, so that he could introduce him to Jo and find out what he knew about Sabden House. As soon as he mentioned the meal would be on him, the journalist was miraculously available. Ted had never known him to pass up on the chance of free food.

'I warn you now, watching him eat is not pleasant,' Ted told Jo as they walked the short distance to The Grapes.

'Is this another sort of initiation, boss?' Jo asked him. 'If I can watch him eat and keep my own food down, I've earned my place on the team?'

'I think that's a given by now,' Ted told him. 'I just need you to keep eyes and ears on Jezza this weekend. She can be a bit impetuous. I don't want her going off being a maverick if she thinks I'm far enough away not to know.'

As usual, the reporter was waiting expectantly at the bar, not having bought himself anything until Ted appeared to put his hand in his pocket. Ted made the introductions, ordered and paid for the food and drink, then the three of them found themselves a quiet corner to sit down.

'What do you know about the Sabden House flats, Alastair?'

'Prime development site. There are big plans afoot, under the radar at the moment, to get rid of the tenants, demolish them and put up expensive new private ones.'

'And when you say get rid of…?'

'I know there have been some deaths there, but just junkies and alkies. I keep being told they're misadventure, at most. Are you telling me there's more to them than it first seems?'

His nose was positively twitching, both at the prospect of a news story and at the sight of the fat steak sandwich and chips which had just been put in front of him.

'You do know that the latest death was Honest John?' Ted asked.

Everyone knew John, especially the press, as he had loved to phone them, as well as the police, with his false confessions.

'Yeah, we got a good story out of that, getting that tub of lard out through the window and all that,' Alastair said, cramming steak and chips into his mouth as he spoke.

Ted fought the urge to punch him for his total lack of respect and human decency. Instead he pushed the press release on their murder suspect across the table to him, assuring the journalist that he had more there than any other paper.

'It's not official at the moment, and I'd like to keep it that way, but we are looking closely into those deaths, too. Jo, here, will be your contact for that. So anything at all you can tell him will be helpful. But for now, I'll have to run and leave you two to it.'

With a shameless wink in Jo's direction, he grabbed his own sandwich, sloped off and left his right-hand man to the delights of watching Pocket Billiards eating.

Chapter Twenty-three

Jezza bounced up behind Maurice and Steve, heading across the car park, as the team members were all going home at the end of the day. The three of them had become good friends since Jezza had joined the team and they had got to know her.

'So how about it, Maurice? You and me, on a pub crawl tonight, round all the town pubs?' she asked, linking arms with both of them. 'Steve will babysit Tommy, won't you, Steve?'

She treated him like a kid brother, completely oblivious to the adoring looks he was always sending her way, when he wasn't drooling over Océane.

'Jezza, it was only this morning the boss said a big fat no to anyone doing anything until he gives the go-ahead,' Maurice reminded her. 'We don't yet know how dangerous our suspect is and I can tell you for nothing, I don't want another knife in the guts, thanks very much.'

'Oh, come on, Maurice,' she wheedled. 'It won't come to that. Just a couple of pals going out for a few drinks after work. Where's the harm? I promise faithfully that if we see anyone who even looks like him, we'll phone for back-up straight away and not do anything until they arrive. Brownie's honour.'

'I bet you were never a Brownie. Too much of a rebel,' he told her, but she could see straight away that he was weakening. Jezza could twist them both round her little finger, and she knew it.

'Go on, please, this evening, just a quick round of the pubs, see what we can see. I'm buying. You can drive the Golf. I'll order in pizza for Steve and Tommy, and I'll treat you to something nice while we're out.'

Maurice laughed.

'I suppose 'you can drive the Golf' is Jezza-speak for you're going to get hammered so I need to be the sensible grown-up to see we get home in one piece.'

He looked down at her fondly. It was hard to say no to Jezza in full-on charm offensive. With her drama training, she could be whatever she needed to be to persuade him.

'You do know the boss is going to kill us, slowly, if he finds out? Especially me,' he warned her.

'Fabulous, thanks so much, Maurice. You'll see, we'll have a blast and who knows, we might just spot a killer to catch.' She flung her arms around his neck to give him a kiss on the cheek, then planted one on Steve's for good measure, making him blush furiously. 'See you at mine, half seven? Pepperoni pizza, Steve? Stay over after, both of you. We can finish off the pizza when we get back, if you leave us any.'

They often did stay at Jezza's place, especially when Steve had been babysitting and Jezza was out late. The spacious flat was big enough, and Jezza's room had a walk-in wet room, as well as the bathroom close by, so there were never problems with four of them in the flat.

Taking it as decided, she was gone in a clunk of the VW's door and a squeal of tyres as she pulled away, waving gaily at them.

Maurice shook his head.

'I'm not quite sure what I've let myself in for,' he said. 'And I still reckon the boss is going to skin us alive, if he finds out. Are you all right with this, Steve?'

'I'll have to be, won't I?' the younger man muttered, looking anything but all right. 'You shouldn't be doing this, and you know it. You should have said no.'

'Eh, Steve, lad,' Maurice sighed, looking across in the

ONLY THE LONELY

direction in which Jezza had just left. 'I wish I knew how to say
no to our Jezza.'

The two of them arrived at Jezza's stylish apartment at the
appointed hour. Steve was in his casual clothes but Maurice
had made an effort to smarten up for the occasion. He didn't
want to show Jezza up, nor to look too much like her dad,
although he was old enough to be.

As usual, they were both met by a barrage of questions
from Tommy, Jezza's younger brother, demanding to know
everything about their plans for the evening, and the exact time
they would be back.

'I told you, Tom, I can't tell you for sure,' Jezza told him.
'We're going out on police business. Important undercover
work. It just isn't possible to say for sure. But we will be back,
and Steve's here with you, so there's nothing to worry about.
And your pizza will be here any time now, so don't eat too
much.'

Tommy liked precision in his life, and his sister's
sometimes erratic hours unsettled him. But he loved the idea of
her doing undercover work like the police he enjoyed watching
on television, in films and dramas.

'Don't let him stay up too late, Steve. And don't you, either.
Make yourself at home, and we'll be back when we're back.
You have the spare room tonight and let Maurice kip on the
sofa, in case you're already asleep when we get back.'

She picked up the car keys from the hall table and, with a
final wave over her shoulder, she breezed out of the door in a
waft of expensive perfume. Maurice trailed in her wake, still
convinced he was doing the wrong thing, though doubtless for
the right reasons.

They had a lively evening and visited several pubs, but
there was no sign of anyone resembling their suspect. Jezza
was taking Maurice's agreement to drive her Golf as licence to
drink freely. Since his operation, Maurice had been drinking

209

much less, partly because of the medication he was on. He limited himself to half a lager, then switched to soft drinks. He was already convinced the boss was going jump all over him if he got wind of what they'd been up to. If he got pulled for driving over the limit as well, that would be the end of him.

'You know, you look really good since the op, Maurice,' Jezza told him, blinking up at him, with the effects of the vodka shots she'd been consuming. She draped an arm round his neck and scrutinised his face from close up. 'You're a really nice bloke. For a bloke, I mean. You should find yourself someone nice. What about Megan?'

'Did you really ask me out to look for suspects, or to sort out my love life?' he asked her, smiling fondly. 'Megan wouldn't look twice at me; she could find someone much better.'

'Rubbish! You're a really nice man. A really, really nice man.' Jezza was clearly rather more drunk than he'd realised.

Maurice thought it was about time he took her home, or at least persuaded her to drink something soft to try to sober her up a bit. He was perfectly sober and had been taking stock of the other drinkers in each pub they'd been in, so that at least one of them was doing what they'd set out to do - looking for the prime suspect.

He went up to the bar to get some mineral water with ice and a slice for both of them, taking the chance to scan the room from a different angle. There was still no sign of anyone who could possibly be their man. No one sitting alone, watching the others. No one who looked the right height or build for the vague description they had of him, and from the CCTV images. It had been a pleasant evening, and he'd enjoyed the meal, but he decided it was high time he was taking Jezza home. Especially if he wanted her to turn up for work the next morning not looking like someone who'd been out on the drink the night before.

'I'm really pleased you're my friend, Maurice,' Jezza told

him expansively when he sat down and put the drinks in front of them. 'What's this?' she peered suspiciously at the tall glass in front of her.

'Vodka and tonic,' he told her. 'I thought it would make a change from straight shots.'

She was clearly too far gone to notice she'd been tricked into drinking mineral water. He hoped it would dilute what she'd already drunk. It was still an unsteady and giggling Jezza he helped back to the Golf and drove back to her flat.

The lights were off and there was neither sight nor sound of Steve or Tommy. Steve was one of the few people who could tire Tommy out enough to make him sleep well, with his patient help in finding endless trivia answers on the Internet for him. Maurice went to put the coffee machine on in the kitchen while Jezza flopped on to the sofa where he would shortly be sleeping, hopefully, if she could manage to get herself off to bed without too much trouble.

He brought in steaming mugs of black coffee for both of them, and encouraged Jezza to drink hers.

'I had a really great night tonight,' she told him. 'You're really good company, Maurice, d'you know that?'

She snuggled closer to him and planted a kiss on his cheek. She could sense his growing discomfort at her closeness, so she reached up and pulled his head towards her, kissing him on the lips.

Maurice groaned and tried to pull away, hating himself for weakening but knowing he was perilously near to being past the stage of saying no, even if he'd wanted to.

'No, Jezza, this isn't right. You're drunk. If you were sober, you wouldn't be doing this.'

She held on to him so he couldn't move away, her mouth next to his ear.

'Come on, Maurice. I know it's what you want. And I need to get back in the saddle. I haven't been with anyone since...' she left the sentence hanging. 'And I can't think of anyone else

I'd rather it was for the first time since then than you. You're a really nice man. Kind, gentle. And you're practically my best friend. I want it to be like that.'

She slid off the sofa and tried to stand up, but immediately overbalanced into a giggling heap on the floor. Maurice stood up, gently pulled her to her feet, and steered her to her bedroom. Carefully, he eased off her shoes, slid her jacket off, then peeled back the duvet and helped her to lie down.

'Come to bed with me, Maurice,' she said sleepily, but she was already nodding off and soon her deep regular breathing told him she was asleep.

He pulled the duvet back up and tucked it protectively around her. Then he took off his own jacket and shoes and lay down on top of the duvet next to her, not close enough to touch her, just watching her sleeping peacefully.

At some point, he must have fallen asleep too as he awoke with a start, some hours later, to find her propped up one one elbow, looking down at him and smiling gently, her features clearly defined in the street light through the curtains.

'You look very cute when you're asleep,' she said softly. 'I'm awake now, and I'm completely sober. And I really would like it, very much, if you would please make love to me, Maurice Brown. My best friend.'

Steve was already in the kitchen by the time Maurice got up the next morning, carefully extricating himself from the tangle of the still-sleeping Jezza's arms and legs. It meant he couldn't sneak past to get his bag from the living room for clean clothes. He decided the only way was to bluff it out, so he went into the kitchen in just his trousers and greeted Steve breezily.

'Morning, Steve, you're up early. I hope we didn't wake you up, rolling in last night.'

Steve had the coffee machine on but instead of returning the greeting, he spun round and landed a punch full in the centre of Maurice's face.

'You absolute piece of shit,' he spat, nursing his hand.

Steve was no fighter and the hand had been badly injured in an assault not long ago, so it didn't appreciate his actions.

Blood spouted from Maurice's split lip and his nose, as he grabbed for a kitchen towel, still trying to bluster his innocence.

'How could you, Maurice? After what she's been through?'

Steve's voice was rising in pitch and intensity, and brought Jezza hurrying in from her room, knotting her dressing gown around her waist.

'Keep it down!' she hissed. 'Tommy's not awake yet. You know how raised voices freak him out. I don't want him starting the day badly.'

Then she appeared to see Maurice for the first time, dripping blood everywhere and demanded, 'What the hell is going on in here? Steve, whatever you think happened, you're wrong.'

At that moment, they heard Tommy's door open and he came padding into the kitchen in bare feet and pyjamas, looking agitated.

'What's wrong? Why is everybody shouting? Maurice, why are you bleeding? I don't like it when you shout.'

Jezza bent down towards him, glaring at Steve.

'Tommy, it's fine. Everything's all right. Maurice and Steve were just being silly and Maurice got hurt by accident. But it's really nothing to worry about at all. Is it, Steve?'

Steve hesitated, but in the face of Jezza's furious look, he climbed down and looked at Tommy.

'That's right, Tom. We were just mucking about and Maurice's nose got in the way of my hand. But it's all fine, we're all still friends. Why don't you go and get ready for school? The child-minder will be here in a minute to take you.'

Jezza smiled her gratitude at him and put a hand on his arm as Tommy obediently disappeared to start getting ready.

'Steve, thank you for thinking you were defending my

honour, or something, but honestly, it wasn't like that. But it's sweet of you.'

The three barely exchanged a word over an awkward breakfast. Steve refused to ride with Maurice in his car, preferring instead to go with Jezza in the Golf. It gave her the opportunity to talk to him, to try to explain how it had been, though he was still angry and unreceptive.

As soon as Ted called the team to order for the morning briefing, he could see that something was badly wrong with the dynamics. He saw Steve's angry face and the way he nursed his hand, the anxious looks Jezza kept throwing at him and at Maurice, and Maurice's cut lip, red nose and guilty expression. He could guess what it all meant and he was not pleased. He was glad he'd told Foster's team they didn't need to come over this morning. They knew what needed doing, and they were also being interviewed by Superintendent Fletcher at some point during the day, so needed to make themselves available.

The whole team felt the tension the three had brought in to work with them and it was affecting everyone's concentration. Jo was able to feed back on his discussions with Pocket Billiards and a lead he had been given on an inquest with a suicide verdict, where mention had been made of bad financial investments.

'It was all very vague, though, he couldn't remember much detail.'

'Give whatever you have to Maurice to follow up. Maurice, check it out with the coroner's officer and see if you can find the detail. Particularly find any next of kin. It's a promising lead,' Ted said tersely.

He was still furious with Maurice and finding it hard to hide the fact.

'Océane, anything else for us from the computers or phones yet?'

'Rather too many photos of Mr Gildyke's not particularly

impressive dick, boss, but so far not much more,' she replied, raising a small chuckle from the team. 'Why do some men think that's something which a woman might find an incentive to date them?'

'Jo, can you work with Sal on Sabden House? I want to know everything about that building and the plans for its future. Do we know when the PM on John is yet?'

'Tomorrow morning, boss, first thing,' Jo told him. 'I spoke to Professor Nelson. Apparently they need to make some special arrangements to handle it, given his size and weight.'

Ted nodded his understanding.

'I imagine so. I'll do that one. I'll be glad of my weekend away afterwards, but it's the least I can do for John.

'Right, you know what you need to be working on, let's get to it. Maurice, my office. Now.'

Maurice was fully expecting the kick-trick and a thorough bollocking. When the boss simply closed the door quietly behind them, he knew he was deep in the shit. Maurice was one of the few who had ever seen Ted close to losing it so he knew that when he reached ice-cold near-silent mode, things did not bode well.

Unusually, Ted didn't ask Maurice to sit down, nor did he put the kettle on. He didn't even sit down himself, he was so angry. He stood behind his chair, gripping the back of it, his knuckles whitening.

'Tell me that what I think happened didn't in fact happen,' he began.

'Boss, it's not like you think, honestly. Steve just got hold of the wrong end of the stick.'

'You're all adults. What you do in your private lives is none of my business. Once it starts spilling over into work, it becomes my business. And I don't like what I've seen this morning. You're old enough to be her father ...'

Ted pulled himself up short, aware that he was about to betray a confidence, if he wasn't careful about what he said.

They were interrupted by a knock on the door, which then opened before Ted said anything and Jezza marched in, wearing her determined expression.

'Please go back to your desk, DC Vine,' Ted told her sharply.

'No, boss, I won't. Sorry, but if you're talking about me, I want to be in here, putting my side of things. I really appreciate you and Steve looking out for me, but I'm a grown-up, I make my own decisions. What happened last night was great. It was two close friends getting closer. But that's all it was. Nobody's business but ours. Just a wonderful one-off that's not going anywhere.'

Ted caught the fleeting look of sadness on Maurice's face and realised that he had held higher hopes and expectations.

'Boss, seriously, it's sweet of you and Steve to worry, but this has nothing to do with work. I'm sorry it spilled over into the nick this morning. I'll talk to Steve again when he's calmed down a bit, and smooth it all over. But it won't happen again. None of it will happen again.'

Ted looked sternly from one to the other.

'It better not,' he warned. 'Now get out, the pair of you, and do some work. And for goodness sake make it right with Steve. It takes something to fire him up to the point of violence. And don't bring your domestic disputes into work again.'

Chapter Twenty-four

'Morning, Edwin. I believe this is someone you knew, so I imagine it's not going to be easy for you,' Professor Nelson greeted Ted as he arrived for the post-mortem on Honest John on Friday morning.

'Morning Bizzie. Yes, this is our Honest John, our local confessor. John Jacobs. A very nice, highly intelligent man with a lot of sadness in his life,' Ted told her. 'He's confessed to every sudden death on our patch for as long as I can remember. It was the fact that he hadn't claimed the last couple that made us send someone round to check on him and they found him dead.'

'Dead for three days when he was found. And I'm assuming, given the degree of his clinical obesity, that he was diabetic? We've had to make quite a few special arrangements for the post-mortem. It's comparatively rare to have to work on someone of this size.'

'Yes, diabetic and on insulin. Very good at managing his condition, too. Just not good at controlling his weight.'

'And I'm assuming, from your interest in the case, that this is something other than a straightforward case of natural causes?'

'We have a theory, linked to the other deaths at the same address,' Ted told her. 'It's vague, at the moment, but I'm hoping your findings today might take it further in the right direction.'

Ted disliked post-mortems at the best of times. Watching

the Professor work on Honest John was particularly hard and he was greedily sucking his Fisherman's Friends the whole time to help him get through it. He kept thinking what a sad waste it was of an intelligent man, and how cynical a way to dispose of him, if his theory was correct.

As usual, between being her usual brisk and efficient self, Bizzie found time to make small talk, of sorts, with Ted. The two had become somewhat unlikely friends. He asked after her mother.

'Mummy's had another fall, and sacked yet more home carers. I fear we're rapidly approaching the time when I will have to think about putting her in a home, and I'm dreading it. She is so independent. She likes to do everything her own way. But I can't see an alternative. I couldn't possibly cope with her at my house and I'm not yet ready to give up work to be her full-time carer. Nor would she let me.

'By the way, Edwin, I should have warned you, this is going to take considerably longer than usual, because of the practicalities. We've even had to call in special implements. I don't want to be indelicate but there's a lot more of him to get through before we reach the revealing bits.'

One of the other pathologists, James Barrington, was assisting her with this one, because of the sheer size of the body they were working on, with one of the mortuary assistants on hand as well.

'It's fine, I've set the whole morning aside. In fact, I'm trying to keep my workload light all day. I'm supposed to be going to Somerset with Trev later on. His kid sister is competing in some horsey event or other at her school. Trev says if I don't go with him, he's leaving me.'

'Then I'd better make sure I work as quickly as possible, so I don't delay you. We've already made a start on blood analysis, as a diabetic coma had been suggested as the likely cause of death.'

'While I'm here, I wanted to ask you about the knife

wounds to our murder victims. I know you saw the wound inflicted by Danny Boy on the victim of our last case, and you commented on its precision. That was confirmed by him being a trained soldier. What about the knife wounds on our three hotel victims?'

'Different kettle of fish altogether,' she said briskly. 'Very haphazard, just a case of slash and stab anywhere that was handy, I would say. There were several potentially fatal stab wounds, but there were also a great many that didn't serve a lot of purpose, other than wanting to inflict pain and injury. I would say a completely different type of attacker. Your soldier was very precise and accurate. He knew exactly where to use a blade for lethal effect. This was much more frenzied, no degree of control or precision at all. Does that help?'

'Enormously, thank you. We're a long way off catching this killer, so I'm trying to form as much of a picture about him as I can. Neither Maurice nor I are keen on being the wrong side of an expert knife-wielder again for quite some time.'

'I can see that Mr Jacobs did take reasonably good care of himself, apart from his weight issues,' she said, turning her concentration back to the task in hand. 'His legs and feet are in particularly good condition, given his weight and his diabetes. In fact, other than the sheer size of him, he's in better shape than I would have expected.'

'His flat was always immaculate, too. It cost him an enormous effort to do any tidying up at all, but he did it. Almost obsessively so.'

'I'm approaching the bit I know you possibly dislike the most, so you might need another lozenge,' she warned him. 'I'm just about to examine the stomach contents.'

She was right. It was the point at which, if he didn't exercise extreme self-control, Ted always risked losing his own stomach contents. He could never get over the smell. He wondered how Bizzie and the other pathologists seemed to have grown immune to it. Unsurprisingly, with a cadaver the size of Honest John, there was rather a lot to come out.

'Interesting,' Bizzie said, peering closely at the dark and noxious liquid with the overpowering smell. 'I'll spare you having to get too close, but I can immediately identify two factors. One is chocolate and the other, unless I am very much mistaken, is some sort of sweet dessert wine.'

Ted was impressed, and had no idea how she could tell that from the foul substance under her nose.

'That confirms our findings at the scene. Someone had sent John a fancy hamper, and it looked as if he'd tucked into the wine and the chocolates, as well as various cakes and pastries. And I should just mention that John's insulin and the rest of his kit were missing from the flat, if that makes a difference.'

'Oh, good gracious, yes,' she said emphatically. 'If he downed that lot with no means of bringing his blood sugars back under control fairly rapidly, I would expect us to be looking at Hyperosmolar Hyperglycaemic State. It's a potentially life-threatening medical emergency, with a high mortality rate.'

'John was always careful with his medication. He ordered all his food in, as he couldn't get out to go shopping. He was well aware that he ate far too many pizzas and crisps, but I've never known him drink alcohol, and certainly not binge on chocolate. He knew the risks.'

'Sometimes if someone is very low for some reason, they do unexpected things,' she suggested.

Ted nodded.

'Agreed. But it doesn't explain the absence of insulin in the flat. He should have had plenty; I checked with the pharmacy which supplied him.'

'Then that would make an extremely cynical and rather effective way of disposing of someone with his medical history, I would imagine. We should get the blood results through quickly. One of the advantages of being based here in the hospital is that I can get such things prioritised when I need to, and I told them you would be waiting for them.'

She carried on working, then said, 'I can certainly tell you that he suffered a myocardial infarction. A massive heart attack. Hardly surprising, given the strain on his system. I'll still be very interested in the blood results as I'm certain there will be something there to explain what precipitated it.'

True to her word, the results appeared rapidly. Bizzie scanned them through then turned back to Ted.

'As I thought. His blood sugar level was catastrophically high. With Type 2 diabetes, his body would produce some insulin of its own, but barely enough for everyday life, and certainly not remotely enough for a sugar overload of this intensity. Based on these results, and the background information you've provided, I will certainly be reporting this to the coroner as suspicious. A heart attack is a natural cause of death, but what led to it in this case raises questions. There will need to be an inquest, of course, and I'm imagining you may well be investigating it as a possible murder?'

'We certainly will. The drugs overdoses could so easily have been just a factor of their lifestyle. Even the alcohol-related death may have been innocent enough. But this? Finding John dead with no trace of insulin anywhere in his flat? That's not right. It's just not right.'

Ted was keen to be back at the station to get Jo and Sal started on the Sabden House case, now armed with the preliminary post-mortem findings on Honest John. He paused to pick up his lunch on the way back, to eat at his desk while he caught up. He wanted everything as under control as it could be before he took his short weekend off. He fully intended to be back in work well within forty-eight hours. After a tough morning, he decided it was definitely a smoked salmon and cream cheese bagel kind of day again, especially as he was not sure where or what time he and Trev would be eating that evening.

At least the atmosphere in the office was slightly better

when Ted got back. Maurice was working away slowly but methodically at his desk, trawling through old reports. Steve and Océane had their heads together over the computers, but at least Steve no longer looked intent on killing Maurice. Just as well, since he lodged with him and Maurice had always been kind to him.

Rob and Virgil were over at South Manchester, keeping an eye on Foster's remaining team, checking witnesses there, still hoping to find more details of the third victim, George Gildyke's, last hours. Mike Hallam, Jezza and Megan were out somewhere, working the case, or possibly taking their lunch break, as the team staggered their hours so that someone was always available.

Jo and Sal had already started a file on Sabden House. Ted suggested they all get together in Jo's office, as there was more room there than in his own. He told them about the findings of the morning's post-mortem, and the likely conclusion to be drawn that someone had deliberately and cynically set out to kill Honest John, or at least to cause his death.

'Pocket Billiards gave me some good leads for the whole Sabden House saga. He's itching to make a big scoop out of it, so I promised him first dibs on anything we get about the deaths. I hope that was all right, boss?'

'Exactly what I would have done,' Ted agreed. 'It's the best way to use him. I hope watching him eat didn't rob you of your appetite?'

'Yeah, thanks for that, boss,' Jo laughed good-naturedly. 'Are there any more of these initiation tests heading my way shortly?'

'With the prospect of forty-eight hours off in the middle of two big cases, I'm not going to do anything to rock the boat,' Ted assured him. 'Right, let's see what our computer experts have for us. I'm hoping our Linda Lovelace will have the decency to behave while I'm away, but I'm interested to know if there's been any chat from him, suggesting he's gearing up to kill again. There has to be a way we can get the jump on him.'

'Boss, Steve and I are monitoring every likely chat group, every possible hang-out, looking for Linda Lovelace,' Océane told Ted, when he went back out to the main office. 'Even where we find a trace of him, we can't go any further as he just seems to make direct contact with anyone interesting, then they switch to email. We've no way yet of tracing him via email, because the only addresses we have are the throwaway kind.'

'So he's going on to these dating sites, targeting men mentioning being involved in financial investments, then setting up meetings with ones who fit his personal profile?'

'Boss, these are mostly not dating sites,' Océane told him patiently. 'They're blatant shagging sites. The kind where anyone looking for a bit of action, purely a one-off, can find some. Ideal for men, and women, like our travelling salesmen, who are going to be in a strange town and looking for a bit of no-strings nooky. I suspect our first lady, Mrs Angus, wasn't quite aware of the site she had enrolled herself in. She, like you, might have thought it was for dating, not just shagging.'

Steve went pink at her choice of words while Ted shook his head in bewilderment. He'd never been much for one-night stands, even before he got together with Trev.

'If, as is looking likely, you decide that we may need to draw him out by baiting him, one thing's for certain. Any mention of investment seems to be a magnet to him. All the people we've found that he's contacted so far have hinted, or even claimed outright, to have a finger on various financial pulses,' Océane continued.

'So if we can't yet trace him, can we contact anyone he's been in touch with and warn them?' Ted asked.

'Theoretically possible, at a pinch, but seriously, boss? The kind of people hanging out on some of these sites would think it was an even bigger turn-on that the supposed woman they think they're going to meet, named after one of the most famous porn stars ever, might actually be out to kill them. I

223

will try, but I wouldn't hold your breath. And I really am starting to think that you will need to be looking at a carefully planned and managed entrapment operation as the best way forward.'

Ted took himself off back to his office to eat his bagel and make sure his paperwork was up to date. He didn't want any nasty surprises at the last minute, preventing him from getting away on time. His instructions from Trev had been clear. He made himself a note to speak to both the Ice Queen and Jim Baker again about trying to bring Linda Lovelace to them, as they weren't having any success to date in tracing him.

He was interrupted in his eating by a knock at the door and Maurice coming hesitantly in when told to do so, looking more than a little wary.

'Come in and sit down, Maurice,' Ted told him. 'Is everything sorted now, between you and Steve? All friends once more?'

'More or less, boss. And it really wasn't like he, or you, thought …'

Ted waved him to silence.

'Water under the bridge now. Let's keep it that way. We have work to do. So, what have you got for me?'

'The suicide inquest, boss. A woman called Elaine Cummings. She lost everything on a dodgy investment deal that went tits up. She was divorced, she'd kept the house, and had a bit of money. Someone she met online persuaded her to do some sort of equity release scheme, safely insured, can't possibly go wrong. You know the sort of spiel these people use. Anyway, it did go wrong. Disastrously so. It was some complicated pyramid-type scheme, and her money wasn't going into the safe as houses investments she thought it was. She lost absolutely everything. The house was repossessed. Of course, none of the insurance policies were worth Jack-shit so no recourse there either. She finished up in a grotty bedsit with a shared bathroom and a wonky electric heater. She sat in the bath and pulled it in with her.'

Ted put his bagel to one side, suddenly robbed of his appetite. He couldn't begin to imagine the level of despair which would bring someone to an action like that.

'Next of kin?'

'Still the ex-husband. He gave evidence to the inquest. He was a maintenance worker on the oil rigs up in Scotland, but they got divorced some time before all this. It seems like he still cared for his wife, stayed in touch, tried to support her as much as he could. When it all went wrong, she broke off contact with him, maybe ashamed of how she'd been conned.'

'So now make my day and tell me you know exactly who this man is and where, because if that's not a motive for murdering anyone selling dodgy investments, I don't know what is.'

Maurice shook his head.

'No can do at the moment, boss. I have his name, from the inquest reports, but they only mention him working on the rigs, no local address. I've been on to the coroner's office for the address where they sent the witness summons, but that was the rigs too. The wife's house was repossessed so no trace there. I've rung the company he worked for but they say he left when his wife killed herself. Had some sort of total breakdown, dropped off the radar altogether.'

'Please tell me there is some good news, so I can go off for the weekend happy?'

'Yes, boss, great news. His name really is John Smith – the wife reverted to her maiden name. And according to Steve's Internet search, there are currently less than twelve thousand of them in the UK.'

Ted wanted a final get-together with Jo before he disappeared for his weekend away. He knew the team would be fine without him, especially with Jo at the helm, but he still liked to be involved at every stage.

'I'm just hoping Linda does the decent thing and gives himself a weekend off, too. I'll be setting off back first thing on Sunday morning, so I'll be in for the afternoon. I know you can cope, it's not that I don't have faith in you …'

'It's fine, boss. You're the SIO, the buck stops with you if we screw up in your absence. Not that we will. And I won't even call you unless it really is something we can't handle. I can always call the Super if I'm worried. You go and have a good time.'

Ted's mobile interrupted them. Trevor. His tone brooked no argument.

'If you're not on your way out of the door already, you are in serious trouble.'

'I am, I am, honestly,' Ted lied shamelessly. 'Well, I'm just putting my coat on as we speak and then I'm out the door. Jo can alibi me,' he looked beseechingly at his DI and handed him the phone, adding, 'But speak English, so I know what you're saying about me.'

Ted had previously told Jo that Spanish was one of the languages in which his partner was fluent. He grabbed his coat and briefcase, so that at least that part of the story was true, as Jo started speaking.

'Hola, Trev, qué tal? The boss says I have to speak English so he can understand. Nice to talk to you, I've heard a lot about you. And yes, it's true, the boss is just putting his coat on and he'll be with you shortly. Have a good weekend.'

He ended the call and handed the phone back with a laugh.

'And I thought I was hen-pecked.'

Ted smiled his thanks and, with a hasty, 'Thanks Jo, I owe you, big time,' he was on his way.

Chapter Twenty-five

It was never easy, waking Trev in the morning, especially at what was, for him, such an ungodly hour. They'd arrived late at their hotel after a long journey down on the bike, stopping for a meal on the way. Trev had promised to be up and about to help Shewee get ready for the event, so Ted brewed up with the small kettle in the room and made sure he got him up in plenty of time to be down at the stable-yard at the appointed hour.

There was no hotel breakfast available so early, but Trev had assured Ted that there would be food available at the event. Bacon rolls would be on the go first thing for grooms, spectators and any competitors whose butterflies in the stomach allowed them to eat before competing.

A part of Ted was worrying about how things were going back at the nick without him, but another part was looking forward to being able to see a different side of his partner, about which he knew little. Trev had enjoyed a privileged upbringing - the best boarding schools, his own horse, endless holidays abroad. All that had changed when he came out to his parents, just before his sixteenth birthday, and they had reacted by throwing him out to go and live with his much more liberal aunt.

Ted often wondered how much Trev missed his former life. He still rode, occasionally, with Willow. But it was a far cry from what he'd been used to. Ted worried whether life with a middle-aged copper in a modest semi in Stockport was enough for him, despite Trev's assurances that it was. He was pleased that Trev would at least have some contact with his previous life, even if it was only acting as his kid sister's groom.

Shewee was already up and busy when they got to the stables. She had her horse, Blue, tied up outside his box and was busily plaiting his mane, while standing on a box. She looked decidedly green round the gills with nerves.

'Can you do tails?' was her only form of greeting, more of a wail of desperation, in Trev's direction. 'I'm crap at tails. Lola was supposed to help me but she was out on the lash last night and she's still asleep.'

'Morning, brother, morning, Ted,' Trev chided gently. 'Morning, sister, morning, Blue, and yes, it so happens that I'm brilliant at tails, though a bit out of practice.'

He moved confidently round to the back of the horse, speaking quietly and putting a hand on its side first, then got to work on the intricate plaiting. To Ted, completely unused to horses at close quarters, the animal looked huge and Trev's position decidedly dangerous.

'What shall I do?' he asked them. 'Apart from stand here like a lemon.'

'Talk to Blue,' Shewee told him. 'He always gets fidgety the nearer to his withers I get, so you can distract him.'

'Will he bite me?' Ted asked warily.

'Honestly, Ted,' Trev laughed. 'You're used to handling armed criminals and you have four black belts.'

'And Blue's a big softy, until he sees a water jump. Then he turns into a total psycho.'

Ted stepped closer, still apprehensive.

'Hello, horse,' he said tentatively.

The other two burst into giggles at his efforts but continued working away, seemingly efficiently. Ted plucked up his courage and reached out a wary hand to stroke the horse's neck. It felt silkier and warmer than he'd imagined, and the horse didn't seem to mind, so he carried on softly stroking.

'You're a natural,' Trev assured him. 'A true horse

whisperer. If you ever get fed up of CID you can put in for the mounted branch.'

'Tell him if he dumps me at the water jump, you'll arrest him,' Shewee said, through chattering teeth. 'I bet you brought your handcuffs with you.'

'If you two are just going to make fun of me, I might as well go back to the hotel and read through the case notes,' he told them, but his tone was good-natured.

The nearer they got to being ready, the more Shewee's nerves were visibly getting the better of her, despite Trev's reassurances and efforts to calm her down. Once she'd finished plaiting Blue's mane, she rushed off to get changed and to try to rouse the sleeping Lola, who was supposed to be helping her.

Trev was busy putting the finishing touches to Blue, applying oil to his hooves and giving his coat a final buff with a silk cloth. It reminded Ted a bit of his days in uniform, with all the polishing he'd had to do for formal occasions. Much as he hated wearing a suit and tie to work now, it was still better than uniform.

Shewee reappeared, smartly dressed for the dressage phase, towing a clearly hung-over friend with her.

'You remember my brother, Trev. And this is his partner, Ted, who is a policeman. His presence here is the only reason I'm not going to kill you for being in such a state when you're supposed to be grooming for me today. At least go and warm Blue up for me while I go and declare,' Shewee told her angrily, thrusting a riding hat at her friend and turning to go.

'Oh, God, I can't ride, I'll throw up,' Lola told her.

Clamping her hand to her mouth, she blurted out, 'In fact …' then raced outside, from where they could clearly hear sounds of her heaving and retching.

'Oh, bloody marvellous,' Shewee said, with not much trace of sympathy for her friend. 'What am I going to do now?'

'Give me the hat and I'll warm him up. You go and declare and calm down. Ted will look after Lola, won't you?' Trev said, taking charge.

He led the horse outside, slapped Lola's hat on his head, where it sat rather precariously on top of his glossy black curls, then peeled off the rug which was keeping the animal's hindquarters warm and handed it to Ted. He adjusted the girth then vaulted lightly aboard.

'I'll be down at the warm-up arena,' he told Ted. 'Just follow the signs. Try and get Lola to come with you, the walk should help her. And put the rug round her. We'll need it later and she looks as if she needs thawing out.'

Shewee's friend had at least stopped throwing up but was still looking rough as Ted went over to her and carefully folded the rug round her shoulders. She looked dreadful, at close quarters. Ted had had occasion before to send the local force round to a pub in the area, which was serving alcohol to under-age teenagers. It looked as if he might have to do the same again.

'Are you really a policeman?' Lola eyeing up his short stature dubiously.

Although clearly not much older than Shewee, who was fourteen, she was taller than Ted, but he was used to that.

'I am. But I'm not going to waste my breath lecturing you about under-age drinking. All of this is completely new territory to me and I have no idea where I'm meant to be going. So if you're up to it, can you show me where Trev has gone? And then perhaps if there's a refreshment place somewhere, I can buy you some tea or coffee?'

Ted had never seen Trev ride a horse before. He was amazed at the effortless way in which he seemed to be making the animal do whatever he wanted it to, without Ted being able to see how. He stood watching him in fascination, feeling incredibly proud and privileged to be his partner. He'd sent Lola off to get them each a cup of tea, once she'd shown him the right arena, and she was starting to look better. When Shewee reappeared, Lola was able to go off and help her.

Trev was grinning from ear to ear after he had he dismounted and handed the horse over to his sister, before going to find Ted. He was obviously in his element. Shewee's horse, Blue, had been bred from the mare Trev used to own when he competed as a teenager.

'That was incredible,' Ted told him admiringly. 'And unbelievably sexy. Watching you wrap your legs round that great big horse and make it do whatever you wanted it to gave me some decidedly un-policeman-like thoughts.'

Trev laughed delightedly.

'Hold those thoughts until later on. And Blue isn't big at all. He's just a little squirt, with attitude. A bit like Shewee.'

A man was walking past them, glancing towards Trev. Then he stopped and turned back, his face surprised. He was wearing what seemed to be the uniform for the day - moleskin trousers, a waxed jacket, a tweed cap. He couldn't have been much older than Trev but his turn-out made him look more middle-aged.

'Armstrong? Good God, it is you, isn't it? Trevor Armstrong? I saw there was an Armstrong competing today. Is that your daughter?'

'Ferguson,' Trev replied tightly. 'And hardly. This is my partner, Ted. Siobhan is my kid sister.'

Trev slipped a possessive arm around Ted as he spoke.

'Oh,' the man said, the look he was giving Ted speaking volumes. Then he remembered the good manners he'd been taught at a doubtless expensive school and said formally, 'How d'you do? I didn't realise you had a sister, Armstrong.'

'I didn't, back then. Ferguson and I were at school together, briefly,' Trev explained, then said, 'You'll have to excuse us, Siobhan is on early and I don't want to miss her.'

He strode away rapidly, his arm still around Ted, pulling him along, heading for the bacon rolls. Ted said nothing. He knew how much Trev hated to talk about certain aspects of his life before they had met.

Ted found the day much more interesting than he had expected to. It was something completely outside his previous experience, not at all the type of people he usually had contact with. But he was an avid people-watcher and he was not short of material. He was glad of Trev to explain the intricacies of the competition. After the dressage phase, while Shewee went off to change for the cross-country, Trev got on Blue again and Ted watched in awe as he popped the horse skilfully over practice fences. It all looked so fluid and harmonious.

It was a different picture when Shewee was heading for the water jump. Trev had led the way over to see the jump which was her bogeyman, and was mentally willing her on. Blue was trying to bang on the brakes, but with a bit of a kick and a shout, Shewee somehow managed to propel him reluctantly over the fence, clearing it, though with not much style. Trev was so relieved for her that he grabbed Ted in a hug and whirled him round, to disapproving glances from several people around them.

They seemed to have to wait around a long time after the last phase, the show-jumping, to find out the results. Shewee hadn't won, but at a respectable fifth, she was squeaking with delight not only to have got over the water jump, but to be told that she was short-listed for the school team.

After it was all over and Blue was happily tucked up in his stable eating hay, they waited while Siobhan grabbed a shower and changed her clothes then took her with them back to their hotel. She would have dinner with them, then Ted would run her back to school afterwards. Lola had already crawled off back to bed, although they'd invited her along.

It had been a good day and Ted had enjoyed the break away from the nick. He'd had his phone on silent and there were not even any text messages to disturb their enjoyment. Jo was worth his weight in gold if he was holding the fort well enough to allow Ted a short break. They almost made it to the dessert course before an insistent muted buzzing warned him of an incoming call.

Glancing at the screen, he stood up hurriedly, excused himself, and headed out of the dining room, muttering, 'Sorry, I really do need to take this.'

'Ted, remember what I said, I seriously will divorce you if you want us to leave now,' Trev called after his retreating back.

'Does that mean you two are getting married then? Cool. Can I be a bridesmaid?' Shewee asked him.

As soon as Ted found a quiet corner, he answered the call and immediately heard, 'Oh shit, I completely forgot you were away for the weekend. Shit. Sorry, Ted. Bugger. Shit.'

It was the Ice Queen, but not like Ted had ever heard her before. Her voice was ragged with emotion and it was the first time he'd ever heard her use language like that.

'Debs, calm down. Just tell me what the problem is, and what you need me to do.'

'I shouldn't have called you,' she said, her voice unfamiliar in its uncertainty. 'I just didn't know who to call. Robin's away and I just needed someone sensible ...'

'What's the matter, Debs? What can I do?' Ted asked calmly.

'It's Justin. He's in hospital. He's ... Oh God, Ted. He's in a coma...'

Justin was her older teenage son. Ted could barely begin to imagine how she must be feeling, especially with her husband Robin away. He was not entirely surprised she had called him. Although their relationship was usually stiffly formal, he doubted she had a lot of close friends, like many career police officers, and certainly few outside the force.

'Debs, I'm so sorry. What happened? Is he going to be all right?'

Her voice was sounding wobbly now.

'They say he should make a full recovery, but the next couple of hours are critical. I'm so sorry to have disturbed your weekend away. I just needed a familiar voice. He looks so young, lying there with drips and everything. I haven't even called Robin yet. I was hoping for good news before I spoke to him.'

'It's absolutely fine. I'm glad you felt you could call me. I'm nearly five hours away, unfortunately, even if I had blues and twos, but this is what I'm going to do. You remember I told you I hoped you would never be in a dark enough place to need to discover DC Brown's softer side? Well, you are and you do, so I'm going to call Maurice and send him straight round. You're at Stepping Hill, I assume?'

She started to protest.

'That wouldn't be at all appropriate ...'

'Bugger appropriate, Debs. You need someone who's a parent, who understands the pain you're going through. Tonight Maurice will come and hold your hand, let you cry on his shoulder if you need to, and buy you hot chocolate. It's his cure for everything. Then on Monday morning he'll call you ma'am again and stand to attention when he sees you. You can trust him, I promise.'

She was struggling to get her voice back under control as she said, 'Thank you, Ted. I knew you'd know what to do.'

Then her tone hardened as she said, 'This was a so-called legal high that went wrong. Robin and Toby have gone off sailing, but Justin really wanted to go to a party with some school friends, so I stayed behind with him. I made him promise to be sensible and not drink or take anything. He clearly thought that something lime that wouldn't be dangerous. His father is going to be furious. If he makes it.'

'He'll be fine, Debs. He's young and strong, and in the right place. You go back to him now and I'll send Maurice round. Please let me know how things work out and feel free to call me again, at any time, if you need to talk.'

He cut short her effusive thanks, anxious to get straight on the phone to Maurice. He knew he would go to the hospital immediately. It was the sort of man he was. It was why Ted had been so disappointed with what had happened between him and Jezza. It still didn't sit easy with him, but he'd accepted Jezza's version. In a way, Ted was glad he would have a chance to let the Ice Queen know why he had been so eager to keep Maurice on his team. He just wished it could have been in better circumstances.

'Eh, the poor lass,' was the first thing Maurice said when he heard the news. 'I'll go straight away. My girls are here but they're in bed now and Steve can watch them well enough for me. Don't worry, boss, I'll look after her. Then as soon as we're all back in on Monday, I'll get started on rounding up the pond life spreading this filth on our patch. Whatever it is they're peddling, we'll get the word out there that it's not welcome.'

Trev was looking daggers as Ted made his way apologetically back to the table.

'If you're going to tell me we have to leave straight away …' he began, but Ted grinned at him and sat back down at the table.

'Crisis averted. I've sent in Maurice, my secret weapon, so all is well,' he said.

He told them both what had happened, anxious to impress upon Shewee the dangers of any type of drugs. He already knew she went to pubs under age and had had stern words with her about it.

'Don't worry,' she assured him. 'Now I've got a chance at the team, I'm not doing any stuff at all, not even a shandy. And I'm going to keep Lola on the straight and narrow too. She can plait tails nearly as well as Trev.'

Ted drove Shewee back to school after the meal, leaving Trev to linger over a cognac, then head up to their room, ready for Ted's return.

'Sorry I had to interrupt the meal like that. Poor Debs. I've never heard her swear before. I hope everything is going to be all right. She sounded in bits, but I know Maurice will take good care of her,' Ted told his partner when he got back. 'Now, you know that mental image you told me to hold on to ...'

Chapter Twenty-six

Martin Wilson was pissed off. Really, seriously pissed off. And horny as hell with it, which was not a good combination. He'd spent all day Saturday at a poxy housing exhibition, trying to flog various types of insurance to would-be house buyers, as well as those planning ahead for their so-called golden years. Most of Sunday would be spent following up leads, a lot of which would probably not turn out to be as lucrative as he'd hoped.

The only thing which would get him through the weekend was the prospect of his pre-arranged meeting with the amazing Linda Lovelace on Saturday night. What she was offering him in her emails had him checking to make certain he had his little blue pills in his pocket. He wanted to be sure he was ready for seconds, following the main course she had promised him. And it sounded like there may be dessert to come after that, possibly even a cheese course, if he got really lucky. Even thinking about it kept giving him an uncomfortable hard-on.

He loved his wife. Of course he did. She was gorgeous. But with her bloody Pilates and sodding yoga and whatever else there was, she hardly ever had time for him any more. It seemed as if the more desirable her body became, the more it was off-limits to him. Lately, it was always, 'not now, Martin, I've got to do my exercises,' or some such excuse. Which was why he no longer minded these trips away. He could usually find someone who was after the same thing as he was – no-strings sex, the hotter and steamier the better.

This Linda Lovelace certainly came across as hot and steamy in the few emails they'd exchanged. And she was nothing if not inventive. Some of the things she had proposed had surprised him, and he was no shrinking violet in the bedroom department. The worst of it was, she hadn't shown up. She was now considerably more than fashionably late. She was definitely in the category of no-show. Leaving Martin with a massive itch he needed someone to scratch and so far, no signs of anyone suitable in the bar where he was sitting.

He still kept optimistically looking towards the door every time it opened, but there were no single women in sight. Few single men, either. Just him, and another poor Billy No Mates sitting in a corner with his newspaper, repeatedly looking at his watch. He looked as if he'd been stood up, too.

Martin fleetingly wondered if they were both there to meet the same woman. Their eyes met at one point and Martin lifted his glass in silent acknowledgement of the other man, who grinned ruefully and did the same.

Oh well, no point sitting there gagging for it and doing nothing about it, Martin told himself, and started looking round the room for a likely target. He dismissed the younger crowd. He wasn't bad looking and kept himself fit, but they hunted in packs and weren't always an easy target. He might be better with more mature meat. Sometimes the older ladies were the most surprising. And the most desperate.

He spotted a group of three, sitting together. All looked to be about mid-forties, dolled up to the nines. Martin was in his early forties and, even though he said so himself, he scrubbed up well. It wouldn't be the first time he'd managed to pull out of the blue. Feeling as he did, he was up for anything. Perhaps even his first foursome, if the girls were game. He had nothing to lose by trying.

He drained his half a lager, all he had allowed himself so he would ready for anything Linda had planned for him, and made his way across towards the bar. He was getting interested looks from three women as he approached, so he paused at their table and gave them his most dazzling smile.

'Good evening, ladies. I was just heading for the bar so I wondered if I could buy any of you a drink while I'm there?'

As chat-up lines went, it wasn't inspired, but it had worked for him before and the way the one nearest him was giggling, he suspected it might just work again. He went off to get himself another bottle of lager, and the red wines the women had asked for. He could feel their eyes on him as he stood at the bar, with his back to them.

'Nice bum,' one of them commented to the others. 'I wouldn't mind getting my hands on that.'

'Kathy! You brazen hussy!' one of her friends laughed.

The third was more serious.

'Just be careful, Kath. Have you seen the stuff in the papers about these killings in hotels? You never know who you get talking to in a pub.'

'Yes, but that killer is targeting blokes,' the one called Kathy said dismissively. 'And it would almost be worth the risk to stick your claws into that bum while he was, you know…'

It was to three helplessly laughing women that Martin returned with his lager, plus a bottle of red and three glasses for them. This definitely looked promising. And it wouldn't even cost him the price of a meal. He noticed that they had already eaten. He rightly identified the one who introduced herself as Kathy as the most likely, so he carefully sat where he could make sure his leg came into frequent contact with hers.

His radar hadn't let him down. After a couple more wines, it was Kathy who accompanied him back to his hotel, a short walk away. Neither of them noticed the man Martin had nodded to earlier in the evening carefully fold up his newspaper, follow them back to the hotel, and up to the floor where Martin's room was, then disappear round a corner.

Kathy surprised him by being more athletic and adventurous in bed than he'd dare hoped. He had to listen to the history of her life in between two rounds of lively sex, which he could have done without, and it wasn't quite what Linda had been offering, but it more than sufficed.

He bundled her out of the room shortly after midnight, being careful to give her his business card in the hopes of maybe selling her an insurance policy or two at some point. She gave him her mobile number and, promising faithfully to call her, and to meet up again, he closed the door behind her and headed for a much-needed shower.

He'd just covered himself in shower gel when he heard a knock at the door. She must be insatiable, he thought, grinning to himself as he stepped out of the small cubicle, switching off the water. He was just going to open the door as he was when a man's voice outside said, 'Sorry to bother you, sir, there's a plumbing problem. I need to come in and look at your shower.'

Martin grabbed a towel and wound it round his waist as he opened the door. The face of the man outside, dressed in overalls, was familiar somehow, but he didn't make the connection before the first blow hit him in the midriff and he doubled over, staggering back.

All he could think, as the subsequent blows started to rain on him, was that this must be a jealous husband. But there was something wrong with the punches. He wasn't feeling pain, so much as a terrible numbness. And why was there so much blood suddenly coming from his mouth, when none of the blows had landed on his face?

He was already slipping into unconsciousness when the wildly slashing knife blade caught the side of his neck and opened up his carotid artery. It meant he was blissfully unaware of the savage assault from the work boots, connecting with his head and face, the minute he hit the floor.

Ted was anxious to get going on Sunday morning, but Trev had other plans. He was hoping for a long lie-in with his partner, followed by a leisurely breakfast in the hotel dining room.

'You'd have heard if there was anything going on,' he told Ted reasonably. 'And you know all's well with the Ice Queen now. So surely, as long as you put in an appearance some time this afternoon, that will be enough?'

Ted had received a text from the Ice Queen first thing that morning. It told him that her son Justin was now well enough to be discharged later that morning, and thanked him for all his help. It ended with, 'Thanks for Maurice. He was a treasure!' then, much to Ted's surprise, two kisses to finish with.

He'd never previously seen the motherly side to his senior officer. There was clearly nothing like almost losing a first-born to lower all defences and show the person behind the rank and the uniform.

'I wish you'd stop tempting fate,' Ted told him. 'It's like a John Wayne film. As soon as you start saying how quiet it is, that's when I'm bound to get a call saying there's been another murder. And that won't be an excuse for you to exceed the speed limit all the way back, either.'

They'd made it as far as Gloucester on the M5 before Ted's phone went and it was Jo.

'Sorry, boss, I know you're still off, but I thought you'd want to know. We have a fourth victim. Manchester city centre this time. I've let the Super know and Mike and I are on our way there now. Another hotel, similar MO, from what the first responders have reported. Duty pathologist and Forensics are all heading there, too.'

'I'm on my way back now. We've just passed Gloucester. I'll get Trev to drop me straight there, then someone can give me a lift back home afterwards. We'll be three hours or more, though.'

'Take your time, boss. Mike and I can handle it, with the local team. No need for you even to go there if you don't want to.'

'Sorry, Jo, that wasn't meant to suggest that I didn't trust you. I know you're up to the task. Certainly Brian Donohue is, and it's his patch. It's just that I'd planned on being in work today, so I might as well come and join you.'

He relayed the information to Trev through their helmet intercom system and again cautioned him against exceeding the speed limit.

'I know you're keen to get there, but we're going to need a short break on the way to grab a drink, if nothing else. I'll drop you straight there then I'd best get back to the cats or they won't speak to either of us for days,' Trev told him.

Ted's mother had been looking after the cats for the weekend. He'd finally relented and given her a key to the house, for just such occasions. They now got on well, but he had still felt reticent about taking that big step. She'd been missing from his life for such a large chunk of it that it still felt awkward to him.

The hotel address which Jo had given him was situated on DI Brian Donohue's patch. He and Ted knew one another well and got on. Ted didn't anticipate any rancour from him about him coming in to his territory as SIO and taking over the case.

In fact, Donohue welcomed him with a smile and a handshake, saying, 'Congratulations on the promotion. About bloody time. Our turn for your killer now, it seems. I'm assuming it's the same man, from what Jo's been telling me.'

'Looks the same, boss,' Jo agreed. 'Another insurance salesman. The hotel was pretty full this weekend. There was a big property exhibition on in town so there were a lot of people here for that. People coming and going all the time, so no one saw or heard very much, from what we've found out so far. Once again our victim seems to have got out of the shower to answer the door.'

'Where's he from, do we know?'

'Northumberland, his documents say. Name of Martin Wilson. And once again, we've got the phone and computer bagged and ready to go to Océane. She's certainly going to be earning her keep on this case.

'The pathologist's been and gone and SOCO are working on the scene now. They confirm signs of recent sexual activity in the bed once more, but our victim had booked in just for himself. I'm betting that his partner wasn't Mrs Wilson, if there is one. We're checking into that now, so we can at least let her know as soon as possible.'

'Is the body ...?'

'About as bad as any of them, I would say, boss. Not a pretty sight, and it's certainly not going to be nice for the next of kin to identify, once again.'

'He's one jump ahead of us all the time so far. I think Océane's right. We definitely need to start thinking of bringing him to us, rather than waiting to see where he strikes next. I'll need to run it past the Big Boss.'

'Just let me know what you need from my officers and we'll get on with it,' Brian Donohue told him.

At least Ted would have no worries about how the local division conducted their enquiries. Donohue was a good officer; his team would know what they were doing. He was a far cry from Foster and his sorry crew.

'I've just come up from Somerset on the bike with Trev. If there's somewhere we can get a cup of coffee, Brian, I can fill you in on everything we have so far.'

He was happy to keep it informal, with just the three of them.

Ted was still in his leathers. Donohue grinned.

'I thought it was unusual uniform for the SIO on a serial case. The management here are being helpful. They've said we can use the dining room when we need to, outside of mealtimes, obviously. We've already started interviewing staff.'

'We really need to get statements from as many hotel guests

as we can, as soon as possible. I'm assuming those up for the exhibition will have left or be leaving first thing in the morning. I'd like to get their statements while things are still fresh in their minds. Can you rustle up enough officers, or do you need me to bring in some reinforcements?'

'I've already got some of my team on to it, and some Uniforms helping out. There's CCTV, too, of the entrance, so that might give you something.'

Ted nodded.

'Right, thanks. Now, a coffee would be good, it's a long ride up from Somerset. Then we can talk strategy.'

'I'll get straight on with the CCTV, boss,' Mike offered. 'I had to wimp out of the crime scene again. I'm not too bad with blood, but when it comes to bits of brain …' he broke off and swallowed hard.

'And I'll carry on interviewing the staff, boss,' Jo told him. 'Let me know when you're ready to leave and I can run you back home. It would be nice to meet your Trevor in the flesh.'

Ted sat down with Brian Donohue over some surprisingly good coffee and brought him up to speed. When he mentioned their prime suspect to date, the DI laughed.

'John Smith, eh? That's not going to simplify things for us. How many tens of thousands of those are there in the UK?'

'Less than twelve, young Steve tells me,' Ted told him cheerfully. 'We've got this new CFI now as well, and she's proving a big help. She suggests springing a trap for our suspect as the best way forward and I think she's right. I'm going on the assumption that he's still local, more to my patch than yours, since that's where the late wife lived.

'I don't know if it's one specific person he's trying to catch and kill, or if he's on a mission to get as many so-called financial advisers as he can. Some sort of campaign of revenge for his wife and others like her who may have lost money. It never came out at the inquest who was behind the scam she fell for, and I doubt there are still any files or documents to be found.

'I know I can safely leave you and your team to this one, Brian, unlike Foster and his useless lot. I need Jo and Mike on another nasty case we've got going on.'

He went on to explain about the deaths at Sabden House flats and how the last victim there, Honest John, had died.

Donohue shook his head in disbelief.

'Well, that's certainly a new one on me. Murder by chocolate? It's some pretty nasty piece of shit to come up with a cynical method like that of getting rid of vulnerable people.

'Leave this one to us, Ted. Me and my team will be more than happy to do the legwork on it, leave yours to get on with what sounds like a nasty case. You can count on us. Looks like we have a couple or more really sick bastards to get off the streets, so we'd better get stuck in, eh?'

Chapter Twenty-seven

'We need this bastard off the street, Ted,' Jim Baker growled when Ted phoned him from Manchester with an update. Jim hadn't been over to the crime scene himself. Ted was SIO. Jim's role was more to do with the politics and purse strings, and he had better things to do with his Sundays than look at blood and brains. Especially now he had a lady friend. Or fiancée, to be precise. He'd never imagined himself being loved up at his time of life, but he certainly was. Given the choice between time with Bella and with a dead body, he'd decided to leave the gruesome stuff to Ted.

'At the moment, the best way I think we're going to do that is to bring him to us, Jim. He's constantly on the move, so he won't be easy to track down, especially with a name like John Smith. I know that will need clearance higher up. Can you arrange it? We'll need to have a strategy meeting to plan how we're going to do it. We can't just wait around to get lucky.'

'It will take a lot of planning,' Jim warned.

'We may not have a lot of time before he decides to kill again. We're trying all the conventional means at our disposal, but with a name like that for our prime suspect, and nothing but throwaway emails, progress risks being slow.'

'I'll run it by the powers that be first thing tomorrow.'

'I'll want everything. Tasers, firearms, the lot. If we succeed in drawing him out, we'll only get one crack at him before he disappears under cover. And I want him, Jim.'

Ted was summoned to coffee with the Ice Queen as soon as he had finished the Monday morning briefing. It could potentially be a bit awkward for both of them, getting back to business as normal after they'd shared an intensely personal moment by phone. Hopefully, they were both grown-up enough to handle it. He first needed to brief all the team members on the latest killing, and to kick some ideas around. Most of all, he wanted a trail to John Smith, as soon as possible.

As usual, Océane seemed to be able to keep one ear in listening mode while she worked, and to chip in when necessary.

'I'm only just starting on victim number four, boss, but he's had emails from the lovely Linda, like the others. Usual steamy stuff. Then arranging a meet at a pub, just off Piccadilly.'

'Is it Linda who suggests where to meet or the men? If Linda is suggesting it, does it mean our killer has local knowledge? If it is this John Smith, then he did live in the area for a number of years.'

'Boss, anyone with a computer can know an area these days, with things like Google Street View,' Océane said patiently.

Ted grinned at her. She'd certainly got his number. He could find his way around a computer just enough to do his job, but was definitely in the novice category for anything else.

Then he asked, 'Do the men ever mention which hotel they'll be staying in?'

She shook her auburn locks.

'No, none of them have done, so far. They've just said that they'll be in the area and staying in a hotel. I suppose Linda could guess which one, from the ones near to the pub they pick? Again, that's easy enough to find with a computer. But then, men like these wouldn't give out the hotel name, would they?'

Seeing Ted's querying look, she expanded on her theory.

'Well, these are not honourable fellows, are they? They're cheating on wives and partners, and from the look of it, they're picking and choosing who they sleep with. So if they don't fancy the person who turns up, they don't identify themselves. Therefore they're not going to say where they're staying and risk some jilted date turning up at their hotel room when they're in bed with someone else.'

'Excellent point,' Ted conceded, 'and very good news if we do try to draw our killer in. If he doesn't know the hotel, he can't check it out in advance, and we can get people in there waiting for him. I've asked the Super to get the go-ahead from upstairs for us to try. In the meantime, I want all the stops pulled out trying to find this John Smith. Maurice, can you contact everyone you can find from the inquest report? Try to trace some family who may know where he is.

'And keep on with witnesses from the hotels and pubs. Océane, can you update the list of pubs, please? If he's following his victims back to their hotel and then waiting around until the woman leaves, someone must have seen him, surely?'

'There are a couple of possibilities there, though, boss,' Jo put in. 'If he's in his overalls, playing the maintenance man, he'd be pretty anonymous. And also, he doesn't need to stay inside the hotel, looking suspicious. He's seen what his victims, and the women they've picked up, look like from the pub. All he has to do is follow them to the hotel, see what number room they go into, then go and wait outside until he sees the woman leave. And again, a man standing outside a hotel to have a fag is not going to attract much attention, when they can't smoke inside these days.'

Tasks assigned for the day, Ted headed downstairs to see the Ice Queen. He paused to put his head round Kevin Turner's office door for a quick catch-up, and to tell him that they were likely to need a joint operation if they got the go-ahead to lure their killer.

The Ice Queen had the coffee on ready. There was a strange brown object of indeterminate shape, in a cupcake case, sitting on a paper plate in front of the empty chair, when Ted sat down as invited. He looked at it questioningly.

'It's supposed to be a chocolate chip muffin,' she told him. 'Sitting next to my son's bedside, not knowing if he was going to make it through the night, filled me with a sudden desire to do something yummy mummy, for when the family were all back together. Unfortunately, they turned out rather like dog turds. But it is sincerely meant as a gesture of appreciation of your great kindness and help, Ted.'

Ted peeled away the paper case and took a wary bite, to be polite. It cloyed his mouth, sticking to his palate and the back of his teeth. When he was able to speak, he said, 'It's very…chocolatey.'

She surprised him by laughing out loud, not something he could remember having seen her do often.

'You're always very tactful. And it is disgusting, I know. An insult to serve to a man who lives with such a superb pastry cook as Trevor. But it's lovingly baked with my heartfelt thanks. And you were absolutely right about DC Brown. Such a kind and compassionate man. Every team should have one.'

Then, abruptly, the shutters came back down and she was frosty efficiency once more while they went over the current case-load.

Virgil went over to Jezza's desk as she was ploughing her way through a pile of witness statements for cross-checking. She looked up and smiled at the welcome distraction.

'Are you still on for tonight, at Nat's? I'll pick you up and take you back afterwards.'

'Shouldn't you be at home with the missus, nesting?'

Virgil groaned.

'I'll be glad of the excuse to escape, to be honest. She's driving me mad. She refuses to be told the sex of the baby, so she's had me paint the nursery in two different colours already and she wants it changing again.'

When's it due?'

'May,' he beamed. 'I'm going to be a daddy! How awesome is that?'

'What are you hoping for?'

'A healthy baby,' he replied, his tone suddenly serious again. 'We lost the first one, a couple of years ago.'

'Oh god, Virgil, I'm so sorry, I didn't know...' Jezza stammered her embarrassment.

'It's fine,' he assured her. 'You weren't here at the time and it's not really something I talk about much. So I'll pick you up at, say, quarter to eight? Have you got someone for Tommy?'

'Maurice and Steve are coming over. I think they'll be watching Star Wars for the gazillionth time and pretending it's for Tommy's benefit, eh, Steve?' she grinned across at him and he blushed guiltily.

At least things were back to normal between the three of them, and Jezza was relieved. She genuinely counted Maurice and Steve as two of her best friends.

Jezza headed for the ladies, as much to stretch her legs as for any pressing need. She also felt awkward for having put her foot in it with Virgil. She was just running her fingers through her spiky, rebellious hair when Megan sauntered in with studied nonchalance and headed for the mirror, alongside her.

'So, are you and Maurice ...' she asked as casually as she could manage.

'An item?' Jezza finished off, and laughed. 'Shit, no. He's my best friend, but we're not going out or anything.'

'So is he seeing anyone, do you know?' Megan asked, fiddling with her hair as she looked in the mirror.

Jezza turned to look at her with a sly smile.

'He'd like to be seeing you,' she said. 'He told me. Do you want me to put in a good word?'

Megan looked embarrassed.

'It's just, he seems like a really nice man ...'

'Oh, he is. And we have. You know. But just the once. So I can assure you – you won't be disappointed.'

Maurice followed Ted into his office when he returned from his meeting with the Ice Queen and took a seat, as instructed.

'The Super has just been singing your praises,' Ted told him as he sat down at his desk. 'Thanks for helping her, Maurice. It sounds as if she went to hell and back, and you were just what she needed.'

'So I'm forgiven now, am I?' Maurice asked. 'About Jezza? I would never harm a hair of that lass's head, boss. You think I took advantage of her. I didn't. Oh, I could have. But I didn't. I thought you knew me better than that.'

There was a chiding note in his tone.

Ted sighed.

'You're right, Maurice, and I apologise. I should have known better. I do know you better. Right, what have you got for me?'

'Hopefully, a possible lead for John Smith. I found contact details for his ex-sister-in-law, the sister of the woman who committed suicide. I phoned and had a brief word. She's not in contact with him now, but she does have some details, so I said I'd pop round there. It may not lead to anything, but it's worth a shot, and it's the best we've got at the moment.'

'Take someone with you,' Ted reminded him, as Maurice rose to go.

It was a sad sign of the times that he preferred his team members to go out in pairs. There had been too many allegations of misconduct against police officers interviewing people when on their own. Fortunately never against his own team, and he wanted to do all that he could to ensure that it stayed that way.

'Jezza, are you free?' Maurice asked her, as he went back out into the main office. 'I'm off to see John Smith's sister-in-law, see if I can get a lead. The boss doesn't want me going on my own.'

'Sorry, Maurice,' she said, pulling files towards her on the desk. 'I'm up to my eyes. The boss wants this spreadsheet sorting as soon as. Perhaps Megan could do it?' she suggested, looking innocently across at her.

If Maurice guessed that he was being set up, he showed no sign. Megan, though, was going pink and looking daggers at Jezza.

'Do you want to go in my car?' Maurice offered. 'It's extra clean at the moment. The twins helped me clean it this weekend.'

Jezza smiled to herself as she heard them talking to one another as they went out of the office.

'Oh, I heard you had twin girls; that must be lovely. I have a boy, Felix. He's eight.'

They were still deep in conversation when they arrived outside the neat terraced house in Heaviley and Maurice pulled up outside.

'Well, we're here,' Maurice said, unnecessarily. 'Let's hope we can get some sort of a steer on John Smith, and that it's a lead in the right direction.'

They were clearly expected as, after Maurice had stepped aside to let Megan through the front gate first, the door opened to a slim woman in her fifties. She introduced herself as Val Baxter, the older sister of the dead woman, Elaine Cummings. She showed them into a small but neat front room and offered them tea, which they both declined.

'Mrs Baxter,' Maurice began, 'first of all, I'm very sorry about your sister. I appreciate it will be painful to go over again, but we really do need to get in touch with her ex-husband, John Smith.'

'I haven't heard from John for a while. It's nearly two years now since my sister ...' she paused to get control over her voice before continuing, handing Maurice a piece of paper. 'I wrote down the last contact details I had for John, but it was about a year ago, I think. He took Elaine's death very hard. He suffered some sort of breakdown. Had to give up work. He was living in B&Bs, never staying long in one place. He blamed himself, because he'd not been able to help her.'

'Did John ever talk about trying to find the person behind the financial scheme your sister was involved in?' Megan asked.

'Oh, yes. He tried to track him down. My husband spent a lot of time helping him. He was very good with computers. That was his profession. Then he died suddenly. A heart attack.'

Both officers mumbled their condolences in the pause which followed.

Then she continued, 'That was the point at which John had a serious breakdown, although he had been going downhill since her death. I think he realised then that he might never find the person behind the scheme that took Elaine's money, and then her life. It sent him into a terrible depression.'

'What was John intending to do if he found the person responsible?' Maurice asked. 'Did he ever show any inclination towards violence?'

'Oh, good heavens no,' she assured him. 'John was always a very gentle man. So kind. Very good with his hands. That's why he worked in maintenance. I think he just wanted to hold someone accountable for what happened to Elaine. Though I'm not sure he could have done. It all appeared to be perfectly legal, or so we were told at the time. Just one of these schemes which should have worked out, but didn't.'

'He was never violent,' Megan reiterated. 'So may I ask you what caused the marriage to break down? Why did they get divorced, if you don't mind telling us?'

'It was the job,' she replied. 'John was away such a lot, as maintenance crew on the rigs up in Scotland. Elaine wanted him to stop. She got so lonely while he was away. But he loved it, and the money was good. She tried telling him she'd be happier with less money and a husband at home. He kept saying he would give it up, but he never did.

'Elaine started going on these meet-up sites online. Not dating, really, nothing like that. Just for some company. She did go out with a few men, but it wasn't for a casual affair or anything. An occasional meal, going dancing, the cinema, that sort of thing. John didn't like it, of course, but he still wouldn't leave the rigs, so they split up. It was about the same time she met this Nigel.'

'Nigel?' Megan prompted.

The woman went on to explain how her sister had encountered the man she knew as Nigel in an online group and met him for dinner a few times. She had always maintained it was nothing physical, just a pleasant companion to go out with, sharing the cost of the meals. At first she had thought him kind and helpful, advising her on where to place her small amount of savings from the divorce settlement, to secure her future.

Elaine had started to believe everything he told her. It was already too late by the time she could bring herself to admit to her sister that she had gambled everything on a dodgy financial scheme which had seen her lose the house, then left her owing thousands. Of course, the charming Nigel had disappeared off the scene and the only mobile number she had for him no longer worked.

'So are you looking for Nigel, now? And do you think John can help you in some way?' she asked them, eyes shining hopefully as she looked from one officer to the other.

'We certainly think he might be able to help us with our current enquiries,' Maurice replied evasively. 'Mrs Baxter, do you perhaps have a photograph of John which we could borrow, please? As you can appreciate, it's not easy finding the right John Smith, especially if he's not at the address you've kindly given us.'

'I do have a photo of the four of us together, from three or four years ago. Me and Eric, Elaine and John. If you're sure I'll definitely get it back safely ...'

'Best lead yet,' Megan said, as they drove back to the nick, with her holding on to the photo. 'At least we have a likely face to put to our Linda Lovelace.'

Maurice nodded then said, hesitantly, 'I have the twins most weekends. I wondered if perhaps you and Felix might like to go somewhere with us, one of these days? I'm not sure what the kids would have in common. The girls love crafting. And picnics.'

Megan smiled.

'Felix adores picnics. Especially if there are cold sausages, and he thinks he might get a chance of seeing a fox. And yes, please, I'd like that very much.'

Chapter Twenty-eight

Ted had to wait until late afternoon for any good news, but when it came, it was a welcome double dose. He'd almost reached the bottom of his in-tray when Jim called and said, without preamble, 'Wednesday morning, first thing. Get together whoever you need for this operation, and get the ball rolling. Start posting wherever it's needed, see if you can get a bite from our Linda Lovelace. I'll be over for the meeting.'

Océane was equally pleased to get the green light, when Ted went out to talk to her and to Steve, who was like her shadow if he was not firmly chased out of the office to do other things.

'Excellent news, boss. Leave it with me. I'll set up a fake profile and scatter it with all the keywords that seem to snare him. With luck, it shouldn't be too long before we have him on the end of our hook and line.'

'It will be helpful to have you at the meeting on Wednesday, as this is very much your side of the operation. But can you tell me, will we have a shot of tracing him if he makes contact, rather than having to set up the whole sting?'

She shook her head.

'Doubtful. He doesn't use a mobile phone for his postings, which would be slightly easier. He's using throwaway emails and it's likely he's only posting from wi-fi hotspots or cyber cafés and not staying online for very long each time, which makes him harder to trace. He seems to know some of the basics of staying under the radar, but then Maurice mentioned that the brother-in-law was a computer expert and had been helping him.

'I'll let you know if and when I can get a trace on him, if he bites, but I still favour bringing him to us. And I imagine that from your side, the logistics will be easier to manage if we do.'

She certainly knew her stuff and, unlike some of the techie types Ted had worked with in the past, she was aware of how her role fitted in with the rest of the team. He liked that.

He was just allowing himself a small sigh of satisfaction as he picked up the last file that needed his attention, when there was a brief knock and Sal came into the office. He was having no success in disguising the look of satisfaction on his face.

Ted took off his reading glasses and looked up at him, motioning him to take a seat.

'This looks like good news. And I'm particularly open to some good news.'

'I haven't really caught up with you with the progress on the Sabden House case yet, boss, and there has been some,' Sal began. 'I've just been waiting on some test results, so now I can definitely give you some good news.

'First of all, Jo came back from his meeting with Pocket Billiards with the name of a supposedly dodgy councillor who's been making noises about selling off council housing stock to improve and develop sites. A man named Jake Gilbert. Our reporter friend said the councillor has a brother-in-law, Seth Hartman, who's a property developer. He's been above board about the connection in most planning meetings, always declaring an interest when necessary, to appear to be squeaky clean. But it's no secret that Hartman is very interested in Sabden House and its potential.

'Now, fast forward to the hamper, which was in Honest John's flat. When I went carefully through it, I found a gift card inside, tucked away under the food where it was easily overlooked. It was just a typed message from the hamper company, from a well-wisher, no name, but it did have the name of the company. I contacted them and they confirmed that it was paid for by Seth Hartman's credit card, but it was sent to him care of another address.

'At first I thought we weren't going to be lucky with prints on the hamper or any of the contents. It looked as if whoever took it to Honest John's flat had worn gloves and been careful. Then forensics managed to find a partial print on the catch. Almost as if someone had started to open it for a quick rummage inside, then remembered to put gloves on. It was a print of someone we have on record.'

'This just gets better and better,' Ted smiled. 'Please tell me the print is either Seth Hartman or Jake Gilbert.'

Sal shook his head.

'Can't do that, boss, I'm afraid. But don't give up hope. The print belongs to a young man, Theo Cowell, who's got form for some fairly minor stuff, like taking without consent. The hamper was delivered to his address.'

Like a comedian with perfect timing, waiting for the best moment to deliver the punchline, Sal paused, watching the boss's face, full of anticipation.

'And the best part is, Theo Cowell turns out to be Seth Hartman's nephew.'

'Yes!' Ted exclaimed, and only just resisted the temptation to do an air punch. 'So, you're going to bring him in?'

'Only just got word on the print a short while ago, then had to check him out. But yes, me and the sarge are going over now to haul him in and see what he has to say for himself. DS Hallam, that is. I can't get used to calling Rob anything other than Rob. I can't think of him as DS O'Connell yet.'

'Excellent news, Sal. Just what we need, a bit of a breakthrough and a morale boost. Go and get him, start questioning him, the two of you. I'll be around if you want me to help. I'll probably let Jo go early, though. He's put in enough hours over the weekend covering for me. And don't forget, with Cowell's pedigree, he will probably have connections, so don't cut any corners.'

Ted knew he could safely leave it to Sal and Mike. They were both experienced officers, well trained, perfectly capable. He knew he didn't need to be telling them how to proceed. He just wanted it to done thoroughly. And he wanted to be there, to watch them at work. He felt he owed Honest John the right to justice.

He phoned Trev, while he had a moment, to warn him that he would be late and couldn't promise what time he'd be back. It would depend how the initial interview went and whether they would need to bring the others in quickly, before they had time to cover their tracks.

'Make sure you eat something, and not just a bagel,' Trev told him. 'I'll keep something here you can just heat up when you're back, but I know what you're like. Eat. Keep your strength up. I have plans for you later.'

Ted laughed.

'I was about to say you sounded like my mother, but I've just revised that. I'll be back as soon as I can. Your plans sound interesting.'

Sal and Mike let him know when they were back and Ted went down to watch and listen to the interview through the two-way glass. Theo Cowell looked no more than a teenager, lanky, awkward, traces of acne. He also looked scared.

Mike went carefully through the formalities, with the tape running, before he began.

'Now, you've already been cautioned, but for now, we just want to ask you some questions in connection with our enquiries.

'Theo, what can you tell me about a luxury gift hamper which was delivered to your address?'

'Shouldn't I have someone here?'

The young man was now looking suspicious as well as scared.

'My uncle, or someone?'

'We've explained your right to legal advice, should you want it, but you don't have the right to have a family member present as you're an adult. So, about the hamper, Theo?'

Now the young man was looking sulky.

'You're trying to trick me. I want a lawyer. I want to call my uncle. He'll know what to do. He'll send me someone.'

'All of this was explained to you before, Theo,' Mike said patiently. 'But if that's what you've now decided, that can be arranged for you, and we'll resume questioning as soon as your legal representative arrives.'

Ted had been working behind the scenes as soon as Sal had told him about the suspect. He'd got the Ice Queen on the case of getting a warrant to search Cowell's bedsit. The break worked in their favour. With luck, they could have the results of the initial search before the interview went very far, with the delay in waiting for the lawyer to arrive.

Ted was keeping his fingers crossed that Theo had not been clever enough to dispose of Honest John's medical kit and his insulin, if he hadn't realised their significance in the case. If they could find those, it meant Theo Cowell was implicated up to his neck in a possible unlawful killing charge. Even if Seth Hartman turned out to be his favourite uncle, Ted wondered how long the younger man would stay silent once he realised that he might be alone in facing a serious charge.

Ted regrouped with Mike and Sal over a plate of sandwiches in his office, taking advantage of the break while the family lawyer was summoned.

'So, do we like him for this, so far?' Ted asked the others.

'I like him a lot, boss,' Mike told him. 'He's not the brains behind it, clearly. I doubt if he has the brains for much, to be honest. Have we got enough to arrest him, without the results of the search warrant?'

Ted shook his head.

'I doubt it. We can't make much of a case out of giving

someone a present. We need to find that insulin. If he took it away deliberately, even on his uncle's instructions, he's possibly looking at a murder charge, but it's so unusual, I'll have to see what CPS say. Removing the insulin must show pre-meditation though, surely?'

'And if we get lucky and find the stuff at his bedsit?' Sal asked.

'Then we bring in the uncle, soon. Question them separately, and see where we go from there. We could be looking at a late evening, so you'd better warn your other halves.'

Virgil arrived bang on time to take Jezza to meet Nat. He grinned at her conspiratorially as she got into his black BMW. 'I can't tell you how glad I am of the excuse to escape. Have you any idea how many different shades of trendy white there are these days? She keeps saying she wants it to be neutral, but they all look the same to me.'

'I'm sorry to be a wimp and need a babysitter,' she told him apologetically. 'It's just, I'm not ready … You know.'

Virgil did know. It would be a while before Jezza would feel comfortable alone in the company of a man she'd not met before.

'Does your wife mind? You being out this evening, chaperoning me, I mean?'

Virgil laughed, a rich, deep, rumbling sound.

'I told her we were going to interview a witness. Which is true, pretty much, except that Nat was a witness from a good few cases ago. It was simpler that way.'

Nathan Cowley, Nat, had been living on the streets when Virgil first met him, and had been witness to a fatal shooting. He was currently living in a friend's flat, to look after the tropical fish, while the friend was working abroad. He was also recovering from a bad accident when he'd once again found himself a witness to a serious crime. He and Virgil had struck up something of a friendship.

Nat greeted Virgil warmly, but looked hesitant as he was introduced to Jezza.

'I do hope Virgil has been frank and warned you about me,' he said warily. 'I hope you realise that I finished up on the streets because I all but bankrupted my former employers when I was a market trader.'

Jezza liked what she saw immediately. Nat had an air of sincerity about him. She liked his honesty.

'That's fine. I suppose it means that if anyone can tell me where not to put the money, you can.'

'Come in, anyway. Go on up to the flat, Virgil, you know the way. I'm still a bit slow on the stairs, I have to do them one at a time, but I'm getting there.'

Virgil led the way, showing Jezza into a spacious, modern flat, with a big aquarium as the focal point of the airy living room.

'Hi, guys,' Virgil greeted the fish. He'd looked after them when Nat was in hospital following his accident. 'Hey Errol, you're looking well. I think you've put weight on, little buddy.'

Jezza shook her head and laughed.

'Virgil, they're fish. Can they even hear you, let alone understand?'

Nat limped slowly in to join them, inviting them to sit down. He offered beer or wine and said apologetically, 'Neither of them very good, I'm afraid. I'm still on a tight budget.'

Armed with a bottle of lager each, they began the reason for their visit; financial advice. Nat had prepared a detailed spreadsheet, showing what he considered to be the best and worst investments currently available. He was careful to keep himself well out of Jezza's personal space. Virgil hadn't betrayed a confidence but he had intimated to Nat that because of a recent incident, she had preferred not to come on her own the first time they met.

As well as the figures, Jezza was looking appraisingly at

Nat. His face was earnest and he spoke with a frank sincerity as he told her his thoughts, then repeated, 'But as I'm sure Virgil has told you, I'm really not the best person to ask, except where not to put your money if you don't want to lose the lot.

'I'll give you my phone number so that if there's anything at all you want to go over, or ask me about, please feel free to do so. Or maybe we could meet up again for another beer, the three of us?' he suggested tactfully.

'I like him,' Jezza said decidedly when they had left the flat and got back into the car. 'He seems sincere. Thanks, Virgil, I appreciate it. Back to the colour charts and the paint-brush now?'

Virgil grinned at her.

'Like him as a financial adviser? Or as something else?'

'Get back to your colour charts,' she retorted, with a laugh.

The Ice Queen certainly had a regal way of obtaining search warrants quickly. Ted had never known anyone quite so efficient. It meant they had their warrant to search Theo Cowell's home almost before they'd finished their plate of sandwiches.

'How do you want to play this now?' Ted asked the others. 'I'd suggest, Sal, that you go round there, with a couple of uniformed officers. You know what we're looking for. We need to find that insulin, if we can, and get it checked for fingerprints. In the meantime, once the solicitor arrives, Mike, I can sit in with you, if that helps, while Sal's out. My own feeling is we won't get a lot out of him without something to shake him up.'

Cowell's solicitor was brusque and officious. He had time alone with the young man before the interview could continue. He'd clearly advised his client against saying anything much at all, until he was able to assess what the police had against him.

Mike was going patiently over the questioning, receiving monosyllabic answers, sometimes, merely a 'No comment'. It wasn't long before the door opened and Sal came back in, keeping his face carefully deadpan. Ted stepped outside into the corridor with him.

'Bingo, boss,' Sal told him, producing a paper carrier bag in his still-gloved hand, a pharmacy logo on the outside of the bag. Inside was the blood testing kit and insulin which were never far from Honest John's reach. 'Too stupid even to have hidden it anywhere or tried to get rid of it.'

The two of them went back into the room. Ted sat down. Sal remained standing and carefully put the bag down on the table, where Cowell couldn't miss it. The young man's spotty face immediately drained of colour and he looked panic-stricken.

'Theo,' Ted said quietly, leaning forward in his chair and looking directly into Cowell's eyes. 'Do you recognise the bag which DC Ahmed has just put on the table?'

'I need a moment to discuss further with my client ...' the solicitor began, but his client clearly had only one thing on his mind – talking himself out of whatever pile of crap was about to land on his head.

'It was my uncle. He told me to do it. He told me to take the hamper round to the fat bloke's flat, a present for him, like, but to take the medication away. He said it wasn't good for him to have that as well as the food. I didn't know it was wrong.'

'I must insist on a short break to take further instruction,' the solicitor was blustering.

'Absolutely fine,' Ted said obligingly, standing up. 'DCI Darling, DS Hallam and DC Ahmed leaving the room at ...' he checked the clock on the wall, 'seven-oh-three pm.'

As the three of them stepped out into the corridor, Ted smiled at his team members.

'If there's one thing which strikes a note even sweeter than Freddie Mercury, it's a suspect, singing his socks off to clear himself and implicate others.'

Chapter Twenty-nine

'Question. You thought you'd committed the perfect murder, or murders. Then you hear that your knuckle-head nephew is being interviewed by the police. You panic, thinking he may have been stupid enough to leave a trail which could lead right to you. What do you do next?' Ted asked.

Mike and Sal answered almost in unison and using practically the same words.

'You go round to your nephew's flat, not knowing if the police have already been there, trying to find anything incriminating before they do.'

'Did you leave it tidy, Sal? Could he tell at first glance that you'd been in there?'

'I'm house-trained, boss. Nothing was out of place. I didn't really need to rummage far. The bag of Honest John's things was on the kitchen table, so I brought that straight in. I didn't look much further. I thought that would be enough for us to be going on with, then go back later for a better look.'

Ted nodded his agreement, then said, 'Good, that's what I thought, and you were right. What I think we need to do now is to arrest Theo, put him in a cosy cell for now and continue our investigations. We can tell his brief we'll let him know when to come back. We've not got enough to charge him with yet, but we'll arrest him on suspicion of murder for now. That should nicely rattle his cage.

'Then I think we - by which I mean me and one of you two - need to hotfoot it round to Theo's place and see if we can't find his uncle there. With the credit card details and the missing insulin, I think we could arrest him on suspicion, too, and bring him in. That gives us twenty-four hours each to question them, and a possible twelve more, if we need them and the Super agrees.

'So, next question. Who wants to arrest Theo then knock off, and who's in for a longer evening with me?'

'Toss you for it, Sarge?' Sal suggested.

'No, it's fine, Sal, I've got this one. You bang up our young friend, and the boss and I can go and find his uncle.'

It wasn't far to the address they had for Theo Cowell. The bedsit was in a smart block, clearly well-maintained.

'Probably one of his uncle's places,' Ted mused aloud. 'Somewhere like this is clearly not being paid for by his benefits, if he's still claiming to be unemployed.'

'I'm betting he's moonlighting for his uncle, and not just for doing his dirty work at Sabden House,' Mike replied, as they pulled up outside.

There were lights on in most of the ground floor rooms, and the address they had for the young man suggested that his flat would be on that level.

'If we just sit here a bit and wait for him to come out, he may save us the job of turning the place over. He might well emerge with other bits of incriminating evidence we don't yet know about.'

'Sneaky, boss. I like your style,' Mike chuckled.

'I'd better just phone Trev while we're waiting, let him know I'm going to be even later than I thought.'

'I'll do the same to the missus, while you're doing that. I'll just step outside the car, save you the embarrassment of hearing me getting a hen-pecked earful.'

He was being tactful, Ted knew. The whole team knew that the boss was besotted with his partner, even after being together for a good few years. Mike was clearly happy to give him a bit of privacy.

'I'm going to be even later than I thought,' Ted began. 'Sorry. But I may just be on the point of arresting the man who had Honest John killed. Am I forgiven, and will your plans keep?'

Trev chuckled.

'That all depends on how tired you are when you get home. But I like it when you catch the bad guys. I like it a lot.'

Ted was still smiling to himself when he ended the call and leaned across to open the car door for Mike.

'I think I got away with it, how about you? Are you in the doghouse?'

Mike shook his head.

'No worries, boss, I just blamed it all on you.'

It was only a few moments later that the light went off in the bedsit nearest to them and they saw a man coming out of the communal entrance to the block of apartments.

'That could be our man. Let's go and find out,' Ted said, as the two of them got out of the car.

The path leading up to the door was narrow. Mike and Ted effectively blocked it as the man came towards them, carrying a bag in one hand. Both officers pulled out their warrant cards and held them up. The man was looking wary.

'Mr Hartman? Seth Hartman? DCI Darling, DS Hallam. Could we have a word?'

'I heard you'd taken my nephew in for something. I just came round to see if he was back yet,' Hartman replied.

It didn't sound convincing.

'No, he's not back yet, Mr Hartman. In fact he's just been arrested.'

'Arrested? What for? What's he done? Or what are you claiming he's done?'

The man was by now looking decidedly anxious.

'What's in the bag, Mr Hartman?'

The man instinctively swung the bag so that it was partially behind his legs, as if that would somehow help him to keep the contents hidden.

'Just some things I thought I'd pick up for Theo, in case he needed them.'

'Yet you told us that you came here to see if he was back. So how do you know he isn't on his way? I'll ask you again. What's in the bag?'

Ted's martial arts training meant he was finely tuned to the slightest hint of movement. Mike Hallam hadn't detected anything, but the moment Hartman made to move, Ted had him by the arm and immobilised him with the speed of a striking snake.

'Seth Hartman, I am arresting you on suspicion of the murder of John Jacobs. You do not have to say anything. But it may harm your defence if you do not mention, when questioned, something which you later rely on in court. Anything you do say can be given in evidence.'

'This is ridiculous. What murder? I don't even know this John whatever his name is. I want my lawyer.'

Ted and Mike carefully installed him in the back of the car. Ted sat next to him, with Mike driving, after he had put the bag in the boot. It didn't feel heavy, but they would wait until they got back to the station to check on the contents.

'If it's the same lawyer who has been advising your nephew, then we can easily call him back to the station for you, Mr Hartman. You are entitled to legal representation, as is your nephew. For now, it might be better if you say nothing, until you've had chance to take advice.'

Hartman was protesting his innocence all the way on the short drive to the station. Ted got him booked in and put in an interview room, while he and Mike donned gloves, found a quiet corner, and had a look in the bag. There wasn't much in it, but what Ted did fish out made the two exchange satisfied looks as Ted exclaimed, 'Bingo!'

'Just as well we're keeping them separate, boss. If Hartman got anywhere near his nephew after us getting our hands on this little lot, he would kill him, for sure.'

The bag contained mostly paperwork. Theo Cowell was obviously not the sharpest knife in the drawer. The delivery note for the hamper was there, screwed up, but clearly showing the destination address, with Hartman's name on it. There was also the crumpled wrapping and address label from the expensive bottle of malt, from one of the earlier deaths. Best of all, there was a notebook with scribbled jottings, the most recent of which mentioned Honest John and his flat number at Sabden House, with the comment, 'Lonley fat bloke, likes to scoff. Diabettick.'

'Clearly not much of a scholar, our Theo. It's going to be very interesting seeing how either of them manage to talk their way out of this,' Ted mused. 'They certainly can't claim they had no knowledge of John, with these details. Everyone locally knew him as Honest John. But not everyone would have known he was diabetic, so they'd been informed by someone who at least knew of him.'

'He must be thick to keep stuff like that.'

'Thought they were too clever for us, I expect. In fact, they might very well have been, if it had been any pathologist other than Professor Nelson. How she can make out any specific smell from stomach contents is beyond me, but it was her nose detecting the single malt that put us on the right track.

'Right, so, let's go and have a crack at the uncle, although I doubt he'll speak before his solicitor gets here. It looks like being a very late one for you and me.'

It was well after midnight when Ted finally got home. Trev was on the sofa, long legs up on the extending rest, buried under a heap of purring cats. He had a black and white film on, in French. Tears were rolling down his cheeks, dripping on to the ears of Queen, who sat on his chest, flicking them each time a drop landed.

Ted flopped down beside him and picked up his arm to

drape around his shoulders. He looked at the screen for a moment, then asked, 'Hôtel du Nord again? How many times is that now?'

'Seventeen,' Trev replied, his eyes still glued on the film. 'Do you want me to turn it off? Are you tired? Or hungry?'

'The ending is probably the same every time,' Ted teased him gently.

Trev picked up the remote and stopped the DVD, then scooped up Queen and used her fur to dry his wet cheeks, to her evident disgust. He turned his full attention to his partner.

'Sorry, you know it gets me every time. So, did you catch the baddies? Are they behind bars where they need to be?'

Ted didn't often talk about his work at home. He certainly seldom shared any of the more gruesome cases, except in brief outline. He had talked a bit to Trev about Honest John, so he explained now how difficult the case might prove to be, going forward to court.

'I really can't see CPS being happy with murder by chocolate, but we're certainly going to try for the best chance we have of putting them away for a long time.'

'Have you eaten? Do you want anything?'

'I had sandwiches earlier on. It's too late really to be thinking about food. I've gone past that stage.'

'Are you tired? It's been a long day.'

'I should be tired but my head's buzzing too much. I doubt I'll sleep easily.'

'In that case,' Trev said, unfolding his long, lithe frame from the settee and pulling Ted up by the arm. 'Let me outline those plans I mentioned earlier.'

Ted went to inform the Ice Queen of the latest arrests, before he and the team started questioning their suspects further the following morning.

'We'll need a meeting with CPS as soon as possible to discuss this, but I don't see how we're going to get a murder charge out of it,' she warned him.

'I've got proof of intent, and the nephew is already spilling his guts.'

'But you know as well as I do there's no murder case to be made out of simply supplying drugs without actually administering them, and I imagine the same would apply to alcohol. And as for the chocolate, I have simply no idea on that. Deliberately removing the medication is significant, but to what degree, I'm not qualified to comment.

'Carry on questioning them for now. I'll get someone over from CPS as soon as I can and let you know when. I'll be more than happy to give you your extra twelve hours, but I honestly think you might need to lower your sights from a murder charge.

Ted left Rob O'Connell to handle the morning briefing for the team. He wanted to get together with Jo, Mike and Sal to discuss strategy for interviewing their two suspects.

'If we can get Theo to make a full confession, implicating his uncle up to the hilt, that's going to help us a lot. He's halfway there. He just needs an extra push.'

'How are they going to manage, both wanting the same solicitor?' Sal asked. 'I'm imagining that Uncle Seth is picking up the legal tab for both of them, so I bet he gets first dibs on the brief. Perhaps the firm will send out a junior to hold the nephew's hand.'

Jo's face took on a cunning expression as he said, 'On the other hand, if the uncle knew the nephew was already singing, he might not want to pay his legal bills at all. He might just cut him loose and let him take the rap for everything. He'll no doubt tell us Theo borrowed his credit card without his knowledge. It would be unfortunate if we were to let slip to him that Theo was already being more than cooperative.'

Ted shot him an admiring look.

'You see, Mike, that's what sneaky really looks like,' he grinned. 'Right, so who wants which? They might be a bit more talkative after a night in our comfy hotel.'

'Uncle Seth will be the harder nut to crack, boss, so why don't you and Mike take that one and Sal and I will switch Theo on and just let him squawk? I doubt he's going to take a lot of prompting. And with luck, we should have the fingerprint results from the medication bag back soon, with his name all over them.'

Ted nodded.

'Give it enough time to be convincing then one of you come in for a whispered update with me, and make sure you're heard using Theo's name and the word confession several times.'

They were all smiling in anticipation as they went their separate ways.

Ted started with Hartman, who had the solicitor with him. It was slow going, as he had clearly been told to say nothing and was doing a good job of following instructions. Jo and Sal went into another interview room with Theo, after waiting long enough for effect. He was sitting alone, looking more worried than ever.

Jo flashed him his friendliest smile, gold tooth glinting.

'Is someone on the way in to advise you, Theo? I suppose your uncle's got the good solicitor, if he's paying the bills? You don't have to say anything until someone gets here. It's fine. Your uncle's already cooperating fully, so you just take your time.'

'I don't know what's happening,' the young man said anxiously. 'The lawyer last night just told me not to say anything, until someone got here. But maybe I should tell you my side of it? Like I told you last night, it was all my uncle, he told me what to do.'

Jo leaned back in his chair, all charming smiles and friendly demeanour.

'Honestly, Theo, it's fine. Don't think you have to say anything, without a solicitor present. In fact, we could take a short break, until one arrives. Perhaps you'd like a drink of water? You look a bit hot. DC Ahmed can bring you one.'

He announced the break for the tape, then the two of them left the room. Sal went in search of the drink while Jo knocked on the door of the next room and went in. He went over to Ted and crouched down to his level, talking quietly but making sure, as instructed, the words 'Theo', 'confess' and 'implicate' were distinguishable.

Hartman's face was a picture of panic. He opened his mouth to speak, but the solicitor abruptly cut across him.

'Mr Cowell isn't to be interviewed further without legal representation. Those were my explicit instructions. Someone from my firm will be along shortly. Until then, he is not to be interviewed.'

Jo straightened up and turned on the Latin charm.

'Oh, we're not interviewing him, sir. He just wanted to speak to us. He really wanted to talk. We were having such trouble getting him to stop that we've taken a short break.'

Ted hid a smile watching Hartman's face drain of colour and the solicitor's go purple with anger.

As Jo was leaving, a PC put his head round the door to tell Ted he was wanted upstairs.

'This would seem to be the ideal moment for us to take a break, so that you can perhaps go and take further instruction from your other client,' he said, as he announced his departure for the tape.

The CPS's Chief Crown Prosecutor was with the Ice Queen when Ted went upstairs. They knew one another of old, both professionally and socially. Ted's partner before Trev had been a Crown Prosecutor. The two men shook hands and Ted sat down.

'Debra has been telling me about your latest case, Ted. Very interesting. But I hope you're not seriously suggesting we go to court on a murder by chocolate charge?'

'I've got intent. And I'll have a causal link with the

fingerprints on the insulin, which was found in Cowell's flat,' Ted began, but was cut short.

'Unlawful Act Manslaughter. You know as well as I do, that's the best we're likely to get out of this. Even then, I have my doubts. Get me a confession, get me fingerprints to prove the unlawful act, charge them with that and we'll see if we can't make it stick. And you'll need the right inquest verdict as well, don't forget.'

'This was murder. A cynical act, deliberately causing deaths. I know we've no chance on the drugs ...'

'Manslaughter's our best bet. I'd go so far as to say it's our only bet. And don't forget, if we all do our jobs properly, they could still get a life sentence.'

Chapter Thirty

Ted wasn't thrilled at the news but he accepted it was the best they were going to get. He called Jo, Mike and Sal together over a coffee while he reported back on the verdict from CPS.

'I need to get on with planning tomorrow's meeting and sorting out a reception party for the lovely Linda Lovelace. Jo, you seem to have established a rapport with young Theo, so you have another crack at him, if his brief is here. Mike, you see what you can do with Mr Hartman. Then charge them both with Unlawful Act Manslaughter. Get them in front of a magistrate as soon as possible, and let's oppose bail. I don't think we'll have any luck, if there's no previous, but talk to the custody officer about possible interference with witnesses, or evidence, or anything you can think of.

'Sal, I want the brother-in-law, the councillor. We're not going to get him on manslaughter. It would be a wing and a prayer to get him on soliciting to murder or conspiracy, but I'm not ruling anything out. I want anything and everything there is on him, even parking tickets, as it's my feeling he may be the brains behind this. He would certainly be in a position to know which tenants were on secure tenancies, and what their personal circumstances were. And don't forget to talk to Pocket Billiards. Tell him he'll be getting a press release soon, before anyone else, about the arrests. Get him on board.'

'Do I have to buy him lunch and watch him eat, boss?' Sal asked plaintively.

'If that's what it takes.'

'Got our first sniff from Linda,' Océane told Ted, when he went up to the main office.

'Already? That was quick. Any trace yet?'

'Negative. Just an exchange which quickly became smutty. I took a gamble and said our man would be in this area at the weekend. I hope that's not too soon to set things up?'

'It should be ideal, thank you. I've got the planning meeting tomorrow, and I'd like you to be at that in case your input is needed. I think it's a great idea to keep him focused on the weekend as, with any luck, it may stop him from killing again before then. We'll need to find a suitable venue. We can hardly entice him back to anywhere he's already killed.'

'What about the Hotel Sorrento, boss?' Rob suggested.

He and Virgil had more or less finished at South Manchester now and were busy collating all the information they had to date.

'I heard it had been taken over already. It's open again, then, so soon?'

'Yeah, part of a small chain now. New management, new name, although I can't remember what. The Ace, I think. Anyway, there are a few pubs within walking distance and it's not quite as busy as a town centre location, which may be easier to manage. Also we already know the layout in there from the other case, pretty much, so it might be a good choice.'

'Good suggestion, Rob, thanks. I'll go and check it out later, sound out the management. They won't be thrilled at having an armed stake-out on their premises, no doubt. But they may be public-spirited enough to go for it. And at least it's a small hotel, so it's not as if they would be turning down huge numbers of bookings. Although at the weekend, of course, we risk there being a wedding party. Steve, can you check out what CCTV coverage is like around there. I'd be happier with an area where there are cameras.'

'I've not even talked days or timings with Linda yet, so we could maybe try for the Sunday evening, if it's quieter? Just let me know what pub and if it looks like we might have a meet, I can float that idea. So far it's mostly consisted of 'you can safely put your valuable assets in my hands' from me, and Linda replying that she may even be able to help my portfolio to swell.'

Ted made a face.

'I'm not too sure that's an image I really want in my head for the rest of the day, but thanks, Océane.'

She grinned at him.

'And you still want me to bring the suspect to us, rather than trying to go after him where he is? He's still using throwaway mail addresses, a different one each time, just the same name.'

'It'll be easier to manage if we do it that way. I'm pretty sure that's what Inspector Jenkins from Armed Response will want. So far Maurice has had no luck with an address for John Smith. The B&B one he had was old, long since gone cold. It's looking like our best bet by far. He must have an accommodation address for his mail somewhere, but even when we find that, it doesn't advance us much.'

Ted paused on his way to check out the hotel to phone Trev.

'I may be flat out tomorrow, but if I get away at a decent time today, do you fancy going for a meal somewhere this evening?'

'A bag of chips and a side order of mushy peas?' Trev asked teasingly.

Ted laughed.

'You make me sound like such a cheapskate. A proper meal. Nothing too fancy, just a nice change. I'll drive, so you can have some wine. Just because.'

'Gets my vote. Does this mean you'll miss club tomorrow? You know how much the kids always miss you, especially Flip.'

'You never know, I might just surprise you and make that,

too. It all depends.'

He started singing Gilbert and Sullivan's 'A Policeman's Lot is Not a Happy One' just before he rang off, and heard Trev laughing.

It was strange for Ted to be back at the Hotel Sorrento, the scene of one of the most distressing cases of his career. One which had had a serious impact on his relationship with Trev. Thankfully, those dark days were behind him now, he hoped.

He was surprised at the speed with which the hotel had been taken over and spruced up. It looked completely different to when he had last visited it, although it was not all that long ago. He knew the staff would certainly have changed. One who had helped them before was now on a Witness Protection Programme and Ted had no idea where she had finished up. He hoped she was enjoying her new life, wherever she was now.

He produced his warrant card and went over to talk to the young woman on the reception desk. Unsurprisingly, when he explained his mission, she said that although she could call the duty manager, who was currently busy dealing with a problem on another floor, she suspected he would need to talk to head office. She helpfully installed Ted at a small side table in the foyer and arranged a welcome pot of tea for him, while he waited for the manager.

When he appeared, the manager was young, eager and oozing efficiency. He took Ted to his office, listened carefully to what he had to say and made some notes.

'We haven't been open long, as you're probably aware, so we're not yet fully booked, especially for Sunday evening, which tends to be a quiet one. I will need to clear it with head office but, looking at the bookings,' he was tapping and clicking away at his computer as he spoke, 'it should be relatively simple to clear a wing for the duration of your exercise. As long as you can reassure us that no lives will be put at risk.'

'It will be a carefully controlled operation,' Ted told him guardedly. 'I don't want to bring any undue pressure to bear, but it is essential that we catch this suspect. We can't rule out the possibility that he could target your hotel for a killing at some point in the future, if he's not arrested, which might be a helpful argument for your management.'

There was surprisingly little resistance from the hotel's head office when the manager phoned through and explained the situation. Ted guessed that, as the new kids on the block, they were keen to cooperate with the police as much as they could. They never knew when they might be in need of Brownie points in the future.

Once consent had been given, Ted asked if he could look at the layout of the rooms the manager was proposing to make available.

'I'll need to come back for a further check with other officers, probably tomorrow, but it's essential that we're able to control access to where we will be. We need to be able to prevent members of the public wandering into that part of the hotel, as well as stopping our suspect from getting away.'

The manager obligingly opened vacant rooms along the corridor to show Ted, who was relieved to find that the four-poster beds which had been there before had all now gone. They would have triggered unpleasant memories from the previous case. Everywhere was now clean lines, modern, minimalist, unmistakably part of a chain rather than the small private hotel it had been previously.

'Thanks very much for your cooperation. As I said, if it's not too inconvenient, I'll be back some time tomorrow with other officers to do more of a detailed recce and talk things through with you again. I'll give you a call when I know an approximate time.'

Back at the station, Ted found Jo, Mike and Sal grinning in a self-satisfied way, which led him to hope things had gone better than expected with the remand hearing of Theo Cowell and Seth Hartman. He had been convinced they would both be granted bail, so he would welcome any better news.

'Don't tell me we got a remand in custody? I'd have bet against that, for sure.'

'And how, boss,' Jo chuckled. 'You'd never guess what went on. As soon as the pair of them were put in the dock together, young Theo started screaming blue murder and saying his uncle was going to kill him at the first chance he got. Which fitted very nicely with our asking for a remand in custody because of the likelihood of intimidating witnesses.

'Between the murderous looks Uncle Seth was chucking at him, and poor Theo wailing and weeping like a baby, begging to be kept away from his uncle and locked up for his own protection, we didn't even have to make much of a case. Both of them remanded in custody for one week. Result!'

'Looks like we may just be on a winning streak all round, hopefully,' Ted said, reporting on his trip to the hotel. 'If we can wrap at least one of these cases up this week, the drinks are on me on Friday. If we polish off two of them, I'll have to think of something more of a treat.'

Ted went back to his office to finish off his preparations for the big planning meeting first thing the next day. He couldn't remember having eaten during the day but decided, as time was getting on, he might as well not bother and save himself for the night out. He phoned Trev again, with an update.

'At the moment, I know of no cause or just impediment why I, Ted Darling, bachelor of this parish, should not take you, Trevor Armstrong, also bachelor of this parish, out to dinner tonight.'

Trev was laughing down the phone at him.

'You sound in a good mood. Does that mean I can go mad and have some fish bits with my bag of chips?'

'You can have chilli sauce on them, too. Let's push the boat right out. I'm happy because we've got two bad guys banged up where they belong, against all the odds, so that's something to celebrate this evening. Then all I need is for this meeting tomorrow morning to go well and we might finally be getting somewhere with this other case.

'I'm just finishing up here, then I'll be home as soon as possible. Book somewhere, if you like. And don't pinch all the hot water. I'll need a shower too, when I get back.'

Trev's tone was suggestive as he responded, 'We could always save water and shower together.'

'Then we'd never get out to eat, and you know it.'

Ted wasn't the only one planning a night out that evening. Jezza had been impressed with the financial advice Nat had given her so far. She'd also been quite taken with him, as a person. There was something broken and vulnerable about him, which she could identify with.

Going out had always presented problems for her in the past, since Tommy had come to live with her. Before that, because of her personal history, she had found it difficult forming relationships. But now she felt like taking a step into that world and, having steeled herself to pluck up the courage, had phoned Nat and asked if she could take him for a drink to thank him for his help. She would drive, as he had no car. That way she knew she would stay completely sober and would be in control of the situation.

Things were back to normal between her, Steve and Maurice, and if Jezza failed to correctly interpret the looks Maurice would sometimes shoot her way when he thought she wasn't looking, it was not through heartlessness on her part. It was simply that their night together had meant something different to her than to him.

Steve was babysitting again and Maurice was keeping him company. He had an ulterior motive for his presence in the flat when Nat arrived, having got the bus, to meet up with Jezza. She let Nat in when he arrived, then scuttled off to finish getting ready, telling him, over her shoulder, to make himself comfortable in the living room with Maurice. Steve and Tommy were in the spare room, playing some sort of computer game together.

Nat limped to the sofa and sat down, while Maurice watched him. Then he moved across the room and planted his bulk next to him.

'So, Nat,' he said, conversationally, although the name was spat out, like a bad taste. One of Maurice's beefy hands landed suddenly on Nat's barely-recovered thigh, injured in an accident, and gave it a hard squeeze. 'You push trolleys for a living. Is that right?'

Nat tried not to make his wince too noticeable as he replied, 'I do at the moment, Maurice. It's no secret that my employment record is a bit of a disaster and I finished up on the streets.'

'And now you're sniffing round Jezza? Who you know has money. Who lives in a smart place like this, and who drives a limited edition car.'

'It's not like that, Maurice, honestly. Virgil just asked me to help, with some advice. Then Jezza phoned to ask me for a drink to say thank you. Really, that's all there is to it.'

This time Maurice's big hand moved with surprising speed and grabbed a fistful of Nat's wedding tackle, squeezing in a vice-like grip, which brought tears to Nat's eyes at the pain.

'I'm glad to hear that, Nat,' with the same note of contempt, his hand still gripping. 'Because let me just tell you something. I love that lass. I'd like to see her with the right person. But if you ever do anything, and I do mean anything, to hurt her in any way, then you will have me to answer to. And let me tell you, I can make your life very, very difficult. And not just as a copper. So think on.'

He gave a final squeeze, then let go, just as Jezza came back into the room, all smiles and looking eager to go.

Nat didn't trust himself to speak, worried his voice would

come out as a high-pitched squeak. He nodded to Maurice in what he hoped was a gesture of understanding. His limp was much more pronounced as he followed Jezza out of the flat.

Chapter Thirty-one

'Morning Ted, congrats on the promotion,' Inspector Paul Jenkins greeted Ted as he pulled up a couple of places away from him in the car park.

'Morning, Shooter, and thanks. Came as a big surprise, I can tell you,' Ted replied.

He and Jenkins had trained together in firearms years ago, until their career paths took them in different directions.

'You did my lads out of their fun last time. I hope you're not going to grab all the glory again on this case. How's the hand, by the way?'

'Getting there,' Ted lifted his palm to show the still impressive scar.

'Aren't you supposed to put honey on scars, to help them to heal?'

'Honey?' Ted asked in surprise, looking at his hand. 'That would be no good. I'd keep licking it off. I've got a terribly sweet tooth.'

Everyone was arriving for the meeting in the conference room. Detective Superintendent Jim Baker was not far behind Ted and took his place at the head of the table, next to the Ice Queen, flanked by Ted, and Kevin Turner. Jenkins took a seat next to Jo Rodriguez. Ted had brought in most of his team, including Océane, but had left Steve and Maurice upstairs for now, to take any incoming calls that might be relevant. He hadn't bothered to bring in the South Manchester depleted team, or Brian Donohue's, as the operation was going to take place on his own patch. Some of Kevin Turner's uniformed officers were also there, including Susan Heap, a trained Taser officer.

Jim Baker called the meeting to order then let Ted outline all they knew so far. He gave a summary, then finished with, 'We're hoping to draw him out on Sunday evening. A date for a drink in a pub near to the old Hotel Sorrento, then hopefully lure him into following whoever we put in there, back to the hotel. That's where we'll have a reception party waiting for him, including Armed Response.'

'What if, for some reason, he changes his pattern and decides to attack on the way back to the hotel?' the Ice Queen asked.

'I want a command post in a van, watching the route from the pub. Everybody wired, plenty of bodies to keep us posted of where he is at all times.'

'I can probably get shooters covering at least part of the walk. I'm assuming it's not far between the two locations?' Jenkins asked.

'Not far, but not many ideal buildings on the route. I already took a look,' Ted told him. 'One or two vantage points, but it may involve being in private houses. You'll want to see for yourself, of course.'

'I'll take a look later on. Chief Inspector Darling, you and I will need to go together to recce all the terrain we need to cover.'

Shooter was keeping it formal in the meeting.

'And there's no better way? No way of us finding him rather than luring him out?' the Ice Queen again, the voice of caution.

Océane jumped in to answer. Her field of expertise.

'He's proving tricky to trace. He's got some basic knowledge and he's using it to make sure he's never in one place for too long.'

'He's an NFA,' Ted confirmed. 'The only address we had

for him has long since gone cold. According to what Maurice found out from his sister-in-law, he no longer works. He has some money from a life insurance policy on his wife, which is presumably what he's using to live on. It was in place long enough for the suicide clause not to apply.'

'And we're sure this is definitely our main suspect, who's in contact now?' Jim Baker asked.

Océane smiled.

'I think the likelihood of there being two Linda Lovelaces prowling the meet-up sites is slim, especially with a suggestive avatar of a slightly open mouth and very full lips. Also, and I'll spare everyone's blushes by not quoting verbatim, but our Linda has a particular way of writing. I agree with the boss and Jezza, the fantasy stuff is more that of a man, pretending to be a woman. We could be wrong but it doesn't ring true somehow. I'll go into the details if you want me to, but this might not be the best place to do so.'

'Quite so,' the Ice Queen said primly, which caused a few smiles, quickly disguised.

'Right, so, down to who is doing what,' Ted continued. 'I want people in the pub, at the hotel, and on the walk between the two. I want this whole operation under tight control from start to finish. We don't really know what we're dealing with here, so no risks.

'If we use a room at the end of the corridor at the hotel, we can put Armed Response in the first couple of rooms as well as in the room itself. Then we can hopefully surround him and take him down quietly with no fuss.

'We need someone to play the part of the person in the profile Océane has set up, plus female officers in the pub ready for the pick-up when Linda doesn't show himself. And it's the male officer in the room at the greatest degree of risk, so that should be me.'

A chorus of voices shouted him down on that the minute he spoke.

'You're just over the last serious injury. You're not going in again,' Jim Baker said in a tone which showed he was not going to accept any argument.

'It needs to be one of my shooters in the room opening the door,' Jenkins put in. 'Our man won't be expecting that. They're in protective gear anyway and if necessary, they can take him down in one shot. I'm imagining there's only room for one of mine in there, realistically? But you still need your man to lure him in. They can put a stab vest on and stay behind my officer when they open the door. That will mean we have him surrounded.'

'With respect to everyone, I'm told by my wife, she who knows everything, that I always look like I'm out on the pull, so I could do it,' Jo offered. 'Anyway, it's my face, or part of it, in the avatar. Océane thought the gold tooth added a little something. I'm not all that brave though, so I'm happy to wear the stab vest and hide behind the bed once the knock on the door comes.'

'And the female officer?' Jim Baker asked. 'Do you foresee a risk to them, as they're leaving? He's not suddenly likely to grab them and try a human shield situation or something?'

Ted hesitated.

'He's always been careful to let the woman leave before he does anything. I think it's unlikely that, at this stage, that he will suddenly change his MO.'

'I could play that part, boss,' Jezza offered. 'I've at least got my kickboxing training if he does try to grab me for some reason.' Seeing his hesitation, she said, 'Someone has to do it. It might as well be me.'

'Just don't make it too hard for me to chat you up, Jezza. We've got to be seen going off together, and it's got to look convincing,' Jo smiled.

Despite the seriousness of the situation, there were a few chuckles. Ted finished off assigning tasks to everyone, then was just about to wind up the meeting when the Ice Queen posed another question.

'Are you sure of stringing the suspect along until Sunday? What if he feels the need to strike again before then?'

'I suppose that's up to me, then,' Océane cut in. 'I'm busy working all the suggestive remarks about investment, asset and growth I can think of into what I'm posting, hoping it sounds both inviting and convincing. Bearing in mind that I'm a woman trying to write as a man, and he's a man trying to write as a woman. If I need any help with the fantasies, who's got the muckiest mind?'

The answer was a unanimous, 'Maurice,' from all of Ted's team.

Ted went with Paul Jenkins to walk the route between the chosen pub and the hotel, and to take a closer look at the hotel layout itself. He had the advantage of having been in firearms himself, so was looking at things from the same perspective.

'It's a bit cramped in here for my team to be working,' Jenkins grumbled, looking at the modest-sized hotel rooms and narrow corridors. 'But I agree, you're right not to try to get him outside, where we've no control over members of the public who might get in the way.'

'Jo will need to have the shower running soon after Jezza leaves. That's been the pattern so far. With the shower room just inside the door like this, it does at least mean he can reach out to open the door but stay safely inside there, out of the way, to give your officer a clear line of sight. And your officers in rooms at the end of the corridor can block his exit. We should have him caught like a rat in a trap.'

'So it's down to your team now, Ted. If you can keep stringing him along and bring him to us, my lads should be able to deal with him effectively. I've seen all I need to for now. Keep me posted on timings and, if all goes according to plan, I'll see you again on Sunday. And this time, don't grab all the glory yourself. Let my lads have a bit of fun.'

There was a strange feeling of anticipation for the team, tempered by inactivity. Apart from Océane keeping in contact with their suspect and stringing him along, there was not a lot any of them could constructively do on the case. Nothing but a collective holding of breath, a sense of hope that their suspect would be patient enough to wait until the weekend before striking again. In the meantime, it was routine paperwork, building as solid a case as they could for when they finally got their hands on him.

Ted even made time to go to the self-defence club and his own judo session to follow on Wednesday evening. The youngsters were always pleased to see him. He had quite a following. Young Flip, in particular, always asked his mother if he could stay and watch the senior class when Ted was there and he could see him sparring with Trev.

Ted's injured hand was recovering well but still lacked a strong grip. It meant he couldn't get as good a hold on Trev's judogi or belt as usual, and his partner exploited the weakness mercilessly. It was fast and furious randori, both men soon breathing hard and sweating. Exactly what Ted needed to concentrate the mind so he could focus on what was to come at the weekend. He had his suspect in his sights at last and he needed to be ready.

Jezza, Megan, and Susan Heap were in the pub well ahead of the appointed time for the meet-up with their suspect. They were dressed up to the nines, three young women, out for a good time, on the pull, if they could find anyone worthy of their attention. Susan's shoulder bag contained her Taser, should the need arise. Rob, Maurice and Virgil were sitting at a corner table, with a clear line of sight to the door, chatting over a drink. They would follow in the car later, once Jo and Jezza left, hopefully with their suspect following them.

There were a few couples and small groups, mostly in for the food, it seemed, but it was not busy. When the door opened and a man on his own came in, Rob said quietly into his lapel microphone, 'Suspect has just entered the bar. He's gone to get himself a drink. Medium height and build, dark fleece jacket with a logo, a holdall, and a newspaper tucked under his arm.'

'Steve just picked him up on the CCTV as he was coming in,' Ted confirmed from the van parked roughly halfway between the pub and the hotel, monitoring the whole operation. 'He did his usual trick with the newspaper so we didn't get much of a look at him.'

'He's got his drink and gone to sit down near the door. I'll keep you posted.'

Jo Rodriguez was next through the door. He certainly looked the part of a man out for action. Jezza almost snorted her drink down her nose at the wafts of aftershave which reached her even across the bar. He got himself a bottle of lager then perched on a bar stool, studiously looking round the room, a man on a blind date looking for his pick-up.

'Suspect has clocked Jo. Just sitting watching him for now,' Rob announced quietly.

Jo was clearly in his element. His eyes travelled all round the room, making flirty contact with any female who returned his glance. The gold tooth kept making an appearance as he smiled widely at anyone he saw.

Jezza was struggling with the giggles, knowing she would be leaving with him before the evening was over. She returned his admiring looks with a smile of her own, noticing as she did so the way the suspect's eyes were now going from one to the other of them. He seemed to be taking the bait.

'I think it's my turn to go and get the drinks, ladies,' she said, standing up and sashaying her way over to the bar, standing just close enough to Jo to look as if she was showing genuine interest. He was playing his part to perfection, openly flirting with her, then looking towards the door and checking his mobile phone, as if he was waiting for someone. All the while, the man in the fleece by the door was watching the interaction between them.

'Still watching,' Rob updated.

'Right, Jezza, we need to move to the next phase,' Ted's voice came quietly through Jezza's earpiece.

They'd decided it would look more realistic to split the women up, leaving Jezza and Jo alone, to head off to the hotel together, hopefully with their suspect trailing them.

'I'm just not in the mood for a curry now, that's all. I think I prefer it here,' Jezza said when she returned to the table, raising her voice slightly. 'If you two want curry, go on then, I'm not stopping you.'

As Megan and Susan flounced out of the bar, Jo stood up and moved across to take his place on the bench seat they had vacated, striking up conversation with Jezza. It was now well past the appointed time for him to meet Linda. Their heads were close together and it wasn't long before Jo's arm was along the back of the seat behind her. It looked the most natural thing in the world when, not long afterwards, the two of them rose and left the pub together.

'He's taken the bait. He's following them,' Rob reported.

'I have eyes on the suspect now. Clear line of sight as he's following the two officers,' one of Jenkins' armed officers reported from the top of a nearby building.

'Just wait. Everyone hold your position. Let's allow him to do as he usually does. Wait until Jezza comes back out before we do anything. That's our best chance of getting him with minimum risk to anyone,' Ted told them, his voice steady, from inside the control unit.

Several pairs of eyes were glued to Jo and Jezza as they walked along the main road, Jo's arm now round her waist as they went. Susan and Megan were not far away, tucked inside a shop doorway, Susan's hand on her Taser so it was ready if their suspect showed any sign of deviating from his normal pattern and putting anyone at risk.

Sal, in hotel uniform, behind the reception desk, studiously ignored all three of them as they went in through the main entrance. Jo steered Jezza towards the ground floor corridor, with the room they were using at the end of it. The suspect followed them.

As they reached the door of the room, Jezza saw the man hesitate, feel in his pockets as if looking for a key-card, then turn and go back through the reception area.

'Suspect has now left the hotel and is in the car park,' Sal reported.

'I have him in sight now.'

It was Mike Hallam, outside, walking around the car park with his neighbour's black Labrador, borrowed for the occasion, which was obligingly lifting its leg at every bush. 'He's just lurking, getting his cigarettes out.'

'So now we wait,' Ted said quietly, aware of the mounting tension of everyone involved. 'Nobody do anything to panic him. Everyone confirm your positions if he does make a break for it.'

'Maurice and me are outside in the car, boss.' Virgil.

'I'm on the petrol station forecourt, looking at flowers. I've got a good view of the front of the hotel.' Rob.

'Still by the shop opposite with Megan, boss, Taser at the ready.' Susan.

'Still have line of sight to the hotel, sir.' Jenkins' officer.

Jezza and Jo had pulled off their mikes for the moment. They didn't want the others listening in to their conversation, which was light-hearted. It was bad enough with an Armed Response officer in the room listening to them.

'So, how long do you need?' Jezza asked Jo teasingly.

'Well, I don't like to boast, but it won't be quick,' he responded with a wink. 'And I'd usually be beyond jumping into the shower straight afterwards. On the other hand, we don't want to keep everyone waiting too long. Do you want to watch the telly, while we're at it, or at least supposed to be?'

They gave it a good hour, then Jezza put her mike back on

and went out of the room. She made her way to the entrance and walked out, noticing out of the corner of her eye that the man was standing a short distance away. This was the dangerous part now. She knew he was going to go into the hotel, intent on killing Jo. She just hoped that the firearms officers would be able to stop him.

She walked out into the main road then got into the back of Virgil's black BMW, parked a short distance away.

'You all right, bonny lass?' Maurice asked her, his tone concerned.

'Fine, Maurice, don't fuss. Just keep your fingers crossed that Jo will be.'

'He's just gone through reception, heading your way now, Jo. He's changed into his overalls, in the toilet in reception,' Sal announced.

'Stand by, everyone,' Ted cautioned, and Jenkins joined in to alert his men.

'Shower's on and I'm cowering behind the door in my body armour,' Jo said, a note of humour in his tone. 'And bang on cue, here's the knock at the door,' then, raising his voice, 'Hang on a minute.'

'Maintenance, sir, can you turn the shower off, please? There's a problem with the plumbing,' came the muffled voice from outside the door.

Jo stuck his head cautiously out of the bathroom and looked to the armed officer, who gave him the universal signal for okay, at the same time speaking quietly into his mike. Jo's hand turned the doorknob, then he pulled back inside the bathroom.

The door flew open and the man burst into the room, knife gripped in his raised hand, looking for his target. Instead, he found himself looking at an armed police officer who was shouting at him, 'Armed police! Stand still! Drop the weapon!'

At the same moment, two more Armed Response officers appeared in the corridor behind him, shouting the same thing.

The man hesitated for barely a second, then dropped the knife and started screaming, 'Don't shoot me, please don't shoot me.'

'Down on the floor. Put your hands on your head,' the first officer was yelling now.

The man flung himself down in terror, visibly trembling. Jo stepped quietly out of the shower-room, handcuffs at the ready, smelling the distinctive, acrid stink of urine as the man lost all self-control.

'John Smith,' he began quietly, issuing the familiar words of the caution, 'I'm arresting you...'

Chapter Thirty-two

It was the wee small hours before Ted got back home. John Smith's state of mental health had given cause for concern after his arrest, so Ted had called out the police surgeon, Tim Elliott. He had administered a mild sedative and ordered him to be kept on close suicide watch, before going on his way, sneezing frequently. Ted made a mental note to finally ask him, next time he saw him, just what it was to which he was allergic.

Trev was already in bed by the time Ted got back. He was, as ever, stretched out across most of the available space, buried under cats, sleeping the sleep of the innocent. Queen opened one baleful eye at the intrusion and Brian rolled on to his back, exposing a fluffy stomach to be stroked, but none of the other felines stirred so much as a whisker.

As he slipped out of his clothes and quietly hung up his work suit, Ted looked fondly at his sleeping partner and reminded himself once more how lucky he was. He just wished he could persuade Trev to marry him, but he was always adamant that it would make too many waves and they were perfectly happy as they were. No use Ted pointing out that a former Assistant Commissioner of the Met was gay and it had been public knowledge. Trev knew that, like a lot of people, Jim Baker could just about cope with them as a couple, but not as a married couple, and could never have agreed to be Ted's best man.

Ted felt selfish even trying to wake Trev, but he was in need of an ear to listen, even if sleepily, while he talked about the tensions of the last few hours, and the overwhelming relief that the case seemed finally to be over. Besides which, on a purely practical level, there was simply no room for him in the bed. He slid under the duvet as best he could then leaned closer to kiss Trev gently awake.

Trev stirred slowly and opened those incredibly blue eyes, smiling softly at the sight of Ted home, safe and sound.

'Hello, you, did you catch the bad guy?'

'We did,' Ted told him, moving further into the bed and into Trev's arms as he made some space. 'Sorry I woke you. There just wasn't much room.'

'Sorry. I meant to stay awake, but you know what I'm like. Do you want to talk about it?'

'It's fine. You're tired, go to sleep. I'll tell you all about it tomorrow.'

Trev moved slightly to get back to a comfortable position which still left Ted a bit of room, his eyelids drooping. Just before he went back to sleep, he said, 'Oh, Shewee phoned. All excited. She got her place on the school team. She said hi.'

As he started to doze off again, he sleepily sang, or more precisely massacred, Queen's 'We Are the Champions'. Ted smiled to himself. His partner seemed to be even more tone deaf when half asleep than when fully awake.

Ted was in early, checking on how John Smith was doing, before he began questioning him. The custody sergeant reported that he had spent a quiet night and seemed to be calm. Ted knew he would have to proceed with caution, if there was any doubt at all about the suspect being fit to be interviewed.

It had been a late night for everyone, with a debriefing after the arrest. Despite that, the Ice Queen was in as early as Ted was, anxious to talk to him before he began questioning. The case was really Jim Baker's but it was her station, she was in charge of what went on in it, and she liked things done by the book.

'I'll get Tim Elliott back to check him over before we even start questioning him,' Ted assured her. 'We've got the knife as well as the boots and overalls now, and no matter how careful he's been, I'm hopeful there will be traces of the victims on those.'

'It was good work, an exemplary operation. We don't want the wheels to come off now if he's not handled carefully. You'll be interviewing him yourself, I imagine? At least I know you will be careful with him. Who will be with you?'

'I'm going to get Megan in, DC Jennings. She looks nice and calm. Between us we shouldn't be too intimidating. I'm hoping it will all go smoothly.'

Tim Elliott had been and gone by the time Ted was ready to start questioning John Smith. He'd have to ask about his sneezing another time.

Smith was sitting quietly and calmly at the table in the interview room when Ted opened the door and stood aside to let Megan go in first. They both took their seats opposite him. Ted started the recording and dealt with the formalities.

'Can you please confirm your name and personal details, for the tape.'

'John Smith, forty-five, no fixed abode, currently unemployed. Widower. My wife – my ex-wife, at her request – killed herself. She committed suicide because some heartless bastard swindled her out of all her money and she couldn't go on any longer,' at which point his voice, which had been rising and getting shrill, broke and he started to sob, burying his face in his hands on the desk.

'Mr Smith,' Ted said quietly, 'you've been told you have the right to legal representation. Are you sure you wouldn't like to have someone here? We could take a short break while a solicitor is called?'

The man took a long shuddering breath and seemed to regain control of himself.

'No, thank you, you're very kind. I don't want a solicitor.

There's no point. I killed those men. All four of them. I would have killed the one last night as well, if you hadn't arrested me. I'm glad you did. It's time it stopped. I did it for Elaine. I couldn't find the man who destroyed her, but I found others, who were clearly doing the same thing.'

'Do you need a drink of water, Mr Smith?' Megan offered.

He shook his head and looked up.

'No. No, thank you. It's fine. Let's do this. I want to make a full confession. I want to tell you everything. In a sense, it will be a relief.'

Once he started, it was like opening the floodgates. The whole story simply flowed out of him, with scarcely a pause. Ted sent Megan out for water for him when his mouth was clearly getting dry, but he talked with no hesitation and made no attempt to deny anything.

He told them that following the suicide of his ex-wife he had suffered a breakdown and been unable to do much. He'd lost his job because of prolonged sick leave, but had then decided to use the money from his wife's life insurance policy to fund a personal mission to try to find the man who had ruined her.

Despite all his efforts, he had been unable to trace 'Nigel', the man his ex-wife had been in contact with. Failure to do so had sent him spiralling into an even worse mental state. But his research had showed him that other men were doing a similar sort of thing. Some were cynically using the dating sites not just for casual sex but also to try to make some money. It was often innocent enough, selling insurance, sometimes extra mortgage cover. But occasionally it would involve get-rich-quick schemes, from which they made a commission, which didn't live up to their promise and could often cause financial hardship for their victims.

'The first time it happened, I didn't mean to do the man any harm, I swear. I just lured him to a pub, then followed him back to his hotel. I was planning on scaring him, making him stop what he was doing. I always waited for the woman to leave. I never wanted to hurt, or frighten, the women, not even to upset them. They were always innocent parties in this. I just wanted to get the men to stop what they were doing.

'I took a kitchen knife with me, not planning to use it, the first time, just to frighten the man. I thought I might be able to get him to cancel any phony investments he'd sold. But when I saw him standing there, so self-satisfied, so pleased with himself, I just lost control. I started slashing at him, and stabbing him. Then when he fell down, I just wanted to stamp that smug look off his face. I couldn't stop myself.

'I carried on and on, even after I knew he was dead. And then I felt really good. Completely calm. I felt I'd done something, at least, to compensate for what my wife went through. I took his key card and left it at reception, as if he'd checked out. Then I decided to do it again, and to keep on doing it until I was caught.'

His voice now was chillingly matter-of-fact. He might just have been confessing to some petty shoplifting, from the dispassionate tone he was using.

'I knew what I was doing. And I wanted to do it. I was luring them in, just like Nigel lured Elaine, and then I gave them what was coming to them. I'm glad I did it. I have no regrets, only that I never caught the one who started it all. But at least now there are four less than there were.'

He looked calmly from Ted to Megan and back again, then asked, 'So what happens now?'

'You'll now be taken and formally charged with all four murders, plus the attempted murder from last night. You will then appear before magistrates as soon as possible and will be remanded, almost certainly in custody, as you have no fixed address. It's likely that you will remain in custody, with further remand hearings, until your trial, at a date which has not yet been fixed.'

'Perfect,' Smith nodded, as if he was accepting the room on

offer to him at his latest B&B. 'I accomplished part of what I set out to do. It's time to stop now.'

'It was quite disturbing, how calm he was about it all, boss,' Megan commented as they made their way back up to the main office, once Smith had been charged and put back in a holding cell until his first remand hearing. 'If he gets a good lawyer, after all, do you think they'll go for a diminished responsibility defence?'

'I don't think he'd let them. I think he's made his mind up that it's over and he doesn't want to fight it.'

All the team members looked up expectantly as Ted and Megan came back into the office.

'Full confession to everything,' Ted told them. 'Drinks are on me in The Grapes after work. Good job, everyone. Now let's get the paperwork sewn up tight.'

There was a collective cheer from the rest of the team at both pieces of good news.

Ted went back to his desk to start on his own paperwork. The legwork may have been over, but there was still a lot to do. Even with a likely guilty plea, they still had to get the file right for CPS. He sat himself down with a mug of green tea and got stuck into the task in hand.

He looked up in surprise as his office door opened without a knock and first Jim Baker then Gerry Fletcher came in, both looking serious. Ted pulled off his reading glasses and stood up.

'Ted,' Jim Baker nodded, not looking his usual amiable self. 'We just came to bring you up to speed. DS Mackenzie is gone, thrown out, no further action in exchange for his testimony. We've got DC Coombs bang to rights, except…'

Fletcher spoke next, his grey eyes boring into Ted's. Ted suddenly had a revelation of what the Elton John lyrics in Nikita meant. Ice on fire. That's exactly what he felt he was looking at, from the fearsome head of Complaints.

'Except that DC Coombs has made allegations against you, of assault, bullying and harassment. And of course I will have to take the matter seriously and start an investigation.'

Ted felt his mouth go dry as he began, 'Sir...'

At that moment, Fletcher suddenly slapped Jim Baker on the back, hard, and let out a great shout of laughter.

'I told you'd I'd get him going, Jim,' he roared. 'That's a pint you owe me. Sorry, Ted, honestly, what a pair of bastards we are, eh? I just couldn't resist, and the look on your face was well worth it.'

Ted was speechless for the moment. Of all the things he knew about the boss of C&D, he'd had no idea he was a practical joker. His legs felt weak, his kneecaps twitching involuntarily with the sudden release of tension.

The two men pulled out chairs and sat down opposite Ted, as he did the same, thankfully.

Fletcher was still chuckling as he said, 'We really came over to take you out to lunch, Ted. I've got my driver outside so Jim and I are going to sink a few jars and you can have whatever the fizzy pop is that you like. It's all my shout, except the first round is Jim's for losing the bet. He said you'd never fall for it.

'I particularly wanted to come and congratulate you in person. You've just had one hell of a run of success. Really very impressive. In particular, the way you went after Foster and his rotten crew. That Cinderella trick was a master-stroke. I watched the tapes.'

'Kopciuszek,' Ted put in, then explained, 'Mr Bosko is Polish. He told me that's what it's called there. Out of interest, what will happen to the rest of Foster's team?'

'There are plans to cut the CID presence there down to a couple of officers. We'll find a decent DS capable of running things and just keep one, or two at the most, of the remaining DCs,' Jim told him.

'Winters has potential. Most importantly, he needs to stay

where he is. He looks after his mother.'

'Noted. I'll see what I can do.'

'Now for what I've really come here for,' Fletcher said. 'It's rare to find someone as straight as you, Ted – no pun and no offence intended. Someone who's willing to go after the rogue cops unbidden, when they already have more than enough on their plate. So if you ever fancy a career change, and if Jim would ever consider letting you go, I just wanted you to know that I'd be pleased to make room for you on my team, any time. At least you'd only be likely to get figuratively stabbed in the back, rather than getting your arm carved up by a knife-wielding nutter.'

Ted was surprised. It was something which had never occurred to him. He was happy doing his job.

'You know what? Given the choice, I far prefer serial killers to the stink of bent coppers, so I'll happily leave that side of things to you. But Trev's always saying my job's too dangerous. So let's just say, if ever Jim's had enough of me, and Trev nags too much, I'll come knocking on your door.'

The End